D0558418

"A supple,   genre with
expert eas   h a rare
power and

                                                  nce Fiction

"One of th   odern science
fiction."

"James V   erb collection,
The Last   to future,
from ri   are achingly
real, d   e are stories
that w   u see
yourse

ration

James   stories are
literat   n that so
often   igorous
scienc   ho writes
across   mmend
him t   tion and joy
of real

author of *The Memory Cathedral*

"I always expect something special from a James Van Pelt story, and yet I'm surprised each time by the depth and beauty of that special something he instills in every one."

—Jerry Oltion
author of *Anywhere But Here*

"James Van Pelt is a teacher, and to read him is to learn. I wish I'd had one of his classes when I was in school. From the Nebula-nominated title story to the stunning "Perceptual Set," he builds and destroys worlds with a meticulous yet effortless craft. Van Pelt's fiction crystallizes the journeys of his characters, examining their lives between one heartbeat and the next before releasing them and you, the reader, to voyage onward, profoundly affected by the experience."

—Jay Lake
author of *Dogs in the Moonlight*

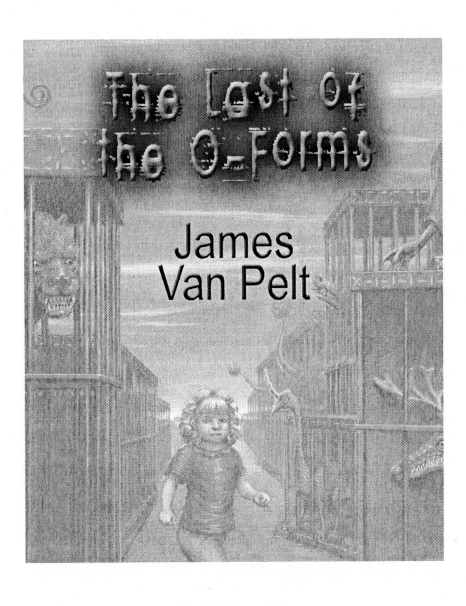

The Last of the O-Forms

James Van Pelt

FAIRWOOD PRESS
Auburn • Seattle

The Last Of the O-Forms

A Fairwood Press Book
August 2005
Copyright © 2005 by James Van Pelt

Fairwood Press
5203 Quincy Ave SE
Auburn, WA   98092
www.fairwoodpress.com

Cover art © 2005 by Alan M. Clark
Cover design by Patrick Swenson
Introduction © 2005 by James Patrick Kelly

ISBN: 0-9746573-5-2
First Fairwood Press Edition: August 2005
Printed in the United States of America

To my three sons, Dylan, Samuel and Teague, who surprise me into joy every day, and to my three sisters, Sharon, Janet, and Ginger, whose brilliant trajectories light my sky. And to Tammy who reads everything and loves me anyway. You're the best.

Acknowledgements

The stories in this anthology first appeared as follows:

"The Last of the O-Forms" first published in *Asimov's*, 2002

"Perceptual Set" first published in *Analog*, 2002

"Once They Were Monarchs" first published in *Alfred Hitchcock's*, 2000

"A Wow Finish" first published in *Amazing Stories*, 2004

"Friday, After the Game" first published in *Analog*, 2000

"The Invisible Empire" first published in *The Children of Cthulhu*,
    edited by John Pelan, 2002

"Its Hour Come Round" first published in *Talebones,* 2002

"The Pair-a-Deuce Comet Casino All-Sol Poker Championships"
    first published in *Talebones*, 2003

"The Stars Underfoot" first published in *Realms of Fantasy*, 2001

"The Long Way Home" first published in *Asimov's*, 2003

"Nothing is Normal" first published in *On Spec*, 2002

"Do Good" first published in *Polyphony*, edited by Jay Lake & Debra Layne, 2002

"The Safety of the Herd" first published in *Asimov's*, 2002

"The Sound of One Foot Dancing" first published in *Alfred Hitchcock's*, 2001

"A Flock of Birds" first published in *SCIFiction.com*, 2002

Contents

The Last of
the O-Forms

Introduction

by James Patrick Kelly

What makes a short story memorable? Some might point to vivid characters, others might prefer a well-paced and possibly twisty plot. Hard SF types might insist on the primacy of the idea, or perhaps the elegance of the worldbuilding. Of course, all of these are important. However, for me what matters most is whether a story has something to say. Understand that I do not mean to denigrate pure storytelling. But often when a writer is truly passionate about his subject, that passion energizes the characters, plot and setting in discernable — although mysterious — ways. After I've read a memorable story, I imagine that the writer spent all those weeks, or even months, laboring to get a vision out of his head and onto the page because he *had* to, not because he'd signed a contract and was up against the deadline or because he just happened to have finished one story and it was time to start a new one.

After you have read some of these memorable stories, I think you will agree that Jim Van Pelt has something important to say. But let's come back to that, shall we?

By the way, excuse me if I call Mr. Van Pelt *Jim* from now on. Some wag once warned that you should avoid meeting your favorite writer since he will almost certainly disappoint you. That may well be true in many cases, but I am here to tell you that my friend Jim is the sweetest and most unassuming writer of talent I have ever met. Not only is he a nimble conversationalist, he is also a great listener. Maybe this comes from all those years in the trenches as a gifted high school English teacher; just this year his school in Colorado recognized him with its teacher of the year award. In any event if you spot Jim across the room, don't hang back. You're in for a treat!

Meanwhile, here's my problem. I need to introduce you to Jim's stories without spoiling them for you. Now if only you would promise to read "The Last of the O-Forms" first, I could point out how wonderfully creepy the ending is. Or else I might discuss what it might mean for humanity when

Carson identifies the species of the flock in "A Flock of Birds." Or perhaps I might revel in the irony of what happens to that nasty little bully Bates when Müller opens his mouth in "Once They Were Monarchs."

But then you'd know far too much, so I must necessarily tread lightly here. To avoid giving away all the best bits, I'm going to limit myself to mentioning just a couple stories. For a start, here is one reader's take on Jim's most memorable character, plot, idea and world.

My favorite character in this collection is Vice Principal Welch, the protagonist of "Do Good," who may be at the end of a long — possibly too long — career at Lincoln High. He's having a crisis of confidence as his retirement looms. You know this guy; he's the one whose office you get sent to if you cut too many classes or are caught smoking out by the dumpster behind the cafeteria. Welch is convinced that students and faculty regard him as a kind of authoritarian pariah. In fact, just to drive the point home, Jim doesn't even give Welch a first name or much of a home life. He is either Welch, or Vice-Principal Welch. What he does at school defines him as a character.

But Welch is way too hard on himself, because in his own way he truly cares about his community of students and faculty. For example, for years he has been opening student lockers after hours with his master key and has been taping $5 and $10 dollar bills to the doors with the admonition "DO GOOD." Like so many of us, he is blind to how others see him, which is where the fantastic enters the story. Welch has been seeing ghosts at school, although Jim puts a clever spin on this conceit. The ghosts are not necessarily people who have passed away but rather those who have passed out of the halls of Lincoln High and Welch's life. And at the end ....

Oops. Almost gave that one away.

There's some excellent worldbuilding in "Perceptual Set," although I also enjoyed this story for its plucky cartographer protagonist Janet. Jim does a convincing job writing from a woman's point of view here, an accomplishment not all male writers can claim. In fact, the story begins with a witty conversation between two women, Janet and her friend Margo, who are trying to assess the personalities of the men in the crew of their mining ship by the way these men eat cheesecake. Jim effortlessly introduces romantic comedy tropes into a hard SF problem-solver. Janet is aboard a mining ship which has been diverted to examine the Gargoyle, a spherical asteroid which seems to have a face carved onto it. Can it be a natural phenomenon, or is it an alien artifact? Before too long it's clear that Janet and Alec, whom we first see in the cheesecake scene and who has previously saved Janet's life, will have to explore the Gargoyle.

Of course, things do not go entirely according to plan after they land and before long Janet finds herself ...

Never mind. We're almost done here. You can read it for yourself soon enough.

Jim is a talented writer who you are catching in the midst of a very promising career indeed. The *Best of the Year* nods have begun to roll in over the past few years for him and of course the title story was a Nebula finalist in 2004. I expect it won't be his only nomination; people are paying attention now, as well they should. The stories collected herein are in the mainstream of our genre — or I should say *genres*, since you'll be meeting up with ghosts and time travelers, spacemen and dragons. There are stops along the way in the late nineteenth century, 1942, 2005 and the far future. And some of these stories are in dialogue with classics by such genre giants as H. P. Lovecraft, Walter Miller Jr. and Ray Bradbury. Always Ray Bradbury. Jim tells a funny story on himself:

"I remember telling my mom once that I was going to be Ray Bradbury when I grew up. This was when I was really young, like seven or eight or six. I was really disappointed a couple of years later when I found out that Ray Bradbury was a person, not a job title. I wanted to be Ray Bradbury like some kids want to be firemen, like some kids want to be policemen."

I mentioned early on that I wanted to come back to that quality which sets Jim apart from lesser writers: the man has something to say. On occasion what he has to say is not easy to hear. Jim has a definite apocalyptic streak; things aren't going very well for *homo sapiens* in some of these stories. However, I don't read them as expressions of an innate pessimism so much as they are cautionary tales. Because even in their darkest hour, many of Jim's most memorable characters cling to a scrap of honor, or make a final gallant gesture. Many of them remain touchingly kind in the face of overwhelming adversity. They accept their fate without being crushed by it.

In "The Long Way Home" the apocalypse *does* happen — don't worry, it's over early and the plot goes on from there. Toward the end of this inspiring story, Matsui, a professor of astronomy, muses over the debate between recovering what was lost in the cataclysm and striking out to make new discoveries. He has been on the losing side in that argument and his career is now over. Nevertheless, Jim brings him to a lyrical moment:

"...when Matsui reached the faculty housing, he didn't stop. He kept going until he reached the bluff that overlooked the sea. Condensation dampened the rail protecting the edge of the low bluff, and it felt cold beneath his hands. Moonlight painted the surf's spray a glowing white. He thought about moonlight on water, about starlight on water. Each wave pounding against the cliff shook the rail, and for a moment, he felt connected to it all, to the larger story that was mankind on the planet and the planet in the galaxy. It seemed as if he was feeling the universal pulse.

"Much later, he returned to his cottage and his books. He was right. Chesnutt replaced him on the committees, but Matsui wasn't unhappy. He remembered his hands on the rail, the moon like a distant searchlight, and the grander story that he was a part of."

My friends, turn the page. It's time for you to take part in that grander story.

The Last of the O-Forms

Beyond the big rig's open window, the Mississippi river lands rolled darkly by. Boggy areas caught the moon low on the horizon like a silver coin, flickering through black-treed hummocks, or strained by split rail fence, mile after mile. The air smelled damp and dead-fish mossy, heavy as a wet towel, but it was better than the animal enclosures on a hot afternoon when the sun pounded the awnings and the exhibits huddled in weak shade. Traveling at night was the way to go. Trevin counted the distance in minutes. They'd blow through Roxie soon, then hit Hamburg, McNair and Harriston in quick secession. In Fayette there was a nice diner where they could get breakfast, but it meant turning off the highway and they'd hit the worst of Vicksburg's morning traffic if they stopped. No, the thing to do was to keep driving, driving to the next town where he could save the show.

He reached across the seat to the grocery sack between him and Caprice. She was asleep, her baby-blonde head resting against the door, her small hands holding a Greek edition of the *Odyssey* open on her lap. If she was awake she could glance at the map and tell him exactly how many miles they had left to Mayersville, how long to the minute at this speed it would take, and how much diesel, to the ounce they'd have left in their tanks. Her little-girl eyes would pin him to the wall. "Why can't you figure this out on your own?" they'd ask. He thought about hiding her phone book so she'd have nothing to sit on and couldn't look out the window. That would show her. She might look two years old, but she was really twelve and had the soul of a middle-aged tax attorney.

At the sack's bottom, beneath an empty donut box, he found the beef jerky. It tasted mostly of pepper, but underneath it had a tingly, metallic flavor he tried not to think about. Who knew what it might have been made from? He doubted there were any original-form cows, the o-cows, left to slaughter.

After a long curve, a city limit sign loomed out of the dark. Trevin stepped on the brakes, then geared down. Roxie cops were infamous for speed traps, and there wasn't enough bribe money in the kitty to make a ticket go away. In his rearview mirror, the other truck and a car with Hardy the handyman, and his crew of roustabouts closed ranks.

Roxie's traffic signal blinked yellow over an empty intersection, while the closed shops stood mute under a handful of streetlights. After the four-block long downtown, another mile of beat up houses and trailers lined the road, where broken washing machines and pickups on cinder blocks dotted moonlit front yards. Something barked at him from behind a chain link fence. Trevin slowed for a closer look. Professional curiosity. It looked like an o-dog under a porch light, an original form animal, an old one if his stiff-gaited walk was an indicator. Weren't many of those left anymore. Not since the mutagen hit. Trevin wondered if the owners keeping an o-dog in the backyard had troubles with their neighbors, if there was jealousy.

A toddler voice said, "If we don't clear $2,600 in Mayersville, we'll have to sell a truck, Daddy."

"Don't call me Daddy, *ever*." He took a long curve silently. Two-laned highways often had no shoulder, and concentration was required to keep safe. "I didn't know you were awake. Besides, a thousand will do it."

Caprice closed her book. In the darkness of the cab, Trevin couldn't see her eyes, but he knew they were polar-ice blue. She said, "A thousand for diesel, sure, but we're weeks behind on payroll. The roustabouts won't stand for another delay, not after what you promised in Gulfport. The extension on the quarterly taxes are past, and I can't keep the feds off like the other creditors by pledging extra payments for a couple months. We've got food for most of the animals for ten days or so, but we have to buy fresh meat for the tigerzelle and the crocomouse or they'll die. We stay afloat with $2,600, but just barely."

Trevin scowled. It had been years since he'd found her little-girl voice and little-girl pronunciation to be cute, and almost everything she said was sarcastic or critical. It was like living with a pint-sized advocate for his own self doubt. "So we need a house of. . ." He wrinkled his forehead. "$2,600 divided by four-and-a-half bucks. . ."

"Five hundred and seventy-eight. That'll leave you an extra dollar for a cup of coffee," Caprice said. "We haven't had a take that big since Ferriday last fall, and that was because Oktoberfest in Natchez closed early. Thank god for Louisiana liquor laws. We ought to admit the show's washed up, cut the inventory loose, sell the gear and pay off the help."

She turned on the goosenecked reading light that arced from the dashboard and opened her book.

"If we can hold on until Rosedale. . ." He remembered Rosedale when they last came through, seven years ago. The city had recruited him. Sent letters and e-mails. They met him in New Orleans with a committee, including a brunette beauty who squeezed his leg under the table when they went out to dinner.

"We can't," Caprice said.

Trevin recalled the hand on his leg feeling good and warm. He'd almost jumped from the table, his face flushed. "The soybean festival draws them in. Everything's made out of soybeans. Soybean pie. Soybean beer. Soybean ice cream." He chuckled. "We cleaned up there. I got to ride down Main Street with the Rosedale Soybean Queen."

"We're dead. Take your pulse." She didn't look up.

The Rosedale Soybean Queen had been friendly too, and oh so grateful that he'd brought the zoo to town. He wondered if she still lived there. He could look her up. "Yeah, if we make the soybean festival, we'll do fine. One good show and we're sailing again. I'll repaint the trucks. Folks love us when we come into town, music playing. World's greatest, traveling novelty zoo. You remember when *Newsweek* did that story? God, that was a day." He glanced out the window again. The moon rested on the horizon now, pacing them, big as a beachball, like a burnished hubcap rolling with them in the night, rolling up the Mississippi twenty miles to the west. He could smell it flowing to the sea. How could she doubt that they would make it big? I'll show her, he thought. Wipe that smirk off her little-girl face. I'll show her in Mayersville and then Rosedale. Money'll be falling off the tables. We'll have to store it in sacks. She'll see. Grinning, he dug deep for another piece of beef jerky, and he didn't think at all what it tasted like this time.

Trevin pulled the truck into Mayersville at half past ten, keeping his eyes peeled for their posters and flyers. He'd sent a box of them up two weeks earlier, and if the boy he'd hired had done his job, they should have been plastered everywhere, but he only saw one, and it was torn nearly in half. There were several banners welcoming softball teams to the South-Central Spring Time Regional Softball Tourney, and the hotels sported NO VACANCY signs, so the crowds were there. He turned the music on, and it blared from the loudspeakers on top the truck. Zoo's in town, he thought. Come see the zoo! But other than a couple geezers sitting in front of the barbershop, who watched them cooly as they passed, no one seemed to note their arrival.

"They can't play ball all day, eh, Caprice? They've got to do something between games."

She grunted. Her laptop was open on the seat beside her, and she was double entering receipts and bills into the ledger.

The fairgrounds were on the north edge of town, next to the ball fields. A park attendant met them at the gates, then climbed onto the running board so his head was just below the window.

"There's a hundred dollar occupancy fee," he said, his face hidden beneath a wide-brimmed straw hat that looked like it had been around the world a few times.

Trevin drummed his fingers on the steering wheel and stayed calm. "We paid for the site up front."

The attendant shrugged. "It's a hundred dollars or you find some other place to plant yourself."

Caprice, on her knees, leaned across Trevin. She deepened her voice in her best Trevin impersonation. "Do we make that check out to Mayersville City Parks or to Issaquena County?"

Startled, the attendant looked up before Caprice could duck out of sight, his sixty-year-old face as dusty as his hat. "Cash. No checks."

"That's what I thought," she said to Trevin as she moved back from the window. "Give him twenty. There better be the portable potties and the electrical hookups we ordered."

Trevin flicked the bill to him, and the attendant caught it neatly in flight as he stepped off the running board. "Hey, mister," he said. "How old's your little girl?"

"A million and ten, asshole," said Trevin, dropping the clutch to move the big rig forward. "I've told you to stay out of sight. We'll get into all kinds of trouble if the locals find out I've got a mutant keeping the books. They have labor laws, you know. Why'd you tell me to give him any money anyway? We could have bought a day or two of meat with that."

Caprice stayed on her knees to look out her window. "He's really a janitor. Never piss off the janitor. Hey, they cleaned this place up a bit. There was a patch of woods between us and the river last time."

Trevin leaned on the wheel. Turning the truck was tough at anything less than highway speed. "Would you want trees and brush next to where you were playing softball? You chase a foul shot into the undergrowth and never come back."

Beyond the fair grounds, the land sloped down to the levee, and past that flowed the Mississippi, less than a hundred yards away, a great, muddy plain marked with lines of sullen gray foam drifting under the mid-morning sun. A black barge so distant that he couldn't hear it chugged upstream. Trevin noted with approval the endless stretch of ten-foot tall chain link between them and the river. Who knew what god-awful thing might come crawling out of there?

As always, it took most of the day to set up. The big animals stinking of hot fur and unwashed cage bottoms, in their eight-foot high enclosures came out of the semi-trailers first. Looking lethargic and sick, the tigerzelle, a long-legged, hoofed animal sporting almost no neck below an impressive face filled with saber-like teeth, barely looked up as its cage was lowered to the soggy ground. It hooted softly. Trevin checked its water. "Get a tarp over it right away," he said to handyman Harper, a big, grouchy man who wore old rock concert t-shirts inside out. Trevin added, "That trailer had to be a hundred and twenty degrees inside."

Looking at the animal fondly, Trevin remembered when he'd acquired it from a farm in Illinois, one of the first American mutababies, before the mutagen was recognized and named, before it became a plague. The tigerzelle's sister was almost as bizarre: heavy legs, scaly skin and a long, thin head, like a whippet, but the farmer had already killed it by the time Trevin arrived. Their mother, as ordinary a cow as you'd ever see, looked at its children with dull confusion. "What the hell's wrong with my cow?" asked the farmer several times until they started dickering for the price. Once Trevin had paid him, the man said, "If'n I get any other weird lookin' animal, you want I should give you a call?"

Trevin smelled profit. Charging $20 per customer, he cleared $10,000 a week in June and July, showing the tigerzelle from the back of his pickup. He thought, I may not be too smart, but I do know how to make a buck. By the end of the summer, Dr. Trevin's Traveling Zoological Extravaganza was born. That was the year Caprice rode beside him in a child's car seat, her momma dead in child birth. In August, they were going north from Senetobia to Memphis, and at eleven months old, Caprice said her first words: "Isn't eighty over the speed limit?" Even then there was a biting, sardonic tone in her voice. Trevin nearly wrecked the truck.

The crocomouse snarled and bit at the bars as it came out, its furry snout banging against the metal. It threw its two-hundred pounds against the door and almost tipped the cage out of the handlers' grip. "Keep your hands away," snapped Harper to his crew, "or you'll be taping a pencil to a stub to write your mommas."

Then the rest of the animals were unloaded, a porcumander, the warped child of a bullfrog that waved its wet, thorny hide at every shadow; the unigoose, about the size of a wild turkey atop four tiny legs, shedding ragged feathers by the handful below the pearl-like glinting horn, and each of the other mutababies, the unrecognizable progeny of cats and squirrels and horses and monkeys and seals and every other animal Trevin could gather to the zoo. Big cages, little ones, aquariums, terrariums, little corrals, bird cages, tethering poles, all came out for display.

By sunset the last animal had been arranged and fed. Circus flags fluttered from the semi-trailer truck tops. The loudspeakers perched atop their posts.

The park attendant wandered through the cages, his hands pushed deep into his pockets as if he hadn't tried to rip them off earlier in the day. "Y'all best stay in your trucks once the sun sets if you're camping here."

Suspicious, Trevin asked, "Why's that?"

The man raised his chin toward the river glowing red like a bloody stain in the setting sun. "Water level was up a couple days ago, over the fences. The levee held, but any sorta teethy mutoid might be floppin' around on our side now. It's got so you can't step in a puddle without somethin' takin' a bite outta ya. Civil Defense volunteers walk the banks everyday lookin' for the more cantankerous critters, but it's a big old river. You got a gun?"

Trevin shrugged. "Baseball bat. Maybe we'll get lucky and add something to the zoo. You expecting crowds for the softball tournament?"

"Thirty-two teams. We shipped in extra bleachers."

Trevin nodded. If he started the music early in the morning, maybe he'd attract folks waiting for games. Nothing like a little amusement before the heat set in. After a couple minutes, the park attendant left. Trevin was glad to see him walk away. He had the distinct impression that the man was looking for something, probably to steal.

After dinner, Caprice clambered into the upper bunk, her short legs barely giving her enough of a reach to make it. Trevin kicked his blanket aside. Even though it was after 10:00, it was still over ninety degrees, and their wasn't a hint of a breeze. Most of the animals had settled in their cages. Only the tigerzelle made noise, one long warbling hoot after another, a soft, melodic call that hardly fit its ferocious appearance.

"You lay low tomorrow. I'm not kidding," said Trevin after he'd turned off the light. "I don't want you driving people off."

Caprice sniffed loudly. "It's pretty ironic that I can't show myself at a mutoid zoo. I'm tired of hiding away like a freak. Another fifty years there won't be any of your kind left anyway. Might as well accept the inevitable. I'm the future. They should be able to see that."

Trevin put his hands behind his head and stared up at her bunk. Through the screen he'd fitted over the windows, he could hear the Mississippi lapping against the bank. An animal screeched in the distance, its call a cross between a whistle and a bad cough. He tried to imagine what would make a sound like that. Finally he said, "People don't like human mutoids, at least ones that look human."

"Why's that?" she asked, all the sarcasm and bitterness suddenly gone. "I'm not a bad person if they'd get to know me. We could discuss books, or philosophy. I'm a mind, not a body."

The animal cried out again in the dark, over and over, until in mid-screech, it stopped. A heavy thrashing sound followed by splashes marked the creature's end. "I guess it makes them sad, Caprice."

"Do I make you sad?" In the truck cab's dim interior, she sounded exactly like a two year old. He remembered when she *was* a little girl, before he knew that she wasn't normal, that she'd never "grow up," that her DNA showed she wasn't human. Before she started talking uppity and making him feel stupid with her baby-doll eyes. Before he'd forbid her to call him Daddy. He'd thought she looked a little like her mother then. He still caught echoes of her when Caprice combed her hair, or when she fell asleep and her lips parted to take a breath, just like her mother. The air caught in his throat thinking of those times.

"No, Caprice. You don't make me sad."

Hours later, long after Caprice had gone to sleep, Trevin drifted off into a series of dreams where he was being smothered by steaming Turkish towels, and when he threw the towels off, his creditors surrounded him. They carried payment overdue notices, and none of them were human.

Trevin was up before dawn to feed the animals. Half of keeping the zoo running was in figuring out what the creatures ate. Just because the parent had been, say, an o-form horse didn't mean hay was going to do the trick. Caprice kept extensive charts for him: the animal's weight, how much food it consumed, what vitamin supplements seemed most helpful. There were practicalities to running a zoo. He dumped a bucket of corn on the cob into the pigahump's cage. It snorted, then lumbered out of the dog-house it stayed in, not looking much like a pig or any other animal Trevin knew. Eyes like saucers, it gazed at him gratefully before burying its face in the trough.

He moved down the rows. Mealworms in one cage. Grain in the next. Bones from the butcher. Dog food. Spoiled fish. Bread. Cereal. Old vegetables. Oats. The tigerzelle tasted the rump roast he tossed in, its delicate tongue, so like a cat's, lapped at the meat before it tore a small chunk off to chew delicately. It cooed in contentment.

At the end of the row, closest to the river, two cages were knocked off their display stands and smashed. Black blood and bits of meat clung to the twisted bars and both animals, blind, leathery bird-like creatures, were gone. Trevin sighed and walked around the cages, inspecting the ground. In a muddy patch, a single webbed print a foot across marked with four deep claw indents showed the culprit. A couple partial prints led from the river. Trevin put his finger in the track, which was a half-inch deep. The ground was wet but firm. It took a hard press to push just his fingertip a half-inch. He wondered at the weight of the creature, and made a note to himself that tonight they'd have to store the smaller cages in the truck, which would mean more work. He sighed again.

By 8:00, the softball fields across the park had filled. Players warmed up outside the fences while games took place. Tents to house teams or for food booths sprang up. Trevin smiled and turned on the music. Banners hung from the trucks. DR. TREVIN'S TRAVELING ZOOLOGICAL EXTRAVAGANZA. SEE NATURE'S ODDITIES! EDUCATIONAL! ENTERTAINING! By noon there had been fifteen paying customers.

Leaving Hardy in charge of tickets, Trevin loaded a box with handbills, hung a staple gun to his belt, then marched to the ballfields, handing out flyers. The sun beat down like a humid furnace, and only the players in the field weren't under tents or umbrella's. Several folks offered him a beer — he took one — but his flyers, wrinkly with humidity, vanished under chairs or behind coolers. "We're doing a first day of the tournament special," he said. "Two bucks each or three for you and a friend." His shirt clung to his back. "We'll be open after sunset, when it's cooler. These are displays not to be missed, folks."

A woman in her twenties, her cheeks sun-reddened, her blonde hair tied back, said, "I don't need to pay to see a reminder, damn it." She crumpled the paper and dropped it. One of her teammates, sitting on the ground, a beer between his knees, said, "Give him a break, Doris. He's just trying to make a living."

Trevin said, "We were in *Newsweek*. You might have read about us."

"Maybe we'll come over later, fella," said the player on the ground.

Doris popped a can open, "It might snow this afternoon too."

"Maybe it will," said Trevin congenially. He headed toward town on the other side of the fairgrounds. The sun pressured his scalp with prickly fire. By the time he'd gone a hundred yards he wished he'd worn a hat, but it was too hot to go back.

He stapled a flyer to the first telephone pole he came to. "Yep," he said to himself. "A little publicity and we'll rake it in." The sidewalk shimmered in white heat waves as he marched from pole to pole, past the hardware, past the liquor store, past the Baptist Church — SUFFER THE CHILDREN read the marquee — past the pool hall and auto supply shop. He went inside every store and asked the owner to post his sign. Most did. Behind Main Street stood several blocks of homes. Trevin turned up one street and down the next, stapling flyers, noting with approval the wire mesh over the windows. "Can't be to careful, nowadays," he said, his head swimming in the heat. The beer seemed to be evaporating through his skin all at once, and he felt sticky with it. The sun pulsed against his back. The magic number is five-seventy-eight, he thought. It beat within him like a song. Call it six hundred. Six hundred folks come to the zoo, come to the zoo, come to the zoo.

When he finally made his way back to the fairgrounds, the sun was on its way down. Trevin dragged his feet, but the flyers were gone.

Evening fell. Trevin waited at the ticket counter in his zoo-master's uniform, a broad-shouldered red suit with gold epaulets. The change box popped open with jingly joy; the roll of tickets was ready. Circus music played softly from the loudspeakers as fireflies flickered in the darkness above the river. Funny, he thought, how the mutagen affected only the bigger vertebrate animals, not mice-sized mammals or little lizards, not small fish nor bugs or plants. What would a bug mutate into anyway? They look alien to begin with. He chuckled to himself, his walking up the sidewalk song still echoing: six hundred folks come to the zoo, come to the zoo, come to the zoo.

Every car that passed on the highway, Trevin watched, waiting for it to slow for the turn into the fairgrounds.

From sunset until midnight, only twenty customers bought admissions, most of them ball players who'd discovered there wasn't much night life in Mayersville. Clouds had moved in, and distant lightning flickered within their steel-wool depths.

Trevin spun the roll of tickets back and forth on its spool. An old farmer couple wearing overalls, their clothes stained with rich, Mississippi soil, shuffled past on their way out. "You got some strange animals here, mister," said the old man. His wife nodded. "But nothing stranger than what I've found wandering in my fields for the last few years. Gettin' so I don't remember what o-form normal looks like."

"Too close to the river," said his wife. "That's our place right over there." She pointed at a small farm house under a lone light just beyond the last ball field. Trevin wondered if they ever retrieved home run balls off their porch.

The thin pile of bills in the cash box rustled under Trevin's fingers. The money should be falling off the tables, he thought. We should be drowning in it. The old couple stood beside him, looking back into the zoo. They reminded him of his parents, not in their appearance, but in their solid patience. They weren't going anywhere fast.

He had no reason to talk to them, but there was nothing left to do. "I was here a few years ago. Did really well. What's happened?"

The wife held her husband's hand. She said, "This town's dyin', mister. Dyin' from the bottom up. They closed the elementary school last fall. No elementary-age kids. If you want to see a real zoo display, go down to

Issaquena County Hospital pediatrics. The penalty of parenthood. Not that many folks are having babies, though."

"Or whatever you want to call them," added the old man. "Your zoo's depressin'."

"I'd heard you had somethin' special, though," said the woman shyly.

"Did you see the crocomouse?" asked Trevin. "There's quite a story about that one. And a tigerzelle. Have you seen that one?"

"Saw 'em," she said, looking disappointed.

The old couple climbed into their pickup that rattled into life after a half-dozen starter-grinding tries.

"I found a buyer in Vicksburg for the truck," said Caprice.

Trevin whirled. She stood in the shadows beside the ticket counter, a notebook jammed under her arm. "I told you to stay out of view."

"Who's going to see me? You can't get customers even on a discount." She gazed on the vacant lot. "We don't have to deliver it. He's coming to town next week on other business. I can do the whole transaction, transfer the deed, take the money, all of it, over the Internet."

One taillight out, the farmer's pickup turned from the fairgrounds and onto the dirt road that led to their house that wasn't more than two hundred yards away. "What would we do with the animals?" He felt like weeping.

"Let the safe ones go. Kill the dangerous ones."

Trevin rubbed his eyes. She stamped her foot. "Look, this is no time for sentimentality. The zoo's a bust. You're going to lose the whole thing soon anyway. If you're too stubborn to give it all up, sell this truck now and you get a few extra weeks, maybe a whole season if we economize."

Trevin looked away from her. The fireflies still flickered above the river. "I'll have to make some decisions," he said heavily.

She held out the notebook. "I've already made them. This is what will fit in one semi-trailer. I already let Hardy and the roustabouts go with a severance check, postdated."

"What about the cages, the gear?"

"The county dump is north of here."

Was that a note of triumph he detected in her voice? Trevin took the notebook. She dropped her hands to her side, chin up, staring at him. The zoo's lights cast long shadows across her face. I could kick her, he thought, and for a second his leg trembled with the idea of it.

He tucked the notebook under his arm. "Go to bed."

Caprice opened her mouth, then clamped it shut on whatever she might have said before moving away.

Long after she vanished into the cab, Trevin sat on the stool, elbow on his knee, chin in his hand, watching insects circle the lights. The tigerzelle squatted on its haunches, alert, looking toward the river. Trevin remembered a ghastly cartoon he'd seen once. A couple of crones sat on the seat of a wagon full of bodies. The one holding the reins turned to the other and said, "You know, once the plague is over we're out of a job."

The tigerzelle rose to its feet, focusing on the river. It paced intently in its cage, never turning its head from the darkness. Trevin straightened. What did it see out there? For a long moment the tableau remained the same: insects clouded around the lights that buzzed softly, highlighting the cages; shining metal against the enveloping spring night, the pacing tigerzelle, the ticket counter's polished wood against Trevin's hand, and the Mississippi's pungent murmuring in the background.

Beyond the cages, from the river, a piece of blackness detached itself from the night. Trevin blinked in fascinated paralysis, all the hairs dancing on the back of his neck. The short-armed creature stood taller than a man, surveyed the zoo, then dropped to all fours like a bear, except that its skin gleamed with salamander wetness. Its triangular head sniffed at the ground, moving over the moist dirt as if following a scent. When it reached the first cage, a small one that held the weaslesnake, the river creature lifted its forelegs off the ground, grasping the cage in web-fingered claws. In an instant the cage was unrecognizable and the weaslesnake was gone.

"Hey!" Trevin yelled, shaking off his stupor. The creature looked at him. Reaching under the ticket counter, Trevin grabbed the baseball bat and advanced. The monster turned away to pick up the next cage. Trevin's face flushed "No, no, no, damn it!" He stepped forward again, stepped again, and suddenly he was running, bat held overhead. "Get away! Get away!" He brought the bat down on the animal's shoulder with a meaty whump.

It shrieked.

Trevin fell back, dropping the bat to cover his ears. It shrieked again, loud as a train whistle. For a dozen heart beats, it stood above him, claws extended, then it seemed to lose interest and moved to the next cage, dismantling it with one jerk of the bars.

His ears ringing, Trevin snatched the bat off the ground and waded in, swinging. On its rear legs, the monster bared its teeth, dozens of glinting needles in the triangular jaw. Trevin nailed the creature in the side. It folded with surprising flexibility, backing away, claws distended, snarling in a deafening roar. Trevin swung. Missed. The monster swiped at his leg, ripping his pants and almost jerking his feet out from under him.

The thing moved clumsily, backing down the hill toward the levee fence as Trevin swung again. Missed. It howled, tried to circle around him. Trevin scuttled sideways, careful of his balance on the slick dirt. If he should fall!

The thing charged, mouth open, but pulled back like a threatened dog when Trevin raised the bat. He breathed in short gasps, poked the bat's end at it, always shepherding it away from the zoo. Behind him, a police siren sounded, and car engines roared, but he didn't dare look around. He could only stalk and keep his bat at the ready.

After a long series of feints, its back to the fence, the nightmare stopped, hunched its back and began to rise just as Trevin brought the bat down in a two-handed, over the head chop. Through the bat, he felt the skull crunch, and the creature dropped into a shuddery mass in the mud. Trevin, his pulse pounding, swayed for a moment, then sat beside the beast.

Up the hill, under the zoo's lights, people shouted into the darkness. Were they ball players? Town people? A police cruiser's lights blinked blue then red, and three or four cars, headlights on, were parked near the trucks. Obviously they couldn't see him, but he was too tired to call. Ignoring the wet ground, he lay back.

The dead creature smelled of blood and river mud. Trevin rested a foot on it, almost sorry that it was dead. If he could have captured it, what an addition it would have made to the zoo. Gradually the heavy beat in his chest calmed. The mud felt soft and warm. Overhead, the clouds thinned a bit, scudding across the full moon.

At the zoo, there was talking. Trevin craned his head around to see. People jostled about, and flashlights cut through the air. They started down the hill. Trevin sighed. He hadn't saved the zoo, not really. Tomorrow would come and they'd leave one of the trucks behind. In a couple of months, it would all be gone, the other truck, the animals — he was most sorry about the tigerzelle — the pulling into town with music blaring and flags flapping and people lined up to see the menagerie. No more reason to wear the zoomaster's uniform with its beautiful gold epaulets. *Newsweek* would never interview him again. It was all gone. If he could only sink into the mud and disappear, then he wouldn't have to watch the dissolving of his own life.

He sat up so they wouldn't think he was dead; waved a hand when the first flashlight found him. Mud dripped from his jacket. The policemen arrived first.

"God almighty, that's a big one." The cop trained his light on the river creature.

"Told you the fences warn't no good," said the other.

Everyone stayed back except the police. The first cop pushed the corpse off its stomach. Its little arms flopped to the side, and it didn't look nearly as big or intimidating. More folk arrived: some townies he didn't recognize, the old couple from the farmhouse across the ball fields, and finally, Caprice, the flashlight looking almost too big for her to carry.

The first cop knelt next to the creature, shoved his hat up off his forehead, then said low enough that Trevin guessed only the other cop heard him, "Hey, doesn't this look like the Anderson's kid? They said they'd smothered him."

"He wasn't half that big, but I think you're right." The other cop threw a coat over the creature's face, then stood for a long time looking down at it. "Don't say anything to them, all right? Maggie Anderson is my wife's cousin."

"Nothing here to see, people," announced the first cop. "This is a dead 'un. Y'all can head back home."

But the crowd's attention wasn't on them anymore. The flashlights turned on Caprice.

"It's a baby girl," someone said, and they moved closer.

Caprice shined her flash light from one face to the other. Then, desperation on her face, she ran clumsily to Trevin, burying her face in his chest.

"What are we going to do?" she whispered.

"Quiet. Play along." Trevin stroked the back of her head, then stood. A sharp twinge in his leg told him he'd pulled something. The world was all bright lights, and he couldn't cover his eyes. He squinted against them.

"Is that your girl, mister?" someone said.

Trevin gripped her closer. Her little hands fisted in his coat.

"I haven't seen a child in ten years," said another voice. The flashlights moved in closer.

The old farmer woman stepped into the circle, her face suddenly illuminated. "Can I hold your little girl, son? Can I just hold her?" She extended her arms, her hands quivering.

"I'll give you fifty bucks if you let me hold her," said a voice behind the lights.

Trevin turned slowly, lights all around until he faced the old woman again. A picture formed in his mind, dim at first but growing clearer by the second. One semi-trailer truck, the trailer set up like a child's room — no! Like a nursery. Winnie-the-Pooh wallpaper. A crib. One of those musical rotating things, what cha' call ums — a mobile! Little rocking chair. Kid's music. And they'd go from town to town. The banner would say THE LAST O-FORM GIRL CHILD, and he would charge them, yes he would, and they would line up. The money would fall off the table.

Trevin pushed Caprice away from him, her hands clinging to his coat. "It's OK, darling. The nice woman just wants to hold you for a bit. I'll be right here."

Caprice looked at him, despair clear in her face. Could she already see the truck with the nursery? Could she picture the banner and the unending procession of little towns?

The old woman took Caprice in her arms like a precious vase. "That's all right, little girl. That's all right." She faced Trevin, tears on her cheeks. "She's just like the granddaughter I always wanted. Does she talk yet? I haven't heard a baby's voice in forever. Does she talk?"

"Go ahead, Caprice dear. Say something to the nice lady."

Caprice locked eyes with him. Even by flashlight he could see the polar blue. He could hear her sardonic voice night after night as they drove across country. "It's not financially feasible to continue," she'd say in her two-year-old voice. "We should admit the inevitable."

She looked at him, lip trembling. She brought her fist up to her face. No one moved. Trevin couldn't even hear them breathing.

Caprice put her thumb in her mouth. "Daddy," she said around it. "Scared, daddy."

Trevin flinched, then forced a smile. "That's a good girl."

"Daddy, scared."

Up the hill, the tigerzelle hooted, and just beyond the fence, barely visible by flashlight, the Mississippi gurgled and wept.

Perceptual Set

Margo said, "**If you really want to know** how a man will treat you, watch how he eats his cheesecake."

Janet poked at her dessert. "That's ridiculous." The second shift filled the cafeteria. From their table near the wall, the narrow room curved up to the other end as it followed the mining and processing ship's long arc, but Janet's attention was on Crew Chief Alec Maier. She noted he'd chosen the cheesecake too, but he ignored it as he listened to a pair of his miners arguing about relief time and compensation for lost work. He never glanced her way.

Janet put her fork down in disgust. "You can't make a decent cheese-cake with rehydrated dairy products. I should have had lunch in my quarters."

"Did you get new scans on the Gargoyle?"

"Where did you get that name?" Janet whispered. "A Strieberist will hear you, and I'll be fending off missionaries again."

"Nut cases. If they had their way, we'd give up on the whole ark project and wait for rescue instead."

Janet remembered how the recruiters sold her on graphic presentations of the ark ships heading for the stars, fleeing the mutagen-wracked Earth, packed from end to end with everything necessary to colonize distant planets. Without the asteroid mining projects, the arks would never be built. They had needed her cartography skills, and now she was the go-to person in the department.

"Maybe, but they see alien fingerprints on everything. I don't care what the company says about hiring diversity. They make my life miserable. You're not supposed to know anything about it anyway. It's secret," Janet said.

Margo dipped a piece of bread into her coffee cup, then popped it into her mouth. "People talk to me. I'm the therapist." Like most of the crew, she'd long ago given up on the regulation work clothes, wearing instead a loose T-shirt and shorts. Her hair was a close-cropped brunette that matched her dark-brown eyes. She grinned while chewing. The only time Janet saw her with a serious expression was when she studied psychiatric profiles. Then, her brow would wrinkle and she'd push her fingers into her cheeks as if trying to squeeze understanding out of herself. "So, is it an alien space station?"

Janet thought about not answering, but Margo's security clearance was higher than hers, and if she really wanted to know, there'd be little Janet could do to stop her. "No, but it's darned weird. The clearer the scan, the more it looks like a head to me, just like the Ceres' flyby recorded." The first clear photos showed a face on the asteroid. At first it seemed as if it was *all* face, but later shots showed it was more like a cameo carved into a larger surface. She'd enhanced the images, then turned in her report.

Margo snorted. "Face, my foot. It's your perceptual set. Giovanni Schiaparelli thought he saw water channels on Mars in the 1800s. He was *prepared* to see evidence of life, and he found it. It's like that head on Mars obsession at the end of the twentieth century. Put three dots and a line on anything, and people turn it into a portrait. That's called 'feature extraction,' taking info you're familiar with and ignoring the rest. A water stain sits on a wall long enough, someone sees the Virgin Mary. Do you ever notice the Virgin Mary doesn't show up on walls in Muslim countries? This asteroid is no different from the rest, an odd-shaped rock we can run through the mill for metals, fuel and chemicals. The Ceres' flyby takes a long-range shot by accident, and third-rate administrators with more imagination than good sense turn shadows and a jagged protrusion into an alien artifact. We're taking a tedious trip for nothing, and I'll be dealing with disappointed alien-hunters for months."

"The main office doesn't think it's nothing. You don't divert an entire mining operation on a whim."

Margo said, "Maybe not, but you're on a deadline. If you don't figure out exactly what it is before we get there, the radicals will get the upper hand. There's more than one Strieberist in administration."

Janet watched as Alec pushed his dessert to the side and started sketching on his napkin. The workers leaned over his shoulder so they could see what he was doing. She admired the way he concentrated while writing on the small surface.

"He's monofocused," said Margo.

Janet turned away. "You're the monofocused one — I'm not watching him. The probe should be within ten kilometers in an hour. We'll get even better pictures then."

"Sheesh, it's half a kilometer long. How close do you need to get before you see it's an ordinary object?"

"That's another thing. The Gargoyle has almost no albedo. I mean, most asteroids are darned dark anyway, .03 or so, but this one's a lump of coal. If it hadn't occluded Ceres, we would have never seen it. That's not natural."

Margo shrugged her shoulders. "A black asteroid, big deal. There, now look at that one." She lifted her chin toward a miner at a near table. He wore his coveralls with a strap down. Sweat marked his shirt in a pattern mirroring his work suit's pressure points.

"What about him?"

"Watch the cheesecake."

Janet thought the man had a rugged competence. Like most miners, he carried the ship's spin-induced gravity carefully, as if he wasn't sure that anything he set down wouldn't drift off. He pulled the plate with the cheese-cake toward him. Then keeping one hand on the plate, he trimmed a third of the slice off with his fork, lifted, swallowed, took the second third, lifted, swallowed and finished the last third, all in fifteen seconds.

"Whew!" Margo said. "That was business-like."

"What does it tell you about him?"

Margo raised an eyebrow. "Isn't it obvious? He doesn't take time for the finer things in life. A woman would be wise to steer clear of him."

"Maybe it means he was hungry. You're a loon."

"And you think a football stadium-sized rock has been shaped into a head. So how did Alec eat his?"

Janet turned to look back at the crew chief, but he and the two miners who'd been arguing with him were gone. His cheesecake sat untouched.

Margo said, "You work with him all the time. Why you have to turn it into such a big deal now that you've decided you're interested is beyond me. What do you guys talk about on those long jaunts in the jalopy?"

"That's business. He's thinking about where the operation will anchor. I'm thinking about navigating and mapping. There's nothing romantic about riding the jalopy from the ship to the next mining site."

"You can't read clues into his every behavior. . ."

"You just told me to look at how he eats his cheesecake, for crying out loud!"

Margo went on, ignoring the interruption. "Yesterday he asked you to pass the salt, and you spent the next two hours deciding what it meant. Tell him you think he's cute."

"I'm thirty, not sixteen. Maybe you could tell him."

Margo laughed. "Oh, that's very thirty. If you give me a note, I'll pass it to him."

Janet looked at her suspiciously. "Does he ever talk about me?"

Margo shrugged. "Maybe."

"I should have never kissed him," said Janet. "He doesn't like surprises."

"He saved your life!"

"Yeah, and there's that, too."

In the cartography lab, Janet shuffled through the new prints. Chief Cartographer Lindsey London held one in her lap, biting her lip.

"It's difficult to ascribe these formations to natural forces."

Janet put a half dozen scans on the table end to end, each one revealing a different look at the asteroid as the probe passed. "Those aren't formations, they're features. It's a face. Two faces, actually, one on each side."

Lindsey stood so she could see the entire set. She was a severe woman in her fifties, rigorous in habit and demanding. She cleared her throat, then rubbed her forehead. Like many on the ship, she suffered from sinus infections. "I suppose it would be hard not to draw that conclusion. They do look like faces." She moved a print closer to her. "Darned ugly ones too."

With enhancements, the asteroid's edges were clear, the shadows and highlights easy to distinguish. Janet turned the photo so the orientation made sense to her. On the asteroid's edges, jagged spikes jammed so tightly there appeared to be no space between them. They crossed each other in random arrangement. With the probe close, details stood out. Janet estimated each spike might be ten or fifteen meters in diameter at the base, although she couldn't see where they anchored, and none were shorter than fifty meters as they tapered to blunt points. Were they crystal structures? What could cause this? If the entire surface were covered with the spikes, it would be difficult to land. There was no place a ship could put its legs down for a secure anchor. In the spike field's middle, however, the face filled a third of the space. It rose from the pointy surface, a nearly perfect ovoid.

Janet turned the photo again, squinting at the new angle. "I don't know about ugly. It looks scared."

Lindsey glanced again. "If it is an alien face, how would we recognize its emotion?"

"How *else* would you describe that?"

The mouth was reptilian and gaping, stretching across the ovoid's bottom, a dark, crooked gap. A slit where the nose would be, and the eyes thrust wide open, like two almonds far apart, pupils dug into the spherical surfaces. Janet squinted at the photo, trying to see it without the starry background. "I don't know what makes me think it, but this is a frightened expression. Whoever carved it knew what fear looked like."

"It's not the same on the other side." Lindsey handed her another scan.

Here the mouth bared huge, stone teeth. The eyes were narrower. Janet shivered. It reminded her of a dog she'd tried to pet once, until its lips curled back and the snout became all fangs and a shuddery growl.

Janet said, "So, are you still going to argue this isn't a manufactured object?"

"I'm not telling the company we've found an Easter Island head in the asteroid belt, but I'm willing to say it's anomalous and deserves further study. Until then, no one Earthside knows about this."

Janet raised an eyebrow.

"Not my decision," said Lindsey. "Word from upstairs. Even on board there aren't a dozen people who know why we've changed our schedule."

Janet started an accelerated animation of the odd object on her computer. It revolved so the two faces alternated. The fearful expression rotated past, the shadows stretched across the stone skin, darkening the mouth, shifting shadows across the eyes so for a moment, they seemed to move. Then the spiny border filled the screen. The fearful face's profile cut across the stars as the second face rotated into view.

"It's a solid hunk," said Lindsey. "Not a rubble pile."

"That's my guess. I read the light bouncing off it — there's darned little — and it comes up nickle-iron. No magnesium. Some iron-silicates."

"Nickle-iron should be brighter. Why's it so dark?"

The second face came into view. As frightened as the first one looked, this one threatened. The same alien features. A different emotion.

"Maybe it's painted."

Lindsey didn't laugh. "Send the probe down to get a sample from the surface of a face. Keep it away from the spiky areas. There *might* be a coating, or it could be just a dark ore, a type of asteroid we haven't observed. If there are others with this little reflectivity, we might never see them. While we're waiting, get a complete map worked up. We're going to want to anchor the drills and mill."

"Has anyone considered the asteroid might be a message?" Janet swallowed dryly. Lindsey didn't like her orders questioned. "If it is artificial, whoever put it there didn't want it to be seen, and if it was seen, they didn't want it to look attractive. Maybe we should leave it alone."

Janet sent the photo probe's data into the mapping programs. She watched the asteroid continue its rotation on the screen. Fearful, angry, fearful, angry.

"Not with Strieberists in upper management." Lindsey stood behind her, her hands on the back of Janet's chair. "Are you going to be able to concentrate on this?"

Janet tore her attention from the Gargoyle. Lindsey's question didn't make sense. "Excuse me?"

"Are you going to be sharp? Everything here has to be perfect. Our reports, perfect, when we send this to the company. There will be political ramifications if this turns out to be artificial. I can't have you mooning over the Crew Chief instead of doing your work."

"I am *not* thinking about that man!"

Lindsey shrugged. "So you say."

"I do say!" Janet's face flushed. She bent over the keyboard, tapping the instructions that would separate the sampler probe from the mapper and send it to the surface.

Janet jogged up the ship's long curve, enjoying the track's yielding surface as it cushioned her bare feet. Behind her, footsteps approached, so she moved to the side, her shoulder nearly brushing the wall to her left until the runner passed. Here the ceiling was low, cutting off the view of the passage sixty meters ahead. She could never shake the feeling she was running uphill. At least, it appeared that way, a steady climb in front, and if she looked behind, a steady climb the other way. Running in the circular station was like perpetually hitting the bottom of a rounded valley. Across the broad sidewalk to her right, she passed doors, hallways and windows. The Infirmary, a long section marked with red crosses at either end rolled by for the third time. Once more would make a five-kilometer workout, her required aerobic ration.

Without the kiss, Alec wouldn't be a problem. It happened a week ago. He'd been reading an asteroid's assay numbers and a mathematical map that showed stress lines, faults, and probabilities of mass shifts once they began operations. The top sheet of papers on a pile near the edge of his desk slid off, fluttering to the floor. They'd both reached for it, her hand on his shoulder as they bent down, and when she looked up, he was there, an inch away. It must have been something in his eyes, or maybe she could feel his muscles tense under his shirt, or maybe it was just a short circuit in all her thinking processes, but she leaned the slightest bit, pressed her lips to his, and then the moment was gone. He bolted straight up, knocking the remaining papers into the air. She fell back, banging her elbow on the chair's edge, and as she grabbed the sore spot, she saw his expression, eyes wide in fear (or disgust?). He spluttered something incoherent, face red, then fled the room.

She blushed to think about it.

More footfalls behind her. She moved to the side again, slowing in thought. The maps showed the Gargoyle was an almost perfect sphere, varying no more than a few centimeters in diameter measured through the poles or the equator, another good argument it was artificial. Bodies this small didn't have enough gravity to pull them into round shapes. Most asteroids were rugged, irregular, nearly solid nickel-iron chunks, or jumbled carbonaceous chondrite rubble piles. The only way she could think to form a small, spherical body in space would be to heat the entire mass to a liquid state, and like a water drop floating in a no-gravity chamber, it would pull itself into a perfect globe. But the Gargoyle wasn't a smooth, spinning bowling ball; it was a designed object. Still, there was a blessing in the shape: figuring orbits around it would be easier. The last asteroid she'd sent a probe to was shaped like a four-kilometer long dog bone with an eccentric wobble, and the gravity going around the long end was three times that of circling the narrow middle. She'd used a lot of the probe's fuel keeping a consistent distance away from it while she mapped.

Alec spoke almost in her ear, "When I run toward the spin I feel faster."

Janet stumbled, then recovered her stride. She tried to speak, but what came out instead was a cross between a cough and an exclamation that sounded like "Gack!"

"It's a funny thing," he said, as if she'd made no sound at all. "I know it doesn't make a difference which direction I go, but when I jog into the spin, it's like the ship rotates beneath me. Going the other way is like trying to catch up, and my strides seem shorter." He had a pleasant speaking voice.

"Have you tried timing it?" she asked finally.

"Same time both ways. Doesn't change how it feels, though."

They ran side by side for a minute without speaking. Janet thought of a dozen things to say, but nothing sounded natural. She almost said, "How do you like cheesecake?" The thought made her smile. Margo would be pleased if she had. When another jogger approached, going the other direction, Alec dropped behind to let him pass. On his chest, the jogger wore the familiar green and white Strieberist button that read, "They are waiting."

The infirmary slid by again on her right. Janet stayed in her rhythm. Why was he talking to her? Had he come behind her on the track by coincidence, or did he want to be with her? Was he just a nice guy who talked to anyone? What was she supposed to read into this encounter?

And he had saved her life. Of course anyone might have noticed the flaw in her space suit before they'd gone on that mission, but he was the one that caught it. How could she date a man who'd saved her life? It was too corny. Knight in shining armor stuff. It put them on unequal footing.

She cleared her throat and said, "This makes me think of a hamster in an exercise wheel."

He didn't answer.

She said, "Where the wheel goes round and round, and the hamster works like crazy to go nowhere."

Without slowing, she glanced over her shoulder. He was gone. She sighed. Just as well. The probe would be near the Gargoyle now, and she wanted to be there when it touched down. It would take several hours to start sending back its analysis, but she felt more in control if she was in the lab while the probe worked.

For a while, the mapper tracked the sampler on its way, showing the tiny craft approaching the Gargoyle, puffing out compressed air to control the descent and to match the slowly revolving asteroid's spin, but the orbiting mapper would be on the other side when the sampler made contact. Sweat tickled Janet's forehead. Landing a probe on an asteroid was tricky business, even with automated routines and computer assistance. There was almost no gravity, so the asteroid didn't help orient the probe, and the probe's kinetic energy remained the same, so a percentage point miscalculation would slam it into the solid surface, and third, she'd chosen the angry face to land on. Now that the probe was within a few hundred meters, all the details were clear. There were lines in the expression, taut skin pulling away from its mouth, a tension in the cheek area, all in black and gray relief. The lifeless pupils seemed to track the probe in as it approached. Dark pocks scarred the surface, as if the face had been disease ravaged. Watching the expression grow larger was unnerving.

"You're closing a little fast," said Lindsey.

"I've got to anchor the probe or it'll just bounce off. If you were standing on the surface there and twitched your toes, you might achieve escape velocity."

The face swelled until there were no discernable features, just the pocked skin. Then the probe's shadow, its spider-like feet reaching closer and closer. Touchdown. Janet sent the signal to fire the anchor bolts in case they didn't deploy on their own. She took half a breath in relief. The probe continued. The feet broke through. Shards flew toward the camera, then nothing. No image.

Lindsey coughed. "That's expensive equipment. What happened?"

Telemetry came in fine. The machine's little nuclear heart still beat. Janet ran through a handful of tests. The internals looked green, but there was no video, and she couldn't tell what the probes' attitude was. "The face must have been a shell. If it's spikes underneath, the probe could be wedged between a couple. The arms are stuck. I can get the sampler to deploy, but it's not reaching anything. For all I can tell, it might be pointing straight up and be nowhere near the surface."

"Can you shake it loose? Take it up and bring it down again?"

Janet shrugged. "I can't tell which way we're facing. Without the video I can't see, and with all the metal around it, radar orientation won't work. It could wedge in deeper. We'll have to wait for the mapper to come around so we can see it. I can bring it in close for a good look, but it won't be in position for several hours."

Later, after she'd made the adjustments in the mapper's orbit, she leaned back in her chair and watched numbers march down the screen. Lindsey had gone to a management meeting, leaving Janet alone in the cartography lab. She tapped her fingers on the table edge. Above the monitor hung the Gargoyle's two clearest images. Fearful and angry.

Was this first contact? The long-sought evidence that mankind wasn't alone in the universe? She knew they were on the edge of something tremendous, but a voice kept creeping into her thoughts, coming from just behind her, not out of breath at all, saying, "When I run toward the spin, I feel faster." She wondered if Madame Curie thought about laundry while she was discovering radiation, or if Buzz Aldrin found himself contemplating a crabgrass problem in his lawn while the Eagle was going down. This would be so much easier if she just knew what he thought of her, but the messages were enigmatic. One day he ignored her, the next he went out of his way to say hello.

She shook her head and studied the mapper's data. Some measurements didn't make much sense. The Gargoyle's magnetic field was what she expected for a body of its size, but there was a ghost image underneath the main one, as if there were a second magnetic source within the asteroid. Deep radar imaging didn't help either, although there were four tiny bright spots on the surface: one on each face and at the poles. She programmed the mapper to take closeups of one of the spots when it made its nearest pass.

The intercom crackled. "Hey, roomie. Cracked the mystery yet?"

Janet said, "Hi, Margo. Nope, and we've just a few hours before the Gargoyle will be at eyeball distance. Some Strieberist working outside's going to catch a glimpse, and we'll have a riot. And you know what's funny? They were right all along. The Gargoyle is alien. Lindsey is confabbing with the upper mucky-mucks about what it might be and what to do about it."

"What's your guess?"

"Maybe it has religious significance." Janet thought about the Sphinx and the pyramids, ancient structures from a long gone civilization. It was hard to imagine why an advanced, technological society would build such an inaccessible shrine. "I lost the sampler probe. It's as if whoever designed it didn't *want* anyone to land on it. I don't know what the ship's going to do when we get there. We won't be able to anchor easily, and it's too big for a controlled melt. We could set up every mirror on board, and it would still take a hundred years to heat it enough."

"When administration says 'jump,' we're not supposed to ask why. Maybe their interest is scientific."

Janet laughed. "Not a chance. If it isn't profitable, they won't do it. They must figure the Gargoyle is a treasure chest."

"Why the faces?"

"To scare off the superstitious?"

On the monitor, video from the mapper streamed by as the asteroid grew in size. Closest approach would be in a few minutes. Janet shivered. No matter how she looked at it, the effect was creepy, like a hedgehog wearing a lizard mask. "Whoever made this was more advanced than us, and it was a tremendous effort. There's some practical purpose here."

"Could it be a tomb like for the pharaohs?"

Janet started at Margo's echoing her thought. "Were going to have to find out. Lindsey will insist on a complete investigation. I'll take the jalopy over for a personal touch. Standard procedure is to pull the ship within ten kilometers, but I'll bet we won't get closer than a hundred on this one. It'll be a long flight."

The mapper's monitor began spitting out images as it gradually swept past the asteroid. "Gotta go," Janet said and broke the connection. First, she looked for the probe. Underneath the face's left eye was a new, dark blemish. What sunlight there was dropped straight into the hole, and she could see the probe canted to one side. A tough angle, but now that she knew, she could get it out on its own power, assuming the jets weren't bent. She rubbed her chin, then directed the camera at what she'd thought were pock marks. They were all holes. They must be from smaller asteroids colliding with the Gargoyle. How long had it been tucked into this orbit? Why weren't there any large meteor strikes? Every asteroid they'd surveyed showed a long, violent past, filled with collisions, but other than these small holes, the Gargoyle was unmarked. She wondered if Texas-sized Ceres, which led the Gargoyle in its long route around the sun, absorbed most of the rocks that should have pummeled the smaller body.

The mapper continued across the surface until it was over a shiny spot the radar had picked up. An image assembled itself on her screen. She enhanced it, then sat back, shaking her head. It was a couple meters wide by a meter high and appeared to be made from polished rock or metal. Even with the monitor's fuzzy resolution she could see illustrations and writing. She contacted Lindsey to tell her the Gargoyle had a plaque.

The jalopy was an awkward looking rhomboid assembly of tubes, compressed air jets for propulsion and maneuvering, and several tool chests loaded with prospecting and mapping equipment. Inserted in the middle were two lightly shielded pods for the pilot and passenger. Alec and an equipment handler were already in the launch bay checking the supplies when Janet walked in.

Alec said, "This doesn't look like a mining operation to me. They ought to be sending an archaeologist." He scowled as he inventoried a locker and then slapped it shut.

"Probably," said Janet, raising her eyebrows. Rather than risk upsetting him more, she moved to where her suit was stored. What's wrong with him? she wondered. Soon, though, she was into the rhythm of getting ready for the mission. Every new asteroid required an initial human survey. There were too many variables in hooking the mining operation up to rely on robot reports. Asteroid composition could vary from one spot to another. A seemingly solid rock could be deeply cracked, or might be a dozen loosely melded pieces. Many turned out not to be suitable for easy mining. Too many silicates, not enough clean ore, not a clear site to base operations. For every five or six asteroids they visited, the ship would pause at one, but tons of usable metal could then be extracted, milled, smelted and shaped, then sent on the long, elliptical path that ended in lunar orbit for assembly into the ark ships. At the same time, chemical processes produced fuels and other usable products. Mining the asteroids reminded her of the Eskimos who used every part of a slaughtered sea lion.

Janet and Alec had worked as a team for three years. It was possible to do the whole job without talking, but they never had. She worked her way into her suit. Next to her, Alec pushed his arms into the thick, clumsy sleeves, his face just as dark and angry as it had been when she walked in.

"Ready," he said a few minutes later. Janet nodded. An assistant hooked her onto the hoist that lifted her over the jalopy and into her pod. Soon they were alone in the launch bay as the engineers left, closing the airlock doors behind them. Her suit stiffened as the chamber was evacuated, then the launch doors opened beneath them. The ship's spin provided the initial velocity. All that was necessary was to orient the ship and time their release, work that didn't need their input. Although launching was routine, it was a team effort, with dozens of others making the trip as smooth and safe as possible.

Janet triggered a private communication line as soon as the vacuum was established.

"What's wrong with Alec?" she asked.

Margo answered. "I thought you'd never get back to me. I've got his med readouts. Elevated pulse and respiration. He's scared. Xenophobia."

Alec's shadow moved in his pod's translucent shell as he checked the instrumentation. Beneath them, the stars scrolled past. "What's our transit time?" he asked.

Janet flipped to his frequency. "Twenty minutes. They pulled us closer than I thought they would." She clicked back to Margo. "Scared? I thought he was mad. You should have seen his expression." Her finger rested on the manual releases as she watched the launch countdown. She'd press her button at the correct time as a backup to the computer. "If he's that bothered, should he be going? I can't have him making judgement errors."

"He's not *that* scared. Check your own readouts."

Above her head, among a plethora of information, were her numbers, all elevated.

The countdown reached zero, and Janet pressed the button, dropping the jalopy from the mining vessel. Her stomach did the familiar lurch from the 1G environment to weightlessness. She rotated her pod so she faced their target, almost invisible in the fathomless black. During the trip, she stayed busy directing the craft to the Gargoyle's surface. In the few jobless moments she had to contemplate their mission, she listened to space's sound, which wasn't silent at all. Her suit hummed and whirred. Air hissed in the helmet's close confines. Behind it, her pulse throbbed. From the unmarked distance, the Gargoyle appeared, grew large, and soon filled the sky.

To anchor, she chose a spot in the spike field to the angry face's side. Unlike the probe, it wasn't her intention to fire explosive bolts into the surface. Instead, she would allow the craft to settle onto the spikes. Up close, they didn't appear as regular as they had in the vids. Micrometeor strikes had scarred them. Some were broken or cracked. Others bore smaller blemishes, like bullet holes. The distant sun's light through the spike forest cast awkward, impenetrable shadows, hiding the base structures.

The jalopy glided a few meters over the spikes until the edge of the angry face appeared on the horizon. Janet slowed the exploration craft until the spikes beneath them matched their speed. They descended onto two blunt tips, and the ship canted to rest on the shattered end of a third.

"We're here," she said. Not a quote for the history books, she thought.

Alec let loose a long, relieved breath. "You wouldn't believe what I've been thinking."

Janet powered the jalopy down, unbuckled herself, hooked a safety line to her belt, and pushed herself from the pod. "Try me."

"It's so obviously artificial. I thought it would open fire. I'm a little jumpy."

"It's dead, Alec." Janet laughed to herself. Odd thoughts had crossed her mind too.

Alec hooked himself in and floated to a tool locker in the Gargoyle's minuscule gravity where he equipped himself with a specimen hammer and sample sacks. "I'll get pieces from these spike tops, then move down to the base."

Janet nodded, then remembered to say, "Yes," as she jetted toward the face's edge, twenty meters away. From this angle she could see it was a thin plate resting on the spikes. She braced herself between two stone spears to examine the material. A hand-width's in thickness, it didn't appear to be either stone or metal. More like black porcelain than anything else. She smacked the top with her hand, but the leverage was bad, and all she succeeded in doing was losing her grip. For a second she floated, unanchored, then she grabbed the edge again, this time to hoist herself to the surface. At this angle, she couldn't tell it was a face. Every few meters, a hole marked the smooth surface, and her light revealed the spikes below. She glanced back to see Alec stuffing something into a sample sack. He waved, then attached his safety rope to a different spot. His voice crackled in her radio. "Looks like typical nickle-iron to me, a dark deposit on top, lighter underneath."

"So they made it from an asteroid."

"Would appear so."

"Okay. I'm going to the forehead to check out the plaque."

Alec grunted, a preoccupied sound. He chipped a bit from one spot, played out the slender safety cable, then glided to the next.

The Gargoyle's gravity was negligible. If she dropped a hammer, it would take minutes to complete its fall, so she drove an anchor bolt into a spike, attached her original line to it so there was now a path from the jalopy to the face's edge. When she reached the plaque, she'd place another bolt. Some asteroids had so many safety lines running across them, they looked like they'd been netted.

A gentle push from her back unit slid her across the Gargoyle's face, past its twisted mouth filled with spiky teeth, past the deep gashes that were its nose, across an eye's smooth bulge, to a knee-high platform on the forehead's edge.

"I'm moving toward the surface," said Alec. His breathing sounded regular, his voice clipped. Janet guessed if she could take his pulse now, it would be normal, while her own heart pounded in her ears. This was an alien artifact, concrete proof there were other sentient beings in the universe. She twisted her hand control to emit gas in a tiny puff that slowed her.

It was a plaque, just as the probe's flyby had shown, packed with symbols, illustrations and hieroglyphics. The largest illustration dominated the plaque's middle: at the top, a diagram of the Gargoyle. Next, a cutaway view showing the asteroid's interior with an odd symbol at the center. She thought about the funny magnetic readings. Was it a storage chamber? Then, a larger circle around the Gargoyle without the cutaway view. A planet? An orbit? The last illustration showed the circle fragmented into broken lines and a series of intersecting lines where the Gargoyle had been. An explosion? She clicked pictures from several angles, then crouched to see how it was fastened onto the platform.

Her gaze was on the horizon.

A screech in her helmet.

Alec shot up from the asteroid's surface, maneuvering jets on full, pushing him away from the asteroid. The safety cable, which was anchored sixty meters from him, snapped taut, pulling him into a parabola. First up, then parallel to the surface, then just as quickly, straight down. He disappeared into the spike field. Too fast.

"Alec?" she transmitted. She'd already detached her safety line, pushed hard away from the plaque toward where he'd gone in, and without thinking, made the corrections that killed a spin she'd picked up. She slapped the emergency "come hither" button, sending an automatic call for help, while flipping through displays until she found his suit telemetry. Pulse, fine. Breathing, fine. Air pressure, fine. She took a few deep breaths of her own. Suit temperature, fine, but falling. Partial system failure.

Questions from the ship. Nothing they could do now. She shut communications down. Concentrated on maneuvering. If she overshot, she'd waste too much time slowing, reversing direction, accelerating, then slowing again. A man in an unheated suit in shadow would freeze. She tried to remember how much time he might have. Couldn't come up with it. Too long since the refresher course. Most suit accidents were instantly fatal.

It wasn't until she paused over the spikes where he'd vanished, that she wondered what had thrown him off the surface in the first place. She directed a light down. His lower torso was visible, feet up, the rest was caught between two spikes as thick as tree trunks. No movement.

He'd yelled, a frightened yip. And his jets had been on, so he hadn't been tossed up, he'd jumped and then blasted. What scared him?

His safety cable pulled at the suit's side, as tight as a piano wire. She unsnapped it carefully, keeping her hand and head clear as it whipped from sight. Working by her helmet light, she inspected the damage. Alec's momentum had jammed him into the space between two spikes. The cover to the power unit on his back was cracked and bent. Whatever was broken inside, she wouldn't be able to repair it from here. The quicker she could extricate him and get him back to the ship, the better. She pulled herself around so she could look into his faceplate. In the middle was a blood spot matching a welt on his forehead. His eyes were partially open, with white slivers showing. He didn't react to the light in his face or to shaking.

The asteroid's surface, where the spikes were anchored was a couple meters below them, but too far for her to push him. She tried bracing her feet on the spikes' steep sides, but there wasn't enough grip and her feet slipped on every effort. Her breathing sounded harsh in her ears. "Damn it, Alec." She rested for a second, her head down.

This deep in the spike forest, the sun didn't penetrate. For the first time, she looked around her. Black, heavy columns leaning every way, marked by shadows that barely showed on their charcoal-like surfaces.

She scanned part way around before she saw it.

A scream stuck in her throat. By reflex, her legs pushed. If she'd been touching, she too would have flown straight up, but she'd drifted just enough that she kicked against nothing.

It was an alien figure, face like the one on the surface, peering around a spike, angry as hell, arms raised, claws extended.

By the time she'd scrambled to the other side of the columns that held Alec, she realized it couldn't be alive, but it took a long minute for her to approach, heart thudding, mouth dry.

The alien was a statue made from the same material as the asteroid. Its skin was polished, details sharp, like finely worked obsidian, her height, heavy in the chest, a short, hairless tail. Beyond it, others crouched behind spikes; some charged, carved in attack. Their frightening forms filled the forest. Janet guessed there was more statuary on the reverse side, mirroring the fright of that face. Angry or frightened. Nothing in between. She took pictures by habit.

Putting the camera away, she pushed herself above the spikes, then jetted to the jalopy. If she could free Alec, she could plug his suit into the exploration craft's power system and get around the break in his own.

It took a few frantic minutes to unanchor and lift off. She tried to eyeball where he was, then realized she hadn't marked the spot. The spikes' tops all looked the same, uniform in their randomness. She started the jalopy forward in the general direction while she tracked down his suit's signal. Soon she was above him. With the jalopy anchored again, she fastened a cable to the sturdy frame, then dove down where he was still stuck and unmoving. Not looking at the statue reaching toward her took will power. Getting Alec off the asteroid was a solvable problem, immediate, without the ambiguity of the message the statues sent. Were they alien gods, represented in stone? Were they art? Were they important at all? It didn't matter now. She fastened the cable to Alec's suit, then measured several meters of slack. Using the jalopy to pull him out by a straight pull wouldn't work. The compressed air jets didn't generate enough thrust. She'd need to use the jalopy's weight and momentum to jerk him out. She played out more cable, cinched it, then headed up.

The jalopy moved away from the spikes. Janet watched her speed and orientation so she didn't drift. It had to be a vertical lift off or she risked pulling the unconscious man across the spikes instead of up. Acceleration was slow. Return trips always took longer than going out.

One meter, two, three, four. How much cable had she left? Five, six. A gentle jolt shook the jalopy. Slowly, Alec rose from the spikes. Janet hit the auto-routines to get them back to the mining ship, then reeled him in. Soon he sat in his pod, plugged into the jalopy's power. His suit temperature rose. She stayed beside him, directing her light at this faceplate, waiting for the frost inside his helmet to melt.

He coughed, a sudden sound in her radio. His eyes opened, then squeezed back shut.

"How do you feel?" she asked. Her hands shook a little. Post emergency shock, she thought. Margo would explain it to her later.

"I saw a monster," he said thickly. He closed his eyes, and lolled his head against the helmet's side.

Medics hustled Alec away from the dock, and Janet had just removed her suit when she was summoned to Lindsey London's office. Lindsey waited inside, a tissue in hand and wearing a pained expression. Behind her were two upper-management types she barely recognized. One, an older man whose hair had gone pure silver around his ears, mirrored Lindsey's discomfort, though Janet doubted a sinus infection caused his; the other, wearing a Strieberist button, smiled widely.

"Oh, you are so lucky," he said, "to be the first person to land on an alien artifact. Let me shake your hand." He squeezed hard, and for a second Janet thought he was going to hug her too. "Your life is in for a change. When the media gets a hold of this, you'll be the most famous person in the solar system."

"We can't jump to conclusions," said the older one. "It may not be alien."

Janet looked at him in disbelief.

Lindsey said, "I did a calculation based on meteor strike frequency on its surface. The Gargoyle's been in space at least three-million years." She blew her nose. "Give or take a million."

"Even if it is. . .extraterrestrial, whoever left it certainly isn't around now," said silver hair. "This find shouldn't impact our basic mission. We'll leave it to scientists who are better equipped."

The Strieberist shook his head. "No, no, no. Don't you understand that this removes the need for our mission? The aliens left this for us to discover. It's their invitation to us. What else could it be? We should find out where the Gargoyle came from, and then bend our efforts to contacting them. It's mankind's most heroic quest yet."

"That's a *scientific* question. We are a *business* operation," said silver hair. "We have neither the expertise to investigate the artifact or the authority to abandon our mining efforts."

"What are you talking about? Investigating? I've never seen a more uninviting spot in my life." Janet looked from one to the other. "Did you see the pictures of the statues on the surface? Have you looked at the plaque?"

Silver hair cleared his throat. "There's some argument about what the plaque means. There appear to be several kinds of writing and diagrams. Our analysts compared it to the messages we attached to our deep space probes early in the space program."

"Which we included to introduce ourselves to other intelligences." The Strieberist sat on the edge of Lindsey's desk. "I agree with that analogy."

Lindsey called up the plaque on the wall monitor. "You saw it close, Janet. What were your impressions?"

"I didn't get to look at it long." She moved to where she could study it closer. The marks made no sense. She thought there would be little chance she could decipher the plaque's intent if it was written in Chinese, and that was a heck of a lot closer culturally to her than this communique. "The only thing I recognize is the diagram in the middle, with the Gargoyle, but I don't think we need the plaque to understand the big message, which is to stay away. I've never seen a clearer no-trespassing sign in my life."

The Strieberist bristled. "There is a message here, and it's a welcoming one to an *intelligent* race. The expressions might represent their smiles. Our evolution is obviously different. What makes you think we could recognize facial expressions in whatever they descended from? When we decipher the plaques, you'll see. There will be formulas for super-science. Maybe faster than light technology, or bio-breakthroughs that will revolutionize human life. See there?" He pointed to the cutaway diagram of the Gargoyle. "They've buried something for us. Why else would they show the asteroid's interior unless they wanted us to get it?"

Janet thought about perceptual set. The Strieberist saw what he expected to see. "In New Mexico there's a radioactive waste dump in the salt deposits. When the government chose the site, they had two worries: one, how to keep the waste from leaking out, and two, how to keep people, generations down the road, maybe long after any record of what was buried there had been lost, from digging it up. The problem was any monument they left could be misinterpreted. It's like the pharaohs' tombs. They were all looted. You can't trust that anything left over great stretches of time won't eventually be disturbed."

She pointed to the diagram. "You know what I think that is? Something deadly. The circle around it in the next diagram is the sun. The last diagram shows the sun exploding. Maybe they had a war and made a sun killer that couldn't be destroyed. Maybe it's their toxic waste. The faces are angry and fearful. Maybe those emotions and expressions are universal. Run away and be afraid."

Lindsey nodded. "If there is something in the Gargoyle, we'd want to study it much longer before opening it up. I'm including a recommendation in my report to quarantine the site."

"That will be my suggestion too," said silver hair.

The Strieberist slapped the desk. "My people won't put up with this. We have a right to know what is inside this artifact."

Janet looked from Lindsey to the older man to the Strieberist. It was a political struggle, and they weren't going to listen to her now. Whatever happened, it might take years to resolve. She remembered the statues at the surface, how they scowled and grimaced, how their hands were poised to rend, and she shivered. If they believed her theory, there was no way they could ever know what was inside the asteroid. She thought about Pandora and Bluebeard's wives.

"I would like to go check on Alec," she said.

Lindsey nodded, then turned back to the argument. As Janet left they were shouting at each other.

Thick bandages wrapped Alec's hands, and a slimy ointment had been smeared on his ears and nose.

"It's frostbite," Alec said. "Another ten minutes, the doctor tells me, and I'd have been frozen to the core."

Janet pulled a chair next to him, not sure what to say.

"They showed me your pictures from the Gargoyle. It was a statue I saw, wasn't it?" His face reddened slightly.

"Anyone might have reacted the same way, Alec. I'm just glad I was there to get you back." She put her hand on his arm.

"You saved my life. That's a pretty big deal."

She shrugged. "It just makes us even."

He leaned back and closed his eyes. "What are they saying about it?"

"I think they're going to haggle for a while, and then somebody will open it up."

Alec shook his head. "If I put one of those statues in the conference room, it would change a few minds. We need to do something to stop them."

"Some day we can, but not today. Today you need to get better. There'll be a lot of arguing among folk with a bunch more pull than we have before anyone makes a decision." Janet was already imagining the report she would turn in. If the Streiberist was right, she and Alec were famous now, the first humans to land on an alien artifact. Their voices might be louder than they would be otherwise. She smiled. There was reason to hope.

A technician wheeled in a cart with a food tray. "Time to eat," he said. "We got you stuff from the cafeteria. No dietary restrictions for you, so dig in." He put the tray across Alec's lap before he left.

For a minute Alec looked at the meal, then at his wrapped hands. He laughed. "I can't hold anything. I don't suppose you could feed me?"

Janet reached across Alec to pick up the fork. On the tray was meatloaf, corn, a roll, and a piece of cheesecake.

He kept his eyes on hers through each bite, and he never tried to move the arm she held. His face fascinated her, how his mouth worked, how he swallowed. Once she wiped his chin and he nodded his thanks.

When she got to the dessert, she cut off   a fork full and held it out for him.

He shook his head. "Too big," he said. "Cheesecake has to be eaten in small bites."

Janet smiled. Maybe she was seeing what she wanted to see. Maybe this was her perceptual set, but she didn't think so.

It was all she could do not to say, "You know what this means, don't you? We're not alone."

She trimmed the piece and fed it to him delicately.

Once They Were Monarchs

From the guard tower, Müller watched Bates circulating among the children in the shallow end. Bates was a fat thirteen-year-old whose bulging fingers turned to pale prunes after a half hour in the water, and whose rounded shoulders glowed dull red with perpetual sunburn. He often cruised the shallows in crocodile mode, his nose barely out, his bleached blue eyes evaluating each child before moving on.

Müller scrunched his hands into fists, thinking how good it would feel to squeeze the little pervert's neck, but he also welcomed the distraction from the lonely heights of the guard's chair. Mostly, life guarding left him too much time to contemplate isolation, his alienation from the screaming children, from the boring regularity of human rhythms. He thought of his unique position, high above the water's surface, looking down on all he surveyed as he had in the old days from mountaintops or from the circling giddiness of summer thermals beneath his wings. But mostly he felt the loneliness of the unending masquerade.

A handful of butterflies fluttered above the oleanders by the pump room. Müller thought about Monarchs and Viceroys.

"Good job yesterday," said Mr. Regin as he walked by the tower. "Quick thinking!" The old man's sandals flapped against his feet as he headed for the exit gate.

A long-haired boy wearing cut off jeans climbed from the deep end to Müller's left and dashed for the diving board.

"Don't run," growled Müller automatically, scrutinizing Bates as he drifted down to the rope that kept non-swimmers from the deeper water. The August, Sacramento sun's heat sank into Müller's skin like a heavy, sweltering blanket while the light glared off waves around Bates in a million, stabbing points. Müller turned his hands over, releasing his fists so they took the sun in his palms. It penetrated all the way to his bones, and he could feel his strength building, his animal inside churning for release, and still he watched Bates.

Müller had warned the pool manager the day before, after he'd pulled the Seigurd boy out of the water. Everyone thought Seigurd was drowning, but after a few seconds, Müller realized the child was having an asthma attack. A quick search of his towel revealed an inhaler, and twenty minutes later the kid was doing cannon balls off the high dive. "The Bates kid is a sicko, Raquelle. He's stalking the little girls all the time." His gravelly voice sounded too loud to him in the manager's office.

Raquelle hadn't looked up from the guard schedule on her desk. "Both Ray and George want the 4th off, and Janille can't teach her Mom-Tot lessons next week. She's taking driver's ed. Can you cover?"

Müller thought about a double or triple shift on the 4th of July, the crowded pool, non-swimmers whom he didn't know showing up the one summer holiday; the sun, like a blowtorch in the sky. "Sure. Now what about Bates?"

Raquelle glanced at him, zinc oxide coating her nose white. "Has anyone complained? Has he touched anyone?"

Müller looked around the room. Raquelle had a shelf full of sun screen by the sink; he smelled a fruity layer of it on her skin. Several floppy brimmed hats hung from a chair by the door along with a thin, light-colored blouse she wore to protect her arms outdoors, although she hardly ever guarded anymore. "I've got a feeling about him."

Raquelle shook her head. "He seems like a good kid to me. Probably should lay off the sweets. Has anyone had him in a lesson or talked to his parents? Maybe they could tell you something."

"I asked. He's never signed up for one, and I don't think he has parents. He walks to the pool."

Raquelle dismissed his concern with a wave of her hand. "You're a good guard, Müller. That was a nice piece of work yesterday with the Seigurd boy. I checked your records. You've been here, what, eleven years?"

Müller nodded, sighing. Raquelle was the fourth manager at the pool since he'd signed on. When someone noticed his longevity, it was time to pack his bags and go to a place they didn't know him, where they'd think he was just another late twenties guy slumming as a life guard and swim instructor. Maybe he'd move to San Diego and do some beach guarding.

"Keep an eye on him if you're worried. And for crying out loud, put up your umbrella. Your skin will turn to boot leather in this heat."

"I'm working on my tan," he said.

Müller squinted against the sparkle off the water. His eyes teared a little, but he stayed focused on Bates. Now the boy had sidled along the gutter until he was behind the Lindsey twins, a couple of blonde-headed, blue-eyed nine-year-olds in matching, pink bikinis who were tossing a ball back and forth between them. They shrieked as the ball went up, jumping to catch it before it hit the waves. Bates submerged, staring for a long minute before coming up for air. In the glare, Müller lost him. The surface caught the sun like an oily mirror, and Müller rubbed the back of his hand across his eyes to clear them. For a second, as Bates surfaced, he didn't look like a young teenager at all. For a second, as the water tumbled off his head, and the fractured sunlight pierced Müller's vision, the boy's skin turned color, a streaked yellow like an old bruise, and where the flesh had been smooth before, it became lumpy as if it were covered with warts. Not little warts, but fist-sized things on the edge of rupturing. For a second, Bates didn't look human. He turned, as if sensing Müller's attention, and the eyes behind the goggles were bulbous. Malice filled them.

Then Müller blinked, and his pulse pounded in his throat. He nearly roared, because now he knew what the creature was. The flickering reflection stopped, and Bates peeked up at him dully, a fat boy on a hot day wandering in the pool.

Something tapped Müller's foot. Beneath her hat, Raquelle shaded her face with her hand. "You looked pretty serious there for a second, buddy," she said. "Something bothering you?"

Müller scanned the few bobbing heads in the water. It was so hot that even being in the pool didn't beat the heat, and play had become listless. The pink-bikinied girls abandoned their game of catch and floated on their backs, eyes closed, blonde hair like nimbuses around their heads, their fingers interlocked so they wouldn't lose contact with each other. They floated in perfect X's, their feet spread, their arms splayed out. Müller had watched them hold this pose for minutes at a time on other days. Best little back floaters he'd ever seen. Some kids were rolling up their towels, readying for the 1:00 break, where the pool was cleared for ten minutes. On really hot days the least crowded time was between the 1:00 break and 5:00, when parents returning from work brought their families in.

Müller said, "Do you know about the Viceroy butterfly and the Monarch?" He nodded toward the colorful display above the oleanders. "Birds find the Viceroy tasty while the Monarch is bitter, so the Viceroy has adopted the Monarch's coloring. Birds leave the Viceroy alone now."

Raquelle looked confused. "And your point is?"

"There are all kinds of examples in nature of protective coloring and mimicry, like the walking stick or the scorpion fly. Sometimes the illusion is to protect the individual; sometimes it's to make it easier to prey. There's a preying mantid in Malaysia that looks like a flower. It eats the insects that come to pollinate it. We even have myths about imitators: the wolf pretending to be Little Red Riding Hood's grandmother, for example."

Raquelle nodded. "You're thinking about the Bates kid still, aren't you?"

Müller shrugged.

"You think he's a forty-year-old in a thirteen-year-old's body?"

"Something like that," said Müller. "He's a troll."

Bates had slid around to where the Lindsey twins still floated. He kept five or six feet away from them, but as the girls slowly revolved in the water, Müller could see he maneuvered himself so when he submerged he could look between one of the girl's legs.

Raquelle studied the tableau before her. "You sure you're not imagining it? I'd hate to confront a kid. Parents, you know, and libel suits. The city sent a memo on just this thing a week ago. He's not doing anything."

Bates sank so only the top of his head was visible, like a tiny hair island in a sun-beat ocean. He turned slowly too, but when he faced the girls, he paused slightly. He looked longer, and a waggle of his fingers moved him slightly closer.

"We just haven't caught him yet," said Müller. "You've got to be patient."

Raquelle clicked her fingernails against the base of the guard stand. "Tell you what. You take a break before you turn into beef jerky, and I'll take the last fifteen minutes. I'd like to watch him for a while."

Müller swung easily out of the seat and dropped to the deck five feet below it. Raquelle mounted the ladder. "How come you know so much about bugs? Are you a student?"

Müller grimaced. "Sort of. For mimicry to work, there can't be too many mimics. The base population has to outnumber the imposter by a huge percent or the adaptation breaks down."

"I don't get you. What does that have to do with anything?"

Müller checked the pool one more time. It was almost empty now: Bates, the Lindsey twins, a handful of older kids in the diving well . . . that was it. "I was just wondering how one Viceroy butterfly would find another among all those Monarchs."

Raquelle shook her head. "You're a strange bird, Müller. Get out of the sun for a while."

In the guard room, Müller checked the job board. This late in June, most positions were filled; even the inner-city rec programs in L.A. weren't advertising. He only looked at jobs south of San Francisco. Years ago he'd been in northern Europe, and the seasons didn't bother him much. Now that he was older, though, he sought the southern sun. Even here, in Sacramento, the rainy winter that never dipped below freezing bothered him. It took a couple of weeks of 90-degree weather in May for him to shake off the winter chill.

He wrote down a few phone numbers, then slouched into a vinyl-webbed deck chair. Summer was coming on, and the heat was beginning to fill him. By late August, it would be all consuming, and the drive to find another like him would make him restless. He brushed a finger against his lip and smiled, thinking about how soft it was. Even now, after hundreds and hundreds of years of hiding in a human body, he marveled at how fragile they were. That they ever threatened him and his kind on their mountain heights amazed him. But they did, and after a century of warfare, humanity had won. Saint George and all the rest like him won.

Only protective coloration and mimicry saved the remaining few. A little magic, a lot of swallowing of pride, and a desire to survive. They spread out. They fit in. They lost touch with each other. How does a Viceroy tell another of his rare kind from the overwhelming population of Monarchs indeed? And how long would it be before a wolf in sheep's clothing would forget what it was like to be a wolf, before he might fall in love with the flock? He wanted to fly above them again, like a tremendous hawk on the hunt, waiting to drop into a long stoop, but he didn't want *them* anymore; he'd been among them too long, he'd *been* one too long. Now, he only wanted to soak up sun and store it, he wanted to find one of his own, and he wanted to guard them, because they were weak, because they protected their young, and because he could. The little boy yesterday with asthma, for a second, Müller had thought he might die, and the thought scared him deeply. It scared him more than any horse-mounted knight ever had.

He folded a towel to put behind his head and rested. Beyond the guard's room, the sounds of the summer pool went on: the steady hum of the pump and filters, the occasional slurp of water through the skimmers, a vibrating thrum of the diving board, followed by the two-beat splash of someone entering the water. He smelled water steaming on the sun-washed cement, the acrid bite of chlorine, and fresh-cut richness of grass in the park around the pool.

Being a life guard suited him. For hours he did nothing except store sunshine. He could sit without moving a finger; only his eyes shifted as he scanned his area of responsibility. And beneath him, the human stories unfolded: there, a teen couple discovered each other while dangling their feet in the water; there, a mother struggled to watch her three boys, all under eight years old, at the same time; there an elderly woman jogged in the shallow end, practicing what she'd learned in the water-aerobics class. People were magnificent at a pool. They were physical and playful and emotional. And some of the time, they too lay still and let the sun fill them.

Then, every once in a while, he stirred to action. A child slipped on the deck and needed tending. Someone in a swim lesson got over his head and needed saving. Boys were too boisterous or young lovers were too amorous or someone lost a parent. And today, of course, there was a Bates, a special problem.

He drifted into a light sleep, dreaming about the undersides of clouds and a forest beneath him like a green, swaying sea.

After a while, outside, he heard crying. He sat up and pushed the door open with his foot. On the verge of grass by the baby pool, one of the Lindsey twins was holding the other. "I don't know why he would do that," said the one between sobs.

The other said, "I don't know either."

Beyond them, the guard chair sat empty; Raquelle stood on the edge of the diving well, chatting with a couple of the kids in the water. Müller wondered how long she'd been standing there.

Without thinking, Müller found himself kneeling by the girls. "What happened?" he rumbled. The girls stared at him, eyes red rimmed and teary.

"Nothing happened," said the crying one.

"It was nothing," said her sister, sobbing a little herself.

"I'm just sad."

"She's sad."

One turned her head toward Bates as he climbed out of the shallow end and headed for the locker room. She shivered a little and held her sister closer.

Müller couldn't move. Inside, things roiled around, raging, raging, but he had to contain them or everything would be lost, so he couldn't move. He knelt by the girls, not speaking for several minutes until they quit crying. Bates had vanished into the locker room but hadn't come out. Raquelle called the break to clear the pool while she tested the water's chemistry, and the handful of kids that were left headed to the concession stand at the other end, away from the locker rooms.

Finally, Müller stood. He was very close to the edge; in all his years, he'd never been this near to letting go of the mask. In his hands he could feel the claws wanting to come out. In his jaws, the long suppressed teeth ached beneath his gums. The ancient way of rending swirled about him. He could see it, could taste it, like a warm, thick soup squeezed from animals' heads.

The locker room door closed behind him. Listening quietly, he heard Bates around the corner toweling off, humming something discordant in a flat key, the notes bouncing off the slick tile and cinder block. Müller closed his eyes and sniffed the air. Chlorine. Hand soap. Mildew. Bates, the odor of sweat and bubble gum, and beneath that, something nasty: the smell of rotted mushrooms under a bridge, what they used to call blood mushrooms, deep red and damp. It was a troll's smell. But nothing else. They were alone in the locker room. The only light came through grimy skylights that dropped foggy shafts of white into the moist air.

Müller locked the door. The click echoed. Bates quit humming.

"Is anyone there?" said Bates, his voice a little quivery after several long moments of silence. A leaky shower head plinked water onto the cement.

Müller couldn't help it; a low growl bubbled out of him. It vibrated through the room.

Bates squeaked, then edged his way along the lockers until he stood directly in a shaft of light and could see Müller standing at the door.

"What do you want?" said Bates. He held his towel to his chest, as if it were a shield, and his goggles dangled around his thick neck.

A part of Müller wanted to say something to him. After all, they were both long lasting remnants of a time gone past, but the fury stilled the small part of him that contained his voice. The larger part of him moved away from the door and toward the fat boy. Bates stepped backwards, and suddenly his eyes narrowed.

"I know you," Bates said, and his voice dropped an octave. He stepped away again, and out of the skylight illumination. For a second, the illusion dropped, as it had when Müller saw him in the pool, and the creature underneath showed through. Now that Müller knew what to look for, it was easier not to be fooled. The clammy, sunburned skin covering the troll shifted, and Müller saw the heavy arms infested with ragged hair and rock-like warts. And the face beneath the face was filled with teeth—two short, heavy tusks dropped out of the corners of his mouth, pulling the lips apart so the cracked, uneven teeth in the middle poked in every direction and were revealed.

"You all are dead," said the troll. He dropped the towel and moved behind a bench, keeping it between him and Müller who continued to advance. "You're extinct, and there aren't many of us left either. It must be hard on you."

He didn't sound like a young boy now. Pretense was gone. The voice gurgled out of Bates' ancient throat, and his stony fingers clenched and unclenched as he kept his distance, moving toward his gym bag on the floor.

"We could share them," said Bates. "How long has it been since you've eaten well? Let me take one, one of those little girls for example. There are two of them — they're the same — one won't be missed. I'll take her to the forest and play my game, then you could have her. We'd both be served."

Müller pushed the bench aside. He eyed the troll's arms; they were inhumanly long and heavily muscled. The troll had changed himself less to fit in. The protective coloration only affected his proportions and surface appearance; he was still mostly troll with all his subterranean powers: his stone backbone and cold earth strength. He still could be incredibly powerful. If they grappled, Müller knew the troll would win. Müller's wings were buried too deep; his hands had been hands for too long while the talons had wasted away. So little was left that wasn't memories, but still, he came forward, the heat from a thousand hours of summer sun coalescing inside him.

Bates stopped at his bag, straddling it, his hands nearly brushing its handles. "The little girls are soooo tasty," he said, and in one motion, plunged his rock hand into the bag, coming out with an obsidian knife a foot long.

"But you'll never know, lizard!" and he jumped forward.

Müller stood still, something quivering inside him, building. His skin could barely hold it, it felt so big, begging for release.

The troll kicked aside the last bench.

The sun stored within Müller focused, became hard, ascended.

Bates raised his knife.

Shaking with the joy of it, Müller opened his mouth as if it were the old days, and unleashed the flame. It roared and roared and roared. And for a minute, the locker room could have just as well been a meadow in front of a castle, and the troll a lance wielding knight charging toward him. For a moment it was like it had always been.

And then it was done.

The sun shone like a white pupil in a blue eye and beat down. Müller stretched on the guard chair so all of his stomach caught the light. He rested his head back so his neck was warmed while he watched the pool. His hands lay palms up, gathering in heat, and within him an empty pocket began to fill again slowly, not like the old days where he'd find a warm boulder on the shoulder of the great mountain to spread his wings, to collect the sun in leathery gulps. No, he was smaller now, and these things took longer, but it still felt good. It felt very, very good to connect this way to earth and light, to the rhythms of the old sol's might.

"The boys' locker room smells bad," said Raquelle. Müller didn't move to look down at her, but he knew her face would be hidden under her floppy brimmed hat. "Can you check it out on your next break?" she said.

Müller breathed deeply, filling his lungs with hot summer air. Beyond the pool, wavy lines rose off the streets. He could see them swaying from black, shingled roofs. "When I'm on my break. Yes."

"Probably a kid lit some trash. I don't know why anyone would play with fire on a day like today. Wouldn't surprise me a bit if it were 115 degrees. Not even 2:00 yet. We ought to close, it's so hot. I'm pumping in city water now to cool the pool."

"It's a beautiful day. Perfect time to be on the tower," he said. In the diving well, the two swimmers who remained were splashing water on the board before they got out to do their dives. Even from here, Müller could see the dark splotches on the cement shrinking. A butterfly fluttered past. It looked like a Monarch, but he couldn't tell. It might have been a Viceroy. He smiled.

"Jeeze, you're a strange one, Müller." Raquelle moved herself so she stood in his shadow, the smell of sunscreen strong on her skin. "You remind me of a woman I guarded with in San Bernardino last year. She's worked that pool forever, they told me, and the hotter it is, the longer she stays out. Regular sun worshiper, she is."

Müller straightened in his seat and looked down at Raquelle intently.

She continued, "There are whole weeks of weather in San Bernardino that make today seem cool. I couldn't stand it."

The first diver went off the board. The second scurried out of the pool, stepping quickly to keep his feet cool as he headed for his turn.

"You've got to like the sun if you're going to guard," said Müller. "Maybe I should look that woman up. She sounds like a kindred spirit."

The diver bounced the end of the board twice to get extra height. At the top of his arc, he grabbed his knees and bent his head back in a tremendous cannon ball. Water flew everywhere, and the sun turned the spray into a flash of rainbow. For an instant, sparkle, color and the reflected diamonds of a million suns hung in the air.

"Yes," said Müller, settling back in his chair. "I might have to go to San Bernardino."

A WOW FINISH

Earle woke up last, on the floor under a sheet. Durance stood at the window, watching the rain, while Hoffman, achingly beautiful sat on the end of the bed, elbow on knee, chin in hand. They were already dressed.

Of all the field trips to all the times in all the world, she had to choose mine, Earle thought, conscious that he was naked beneath the thin covering. He wondered which of them had put the sheet over him.

"It's a pity we always arrive in a storm," said Durance. He tugged at his dark tie. "And the outfits are uncomfortable." He wore a beige double-breasted suit with matching pants creased so sharply Earle thought he could cut paper with them.

"Allergens," said Hoffman without moving. "The air's cleaner on a rainy day. God knows what you'd react to here. Street dust. Pollutants. Pigeons. It's safer on wet days. Cowardly, perhaps, but safer." She smiled at Earle. "You going to lay there all evening?"

Earle rolled to his side. His clothes were neatly piled beside him. He pulled them under the sheet and dressed there, aware that Hoffman only had to shift her gaze a foot to be looking right at him. It was a struggle to get into the shoes. The stiff leather bit into his ankles, but they had a nice shine to them, and putting them on made him feel more there. More real. Somewhere distant a bell rang. He realized he'd been hearing it for a while. Beyond that a steady rumble quivered just on the edge of his perceptions.

"Look at this phone," said Durance, picking it up. At first Earle thought that it was tied to the table. Durance said, "Wires *and* a dial. How do you work it?"

Hoffman stood from the bed, smoothing the front of her skirt with the edge of her hands. She'd cut her hair short for the trip and given it a curl. "Honestly, it's like you've never been in the field before."

"Nothing before 2020. My master's was on post-rock pop, but I got interested in the roots of neuro big band. Earle has been in the Twentieth

Century, though. I sampled that thing you did on the *Hindenberg*. Nice work."

Earle struggled with the shirt's buttons. "Beginner's luck. I was a last minute replacement."

Durance shrugged, then put the phone back on the table. "Hard to believe the trouble I'm going through to put in an extra footnote. Tiny Hill and his orchestra are in the Green Room here in the Edison. Harry James is uptown at the Astor, and Benny Goodman opens there tomorrow. Cab Calloway plays the Park Central."

"Pretty good lineup," said Earle.

"I tried talking Hoffman into going with me. A live band has to be better than a dusty old movie. So why go?" Durance laughed and put his hand on Hoffman's shoulder. She leaned into him. Earle turned away, concentrated on tying his shoe.

"Ask Earle. It's *Casablanca*," she said. "Opening week. I don't get it either. The *Hindenberg*, now that was important, but a film? Well, for a me a theater's as good a place as any."

Durance sniffed. "I read up on the movie. Who can watch this stuff? Ancient black and white that you can't edit while you watch, and bad piano bar music on top of that. Dooley Wilson didn't even play the piano. He was a drummer. Then there's a bunch of Germans singing an off-tune version of 'Die Wacht Am Rhein' instead of 'Deutschland Uber Alles,' which would have made more sense. I wouldn't get anything useful. Hard to believe people would get worked up over it. Twentieth Century sentimentalism."

"I've never seen it," said Hoffman. "Studied the background, though. Vichy France. The German advances. The resistance movement. Bogart. Bergman. I'm ready."

Earle paused in straightening his jacket. He didn't know that she had never seen the film. There might be hope yet. He dropped the sheet on the bed as he walked to the window. Traffic flowed below, rumbling. "Broadway," he said. "The Great White Way. 1942. Three and a half weeks until Christmas, and an entire world that hasn't seen *Casablanca*." He could feel the cars passing through his fingertips resting on the window sill. "Bogart said, 'When it's December 1941 in Casablanca, what time is it in New York?'"

Durance shrugged. "That's 47th. Broadway is around the corner. It's just an old movie. You could have stayed home and watched it on video."

"And you could listen to big band recordings whenever you want. Why'd *you* make the trip?" said Earle.

Durance glanced at Hoffman. He said, "Experiential research. I'm nanoed to the gills. Download the lot uptime, and I'll have a couple years' work worth of data in my twenty-four hours. No paper's complete any-more without actual field hours," but his glance said it all.

"Me too. Serves me right for asking a direct question," said Earle.

Hoffman slipped her arms into a coat, then flipped the white blouse's collars over the blue wool, as if she's always worn the style. She pulled on a pair of white gloves. Earle could hear Bogart's dialogue in his head: "I remember every detail. The Germans wore gray. You wore blue."

"We'd better get going, Earle. It's a four-block walk, and I want good seats."

Durance said, "I've got a half hour before the band starts here. Last chance at some decent music, Hoffman."

She shook her head at him as she headed for the door.

In the hallway, a sign read, WHEN IN DOUBT, PUT IT OUT.

She ran her fingers along the sign. Earle knew she was calling for info out of habit, but they weren't tied in here. No instant details about what-ever they wanted. No augmentation at all. They had to fit in. "Cigarettes?" said Hoffman. She buttoned her coat. "I didn't think the anti-smoking trend came along for another fifty years." She sniffed. "It doesn't smell like it's working either."

Earle adjusted his hat, a dark snap-brim with a black silk band above the brim. "It's a light-dimming measure. They were afraid German subma-rines might cruise up the Hudson River to shell the Rockefeller Center or something. They never really turned the lights out on Broadway, though."

Hoffman laughed, "That's funny. For a second there I tried to edit out the smell. It's weird to be stuck with one version of the world."

"Nope. Can't change a thing. Just like the natives. No VR ghosts. No info on demand. It's a single-track existence. Besides, you'd stick out wear-ing your regular headgear."

Earle looked down the long hall, doors opening on each side, a serving tray on the floor next to the nearest room, on the tray a partly eaten sand-wich on a plate beside an empty cup. That's exactly it, he thought, that makes this so good. One reality. Of course, even in the editable world, Hoffman had left him.

A bell chimed, and the elevator arrived. Earle started in recognition. That was the bell he'd been hearing. The doors opened to reveal a mirrored back wall. His coat looked good next to hers. Wide lapels. Plain epaulets on the shoulders. Buckled cinch bands at the wrists. He turned his collar up.

"You look like Bogart," Hoffman said.

"In a raincoat and hat, everyone looks like Bogart." He tried not to consider her face in the mirror. "Why'd you choose this trip? There were others to this era."

"I wouldn't have come if I had known that you were here. I'm still research assistant for Dr. Monroe. She's doing that monograph on women's social development in the mid-twentieth. This slot was open. Besides, she wanted me to see how contemporary women react to Ingrid Bergman saying"— she pulled a notecard from her pocket and read — "'I don't know what's right any longer. You have to think for both of us.'"

"You'll love Capitaine Renault then. His hobby is preying on pretty girls who need exit visas but don't have any money."

Hoffman raised her eyebrows. "And this is the classic film you argued was 'the cultural pivot point in American consciousness?'"

If that bothered her, Earle thought, he couldn't wait to see her response to Renault saying, "How extravagant you are, throwing away women like that. Someday they may be scarce."

The elevator opened onto the lobby level.

Hoffman stepped out first. "Heavens. If you love art deco, this is the place."

Gold-rimmed half-dome chandeliers hung from gold chains above the gold and brown carpet. Overstuffed chairs nestled up to tiny tables where a handful of people sipped from china cups.

A pair of sailors in dress whites walked by. "We could catch *The Skin of Our Teeth* if you wanted to see a show," said one.

"I hate Thornton Wilder," said the other. "We've only got two days. I'm going to spend the time snuggling up to that hat check girl or someone just like her."

Hoffman took a step after them, then turned to Earle. "That's the kind of material I need. They're so primitive."

"I don't know. You'd get the same talk in the grad dorms on a Friday night."

"Really?" Hoffman looked offended.

She took a complimentary umbrella from the doorman. Earle waved off the offer. He wanted to feel the rain tapping against his hat, to get more into the moment of time that was *this* time. He needed to submerge in 1942 so that it would be visceral. He couldn't just watch the video because the video wasn't theater. Experiential research meant that there was no substitute for being there. Like Durance, his system practically leaked nanos. They recorded everything he sensed. They made a duplicate of the experience he could return to again and again for study. Better than eyewitness reporting. So, no umbrella. Connect to the moment, walking in the rain with Hoffman, like Paris, where Bogart waited in the rain for Bergman at the train station. "Where is she? Have you seen her?" Bogart asked. The storm poured down. "No,

Mr. Richard," said Sam. "I can't find her." Sam handed Bogart a note. It read in part, "Richard, I cannot go with you or ever see you again." The ink ran in the rain.

They stepped through the doors onto the sidewalk. Earle held his hand out. Droplets pelted his palm. He could imagine the note in it, the ink leaking off the page. A car passed, splashing water onto their shoes.

Hoffman said, "I thought it would be louder. You know, all the gasoline engines."

Rain hissed off the street, drummed steadily against the buildings. Tires whined on the pavement. Lights glistened on the wet surfaces. Two couples, huddled under their umbrellas, hurried into the Edison's doors. This is New York at war, thought Earle. You couldn't tell. Despite gasoline rationing, traffic was heavy. A restaurant sign advertised a variety of steaks. Other than the sailors in the lobby, he hadn't seen military personnel or equipment. Were there anti-aircraft guns on the roofs?

He wanted to ask her about Durance. Hoffman hadn't seen the film. He could say Bogart's line without a hint of irony, "Tell me, who was it you left me for? Was it Durance, or were there others in between?"

Hoffman said, "It's breezy wearing a dress. These nylons aren't insulating at all. What did women do when it snowed?"

"They toughed it out, but they suffered. They took jobs in the factories and raised kids on their own, and waited for terrible telegrams to tell them their husbands weren't coming home." Cars eased by, dripping water from their fenders. Earle strained to see the people within. God, it's 1942, he thought. Soldiers are dying by the thousands. Northern Africa, southern France. Drowning next to the flames of their burning freighters. Broken airplanes tumbling. Many, many more are yet to die.

Hoffman shivered.

They crossed 48th. Low-hanging clouds hid the buildings' tops. The few pedestrians walked briskly under their umbrellas.

"It's amazing how every place in the past feels just like home," Hoffman said. "I mean, the air smells different–all those hydrocarbons–and the architecture's dated, but *I'm* the same. I could have been born here just as easily as any other time. Of course, half of my brain feels like it's turned off, but other than that . . ." She stepped around a puddle.

She doesn't see it, thought Earle. There's *nothing* here that's like home. Life here was both straightforward and mysterious. Everything was what it appeared to be, but nothing provided answers. The buildings, the sidewalks, the stores, the people, unaugmented and uneditedable, but all mute, their histories hidden. All of it's different. How could he explain that to her so that she'd know? "If you want to see sights unique to the era, we could

cross over a few blocks. St. Patrick's Cathedral and the Waldorf-Astoria
are that way." He pointed east, across Broadway.

"The cars are huge!"

A yellow Nash coup cruised by, rain water running off its long hood,
the silhouette of a couple, visible for just a moment in the front seat.
Packards, Olds, Mercurys, Studebakers, Plymouths, De Sotos, Grahams,
Fords, and others he couldn't identify splashed through the shallow pools. A
car twice as long as any he'd ever driven in glided on broad whitewalls, a
covered spare tire mounted on the running board behind the front wheel. A
Cadillac, probably, or a Rio. He whistled in appreciation.

Hoffman walked several steps ahead, hidden beneath her umbrella.
What I need, thought Earle, is something she wants. I need a Ugarte to
give me letters of transit. A passport to her heart. Ugarte, Peter Lorre in a
beautifully done small part, said the letters were "signed by General DeGaull.
Cannot be rescinded. Not even questioned." Ugarte killed a pair of German couriers to get them.

Earle shook his head. How did Bogart get Bergman back? He practically called her a whore, but she still loved him. *Casablanca* started as a
story of a jilted lover's bitterness. Bogart wanted to punish Bergman for
leaving him, but the vengeance went awry. Instead of hurting her, he drew
her in. Bergman said, "I can't fight it anymore. I ran away from you once.
I can't do it again."

"Tell me about the movie," Hoffman said.

Earle sped up so that he walked beside her.

"*Casablanca* is a pivot point for Americans' attitudes about themselves and the war. They didn't think that at the time. It was just another
movie, but when cultural historians look back now, they see it. It's a slice of
the times. Go in with an open mind; maybe you'll get more out of it than you
believe. If you keep your eyes open, you'll see all sorts of gender attitudes."

Hoffman peeked from under the umbrella. "These gloves aren't very
warm either. December in New York is cold," Hoffman said. She jammed
her free hand under her armpit. "So what should I be looking for?"

He smiled. "Start with Yvonne. It's implied that she and Bogart have a
relationship, but he dumps her in an early scene. She says, 'Where were
you last night?' and he says, 'That's so long ago I can't remember.' It's a
classic demonstration of Bogart indifference. The really interesting moment is with a Bulgarian girl later in the film. She wants Bogart's advice on
love and sacrifice. I don't want to spoil it, but her quandary reflects on
what's going on between Bogart, Bergman and Henreid."

"Henreid?"

"Victor Laszlo in the film, Bergman's husband."

"Right. Sorry. I got him mixed up with Greenstreet."

"He owns the Blue Parrot. Another big actor doing a nice turn in a small role."

Hoffman lifted the umbrella so she could look at him. Her eyes caught the oncoming car lights. "Just how many times have you seen this film? You never talked about it a year ago."

"Maybe a hundred."

"Heavens! So you've been a *Casablanca* fan your whole life?"

They crossed 49th. "No, not really. I saw it the first time in January." He blushed. "Well. . .um. . .I was doing a lot of other things too. Have to keep busy, you know."

"It's just hard to believe that a piece of film could be worth the trip." She kept glancing at the traffic to her side, but didn't say anything else as they approached the theater. Her silence was disconcerting. A hundred times, he thought. She'll think I've spent all my days watching romances. How pathetic. But he did watch it a hundred times, reclining in his academic's cubical, the film playing on the ceiling. Sometimes, while walking on campus, he had edited the world into black and white, and Sam playing "As Time Goes By." University noir, he had thought.

The line into the theater was short. Earle fingered the unfamiliar paper cash in his pocket. Seventy-five cents each for admission. For a moment he panicked when he couldn't remember if dollars were more than cents as he handed the woman at the ticket window a five. She smiled and pushed back a pair of quarters and three dollars.

In the lobby, Hoffman folded the umbrella, after fumbling with the mechanism for a moment, then looked at the change. "Is this any way to run an economy? It's so clumsy, passing around metal and paper. How many people do you think *touched* this? Yuck."

"You sound like Durance," he said.

She laughed. "Sorry. He can be a bit overwhelming. Infectious cynicism. Most of the time I edit him down. I'm going to mingle a bit before the show. See what I can learn."

Earle moved to the edge of the room so he could survey the area. Like the Edison, the lobby was opulent, more like a museum than a theater. He laughed to himself. Experiential research always affected him this way, and it was hard to shake the idea that the world he was walking through was virtual and augmented instead of being actual. This was the *real* world. 1942. A paranoid world at war, although, as someone once told him, it isn't paranoia if they're really out to get you. All kinds of history happened in '42. The Japanese captured Manila, Bataan fell, Roosevelt interned Japanese-Americans, MacArthur left the Phillipines, an oil refinery in California was shelled by a Japanese sub, the civilian draft began. The war hit close to New York too. In June, the FBI arrested four German saboteurs after a U-boat landed them on Long Island.

The people waiting to see *Casablanca* didn't look nervous. They chatted in the low murmur people use when in public. He wondered if the first audiences for *Romeo and Juliet* were the same way. No idea what awaited them inside. It is just another play, they would have been thinking. An idle way to spend a few hours. But the world was different afterwards. Those first audiences were there at the beginning, like people standing in a mountain meadow, unaware that the tiny stream at their feet was the progenitor of the Mississippi.

A handful stood near the coatroom. A couple leaned close together under a BUY WAR BONDS poster. Others entered a door into the theater.

"Shall we?" said Hoffman.

They took seats near the front. The room smelled of plush and colognes, and the wet street on people's shoes. Earle eyed the curtain at the front of the room apprehensively. It stretched nearly the length of the stage. "We could be too close. The image might not hold up when you're near the screen."

"They wouldn't have chairs here if it wasn't good." Hoffman sat, then squirmed a bit. "You wouldn't believe what I'm wearing *under* this," she said. "It's all seams and scratchy cloth."

Earle surveyed the theater. *Casablanca* had its opening night three days earlier. Now, fewer than half the seats were filled, almost all folks in their twenties or older. He breathed deeply. His record of the experience would be clearer if he stayed focused and calm. Hormonal imbalances could throw it off. He tried to forget that Hoffman was sitting next to him, her arm against his on the armrest. Slow breaths. Calmness.

The house lights dimmed, and the ceiling to floor curtains drew aside, revealing the screen.

"Very dramatic," said Hoffman. She settled deeper into her seat.

Behind them, a ratchety noise clicked into being, then a beam of light cut through the air to illuminate the screen. Earle turned. Through a small window high on the wall at the back of the theater, the projector glowed as the first film rolled. He nodded. The clicking would be the film pulling through the sprockets and the shutter flicking in front of each frame to give the illusion of movement. *That's* what I'm here for, he thought. All the reading about *Casablanca* had never told him how loud the projection equipment could be. He faced the screen. Movie Tone News, the title said. Reading hadn't told him that the floor would be sticky, or that watching a film in a huge room in the company of strangers felt so. . .well. . .so theatrical. No wonder people went to movies by the millions. This was the era before television, before computers and home theaters and specvids or tactiles or any of the entertainments he was used to. Black and white images of battleships at sea filled the screen.

The narrator's voice boomed through the theater. "Brave sailors on the USS Dakota shot down a record thirty-two enemy planes in a valiant effort in support of the South Pacific campaign." A shadowy plane raced across a gray sky, chased by tracers.

A woman a few seats to his left sat with her hands up to her mouth. Did she know someone in the navy? She might have been twenty, hair curled below her ears, a crucifix dangling from her throat, and she wore a long white skirt covered with a floral pattern, her coat folded on her lap. She appeared to be alone.

In the row in front of them there were three couples, all with the man's arm around the woman's shoulder. More than half the people in the theater were coupled up. It's a *social* occasion, Earle realized. Going to the movies wasn't just about seeing the story, it was, oddly enough, in the darkness of the theater and the noise of the movie, a way to be with someone. Granted, the communication was nonverbal, but the people must have come together to be together.

Hoffman sat beside him. He could put his arm around her. How would she respond? Her hands lightly gripped the armrests. Her legs were uncrossed. Nothing about her body language gave him a clue one way or another about what she was thinking. If he just raised his own arm, he could reach around her. Would she move in close? Her violet perfume filled his nose. From the corner of his eye, in the flickering light of the Movie Tone News, he could see the curve of her cheek, the reflected shine in her eye.

Earle's arm twitched. It would be so easy to make the motion to hold her. He could tell her that it was part of the experience of seeing a movie in 1942. He leaned to the left so he could raise his arm.

Something bumped the back of his chair. Earle turned. It was Durance, his forearms resting on their chair tops. "I figured I could catch Tiny Hill's Orchestra's late show. Thought I'd better see what this *Casablanca* fuss was all about. I had a tough time finding you in the dark!"

A sibilant "Shh!" hissed from a row back.

"It's not etiquette to talk in a theater," whispered Hoffman. She didn't appear happy to see him.

"Why not?" Durance said, his voice still too loud. "It's not a live performance."

"Shh," said Earle.

The Warner Bother's theme trumpets and drums theme filled the auditorium, and the film began.

Earle slid down in the chair until his head rested against the plush. The opening credits played over a map of Africa. He trembled. An arrow traced its way from Paris, across France, through the Mediterranean to end in Casablanca where all refugees without exit visas "wait and wait and wait."

He'd seen the picture a hundred times before. The rhythm of it was familiar — the report of the dead couriers and the stolen letters of transit, the roundup of suspects, the English couple talking to the pickpocket — but he'd never seen the movie like this, in a huge theater, and the atmosphere was different. The people sitting all around him had no idea that they were in the presence of greatness. Earle felt the same way he had at the *Hindenberg*. 1937. The ship was ridiculously large, only eighty-seven feet shorter than the *Titanic*. Earle had stood with a crowd to watch the docking. The people oohed and ahhed at her girth. They didn't know. They didn't know, but Earle did. To the unprepared, great moments felt like common ones until they were over.

On the screen, a model airplane flew over a crowded, Morrocan street. The people stared hopefully. Hoffman leaned into him. "That's not a very realistic looking airplane."

"Production costs," he whispered back. "Almost everything you see was done in the studio or back lots. No computer help."

She wrinkled her brow. "It's distracting."

"The story is not about the plane."

Scenes flicked by: Germans stepped onto the runway where Renault waited. Bogart played chess by himself at Rick's. Ugarte bragged to Bogart about selling exit Visas cheap. "I don't mind a parasite," said Bogart. "I object to a cut rate one."

Earle craned his neck to see other patrons in the theater. What were they feeling? How did the movie effect them? The woman in the floral print dress leaned forward, but he could see nothing in her or the rest of the audience's attentive faces. For a second, Durance met Earle's gaze, but he looked back to the screen.

Earle turned around. Within minutes, Bergman entered, saw Sam. She had to know right then, Earle thought. Rick was back in her life. The bar was called Rick's and Sam was Rick's best friend. Sam knew too the heartache she brought. Earle could see it in Sam's face. Sam must have been thinking, run boss! Later he would beg Rick to leave. "Please, boss, let's go. There ain't nothing but trouble for you here. We'll take the car and drive all night. We'll get drunk. We'll go fishing and stay away until she's gone."

But Rick waited for a woman. He made Sam play "As Time Goes By."

Earle's hands rested on his knees. Hoffman had taken the armrest. She stared at the screen, the changing light brightening then shadowing her features.

Bergman walked into Rick's. "Can I tell you a story?" she asked Rick.

"Does it got a wow finish?" he said.

"I don't know the finish yet."

I don't know the finish either, thought Earle. He felt Bogart's pain in his loss of expression. Despite his tough-guy posturing, it was all there beneath. And the film played on, uneditable, inevitable, like history. He wondered what the script of the evening held for him. Was there an inevitable crash coming? Was his *Hindenberg* moving toward the docking tower, with him on board instead of those poor, doomed people? But, gradually, as the film clicked on, he forgot about Hoffman sitting next to him and Durance behind. He forgot about the other people in the theater. They were all in Casablanca, holding letters of transit close to their hearts, bargaining with bitterness for love. Ignoring the Nazi Major Strasser and his arrogance. Ignoring the pain in the world around them, until the passion became too much. Laszlo lead the café's band in "La Marseillaise," overwhelming the Germans' singing of "Die Wacht Am Rhein." Even Yvonne, Bogart's spurned lover who came to the bar with a German officer on her arm joined in, tears on her cheeks. Bergman looked at her driven husband across the room, who was not thinking of himself or her or of love, but of his occupied France and the German heel in its back. It was an instant where Earle often paused the film to look at Bergman's eyes. The world was in them, filled with respect for Laszlo's courage, with admiration. Anyone would give a lifetime to earn the look that Bergman considered him with, and Laszlo didn't know. He sang the song to its end, the expatriates in the café on their feet, for a moment joined in emotion.

But Earle couldn't pause the film. It rolled on. "Viva la France!" they roared. "Viva La France!"

Like he had a hundred times before, Renault closed the café under Strasser's orders. Bogart said, "How can they close me up? On what grounds?" Renault said, "I'm shocked, shocked to find that gambling is going on here." Just then the croupier handed Renault a handful of cash. "Your winnings sir." The audience laughed, which woke Earle to his mission. He broke his gaze from the screen. The woman in the floral dress didn't laugh. Her posture was tense. Earle could see she was mesmerized. What's going to happen next? she must be thinking. Her life was involved now, like the audience to any worthwhile story. What's going to happen?

In a few minutes, Bergman would wait for Bogart in his apartment. She'd plead for the letters. Finally, she'd pull a gun on him. "Go ahead and shoot," he'd say. "You'll be doing me a favor." She will put the gun down. "Richard, I tried to stay away. I thought I would never see you again, that you were out of my life." She'll weep. "The day you left Paris, if you knew what I went through. If you knew how much I loved you, how much I still love you." They'd kiss.

Why didn't Bogart see what she was doing? Earle thought. The Bulgarian girl not ten minutes earlier in the film had said, "If someone loved you very much so that your happiness was the only thing she wanted in the world, and she did a bad thing to make certain of it, could you forgive her?"

But that was the beauty. Bogart didn't. He couldn't replay the Bulgarian girl's words. He couldn't edit what Bergman said to him, nor could he tinker with his own heart. Maybe by the end of the film he figured it out, but right then, Bogart went with his own emotions. He forgot his anger and held her, Bergman, with her luminous eyes and high cheekbones and smile like a sunrise.

Hoffman whispered. "You didn't tell me the film had a sense of humor."

Earle felt her breath in his ear, her hand on his arm. "It has irony," he whispered back, keenly aware that Durance sat behind them. Did Bogart send Bergman off with Henreid at the end of the film because he knew she didn't love him? Was he that keen-sighted? And how did he know?

What was Hoffman thinking? Did she care for him in the least?

Earle forced himself to look away from the screen again. He was here to experience *Casablanca* in a world where it hadn't existed before. He had a job to do.

The woman in the floral dress held a handkerchief to her cheek, not moving. Her face was wet with tears. Henreid asked Bergman about the time she thought he was dead. "Were you lonely in Paris?" he asked. "I know how it is to be lonely," he said. Was Henreid forgiving Bergman for the affair with Bogart without even knowing about it? The woman in the floral dress sobbed silently. What was her story? Was her husband at war? Did she believe him to be dead? Even now, was there a lover?

Earle watched, awed. How seldom had he been able to feel the world through someone else. The bend of her wrist. The handkerchief's dangling end. The quiet, wracking sobs that shook her sides. How privileged he felt to be a part of her moment. What a moment of trespass on his part. Everything he hoped for in coming to see *Casablanca* was encompassed by this scene. This would be bigger than his *Hindenberg* experience.

He looked away, blinking against a momentary sting. It didn't take much to see that his problems didn't amount to — he sought for a comparison, then smiled — a hill of beans. It was Bogart's line. Whatever the woman in the floral dress was going through, his own anxieties couldn't measure up. Earle couldn't know Hoffman's mind any more than Bogart knew Bergman's, and in this time he couldn't edit in messages from her or create pictures of the two of them at romantic vacation stops, or even replay their times together. He was a time traveler stuck in the ever-present and always receding now with the people around him an enigma, like the woman in the floral dress.

On the screen, Bergman slipped away from her motel room to meet Bogart, to tell him of her life after she married Laszlo, how she thought Laszlo was dead when she'd met Bogart in Paris. Earle slid his arm out from under Hoffman's hand, then walked to the rear of the theater. From the back, he could see all the still heads. Earlier in the film he'd heard conversation, but now there was nothing but Bogart and Bergman's voices. Bergman buried her head in Bogart's shoulder. She said the line: "I ran away from you once, I can't do it again."

Earle nodded. He'd seen this moment over and over. It seemed to him that Bergman was exactly torn. She loved her husband, but she also loved Bogart. It was a perfect scene, balancing the two men she loved against the sureness that she would have to leave one behind. Maybe she believed that Laszlo really lived for his work and could go on without her, or maybe she knew that no matter what happened, if she demonstrated her love for Laszlo by deserting him for another man that she had done the right thing. There was no way to tell. Regardless, she chose Bogart and set him in motion for the end of the film.

Who was the audience rooting for? Laszlo seemed a bit of a cold fish, but he was absolutely blameless in his love for his wife and devotion to his anti-Nazism. Bogart was flawed and scarred, but his passion for Bergman redeemed him. And now, in the time the audience watched, France was still occupied. The Vichy government still danced to Germany's pipes. Soldiers were dying over what song the people would sing, "Die Wacht Am Rhine" or "La Marseillaise."

Earle moved to where he could see more of the audience. He imagined how the sequence would replay when he downloaded the nanotech recordings. The noisy projector clicking away in the background. The feel of plush beneath his hands. The hint of rain held in wet coats dripping onto the floor.

Now came the plan, the thinking that Bogart did for Bergman. Bergman believed she was leaving Casablanca with Bogart. They went to the airport. Bogart told Renault to fill out the letters of transit with Laszlo and Bergman's name. Bergman was confused. Bogart explained, the time travelers lament, that if she didn't leave she would regret it, "Maybe not today, maybe not tomorrow, but soon and for the rest of your life." The plane took off. Major Strasser was shot. Bogart and Renault walk into the fog together.

Earle closed his eyes and leaned against the wall. The soundtrack boomed out "La Marseillaise." People clapped. He opened his eyes. Some of the audience was standing, applauding the screen as the curtains closed and the lights came up. They kept clapping. Even though there were no live performers to appreciate their reaction, they applauded. Finally, they turned, gathered their umbrellas and coats to head toward the exits.

"I loved that," said a woman to her companion as they passed Earle on the way out. "Who would have believed Bogart could play a romantic lead?" said another.

Hoffman walked up the aisle, the houselights catching the shimmer in her hair. "You were right to come here. I had no idea," she said, her hand brushing his as she passed. "I'll see you in the lobby." She nodded back into the nearly empty theater.

Only Durance and the woman in the floral dress remained. Durance stood next to her, leaning down over where she was seated, speaking earnestly.

Earle glanced to the exit. Hoffman was already gone. He walked down the aisle toward Durance and the woman. It wasn't until Earle was close enough to touch them that Durance looked up.

"She seemed upset," said Durance.

"I'm better now, really," said the woman. She'd dried her face, but her mascara had smudged. "I don't know what came over me."

"I understand," said Durance. "Look," he said to Earle. "You were right." He fumbled for words, "I didn't think a film . . . it wasn't sentimental." He inhaled deeply, and in the exhalation was a hint of an emotional quiver. "They're doing the show again, aren't they, in a half hour?"

Earle nodded.

"And it will be exactly the same, won't it? They can't change it?" said Durance.

The woman looked at him quizzically.

Earle understood. The film would always play out the same way. Like the *Hindenberg*. Like all of history, unrolling in its immutable way. That was its charm. "Yes," he said. "Of course."

Durance took a seat next to the woman. "We thought we'd see it again." He gestured toward the exits. "Could you pay for our tickets?"

Durance and the woman faced the screen, waiting for the lights to go down and the curtain to open.

In the lobby, Hoffman stood by the door. They stepped onto the side-walk without speaking, where the rain had slowed to a gentle patter, hinting of snow. A block later, while they waited to cross the street, Hoffman said, "It was a good story."

She was looking into the distance. Not at him.

"Yes," he said.

"It had a good finish."

"Yes."

As they crossed, Hoffman took his arm. He realized she hadn't brought her umbrella. Water ran off the edges of her hat. She said, "What should we do now?"

When they reached the sidewalk, she still held his arm.

Earle thought of Bogart walking into the fog with Renault. It *was* a good ending, a wow finish. Earle said, "I hear that Cab Calloway is playing at the Park Central."

Hoffman smiled in a lingering way that seemed very much like Ingrid Bergman. "Do you know how to dance?"

A passing car splashed water on their legs. Earle didn't care. They had another twenty hours or so in New York, in the city that never sleeps. Meanwhile, in *Casablanca*, Sam sang at his piano, the old song, Bogart's and Bergman's song. Everybody's song.

It's true, Earle thought as the rain came down, as the water gurgled in the gutters, as the undersides of clouds glowing in New York's evening lights twisted slowly above. Sam was right: it's still the same old story, and it would always be, as time goes by.

Friday, After the Game

Arien never considered playing football for Wells High to be *real* football even though the senses were accounted for: the concession stand oozed popcorn and hotdog odors; the home crowd roared at good plays and moaned for poor ones. The opposing players' stentorian breathing when they took their stance filled his ears. The helmet squeezed his head. Of course, he tasted the mouth piece's hard plastic; it was the only part of the game that *was* real. Despite the vividness of those senses, the grass beneath his fingers didn't feel grassy. All his hands sensed was hard or soft, warm or cold. No detail. No texture.

Also, he missed cheerleaders, mostly Margo. It wasn't that they weren't there; they were, stunningly beautiful, energetic, spirited, rousing the fans with intricate stacks and clever cheers, but as soon as the game ended, the field flicked out, and he was alone in his room, wearing his port gear. The cheerleaders were gone, including Margo.

The experience didn't satisfy him.

But after tonight's game, this could change.

Wells archrival, West Kimono High, owned the same six-and-two record, and the game would settle the league championship, but, more importantly two of West Kimono's players, Broncho Martinez, an offensive lineman, and Bernardino Li-Chen, an option back, lived within sixty miles, while Wells' quarterback, Harmon Byers, lived in Sante Fe, only forty miles from Albuquerque where Arien lived.

What were the odds, Arien thought, that *four* players from two opposing high schools lived within commuting distance? West Kimono's quarterback ported in from Fairbanks. He threw passes to a pair of wide receivers, one who connected in Buenos Aires, and the other played from Sydney.

Arien's senior class was spread over the globe, and were sim-students at Wells because their learning styles matched the teacher's techniques. They ported to classes in the morning, studied all day; then the athletes practiced, squaring off against virtual opponents for a couple of sweaty, afternoon hours.

Their proximity was rare, almost amazing, and out of that unique circumstance, the plot was born.

Harmon, who *looked* like a quarterback, classically chiseled cheek bones, long, smooth muscles bulging in his upper arms, always in his letter jacket, sat behind Arien in their Information Exploration class, a boring study of how and where to find problem related data. The assignments mostly consisted of scavenger hunts for obscure facts: How was the *Maine* sunk? What were religious reactions to the discovery of Martian lichens? Miss Davenport said for the umpteenth time, "Finding information defines the modern thinker."

Harmon whispered in Arien's ear, "Are we ready?"

Of course, he wasn't really whispering in Arien's ear. Harmon sat in his port room at his home forty miles away whispering into Arien's virtual simulacrum.

Arien checked Miss Davenport. She lectured unperturbed. Harmon's "whisper" would register on her monitors — teachers received way more information about their students in a virtual classroom than they did in an old-fashioned one — but she still needed to pay attention, and Harmon's question was too vague to trip alarms.

Arien nodded.

Miss Davenport said, "What would be a productive sub-search routine to run if you wanted to know a foreign visitor's cultural differences while you made your initial introductions?"

After a pause, Martin, who sat to Arien's left, put up his hand. Arien moaned. Martin always answered questions, or asked them, or initiated discussion, or prompted debate, or looked interested, or otherwise kept the class moving. He was a Turing, an AI student. Most of the first week of school Arien spent discovering the Turings. Every class had at least a couple of them, digital shills who made the classes lively when the real students were sluggish.

After Martin answered, Miss Davenport moved on to another topic. Arien leaned across the aisle and said, "How'd you do on the test yesterday, Turing?"

Martin smiled — Arien thought he detected a nanosecond delay in the programming; the smile showed up a shade late — and said, "My name's Martin. Ninty-two percent. How'd you do?"

Arien considered lying, just for the reaction. If he said sixty-percent, for example, the Turing would know that was twenty-five points low, and instead of whatever canned reaction the higher score would produce ("That's a great grade, Arien!" Fake smile.), the AI would have to decide how to respond to the lie, all the time behaving as if it didn't know it had been lied to. However, Arien knew the prank would get him a session in counseling inside of a couple of days where they'd poke and prod him about his self esteem.

"I did O.K."

"That's great, Arien." Fake smile.

The Turings were unfailingly chipper in class. Also, they never went out for football.

Margo sat in the front, a row to his left. She wore her cheerleading uniform today, taking careful notes in her perfectly formed script. She'd shown him her notebook once after he'd missed a day sick, each "i" dotted with a heart. Her head rested on her hand, and long, wavy red curls spilled down her arm. Rather than take his own notes, he studied her shoulders, the way she held herself tilted a bit to the side, her cheek's roundness.

He wished he could meet her for real, but he wasn't even sure where she lived. Her snail-mail address was an international post office box, which just meant the mail was forwarded elsewhere. Most people chose to keep their home addresses unlisted.

They'd gone to the virtual Homecoming together, which hardly counted. Parents and the school monitored the dances closely, and other than dancing, and a chaste hug at the end of the evening, they'd barely touched. It wasn't worth it. Although the port-suit was good for football's heavy impacts, a caress left something to be desired.

After class, they met in the promenade. Theoretically, conversations out of the room weren't monitored, but Arien, like most of the kids, didn't believe that. Comments were elliptic.

"Are you still going to do it?" Margo asked. She had a musical voice. Arien thought it sounded like a pipe organ, a small one, each note ascending through golden tubes. Sometimes they'd meet in study hall, and he'd ask her to read his notes back to him, just so he could hear her speak.

"It's a once in a lifetime chance," said Arien. The passage between classes was airy and wide. Students strolled or gathered in small groups. Wells High adopted a classic Greek look this year — last year had been ivy league Victorian — so the walks were marble, and tall colonnades flanked doors into classrooms. The administrators at Wells reveled in digital remodeling. The teachers were the same way. Last week Davenport's class met in sawgrass covered sand dunes with the ocean pounding away in the background. This week she'd gone to a kind of a post-Disney, pseudo-dental office burnished chrome and porcelain motif room under twenty-foot tall ceilings.

Margo held her books close to her chest, arms crossed over them, her expression serious. "Will the place work?" She'd suggested the site weeks earlier, when he'd told her about the plan.

Arien nodded. "There's enough light. The grass is flat. I lined out yard-markers a couple days ago. The ground up chalk worked just like you said it would."

She said, "What if you. . .you know?"

He knew she meant to say, "What if you get caught?" a phrase that would surely alert a monitor.

They were at the door to his next class, Advanced Placement World History. "There would be a price to be paid. We won't get. . .you know." He thought about consequences. How many rules had he broken already? There was the stolen equipment, of course, and the lying to his parents about where he was going. The worst, though, the ones that might really get them, were the quarantine violations.

"It's just too paranoid," Arien said angrily. "I don't think I'm going to get the flu or a cold or something from everyone I meet. You know they used to play football in front of big crowds. A hundred-thousand real people in the same stadium, and they didn't all get sick from each other."

Margo looked panicked for a second, then recovered. "Thanks. I hadn't thought about it that way. Maybe I can use that idea in my paper on archaic practices."

"Yeah," said Arien lamely. "Anything I can do to help." He kicked himself mentally for almost blurting out the plan.

She turned and started to walk away, then stopped. "I wish I could go," she said. "It'd be nice to spend some time with you."

Pressure constricted Arien's chest. She really liked him! He said, for the invisible monitor's benefit, "Well, study hard and you can get into this class too."

Coach practiced the new plays that afternoon, but they walked through the formations without hitting. On defense, Arien lined up to the left of the nose guard. For West Kimono, Coach had put in several twist plays where Arien switched places with the nose guard or the defensive end after the snap. Mostly Wells ran slants on defense, and the extra steps threw Arien's timing off.

Arien took his stance, almost helmet to helmet with the offensive tackle. On this twist he was supposed to go around the nose guard and into the hole between the other team's center and guard. They repeated the play a half-dozen times.

Football's a thinking man's sport, thought Arien. While he trotted around the nose guard, his heads-up display scrolled fundamental instructions. "Remember, a stalemate means the offensive lineman won. NO ARM TACK-LES! Listen to the linebacker for the defense." The scrolling was endless, as were Coach's canned speeches playing in his ear, and Coach's real-time comments. A diagram appeared in front of him, showing where he was supposed to go and where he was now. His position glowed red.

"Arien! Get to your mark! If you're not there on time, they have an alley my grandmother could run through!" bellowed Coach.

After practice, Arien carefully disconnected himself from the portage. He put the helmet on its peg, pulled off the gloves, unzipped the sleeves, stepped from the pants and hung the suit on a hanger. The porting equipment filled one corner of the room. Arien's parents believed in waiting until technology was proven, so he didn't have one of the new units that was no bigger than a wastebasket. Regardless of the size, the ports worked the same way, transmitting data to the gloves, suit and helmet, creating any sensory environment. Within the outfit, he could run, swim, free fall, climb mountains, and hunt tigers, but mostly he went to school and played football.

It isn't *real* football, he thought, as he dragged the box from under his bed. His parents were locked in their offices, but still, they might come out for some reason, so sweat beaded on his forehead as he carried it down the hallway to the garage. It wasn't until he'd locked it in the trunk and returned to his room that he could breathe easily.

At their pre-game dinner, Mom said, "I don't see why he has to *go* to the musical revue."

Arien fought the urge to roll his eyes. "It's not a 'musical revue.' It's a retro-concert. The musicians play their own instruments, and you promised."

Dad said between bites, "We did wild things when we were kids, dear. He has a bio-mask. He'll be perfectly safe. You do have your mask, don't you?"

Arien nodded. "It's a state of the art concert hall. They said all the air will be filtered and irradiated four times an hour. It's safe."

Mom looked doubtful. "Won't you be too tired after your game?"

Dad said, "He'll be fine. After we win, he'll have earned a little relaxation."

With any luck, Arien thought, he might be able to make the concert too. It was the concert that gave him the co-conspirators' addresses. He had ported to a chat room about it, a pleasant oak-shelved music library with deep-pillowed couches. Harmon was there, and Harmon had seen Bernardino and Broncho earlier. They all wanted to see the concert, and the plan was born.

After dinner, Arien showered. The suit seemed more responsive when he was clean, and the pounding water cleared his head. If Wells beat West Kimono, they'd qualify for regionals, but he had a hard time concentrating on the game. He thought about the box in the car. It wasn't too late to chicken out.

The first defensive playoff scrimmage convinced him he wouldn't.

As always, the stadium smelled appropriately grassy; the concession stand oozed popcorn odor; the home crowd roared appreciatively at good plays and moaned for poor ones, and opposing players' breathing when they took their stance filled his ears. It was *exactly* the same as the last game he'd played. The virtual playing field never changed, was absolutely regular. Shadows never varied (They played under the lights). Weather conditions always within parameters.

The West Kimono kickoff man returned the kick to their own twenty-five. Arien trotted in with the defensive unit. The linebacker called one of the twist plays they'd practiced. Arien put weight on his hand, ready to dash right on the snap (careful not to *lean* right or look right so as to give away the stunt). Their quarterback started his cadence. The ball moved. Arien jerked right. Drove around the nose guard. Turned toward the quarterback who'd backed to pass. Open ground. No protection for him. The twist worked! Arien plunged forward, already counting the QB sack on his stats. A hit from the side, and he was flattened.

They'd anticipated the twist and set up trap blocks. Arien stared through his face guard. The West Kimono man pointed at him. "Got ya," he said.

The hit was a surprise, and his side ached where the shoulder pads drove into him, but it didn't hurt anymore than any other hit. Arien pushed himself up, pulled grass out of his face guard. Another shortcoming in virtual football was the game had become risk free. No chance for *real* injury. The port suits gauged the strength of the blow and the ability of the athlete to absorb it. A couple of years ago there'd been a scandal in high school ball because a player actually broke a leg. For weeks officials suspended the schedule as they investigated. Eventually it came out that the boy had an undiagnosed calcium deficiency. The game was deemed safe once again, and play resumed.

Well done trap blocks made a defensive lineman's life miserable. West Kimono mixed their blocking routine, sometimes taking him straight on, sometimes double-teaming, and every third or forth play, letting him through for a blindside. He didn't lay a hand on a runner in the backfield or even hurry the quarterback until almost halftime when he side-stepped a blocker, lowered his head, and buried it in the quarterback's ribs. They whistled him for spearing.

As the team filed into the locker room for half time, Arien looked for Margo. The cheering squad knelt on the sidelines, waiting for the band to play. No Margo. He wondered if she was sick.

Coach prepped them on defensive adjustments, adding two new alignments to their heads-up displays. Arien studied them. Pretty routine stuff. He supposed the game was exciting, the teams were tied at seventeen points each, but he was counting off the minutes until the end. The four players were supposed to meet an hour after the last snap. They'd have maybe an hour before heading to the concert. Would they show up?

Arien fidgeted on the bench. He didn't dare display the driving route. Coach would see he wasn't paying attention. Dutifully, he scrolled through the new plays. The band started their next song. Coach huddled them in the middle of the room. "Wells, Wells, Wells," they chanted.

The second half went their way. Arien flushed the West Kimono quarterback out of the pocket on their first possession, and the Wells safety ran the interception back for a touchdown. But time passed slowly. Arien kept checking the game clock.

Wells won. The crowd went crazy, and Arien ported home before anyone congratulated him. He peeled the suit off and headed for the garage.

"Good game, son. Enjoy the concert," called Dad as Arien passed his room. Dad held his port helmet in his hands. Mom still wore hers. "Go, Wells! Go, Wells!" she yelled, still at the stadium.

Arien punched the destination into the autopilot, and the car pulled away from their house. A projected map showed his progress as he moved through the neighborhoods. Arien liked to keep the windows transparent. The few cars he passed were opaqued. A light rain fell. Maybe they won't come, he thought. His stomach tightened. Arien had the greatest distance to cover, seventy miles. If everything went well on his end, he'd hit the super-way and make the trip in under thirty-minutes. The others lived closer to the field.

The car turned into a retirement community. Lots of individual cottages with real windows, some with lights behind their curtains, then back into a newer area where the buildings crowded the streets, their unbroken faces as dark as the night sky behind them. Arien rubbed his arms briskly. He was only minutes away from the field, a long and wide grassy stretch at the back of a cemetery. He chewed his lip. If everyone showed up, they'd have maybe an hour. It had taken him about an hour to line the field, and he hadn't seen anyone. The tombstones at that end were all more than a hundred years old, so there were no visitors, but light poles circled the area and lined the path. They'd be able to see.

Under the cemetery entrance. Up the winding path through trees and crypts. Over a rise and into the older grounds. Some stones leaned, their names nearly worn away. They were the influenza stones. Thousands of them the same size and shape. The city left the field as a reminder–most victims were cremated, but these were buried, and the stones served as a monument.

Three cars were already parked when Arien pulled up. A skinny boy wearing a jacket looked up from his car's trunk and waved. Arien's motor turned off, and he climbed from the car. For a moment he considered putting on his bio-mask, but decided against it. If they were going to play, they might as well breathe on each other too. The boy looked familiar, but barely. He was baby-faced, and his wrists were thin. Arien guessed he might weigh a hundred-and-thirty pounds.

Arien said, "Harmon?" Rain drizzled down. He wished he'd brought a hat.

"Is that you, Arien?" the boy said. "Wow. I thought you were bigger." He pulled a set of shoulder pads and a helmet out of the trunk. "Did you bring the ball?"

Arien blushed. He'd tweaked his simulacra over the past few years to reflect what he wanted to be. After all, he played on the defensive line. It wouldn't do for him to appear unintimidating. But Harmon was a god in the classroom, a *quarterback* god, and this boy didn't look like he could toss a ball twenty yards.

Harmon said, "Broncho and Bernardino are here already. I don't know if we want to go through with this."

Arien opened his trunk. From the box he extracted his own shoulder pads, helmet and a ball, all ordered from an e-collectibles site. "Come on. We've gone this far. Don't you want to know what real hitting is like?"

Harmon swallowed nervously. "It's not that. Have you seen Bernardino?"

"Sure," Arien said. Then he thought about how he'd "seen" Harmon. The Bernardino he knew from the games was a lithe option back. Solid, quick footed. Soft hands that never fumbled. Arien had tackled him twice during the game, once for a fifteen-yard loss.

A chubby kid wearing shoulder pads that were too big for him, carrying his helmet in one hand and an umbrella in the other came around the cars. "Hi, guys," he said. "Is this Arien? I thought you were bigger."

"You're Broncho?" Arien almost said, "I thought you'd be more fit," but he bit his tongue. "Nice to meet you. Did you have trouble getting out?"

"Naw. Coach chewed on us for a while about losing, but he got disgusted early and dismissed the team. You really took us to town in the second half."

"You guys played a good game," said Arien. "Where's Bernardino?"

The other boys didn't say anything. Then Harmon pointed across the field. "Warming up."

In the darkness beyond where Arien had marked the sideline, a shadow moved. Then Bernardino stepped into the light.

He was huge! Six-and-a-half feet tall. Two-hundred-and-fifty pounds. Shoulders too wide for pads. "Hello, guys," he said, his voice a well-tuned avalanche.

"Wow," said Arien.

"Yeah, I thought so too," said Harmon. "I want him on my team."

"Sorry, boys. He plays with me," said Broncho.

"Wow." Arien had studied the old football films. Seen pictures of the greats. Bernardino looked bigger and stronger. He moved like he was barely containing an explosion.

"I apologize my simulacrum looks differently. The league handicapped me so I could play the game."

"They can do that?" said Arien. He felt like he'd discovered a new sin.

Harmon said, "Yeah, it's a parity thing. My dad knows all about it. He used to be on the high school activities board. Player's skills are augmented or limited so no one feels bad about being understrengthed or slow."

Arien shook his head. "Sheesh. Well, who would have guessed that? Let's play anyway. If we don't get started, the opportunity will be gone."

Bernardino grinned and picked up the ball. It disappeared in his hand. "We will kick off."

Arien helped Harmon into his pads. Then they trotted to the field's far end. Harmon said he'd take the kick. Arien would block. He looked up. The rain continued, the drops suddenly appearing in the light to splatter on his face.

This is the way it should be, he thought. No crowd. No virtual concession stand. Beyond the sidelines, rows and rows of tombstones glistened under the lights. The pads felt good on his shoulders, even if they didn't quite fit. They were weighty and sturdy and *real*.

In the mist, fifty yards away, Broncho looked like a midget standing next to Bernardino.

"Go ahead," said Arien.

Harmon raised his hand above his head, then dropped it. Bernardino kicked. The ball sailed out of sight as Arien charged forward. Special teams. His job was to give Harmon a clear path. His legs drummed. Rain tapped against his helmet, and a glorious rush of feelings consumed him. I'm playing ball, he thought. Real ball!

A dark mass moved down the field toward him. A tackler. Get him! thought Arien, his consciousness now reduced to instinct. Stop the tackler. Protect the ball carrier. He changed his angle, all his practice coming into the forefront. Even without a heads-up display, he envisioned the lines forming on the field. Bernardino converging on the ball. Harmon cutting behind Arien for protection. Broncho following the lead tackler, swinging to one side to drive Harmon away from the open area. Hit him low, thought Arien.

In the back of his mind, Arien analyzed the situation. Bernardino led the charge, his long legs chewing up distance. Broncho lagged behind. If he could engage Bernardino for an instant, he might be able to break the block and also take on the second defender. They would score a touchdown on the kick! There were only two men between them and the goal. Arien took on two players all the time during games.

For an instant, the scene was poised and beautiful. No virtual set pieces. No synthesized crowd urging them on. No simulacra. Real air. Real grass. Real inertia. Arien saw it as a painting, a grim look set in his features, shoulders hunched for the block; Bernardino getting ready to juke left or right around him. This was better than his imagination. Then the scene continued, Arien swooping forward, waiting for Bernardino to commit to one side or the other. Another stride. Bernardino grew, came closer, details focused: a button on his shirt, a string flapping on his pads.

He loomed.

He didn't juke.

The world went black.

Sometime later the world was still black. Arien's back felt wet.

"Do you think he's okay?" someone said.

Arien considered his position. For a while he thought the port-suit had fizzled out. Soon the screen would flicker and he'd be back in the classroom or at practice. He waited. A light patter of sound caught his attention. "What is that?" he thought.

"Maybe he's dead."

"I didn't mean to hurt him," said a deep voice.

Arien thought, "It's rain. I'm hearing rain. Why can't I see?" Slowly he raised his arms. The right one ached from the shoulder to the elbow. His hands met a smooth surface in front of his face. He turned it, and above the face-guard Bernardino, Harmon and Broncho's concerned expressions floated.

Arien pulled the helmet off. Rain fell straight down, tapping against his skin. "That was a heck of a hit." He shut his eyes. "Did we score?"

"No," said Harmon.

"He dropped the ball and ran the other way," said Broncho.

"I'm sorry, Arien." Bernardino crouched beside him. "Can you move your legs?"

Rain stroked his face, sending drops down his neck. He thought about it for a while before sliding his feet toward him. "Yeah."

Bernardino looked so relieved that Arien nearly laughed, but breathing hurt, and he wasn't sure that he hadn't broken a rib.

"Maybe if I sat up," said Arien. They bent to help him. He wrapped his arms around his knees. Nothing grated in his chest, so he decided the rib was whole, but it wouldn't surprise him if he was bruised tomorrow.

In the rain, by the cemetery lights, the grass glistened. The ball rested in the middle, someone's helmet upside down beside it. If Arien could pre-serve an image, that was the one he wanted. The rain, a helmet, a ball — an unevenly lined field and four warriors (three a little smaller than he'd pictured them). He smiled.

"Someone's coming," said Harmon. A car crested the hill and pulled next to theirs.

"Oh, jeeze," said Broncho, "What if it's one of our parents?"

The headlights winked out and the door opened. In the rain, Arien couldn't tell who it was, but there was only one of them. He forced himself up, grimacing as he did.

The figure approached, wearing a bio-mask. It was a girl, a slender one in a rain coat. Arien didn't recognize her. She was shorter than he was by a couple inches, and the rain dampened her thin red hair — strands stuck to her forehead. Her nose was narrow, and her eyes, above the mask, were dark.

"Arien?" she said, in a voice like a delicate pipe organ. "Did I miss your game?"

"Margo?" Arien said. He dropped his helmet.

"I did, didn't I?" She put her hand to her mask, hesitated, then, looking at the other boys, removed it decisively. Her cheekbones were high, per-haps even a little sharp, and her chin wasn't as round as it appeared in class, but now that he'd heard her voice, he could see the Margo he knew.

"Yeah, it wasn't much of a contest."

Harmon said, "We did a kick off, but I don't think we're going to run any more plays. Maybe we could catch?" Broncho and Bernardino nod-ded.

Arien rotated his shoulder to a chorus of sharp pains. "I'll watch."

The other boys trotted onto the field. Holding the ball, Harmon set them on a line, called a cadence, then yelled, "Hike!" He faded back and threw a tight spiral to Bernardino. Arien whistled appreciatively. Harmon might be small, but he had good technique.

From the corner of his eye Arien glanced at Margo standing at his shoulder. Caught her looking at him.

"Missed you at the game," he said.

She scuffed the ground with her foot, and put her chin into her coat's collar. "I've been on the super-way since breakfast. I really wanted to see. . .you know. . .you guys play. I live in Toronto."

Broncho threw the ball this time. His wobbly pass didn't reach Harmon, who dove to make the catch. He came up laughing. "Look, grass stains!" He held his forearms up for them to see.

"That's a long way," said Arien. He didn't know what else to talk about. The Margo at school he could talk to for hours, but she wasn't *there* actually. He was safe behind his digital image.

"Was it worth it. . .to play like this?"

Bernardino threw the next pass. It knocked Harmon off his feet.

Her voice was the same. He thought about her sitting in class, about walking with her in the courtyards between their rooms.

"Yeah, I'm glad we did it. I don't need to do it again, though."

The silence stretched uncomfortably. Finally, Arien said, "There's a concert we're all going to. Would you like to go?"

He could hear the smile in her voice without turning to see it. "Oh, I'd love to. That would be lovely."

They didn't move toward the cars. They watched the three other boys playing catch, yelling with joy in the rain.

After a while, Arien took a shaky breath, then reached out slowly, blindly from his side, until he touched her hand. They touched. She nestled her fingers between his. He could feel her palm's silky texture, the fine strength in her hand and wrist. The rain had turned into a mist, and just before the boys quit throwing to each other to return to the cars, Arien, his heart careening in his chest, squeezed her hand.

She squeezed back.

The Invisible Empire

W hat the beginning of my tale must do is to convince you that a
man of science like myself could do what I did at the end of it. I
don't know if I can. Some actions are too hard to explain. Maybe it was the
fever born of living in a foreign land. Maybe Charlie Crumb and his super-
stitions affected me. Perhaps I became insane for a moment. All I can tell
you is that the events are true, and for what it's worth, I did what I did.

It started with young Colonel Montgomery Thomas, eyes bleary with
drink, sitting on the edge of the vertical shaft into the Epitome, facing me as
I cranked the windlass that lowered four Negro miners in a bucket to the
tunnel a hundred feet down.

When I'd arrived in the Colorado territory two weeks earlier, Montgomery had squinted at me from under his hat. "What kind of black boy are
you?"

"I'm mulatto," I'd said a bit stiffly, and quite a bit better educated than
you, I thought.

"Neither fish nor fowl, eh?"

In a few days the Colonel seemed to have forgiven me for my African
mother. I believe he found in my English accent a sign of kinship not present
in my American cousins.

"Surly bastards," he said, gesturing toward the men, now vanished
below. "Before I surrendered with the Western Army in North Carolina,
Jonas, they were *properly* scared of me. Hell, Charlie Crump served as
my house boy." Charlie Crump was the crew chief, a likable man of
twenty-five or so, about my age. He'd tipped his hat at a jaunty angle and
grinned at me as I lowered the crew. Montgomery rolled a whiskey bottle
between his palms. Only a swallow or two remained. I concentrated on
holding the bar against the cable's tension. If the bucket jerked, it could
spill the miners.

Looking into the shaft, he said, "I should have become a raider. There
would be glory in that." He pulled a drink from his bottle. "For my service,

the Confederate government gave me one Mexican dollar for food and a mule to get home on. You know what I found there? Do you? Surly, superstitious, brown bastards from pantry to parlor. No Klan then. I should go back, you know. Give them a bit of the white sheet. Give them a bit of the ghost. You can scare a man into better behavior. Nothing like a little terror to keep him awake at night. Better than guns. Better than nooses." He sounded introspective suddenly. Very quiet. "Plant an imp in a man's head, and he'll walk always in darkness."

I nodded. Some variation of this story came whenever he drank, and he hadn't missed a day since I joined him. He was worse than usual, swearing more, slurring his speech.

Keeping the bucket ride smooth was my job now, not listening. They didn't warn me at Oxford's School of Mines about drunken, southern expatriot owners who knew nothing about hard rock mining. He tunneled on whims, overworked his crews and stored blasting powder too near the machinery. Reading the American authors, Nathaniel Hawthorne, Ralph Waldo Emerson and Edgar Allan Poe had not prepared me for this land either. Well, perhaps Poe, who said, "There are moments when, even to the sober eye of Reason, the world of our sad Humanity may assume the semblance of Hell."

Across the canyon, a puff of smoke billowed from the Daedelus. A few seconds later the explosion echoed sharply. Up and down the gulch, yellow tailing piles marked the slopes. Powder blasts resounded regularly, and when no wind rattled through the trees, the sound of hammers on drills filled the air. Below, tents and rude log structures occupied nearly every flat spot, and in the middle, Clear Creek oozed like muddy soup.

I wasn't thinking about the Colonel, though. In my mind's eye, I pictured the shafts and drifts and crosscuts underground. One-hundred-and-eighty feet down, we had hit water. If we were to go lower, we'd need pumps or a drainage tunnel.

More troublesome, however, was the cavity in Bernice, the middle of three coyote tunnels Montgomery had extended. A miner lost a hand drill while setting a powder charge the day before. He'd placed the drill, whacked it twice, and the third time it disappeared into the hole. He'd fled, blubbering about witches and demons. Now none of the men would go into Bernice. I went down by myself and widened the cavity until it was large enough to extend a lantern into. Light reached no walls or ceiling, and when I pitched a rock through, it clattered once against something, making no other sound as it fell. Suddenly I'd felt nauseous. My light dimmed, and I backed out. Bad air. How could there be a natural cavern in granite? This was a conundrum more interesting than any story I'd heard from the Colonel.

He droned on, "I didn't *have* a home to go to. That damned Sherman gave the land over for slave occupation. Camp followers, the whole cursed lot. I could see the Atlantic from my porch, you know, the clipper ships. I remember their sails, full of the sea breeze. It's been two years, now. You think they've grown a decent crop yet? You think they can care for themselves without proper direction? Might as well have burned the building to the ground."

"You did well with your dollar, sir," I said absently. The bucket would be nearly to the new shaft now. I waited for the signal. One bell meant "stop," or "lower the bucket." Two meant, "bring it up."

"Investors," he said, leaning over the hole. From where he sat he would be able to see the men's candles eighty feet down, if the air was clear. "Not *everything* ended in Yankee banks." He flicked a pebble over the edge. I cringed. If it hit one of the men, it could sting. They were runaways who'd fled west during the war. That's all Montgomery hired. At first I thought it was because he paid them less than white miners, but I think it was his hatred of them and the chance to make their lives miserable.

He swung his feet out of the shaft, and stood. "The air's too dry here. Too damn thin. The work's dangerous. The gold, what there is of it, is impossible to dig out, and what I ship to the stamper mill is stolen. I can't get a decent breath that doesn't smell of Chinese, Yankees and darkies." He paced around the shaft, the empty bottle dangling from his hand, a dangerous scowl in his eye. "Did you see how they looked at me before they went down? Insolent. Pure disrespect. In Atlanta white women walk on the street because the Negroes won't give way, and the law, Northern law, protects them. Used to be they knew their place."

I watched the bell, a hammer strung next to a panning plate. When they tugged on the cord, the hammer struck the metal. They were working the new dig, and I didn't have the cable marked for the proper depth.

After I'd explored the odd cavity within Bernice, I'd spent most of the afternoon collecting samples from the shaft walls. Before I'd arrived, the Colonel had found the main vein, much thinner than he hoped it would be. Several tunnels followed it through the mountain, the coyote tunnels, so named because they were exploratory, not like the engineered shafts I was used to seeing. The support timbers gave me nightmares, roughly hewn beams jammed haphazardly into place. A good nudge would knock any one of them down. My first day in the mine, while Charlie gave me a tour, a foot-wide support timber fell over, nearly smashing my foot. Neither of us had touched it. Charlie grinned and wedged it against the floor and ceiling. I'm not claustrophobic, but the Epitome gave me shivers. The mountain's weight hung over me. The ore was low grade, too. Colonel Montgomery hoped for better luck at other levels, which is why he'd hired me. "Expertise," he said, "Solves problems."

I'd noted the promising spots. The assay numbers were posted on a beam by the windlass. I studied them. The rock was thick with quartz, but it was difficult to tell with small samples what bore gold thread and what was worthless bull quartz. I ignored the Colonel as he continued his rant. Work went better when he stayed in his tent farther down the mountain, or rode his horse into Blackhawk where there was a proper saloon, with wood floors and glass in the windows.

The hammer clanged once. I leaned against the bar, stopping the bucket's descent. The Colonel stood on the shaft's edge again, his back bent, looking down. At first I didn't realize what he was doing. His posture seemed so odd, as if he were praying. Then I saw: he held a rock the size of a human head. He swayed a little, from the weight or the drink I couldn't tell. I opened my mouth to speak — I have no idea what I would have said — but he lurched forward and pitched the rock into the opening before I spoke. Whatever I might have uttered stayed frozen in my throat. The Colonel stood perfectly poised, his hands empty, while the rock — it must have weighed fifty pounds — hurtled down the shaft.

The retarding bar jumped out of my grip. I didn't hear the rock hit. Everything seemed silent, but I felt it in my hands, the vibration leaping up the cable and through the bar. The windlass spun a half turn before I grabbed the bar to stop it.

Stunned, I looked at the Colonel. He never raised his eyes. If he had, the spell might have been broken, but he stood like a dusty statue, head down. Behind him the mountain rose steeply. Pine spotted the slope, clinging to gaps between dark granite outcrops. A lone bird, a hawk, glided overhead at a level with the ridge's top. I held the bar, the vibration no longer alive in my fingers, the metal, a deadly still, cold weight against my hand.

Two bells. I watched the hammer, not believing it had moved. Two bells again, insistently.

I started the laborious process of bringing the bucket up.

The Colonel stepped back, dusted off his hands, then strode past me. "I'm getting a drink. You tell those men I don't pay salary if they're above ground." His voice was absolutely steady.

Time crept as I turned the windlass. They didn't ring the bell again, and they made no noise. I'd almost convinced myself that the rock must have missed. Maybe it clanged off the bucket's rim. They were just scared. The walls weren't steady if rocks were falling off, they'd be thinking. They wouldn't suspect the rock had been dropped intentionally. Who would toss a stone down a mine shaft on purpose? They were frightened and coming up to tell me we needed to stabilize the walls. The buckle holding the bucket to the cable appeared, then the men. Three held one like a broken toy. Blood soaked them all. At first I didn't recognize what I was seeing. They've covered his head, I thought. Why would they do that? But his head wasn't covered. That *was* his head, not head shaped anymore, and his shoulder hung awkwardly. They didn't move, the three men, they just held him, as if by supporting him they could put him back together.

I shifted my gaze down. On the bucket's edge a deep dent bent the metal. A single bloody drop and a clump of hair marked the dent.

"We need a mortician," Charlie Crump said. All the Negroes spoke with thick accents, but this was clear. He didn't ask for a doctor. He didn't ask what happened. He just held his dead companion. "We have to be burying," Charlie said. They carefully lifted the dead man from the bucket and laid him beside the shaft. I covered the corpse with a tarp.

One of them said to another, "It's dat debil man, Montgomery again."

"This has happened before?" I said, unable to take my gaze from the lump under the tarp.

They nodded.

There was no constable in Veronica Falls, which wasn't a full-fledged settlement yet like Idaho Springs or Central City, so I walked along the cart trail to the jailhouse in Idaho Springs, about a five-mile trip. The air shook with explosions and smelled of blasting powder. Sawing, hammering, cursing. Enduring their looks, I stepped aside for men on horseback or leading mules hauling supplies in huge baskets draped over their backs. The farther west I'd gone from Boston, the worse this country had become. Boston, at least, had a sense of civility. A man wearing a jacket over a white shirt with starched collar would be considered properly attired. Here, I couldn't tell if it were the color of my skin or my dress that attracted so much attention. It cost fifty cents a shirt to have them laundered, which was what I paid for them new, but a person must keep an appearance of dignity about him or be reduced to the barbaric. Men lying in open tents, waiting for their shifts, stared at me. Signs advertising tools and dry goods hung from log buildings that weren't even chinked yet. I could see tables and chairs through the cracks.

"You're that fancy, European mining engineer Montgomery's hired on, ain't ya? Heard you were a bit of a dandy. Didn't know you were a black fella, not that you're all that dark," said the sheriff, sitting on a stool outside his cabin that also served as a jail. "What are you, some kind of Arab?"

"I'm British," I said.

Like everyone else in the camps, he was desperately in need of a bath. Grease and dirt stained his shirt so heavily, I couldn't tell what pattern it was. I don't know why I thought I would get justice from a man such as this. "Did anyone else see this happen? How 'bout the colored boys. They see it?"

I shook my head.

He rubbed his hand down his beard. "I've been out to Montgomery's claim before. Heard a rumor, but the darkies wouldn't answer questions. You being foreign, I reckon you don't understand how things work around here. We need proper, believable witnesses to make an arrest."

"*I* saw it," I said.

He rubbed his beard some more. "There is that," he said, "but it's just you. One witness won't do."

"That's outrageous! If Montgomery came to you saying I dropped a rock down the shaft, would he need a corroborator?"

The sheriff laughed. "Of course not. He's white, even if he is an ex-Confederate."

My mind reeled at this turn of events. "I thought the war between the states was to emancipate the Negro race."

He seemed to think that over, then said, "We freed them. That doesn't make them the same as everyone else. I hear the plan is to round them all up and ship them back to where they came from."

"Are you going to arrest Montgomery or not?"

"Look, I don't like him any better than the next man, but there's no use in me going up there if there's no case. You could be mistaken. It'd be your word against his. If he's stupid enough to kill his own crew, then he won't last long out here. Anyway, miners die all the time. If I'd had any sense, I'd have bought a hearse instead of a mining kit. That way I'd be one of the few to *make* money from digging holes."

I left his cabin. By then the day was nearly done, and the tree stumps cast long shadows behind them. When I got to Veronica Falls, night had fallen, stars glittered in the dark blue. Lanterns lit mine entrances in the slopes above, while silhouetted forms sat in glowing tents along the creek. Woodsmoke filled the valley, carrying the smell of cooked beef and vegetables. It had been six months since I left London, and I missed the rain-washed streets, the pubs, the way boat lights reflected on the broad Thames, waiting for the tide to turn. I missed an enlightened city where even a street urchin's death deserved an investigation.

I made my way toward my quarters in Brown Town, where the Negroes, Chinese, and Mexicans pitched their tents. Montgomery's crew tent might have been built for ten men, but twenty-four slept there. Generally eight-man teams worked the Epitome, so we weren't stacked on top of each other all the time. It made even the primitive conditions of the Pakistani gold dig, where I'd worked with my Oxford mentors, look palatial in comparison. No native servants taking our laundry in the evening here. No break for tea in the afternoon, even if field rationing meant boiling the leaves twice.

Somewhere in the dark, a gun shot echoed. Then two more. I shuddered and drew my coat closer. Americans!

I'd spent nearly all my money to get to Montgomery's mine. He'd promised to reimburse my traveling expenses in our correspondence, but now he said I needed to "earn it out." If I quit his employment, I would have no way to get home again. But I swore to myself then, as I wandered up the darkened cart path, Clear Creek gurgling in my ears, that I would stand in harm's way rather than let him hurt another miner. Accidents can happen both directions. There are many ways a man can be killed in the Colorado mine fields.

A strange scene greeted me in the crew tent. Rather than the still forms of men bedded down for the evening, a circle of heads bent over an oil lantern. They chanted low, deep words that made no sense to me. They might have only been nonsense, but it sounded like language. The lantern lit the faces nearby, serious, white eyes, flashes of teeth. Charlie Crump saw me. He pushed his way out of the circle, grabbed my arm and took me from the tent.

"I must ask you this question," he said. Of course, it was in his southern dialect that sounded to my ear like, "I mus'as' ya dis question. What kind of person is ya'?"

This confused me. "I'm an academic, an educated man," I offered.

The men in the tent still chanted, and I could not shake the sense of unreality. He said, "No, I mean are you for Master Montgomery, or are you for us?"

I didn't have to think to answer. "He must not kill again."

Charlie nodded. "Master Montgomery is a devil." Charlie's voice dropped, and he moved closer, as if he was afraid to say the words loudly. "He is in league with the 'Invisible Empire.' He boasts of it. If we are not respectful, if we forget that the white man is master, then we will be punished. He took tokens from all us and made evil signs so we could not leave."

In the darkness outside the tent, I looked around. The stream still gurgled, and pans rattled against pans in another tent down the hill. Rough laughter came from the opposite direction. Everything still appeared real and definite. Even Charlie's hand grasping my arm felt solid, but it seemed as if I'd entered another world, where Satan and madmen coexisted. I shook my head in sudden understanding and said, "No, no. That's the Klan. Montgomery is part of a group that terrorize freedmen so that you will be slaves again. There is no invisible empire."

Charlie whispered vehemently, "I have seen its messengers in Carolina. Ghosts on horses with fire in their eyes and lightning at their hooves."

"Men in sheets," I said, wondering if it were true.

"He means to kill us all. The mine holds no gold, so he is returning home. Before then he will make a sacrifice to the empire. He's told me when he was drunk. He'll seal the mine with all the men in it." Charlie squeezed my arm harder. "We have his book of spells. He collects witchy papers that he keeps locked in a trunk, but I have the key. I've always had the key. If we are to beat a devil, we must use his magic against him."

Charlie looked around us, and he spoke so nervously I thought Montgomery might jump out from behind a bush any moment. "While he was away at the war, a special book was delivered to the house. It came in the middle of the night. The courier was not human. I saw him. His cloak slipped when he handed me the book, and I saw his demon eye." Charlie shuddered, as if he faced the man now. "I have that book, but I cannot read it. Will you read it for us?"

So I found myself back in the tent, crouched before the lantern, the black miners surrounding me as Charlie handed me the volume. It's cover crackled unpleasantly against my hand. The men hummed in their throats like huge bees, pressing against me when I opened to its first page. In the lamp's yellow light, I could barely make out the spidery writing. "It's in Spanish," I said. Fortunately I read Spanish well, along with French and Latin. Many of the best mining texts are in Spanish. I canted the book toward the lantern to show the letters better. The title was, *El Libro de los Normos de los Perdidos*, and below that was the date, 1579. "It says the author was Miguel Cervantes, 'Upon My Captivity in Algiers.' Ah, not the author, the translator." I wondered if this was the same Cervantes of *Don Quixote* fame. I turned to the next page carefully, although the nearly two-hundred-year-old paper seemed supple. I only read a few lines before I came upon an epigraph, which I translated out loud, "That is not dead which can eternal lie/and with strange eons, even death may die." The lantern guttered and nearly went out.

"Do not say the black magic words, Master Jonas," hissed Charlie.

His beliefs that would under any other condition provoke incredulity, chilled me. The men leaned away, some with their hands over their ears, still humming. Their fear and sweat hung in the air.

I nodded my assent and read on silently. This was no Christian super-stition. Nothing of witchcraft in this book. It was cosmology and history and strange references to monarchs or gods with unrecognizable names who existed as exiled sovereigns. Most of it I didn't understand, but my bile rose while reading, and I felt the same kind of nausea I'd felt in the Bernice. Is it possible that there is the equivalent of bad air in words? "There are incantations here for calling forth a creature named the Lurker at the Thresh-old. See, there are notes in the margins." My finger shook while pointing. Charlie moved to where he could see.

"You will have to tell us how to speak it."

"The notes are a warning, not a translation, but commentary from Cervantes. He says, 'Under sanity's blanket lies chaos.' Then he writes, 'The spell of summoning costs a human life. Yog-Sothoth consumes.'"

One of the men started shaking. His lips drew back from his teeth, and his teeth ground together. Eyes rolled back so there were only white marbles in his head. He collapsed, falling slowly between the men crammed so close together. No one paid him heed. They continued their moaning, rock-ing back and forth. I looked down at my hand on the page. For an instant, it seemed the spidery writing glowed black on the paper, as if the volume couldn't contain the letters anymore, and the ink wasn't ink at all, but thin slits to nothingness behind them.

I dropped the book and fled from the tent.

When the sun rose, I was still walking. My agitated pacing had taken me past Idaho Springs, past the stamper mills and abandoned sluice troughs. Down river, below the town, broken equipment sat in piles beside the path. As the sky lightened, I saw first the black holes opened into the mountain, lost claims, dead-end shafts that led to nothing, abandoned when their own-ers ran out of money or patience, left as futile evidence. In my exhaustion, I fancied the mountain was a great face and the mines were eyes. If eyes are the window to the soul, then the mountain's soul was blank and heart-less. No compassion twinkled in those inanimate sockets. I thought about the tunnels burrowing through the canyon's sides, some beneath me, miles and miles of lightless passage stretching through the rock.

During my life in mining, I had never thought of mountains this way, not the way I did that morning after reading Cervantes' horrifying translation. For me, a mountain presented itself as a beautiful, ages-long story. An open, striated cliff face, bands on bands of mineral and different colored rock told a geologic narrative, as moving as any of Shakespeare's greatest plays, as epic as Homer's *Odyssey*, but that day I didn't see them as lovely. The yellow tailing piles seemed pestilent, as if the mountain oozed from sores. From one end of the valley to the other, no trees hid the granite bones. Only stumps until just below the ridges, and if the mining continued, those would be gone too. The creek splashed up ocherous, scummy water where no fish could live.

I would stop Montgomery, then leave this terrible valley, where black miners trusted frightening books, and a crazy Confederate dropped rocks on his men.

But as the sky grew lighter, and the sun crept down the mountain wall, my fears lessened. Montgomery was evil, this was true, but last night's performance in the tent had nothing to do with him. Perhaps I had a touch of fever myself. Who knew what diseases passed from man to man in these filthy conditions? Certainly nothing I'd seen in London, where a doctor was no more than a few blocks away at the worst.

I'd deal with Colonel Montgomery, and I'd do it without "supernatural" aid, but I could use his own fears against him, his ignorance of the mines. What man would own a collection of witchcraft and superstitious drivel who didn't believe in it a little himself? No wonder he wanted to scare the Negroes. He was nearly heathen himself.

All I needed was preparation, and then to get him into the claim.

"You need to see the vein yourself," I said, holding the gold-threaded quartz in my hand. "It's the richest ore I've ever seen."

Montgomery lounged in his chair like a slothful cat, his arms draped back over the low top, his feet on the table next to the open bottle. Behind him, his travel cases lined the tent's walls, each with a huge clasp lock. Charlie told me that some contained liquor, but books filled many, his entire collection of supernatural studies. From what I remembered of American history, if Montgomery had been caught with the same books in Salem in 1692, he would have been hung.

His feet came off the table.

"Give it to me," his whiskey-roughened voice growled. He found a hand lense in the desk's clutter to examine the pebbles. At length, he said, "This came from my mine?" The lense magnified his eye into a black ball as lifeless as those dead-end shafts I'd seen that morning.

"There's a cavity at the end of Bernice. I wanted to find out how deep it was, so I chipped a wider opening. It wasn't until I got to the surface that I thought to look at the stone I'd removed. I exposed a band the same as that at least six-feet wide. It could rival anything in California." I tried to sound optimistic, but not over-eager.

Montgomery bent over the rocks again. "We'll need to do an assay to be sure. I want to inspect it first, though. Get Charlie Crump to run the bucket. I don't trust any of the others."

He noticed my hesitation.

"Oh, Charlie has been with me a long time. I swore to him if anything ever happened to me, I'd haunt him. These African folk are big on hauntings. Very simple that way, so don't worry about riding down with me."

As we took the steep path to the shaft, Charlie bringing up the rear, Montgomery said to me, "You're not superstitious, are you? A man died in here yesterday. Lot more ghosts than him in this mine." He laughed, and I remembered what the sheriff had said about coming out to this claim before. How many other "accidents" had there been?

"Are *you* worried about ghosts, Colonel? I don't remember you in the tunnels before."

His hand went to his chest, feeling something under his shirt. "I don't believe in ghosts, Jonas. A schooled man like yourself should know better. It's the coloreds who live in a spiritual world. That's why the Klan will be so effective. Properly funded, they will win back the South." He paused, then said without irony, "Just in case, I wear a warding. My kitchen woman made it for me years ago. If there were ghosts, it would keep them off. Belts and suspenders is what I always say. Besides, the richest gold strikes in history are associated with tragedy. The Buluma deposits in Austria were discovered after a cave-in killed fourteen miners. The ancient Egyptian kings shored up their mine walls with slave bodies. The greatest treasures in the world were founded on death."

Charlie made no noise as he followed. I couldn't help but think of him last night, as I read from the book, eyes wide, too frightened for me to even read the words out loud. Belief is a powerful thing. Charlie and the others believed in haunts and witchings and ritual. I'd seen them pinch spilt salt to toss over their shoulders. I'd seen one spin counterclockwise three times after accidently killing a spider. I'd seen the small sacks they wore round their necks filled with little bones and bits of feather.

I'd seen mine owners too, on a "hunch" pouring thousands of dollars into worthless projects in the belief their fortune resided only a few feet deeper. I'd seen prayers said over open pits, hoping divine intervention would put wealthy deposits in that day's diggings.

That's what I learned to resist during my geologic studies. Minerals congregated when the conditions were right. No "belief" or ritual would put gold ore where the geologic conditions were not favorable. Science guaranteed success where faith could not. That was why I studied Earth's stony mysteries and turned away from men, like Montgomery, who were too puzzling to fathom. I longed to return to the classroom. Perhaps I could become a lecturer in England, where a man of learning could be respected for his education and not be relegated to sleeping in Brown Town because he was not white.

I reached for the square shape in my ore bag. The book was there. If this worked, the men would be rid of Montgomery one way or another. No matter what, when I left, their lot would be better. If I'd felt my brow then, would I have felt fever? The plan was insane. The sheriff in Idaho Springs wouldn't arrest Montgomery, but there was law farther east. I could write to the magistrates in Kansas City. Still, we pressed on. My memory of the trek up the hill is filled with garish color: igneous rocks so dark no shadow showed on them, clouds bleached as if the sky had been erased and the stark parchment of the universe shown through. More than once I stumbled. Granite scree imbedded itself in my palm. I put my mouth against the wound and sucked.

Charlie manned the windlass. Montgomery lit an oil lantern, a luxury he never allowed the miners. They carried shadowgees, tin cans or buckets shaped to hold candles. I stepped into the bucket beside him. Overhead, the noon sun beat down, but a cool draft blew from the mine. The cavity at Bernice's end must be vast indeed to push this much air from the tunnel.

I nodded to Charlie, and he unlatched the windlass. The headframe pulley creaked as the cable played out. Ground rose to our eye-level as we started the long descent. Crudely carved granite walls replaced the sun-washed mountainside in our view. Montgomery bumped me when the bucket lurched. "Be more careful, you charcoal buck!" he shouted to Charlie. In the shaft's close confines, his voice resounded. The lantern smoked and stank. He had not properly trimmed the wick. He smelled of unwashed clothes and old liquor. I half hoped Charlie would drop a stone himself. Surely providence would have it hit him and not me. I looked up. The opening glowed like a white-hot coin.

"If this ore assays out, we'll hire more crew," he said. "Cornish miners who know what they're doing. Not this shiftless crowd of buffalo heads. My investors, my *Southern* investors, will be very happy."

"Always proper to turn a profit, sir," I said to keep his suspicions away. Would he notice the new timber work in Bernice?

At seventy feet we passed the northward-wandering Agnes, the oldest of the Epitome's three tunnels and the only one with track for ore carts. As always, I grimaced at the few support pillars the light illuminated. They were ill-fitted, coarse beams that needed to be hammered back into place periodically as the uncured wood contracted.

At a hundred-and-ten feet, Charlie stopped the bucket with nary a jostle only a foot shy of Bernice's floor. We stepped out. Montgomery's oil lantern cast a much brighter light than the candle in my shadowgee. I checked my pockets. There were plenty more candles there, not that I expected to use them all.

"You should lead, sir," I said.

Bernice bore north-east into the mountain, following quartzy rock in a zig-zag fashion for hundreds of feet. We passed short exploratory adits, horizontal tunnels that petered out in a few yards. The farther in we went, the lower the ceiling became. I kept one hand above my head, running it across the rough rock. Something felt wet, and I brought my fingers down to the light. They glistened from seep. I'd seen no sign of water this high in the Epitome before. I rubbed my fingers together. The water was slimy, and the tunnel smelled fetid. I wiped my hand hard against my pants.

Soon we were bent at the waist. Even shrouded in glass, Montgomery's lamp flickered from Bernice's steady, moist exhalation. The light surrounded him in a circle, while his black form eclipsed the lantern itself. He passed two newly-hewn timbers without pausing. I stopped. The cavity was only thirty yards farther around another bend. Over his head, fresh boards covered the ceiling for ten feet. He didn't even remark on the change. Perhaps he never had been in his own mine. I put my shadowgee in a niche on the wall, waited until Montgomery went past the corner, then kicked the first support under the new boards. It didn't move. I kicked it again. What if he heard? What if he discovered me at work? Maybe I'd miscalculated the weight. I sat, braced my hands behind me and kicked the beam again with both feet. It slid over a few inches, and pebbles dropped from between two boards.

"I don't see your vein," said Montgomery, his voice echoey and small. "Where the blazes are you, Jonas?" The turn in the tunnel brightened. He must be coming back. I scooted closer to the beam and kicked a last time with all my strength. The timber slid another half foot. A board cracked farther along. More dust dribbled from the ceiling. Montgomery's lantern came around the corner, and I reared back for one more desperate kick, but I didn't need it. With a loud pop, the center board snapped and rock roared into the tunnel.

Instinctively, I rolled away, covering my head. Rock on rock makes a particular sound, a crisp clack. For several seconds, lying on the stone floor, I heard the rocks hitting each other, clack, clack, clack. There was dust. It took me a minute to light a new candle. Broken rock choked the tunnel closed from floor to ceiling, and shards reached to my feet. If I had not moved, the cave-in would have killed me. The flame bent toward the shaft. My blockage had not stopped air flow. If my calculations were correct, there was no more that twelve feet between Montgomery and myself. Of course, he wouldn't know that. He would have no way of knowing if the entire drift had collapsed.

"Montgomery," I called. "Are you still alive, Montgomery?" I placed my hands on the jumbled rock.

"Thank God!" came his answer, his voice clear through the breakdown. "Jonas, is the drift clear behind you? Can you get help? My leg . . . I'm hurt."

I didn't say anything for a while. He had stood on the edge of a mine shaft and dropped a stone on four men, killing one. I remembered his eyes when he looked up, no different than if he'd stepped on an insect. The breeze blew cool air through the rocks beneath my hands. I let it play off my face. "Who would come to help you, Colonel? Should I call Charlie Crump? How about the other men on the bucket yesterday? Do you think they would come down the shaft for you?"

No answer.

You may think at this point that surely I meant to kill him, but I didn't. I'd loosened the ceiling, but only enough to fill the passage. Montgomery could dig his way out in a day or two, all the while without light, an unknown cavity behind him, my planted fears flourishing in the dark.

I sat on the floor, extricating the book from my ore bag. It seemed even more repugnant than when I'd held it in the tent the night before. Perhaps the moist air penetrated its cover, or maybe the environment — my heightened senses — affected me, but the tome felt heavier, more gruesome.

"How much oil do you have for your lamp, Montgomery?" I knew exactly how much he had: no more than a half-hour's worth.

Rocks rattled on the floor. He grunted in pain. I imagined he was trying to remove the fall. Had he seen the cavern at Bernice's end? Even a man of limited imagination might conjure up a monster from such circumstance, but Montgomery was not so limited. I wondered too if the bad air had cleared out. The air's movement was brisk enough, but there could still be patches. If they were concentrated enough, they could render him unconscious, possibly kill him.

The book rested on my lap. My single candle cast enough illumination for me to see a few feet of tunnel back to the shaft. All tunnels look the same when you are by yourself. The walls around glow with light, the tiny minerals catching the flame, reflecting it in glisters, but the light fails so soon, and the circle's middle in both directions is darkness like an eye's pupil, surrounded with color, centered in black.

I began reading the words. They were different underground. Even a rational man like myself can be affected by the mine's solitude, by odd echoes and tinkly drips tapping into unseen pools. Any miner can tell you that a mine is not a quiet place. The silence itself creaks.

"What is that you say?" shouted Montgomery. He sounded frightened. Stones continued to clatter on his side.

I spoke a bit louder. For this to work, he had to hear what I was reading and realize what it was. The sentences hurt my throat. Saying them was like a vomit.

When I reached the spell's end, I started over. When I finished the second time, there was no sound on the other side. Either Montgomery was resting or he was listening. He'd said to me once, "Plant an imp in a man's head, and he'll walk always in darkness." If he was scared to the bone, so scared he'd flee the mines, then his men would be safe.

"Is that the Spanish book?" he yelled.

I took up the chant. Somehow it was easier to say now, and the rhythm fell more naturally.

"Don't read from that one, Jonas! It's not safe, Jonas!" He swore vehemently.

My eyes no longer strained to see the words on the page. Without stopping, I looked up. The candle flamed brighter, unnaturally radiant, and the wax gave way before the assault. It wouldn't last a minute at that rate. Shaking, I drew another from the bag. When lit, it too burned like phosphorous. By the light of the twin suns, the pages became transparent, and the text hung suspended, all the words visible at once, but it didn't matter; I wasn't reading anymore. My voice became powerful, not my own, and the spell boomed the tunnel's length.

Montgomery screamed through the stone, his imprecations no longer coherent.

Then, all became still. The chanting stopped; I did not stop it. It was as if a presence that had taken me had left. Montgomery cut off a curse in mid-utterance. Since I'd entered Bernice, the candle's flame had bent toward the entrance as the breeze exited the mountain. Now, they stood straight up. Then they tilted the other way, as if a door to a much larger universe than our own had opened on Montgomery's side.

Something was coming. Montgomery screamed again, a pathetic whine like a kicked mongrel.

"Let me out, boy! Let me out, you goddamned nigger!"

The wind pushed at my back and whistled through the rubble. Whatever lived on the other side drew everything toward it. Fine sand peppered my neck, then disappeared into the broken rock. The first candle went out.

The entirety of my being demanded I run away. I felt it in my muscles and bones, an instinctive aversion, but I forced myself to stay. The thing that approached could not be of this world. I imagined it rising from the cavity, flowing into the opening I'd made, filling the small shaft. By lamp light, what did Montgomery see? He made a non-human screech, then a soggy gasp. Green-limb snapping. Hollow slurping, and Montgomery continued to scream, a mindless, noisy babble. Finally, there were only wet noises. Moist rippings. Damp slaps.

Rocks slipped from the top of the pile, and the jumbled stack lurched toward me. Twelve feet of rock, four-feet wide and high, chocked tightly against the mine's wall slid a foot toward me. There were two or three tons of rock blocking the mine, and it moved!

I scrambled down the tunnel on all fours, stood too soon, whapped my head against the ceiling, reeled from wall to wall until I collapsed in the bucket. Behind me, rocks tumbled. The thing beyond was dismantling the blockage. Weakly I pulled the bell cord twice and prayed that Charlie Crump could pull me up before the thing from the mountain broke through.

No trip in my life was ever longer. As the bucket crept up the shaft, the wind vacuumed me back, whistling by. Slowly, ever so slowly the light at the surface grew larger, while every second I expected a clawed hand or a tentacle to drape itself over the edge, and when I reached the top, I didn't talk to Charlie. Instead, I staggered up the slope to the powder cache.

The explosion shook the valley. By the time I made my way to the tents, a crowd had gathered, a hundred miners, picks resting on their shoulders or shovels at their sides, expecting to hear the news.

"Was anyone in the mine?" someone shouted. "Do they need rescuing?"

I must have presented quite a picture. Blood from the bump on my head streaked my face, my fine coat was torn. Dark smudges streaked my white shirt, from starched collar to the belt. They waited for my answer.

"The Colonel was in the dig, but no one is alive," I said, finally. "There's no mine left."

Shaking their heads, they dispersed until only the Idaho Springs sheriff stood there, his hands deep in his unwashed pockets.

"I came by today to talk to Montgomery," he said. "Don't seem like I'll get the chance now." I couldn't discern his purpose in eyes shaded under his hat, and I didn't care. My hands started quivering. My legs lost their strength. I sat on the ground. He sat beside me. A hundred yards downhill, Clear Creek roiled in sullen, muddy, sun-drenched muttering.

"Nobody will miss the bastard," he said.

I tucked my head between my knees, on the verge of sickness. I'd left a monster in the mines. Poor Montgomery. I'd only meant to scare him.

What would happen when the next prospector broke through into the cavity? Did the Lurker on the Threshold wait there, or did it only appear when I read the spell? Had it gone back to the nether regions past the stars that Cervante's book talked about? I could still hear it pulling rocks down, coming toward me.

In the meantime the sun pressed like a warm kiss on my shoulders. The sheriff sat with his hands wrapped round the top of his hob-nailed boots.

He said, "Guess you'll have to find another employer, although I don't know what luck you'll have, being you are. . .what was it you said you were again?"

I looked up. There are awful things in the world, beneath it, beyond it. The sheriff waited for an answer. I'd thought of him as an unwashed, white, ignorant American, but now his fingers laced firmly across his boots, and his hat shaded curious eyes. He had arms, legs and a familiar torso. Our differences were small. Whatever he was, he wasn't claws or tentacles or a rending thing that rose when called. He wasn't a part of the real invisible empire.

"I'm human," I said.

Its Hour Come Round

Bad news should be held to the end, don't you think? Especially the kind that unbalances everything else you've said, erases it even? So I'll wait until I've told you about how I love working in the orchards in the spring. We hoe around the tree trunks, loosening the soil for rain and fertilizers; we rake away twigs and dead leaves, and a few dried apple husks that are all that's left after the winter, until the ground beneath the trees is smooth and clean and almost holy.

I love climbing the long ladders to inspect the buds. Are they green yet? Have they begun to bloom? I love the pace of prison work. An old-school lifer named Blue Buck Johnny told me once, "Drink plenty of water and walk slow. You're going nowhere fast." He started his term in Soledad fifty years before I met him, before the Mars colonies, before the 21st Century was properly rolling. Soledad was the last of the big houses where they warehoused criminals. No real treatment there, hormonal, psychiatric, genetic or otherwise. No ET. Just a bunch of maladjusts teaching each other how to be bad. That's when they held cons for "time served" rather than reforming them. They grandfathered Blue Buck into the Mola Correctional Facility. He was never going back to the world, but he didn't mind. He liked the inside and the shunt that stifled his urges.

So do I, sometimes. Did I mention I read poetry too? Yeats, I read him a lot, but I like Houseman and Neruda and Walt Whitman too. I speak the poems out loud to the bare branches when I'm hanging on a ladder, looking for beetle bore holes or frost damage.

I love breathing spring air. It's rainy here in the valley, not your California rain that settles in for months, where you don't see the sun from January to May, but the sudden Colorado rain that sweeps up the valley in a heady gust that smells of Utah canyons and wet grass. The wind comes across the treetops, bending the far ones first, so they shake their heads, and then the next and the next and the next, until it's on you, loaded with dust and litter and fat, stinging drops that make dark bullet holes in that perfect dirt beneath the trees.

I love all that, and I love people too. Can you believe it? There's slang for people inside: white guys are peckerwoods, and most affiliate after a while. AB's a popular choice, the Aryan Brothers. Blacks go for the BGF, the Black Guerilla Family. Border Brothers for the Hispanics, or the NF, Nuestra Familia — they're northern Hispanic. The BGF is the power broker at Mola. Even the guards step lightly around them. You want something done, you go to the family. Prisons may be different from Blue Buck Johnny's day, but the power games, intimidation and supply and demand are the same.

I, of course, don't affiliate. They've got names for me too. This is the bad news I've been holding back. It doesn't matter that I like the sun on my face, or on any ordinary day I'm the most generous guy in the world, or I have parents and a sister I love, or in the fifth grade I won a citizenship award for collecting the most tin cans for the senior center fund raiser. I'm a cho mo. A diddler. A chester. A BGF lord named Grover Lincoln Douglas outed me at lunch my first week here. Grover said, "This peckerwood's name is shit. He's on a drug charge." I didn't know what he meant then; I'd never done pharmaceuticals in my life. Later I found out a "drug charge" was shorthand for, "He drug them out of the sandbox." I'm a child molester, and a child died.

See, I told you. It doesn't matter what else I say. You might have even started to like me. I might have invited your sympathy. The man loves books. He appreciates nature. He has a pleasant, measured voice. I could have been your friend until you heard that. No matter how long my story is, the one deed will color the rest of my words. My life is measured, evaluated and overbalanced by that one fact. Some mistakes never go away.

But there, now you know.

This spring, my fourth at Mola, I first saw Chika Achutebe as she arrived on the morning bus. I watched from a treetop when the stringer of fish, all newbies, filed by to housing orientation, their shunts so fresh that infection still streaked their biceps. Chika's blonde afro stood out, her dark face shining beneath it, all Arabic and sleepy eyed. I thought she was on depress already, but that's just the way she looks. There were seven fry, a big shipment. Blue Buck told me at Soledad they'd get fifty cons on a bus, and they'd get a couple busses a week, all men. No coed populations then! No wonder time was so violent. Hard to imagine that much fresh meat, and Soledad was just one of hundreds of lock-ups. Of course, most of the cons were returners. Revolving door justice. Lots of recidivism back then, before they started grading the prisons. Before the shunts and ET and that whole therapeutic cocktail they've cooked up to keep us from coming back.

So these really were cub scouts, so scared they didn't know if they should shit or go blind. But I picked out Chika; she was huddled up on herself, shoulders pulled in, hands squeezed so tight together, and taking little steps like she was afraid that if her feet got too far in front of her they might not come back. Gang bangers checked them out as they went by. Grover Lincoln Douglas leaned on his hoe (the long-handled kind for breaking up dirt), marking who to recruit. Couple of the Aryan Brothers worked as trustees, handling paperwork for the transport bulls, and they wracked up the possibilities too.

You'd think in a controlled environment like this there wouldn't be much violence, and there isn't. The shunts, ET and therapy out the wazoo work, but it's still dangerous. You don't go from crime to cure in a day, you know. Some urges don't ever go away, and most the cons are Coving it, Crimes of Violence. When you get off on hurting people, you're an ET candidate for sure. Mola pulls a Clockwork Orange on you and that old blood music never sounds the same.

It would be a week before I saw her again — it takes the medboss that long to put them on a program — but then she was out. Best chance I have to make friends is to break in the new ones, so they know me before they know my time. I'm gregarious by nature. Talkative. It's a craving the shunt doesn't manage.

We met at breakfast. "Can I sit here?" I asked. The cafeteria is big enough for two-hundred, but there are only eighty prisoners and a dozen staff members at Mola. Blue Buck told me Soledad housed over 7,000. Hard to believe there was that much crime. Here, big windows open onto the orchards. Some of the apples had blossomed all white and pink in the sunlight, and I could see apricots and peaches farther off. Pancakes that morning. The room smelled of maple and sizzling butter.

"Yes, thank you," she said without looking from her food.

Up close she was even more striking. Hair so blonde it was nearly translucent. Classic cheekbones. Skin as dark and smooth as chocolate pudding. Heavy, long lashes over those sleepy eyes. Narrow shoulders. Trim figure under the khaki work shirt. My shunt kicked in. Sometime you can feel it: a tiny click under the skin as a microdosage releases. Sexual depressant. I hadn't had a hard-on in four years.

She said, "Sometimes I wake up in the middle of the night, and I'm sad." She looked toward the windows, but I don't think she was seeing anything. Her eyes were red-rimmed. "I used to have a dog named Fardel, but she's gone now. When I wake up I think I hear her barking, but it's never her."

Her voice was tiny and soft. She frowned when she turned back. "If I got a puppy, I'd name her Fardel Two, because she would be the second." There were no lines in her face, no worry marks above her eyebrows, no creases anywhere. Absolutely pure, unwritten-upon skin.

"How old are you?" I said. My shunt clicked again, and then twice more. Different doses. My brain fuzzed a little bit; the room got sort of whispy and underwater.

"Twenty-seven," she said in the voice of a ten-year old. "Twenty-eight this June. How old are you?"

"Thirty-six," I whispered. "Thirty-seven in November." She's retarded, I thought. What could this little girl have done to earn a stay at Mola Correctional?

The medboss ordered an unscheduled ET for me that afternoon. I was stacking bug powder for spraying next week. "Empathy Training, 3:00, Knavely," she said. She wore scrupulously clean pants suits, razor-like creases pressed into the legs and arms. Short, black hair, streaked with gray, like a maiden aunt. A pleasant smile that showed her gums, although she didn't smile often. Old-fashioned glasses.

"Yes, boss," I said, without breaking rhythm.

The Adjustment Center dominates the housing yard. Single-story prisoner bungalows line the four streets that lead to the circle drive around the AC. From the air, I imagine Mola looks like a sniper scope. An eight-foot high fence to keep deer away from the fruit circles the compound. Inside that, a two-hundred-yard clear zone to the trees, the orchards; then the roads, which form the crosshair, the Adjustment Center in the middle. Administration, medical services, counseling, parole and the warden's office fill the upper floors while ET takes the entire basement. A placard next to the entrance reads, "NEITHER NATURE NOR NURTURE IS DESTINY." They're serious about it too.

My hand barely shook as I signed in. This would be my seventy-eighth ET in four years. One a day for the first month, and then one a month after that. I knew the drill.

Take a chair. Strap my feet in. Plug the IV into the shunt. It's pretty easy once you've practiced. The access port is under a skin fold on the bicep. The shunt itself, an inch wide and three inches long, is buried in the muscle. You don't feel it after the first few weeks. Hard to believe it analyzes the patient, makes dosage decisions, transmits and receives all in that little unit.

The medboss bustled in, checked my straps, then locked down my hands and chest. She looked me in the eyes before lowering the diving bell over my head. "Pretty routine now, eh?"

I nodded, feeling anything but.

Empathy Training. I don't know what you've read, but it's not like that. Not virtual reality. Not "Electro-psychotropic Simulation." It's total immersion in fear and pain.

The helmet came down, covered my eyes, fastened under my chin. My shunt rattled a complicated series of clicks in my arm. I waited for the scenario. Different one each time. I have no idea how they make them. Then, I'm squatting on a beach, packing sand with a little shovel. My feet are tiny. I slip them into a puddle and squish the water between my toes. The sky's bright, the sand is crisp and smooth, lazy waves slide toward my castle to slip back into the sea. Tomorrow's my birthday, I think, and I'll be seven. Seven, seven, seven, I sing to myself. A shadow covers my work. I look up at a dark silhouette. My mouth goes dry, and he picks me up. Already I'm scared. My legs don't straighten. I stay curled, shovel in hand, and he carries me that way, hustling me toward the bathrooms.

I know it's chemically and electrically induced anxiety. The diving bell reaching into my cortex, stimulating the right reflexes, but it feels real, not simulated. I'm genuinely terrified. Sometimes I scream. After ET I can't talk from the hoarseness, but this time I'm silent. The door opens and closes. He turns the light off. My head bangs on something, a bathroom stall maybe.

He's so big. I'm small and weak and scared, scared, scared. Wet myself scared, and I do. My pants come down. He turns me and my chest is pressed against the ceramic edge of the toilet bowl in the dark. A noseful of unflushed urine smell, my face nearly in the water. Then I scream. His hand's on my mouth. I can't breathe. It goes on.

It goes on.

It goes on.

When the diving bell came off I was weeping. "Oh god oh god oh god," I heard myself saying.

"I know," said the medboss. "I know, Knavely." She was not unkind. It was the job.

"Why don't you just kill me?" I gasped.

The chest belt fell away, and I leaned forward, still strapped at the hands and ankles, to throw up. They'd hose the room down later. The medboss patted me on the back until I finished.

"There's no such thing as a throw-away person," she said.

I staggered out of the AC. His hands still on me. My ribs hurt. My ass hurt. I was afraid to feel back there. Surely I'm bleeding, I thought. Sometimes cons develop bruises. There was a guy in here a couple years earlier on an assault and battery beef whose face would be puffy, his eyes black, after ET. Psychosomatic symptoms. Stigmata. No one touched him, but he'd take days to heal.

Nobody talked to me as I walked through the apple trees, through the peaches and apricots, past the last tree and into the clear zone. The fence was two hundred yards away, but I wasn't trying to escape, nor going for a "bush pass." No one escapes Mola. I kept walking. There was a proximity guard in the AC. I was on a grid, and when I got far enough away from the center, long before I reached the fence, it knew.

Tears rolled down my face. My legs shook. I did that to someone. Who was I? There's this poem by Yeats where he says, "What rough beast, its hour come round at last, slouches toward Bethlehem to be born?" There was a beast in me, or I was the beast, I don't know, but how can one live with knowledge of what he has done when the victim's pain is so fresh? And so, for the seventy-eighth time, I walked toward the fence until the proximity alarm sent a signal to my shunt. It clicked. Suddenly, I was drowsy, and unconsciousness washed over me. Vaguely, I felt myself falling, but I don't remember hitting.

Sometimes a con pisses a bull off, and the guard orders a cho mo double feature. Not all the staff at Mola is as compassionate as the medboss. There's sadism; there's violence, even with the shunts. Sometimes it's the inmates; sometimes it's the staff. On goes the diving bell and the poor bastard gets a long load of my normal treatment. Nothing worse than being a diddler in prison. Nothing worse than being one, period.

By the next afternoon, I was in the trees again, pinching buds. I culled out every other one so the crop would be more robust. It was non-thinking, physically trying work involving moving the ladder often and climbing up and down it scores of times.

Maybe I was the only one *not* to hit on Chika the first day — most cons aren't at Mola for COP stuff, crimes of passion, so they don't get chemically castrated every time a sexual thought crosses their minds — or maybe it was just another of nature's cruel tricks, but when I came down the ladder the umpteenth time she waited for me.

Even the way she wore her clothes was childlike. An adult makes adjustments, draws the shoulders square, smooths away the wrinkles. Not so with Chika. She'd missed a button three down from her collar. "Can I watch?" she said in her little girl voice.

I shrugged. "It's a free prison." The day after ET, I'm not nearly as chatty. It's sort of like that old joke about not wanting to belong to a club that would have you as a member. A person who wanted to talk to me probably wasn't worth talking to.

She sat cross-legged at the foot of the ladder and played with her shoelaces. "I have a tree at my house, but there's a table for tea and two chairs."

Not many branches left to do on this tree. It'd take me another twenty-minutes to finish, but I was tired. When I reached the ground, she moved aside by scooching on her bottom.

"My new bed's nice," she said, her expression totally innocent.

I leaned back against the tree a yard from her and slid until I was sitting too. She looked around, her slender fingers cupping her knees, hair like a halo, wide-eyed, as if she was on a field trip.

"Do you have any idea why you're here?" I asked.

She ducked her head. "I did a bad thing I shouldn't have. They'll keep me until they're sure I won't do it again. That's what my attorney told me." She said "attorney" carefully, getting each syllable right. "What are you here for? Did you do something bad too?"

Nothing I could say to that. There is this phrase, "Do your own time." It means, mind your own business.

"Yeah, I did something bad too." I wanted to hold her. She trembled even though the day was warm, pulling her arms in close. It was weird: her size and build said she was adult, but her expression and posture said she was a child, a frightened kid who didn't know who to turn to. I kept my hands firmly still. Everything in me wanted to reach out to comfort her. I could picture it, her leaning into me, her blonde hair against my face. I shook my head and moved a few inches farther away, waiting for the shunt to click, to save me, but it didn't, so I tried to think about the night that put me here.

The funny thing about it is that I could hardly remember the actual event. For so long, my life had been bound up in Mola's orchards that everything before, my schooling, my work, my marriage, my own children, my crime, seemed to belong to someone else. All I kept from that former life is the burden.

She shifted on the ground so she faced me more, her knees apart, ankles crossed. "Do you get scared at night, Knavely?"

Before I go to sleep sometimes, there's an image from the trial that gets me. It's the mother. I'd been sentenced like everyone else to an RTL, "reformation to life." They were taking me from the court when the mother leaned out of the crowd at the door, her face white and dead. "I hope you never sleep peacefully again."

After sentencing I'd gone straight to surgery for my shunt. I didn't know if I slept peacefully or not. When I stayed awake too long, the shunt took care of me, then I slept. Who knew if it was peaceful?

"I get scared," Chika said. "People moan, and I ask them if they're all right, but they don't hear me. I think they're having nightmares."

In my unit people moan. Six cons per apartment. Blue Buck told me that prisons used to be noisy all the time. People screaming, doors clanging. Never a quiet moment. Mola's not like that. No slamming, barred gates. Much calmer. Half the pop's on depress, though, so it's hard to tell what it would be like otherwise. From where Chika and I sat I could see a dozen other cons just standing among the trees, too tanked to make a move. Sometimes in the summer I'd go and turn them if it was a sunny day. They could get a bad burn if they weren't wearing a hat.

Chika leaned toward me and whispered, "A man comes to me every night. He wants to get in, but I won't let him. I can't see his face."

I found myself standing over her — I have no idea how I leapt to my feet so fast. I yelled, "What?" She fell back in the dirt. Her hands covered her mouth, and she cried.

"No, no. It's okay. I'm sorry. . .I didn't mean to startle you." Sweat dripped into my eyes. I wiped my face with the back of my wrist. A steadying breath, then I counted to ten slowly.

Chika rolled to her side away from me, drew her legs in, and sobbed. I squatted beside her until she suddenly relaxed. Her shunt had dropped a load. When she sat up, her eyes glazed over. It was as if I'd never said anything.

"My new bed's nice," she said again. "I like pink sheets."

Her thumb went into her mouth.

"She's mentally incapacitated," I said. "She shouldn't be here."

The medboss sat behind her desk in her corner office. She could see half the facility through the floor-to-ceiling windows. "I'm not in a position to judge," she said. "The courts found her competent. Chika's very high functioning, considering her IQ, capable of making choices. She's made some poor ones."

I forced myself to stay calm. Sun bathed almost the entire office, warming my legs. It would be only a couple hours until nightfall.

"I think she needs protection. She's not safe."

The medboss consulted her records. Screen after screen flickered by. When she stopped, it wasn't at Chika's profile; it was mine.

"Knavely, I appreciate your concern, but, really, she's much safer in here than she'd be outside." She studied my charts. "You have a parole hearing next week. I'm recommending your release. What do you feel about that?"

I didn't even have to think. "No. I'm not ready."

She appraised me from her chair, her dark eyes steady behind her glasses. "The state pays us to cure you. If you recid, we lose money. If we keep you too long, we lose money. When the therapy team says you're turned, and the board agrees, out you go. Assuming we did our job, you're a new man, society is safe, and you can get on with your life. You'll be relocated, renamed and be given a whole new background. The state wants you to have the best chance possible of making it."

My tongue stuck to the top of my mouth, and I had a sudden flashback to yesterday's ET session. The room smelled like unflushed toilet. "I haven't been punished enough."

"We can't punish you, Knavely. Punishment is old-school. This is a reformation facility. All we're worried about is a relapse. Do you think you'll commit another crime?"

I thought about Chika. I *wanted* to hold her, but there's lots of ways to hold someone. "I'm not confident."

The medboss shrugged. "Nothing's certain. All we can do is look at your profile. I'm recommending dismissal. I'll bet you clear 369, and we'll collect triple bonus." She smiled, lots of gums. If I didn't recid in thirty months, the prison received performance pay. Sixty months later, they collected again, and ninety months earned them a third. A full 369. Mola Correctional guaranteed their freebirds.

"But what about Chika?" I said. My legs shook. I doubted I could stand.

The medboss turned back to her display, called up Chika's charts. "Oh, I wouldn't worry about her. She's tougher than she looks."

"She's just a little kid. She can't make decisions for herself."

Outside an inmate crew unloaded smudge pots from a flatbed. The prediction was for a frost tonight, and if it was too cold for too long, the buds would die. There wouldn't be a crop. Rather than look at the medboss, I watched them wrestling the unwieldy furnaces into position. A pressure itched at the backs of my eyes.

She said, "Five months ago your 'little kid' killed her father with an ice pick. She *decided* to do that."

"Surely it wasn't premeditated," I said.

"Daddy was tied up. The coroner testified she took two hours to finish him. Don't know what started her, but she had plenty of time to change her mind along the way. I wouldn't paint too pretty of a picture of her in your mind. Your girl has some anger management issues."

After dinner I walked Chika to her dorm, trying to decide what to do. "I like you, Knavely," she said, and held my hand.

The hairs flew up on the back of my neck. My arm went rigid as an impulse to jerk it away was answered by a fear of frightening her again.

We stopped at the door. In the orchards, the bug lights were on. So was the one hanging from the dorm's gutter, five feet away. A cool, polar light washed over the wall, turning the windows into icy squares. Bugs zapped themselves into ash all around us. A front was coming in, and I felt frost in the air. They'd be lighting the smudge pots soon. Chika didn't let go.

"I don't want to talk to that man again," she said. She kept her head down, so I could just see the top of her head. Her feet shuffled on the cement. "He scares me. He said, 'I can be your honey, Chika.'" She looked at me, her eyes shiny, reflecting bug light blue.

"Tell the dorm bull you don't want visitors."

She giggled. "What's a dorm bull?"

"The guard in your unit."

She squeezed my hand, serious again. "No. . .not the guard."

And then I knew, it wasn't an inmate.

A faint squeaking filled the night air behind me. Bats dipped and circled through the trees. She watched them, the corners of her mouth turned up in delight. "Did I tell you I had a dog?" she said. "His name was Fardel."

"Yes, you did."

"I like animals. I'm going to ask them for a puppy."

I was ready to go. How could I help tonight? And what about tomorrow night, and the one after? The medboss said she'd recommend parole. I might not even be here in a week.

"Could you stay with me, Knavely?" she said. "If you're with me, the man won't come." Her grip was intense. "I could. . .do things for you."

My gut twisted. "No," I said. "Oh, no. I can't." I paused, waiting for the shunt. This was when it should click, sending a soothing dose through my veins, but it didn't. Was she a child or an adult. And what was I? I felt a stirring. Holding my hand, Chika looked at me, pleading. I gasped, "You'll be fine. Really. You'll see," and I disengaged my fingers.

* * *

There's no curfew at Mola, but most go to bed early. A hard day in the orchards'll take it out of you. I walked from Chika's apartment, afraid to look back. She'd still be on the porch, her bed awaiting her, and the long night. The late shift moved between the trees, carrying torches. A few smudge pots were lit, and an oily smoke eddied in the cold air. Without a coat, I shivered.

Grover Lincoln Douglas and three of his BGF cronies bunked in the last unit on North Street. I went in without knocking. Cigarette smoke twisted around a desk lamp in the middle of their card game. He put his cards down when I moved into the light.

"I need to buy something," I said.

"What do you have to offer?" He spat on the floor.

"Name your price."

Grover leaned back in his chair. Shadows surrounded him. Only the beds' edges were visible, then I realized that two of them were occupied. Eyes glinted, watching like coyotes.

He glanced at his cards on the table as if he'd rather be playing, then folded his hands across his chest. "It might be too expensive for you. What do you think I have to sell?"

"Protection."

He laughed. "Nothing can buy you that, Cho Mo. No soul here would slap your back if you were choking on a chicken bone."

"It's not for me."

His chair flopped forward so he could rest his elbows on the table. "That's different. Maybe we *can* deal. It just so happens a pair of fish I know have a desperate urge you can help them with, and they're willing to owe me big for the privilege."

I swallowed, knowing what he was talking about. Grover specialized in fulfilling urges.

Grover said, "No charges. Not a word." He drew a finger slowly under his chin.

We worked out the arrangement. Last thing I said was, "She stays safe. No predators. No coercion."

"I'll put the word out." He tilted his head and looked up at me, eyes narrow. "Funny request for someone on a short ticket. I heard you're riding the 369 out soon. Why should you care?"

It was a tough question. "Sometimes I don't know why I do stuff, but I've got to do it anyway."

A coyote grunted on one of the bunks, "Ain't that the truth."

Grover picked up his cards, "Be at the peach tree blind in twenty minutes."

I nodded and left. By now all the smudge pots were fired up and the orchards stank of kerosene and diesel smoke. No wind, so there was a chance the buds wouldn't freeze, even if it dropped into the mid 20s.

There are several blinds at Mola, places where surveillance cameras don't reach. Activity happens there in private. While I walked between the night-blackened trees, I thought about Grover and the shunts. He'd been out of the world for fifteen years. Whatever he'd done, the medboss and the rest of the staff weren't convinced he wouldn't do it again. They were planning on kicking me after only four years on a manslaughter and molestation conviction. Some folks must be harder-wired for their lives than others. I walked a slow circuit around the orchards, checking the smudges, thinking about reformation, redemption and punishment. Mola only offered one. The others I'd have to find on my own. Dull yellow flames undulated within the smudges, belching warm smoke. A con nodded in acknowledgment as I went by. He must not have recognized me.

Grover and two others waited at the peach tree blind, a distant fence light illuminating their heads and shoulders but leaving the rest dark. He was talking to them. "Here's the package. You take your shot, best you can. I'm not responsible for administrative follow-up. You can't perform, it's your fault, not mine. Payment in full on your side regardless."

They nodded. Both held something a foot-and-a-half long. Hard to tell in the shadows. Probably rubber hose. The light showed their faces clearly enough, though. Fresh fish. One I recognized from Chika's bus. Young, hard, wary. Asian eyes on him; a twisty scar across his cheek and the corner of his mouth. The other was bland, peckerwood suburbia. Straight teeth in his smile. He smiled now. "I want to go first," he said.

As I said, there's violence in Mola. Not much, since meds and therapy work hard to stomp it out, and, of course, recidding in prison is a short route to another month or two of daily ET., but the urge is there, even when there's little opportunity.

Suburbia said, "Are you scared, asshole? I like it better when they're scared." He popped the rubber hose across the palm of his other hand. "Grover here says I can't kill you, but he didn't say I had to leave anything for anyone else either." He whacked his palm again.

He looked at Grover. Grover nodded. Suburbia stepped forward, his smile wider, eyes bright. I didn't flinch. Maybe somebody had molested him when he was young. Maybe he was abused. All those nurture arguments. Or maybe nature programmed him for violence. Too much of one hormone, not enough of another. Maybe a genetic flaw. Lots of reasons people behave the way they do. There's no discussion of evil in technological corrections, no room for it, and no treatment.

He got close, exhaled in my face. "Damn, this will be good!" He breathed hard. Licked his lips, working himself up. Raised his hand, and I could see the hose clearly — he'd jammed glass shards in it.

The hose would hurt, when it hit, the glass would rip, and I would deserve it. I clasped my hands behind me so I wouldn't protect myself by reflex.

Then, his eyes crossed. It would have been funny in any other context. When his eyes crossed, and all the tension went out of his face, he sagged as if he'd been erased inside. Shunt magic. He struggled for a second, raising his hand again, but the hose rocked loosely. He gasped, then dropped his arm to his side. "Damn," he said, no force behind it. "This isn't fair."

"I told you that might happen," said Grover.

"Huh?" said Suburbia. He sat at my feet. "Can't shtand anymo'." With his legs crossed, he fell over backwards, his eyes shut. A soft snore bubbled in his throat.

Grover looked at the other one. "Your turn slant-eyes."

The boy murmured under his breath, chanting a mantra. "Stay calm," he said. "Stay calm," but his brow oozed sweat. His shunt was already working on him. He approached anyway, hand pressed against his stomach, hunched a little like a washerwoman. In the mellow light, he grimaced, paused, then shuffled forward another couple steps. "Oh," he moaned. "I'm gonna be sick." The rubber hose plopped onto the dirt, and he shambled off, bent almost double now, into the swirling smoke.

Grover laughed. "You did those boys a favor, Knavely. They're seeing the errors of their ways through you. Bet they're out of here a year earlier each because of this." He picked up the hose. "You get what you want, and I collect my fee anyway."

I took a shuddery breath. They'd been so close. Another step, and either would have been on me. The strong arm. The quick lash, and I'd get my inadequate payback, but they'd faltered. Reformation without punishment. The medboss would send me into the world unmarked. My hands unclenched. I hadn't realized it, but my fingers had been squeezed so tightly my fingernails had dug into my palms. Blood seeped from both.

"Pity to waste the opportunity, though," Grover said.

The hose whistled in the air, and the first blow took me across the chest, knocking me against a tree. The second snapped a rib. My hand went up, and he broke my wrist. Grover reeled back drunkenly. His shunt must have been dumping everything at once, but he came forward again, arm high, and I looked up in time to see retribution coming down.

* * *

The medboss sat at my bedside, peering over the glasses that had slid to the end of her nose. "So you fell off a ladder?"

I nodded, the thick dressing clinging to my face. The drainage tube running out of my cheek brushed my neck.

"And this happened in the middle of the night, not only shattering your cheekbone, but also breaking a pair of ribs and your arm?"

From the high infirmary window, only clouds were visible. I turned away from her to look at them. My head made the maneuver in a pulsing, oceanic slosh that didn't settle down for several seconds after I'd stopped moving.

"How's the crop?" I said carefully. Talking sent razored slivers through my jaw.

In the corner of my eye I could see her studying me. Her hands came up and templed against her lips. "No frost damage." She sighed. "You know, we can't help anyone if you stick to this story. We don't know what happened out there. I have some medical clues. I know what the shunts did, but I don't know why they did it. I don't know which of my records correlate to what you're covering up. There's sick folk in here. The only way to treat them is through knowledge."

I shrugged, and that hurt too.

Two weeks later I met Grover under the apple trees, thick with blossoms now, and the air so pollen-filled my eyes watered. He worked a weed pick, uprooting anything small and green with a twist of the wrist.

"I hear you're on the next bus," he said without looking up.

"They're waiting for me at the gate." My arm ached hollowly from where they'd removed my shunt. "I never said anything."

Another weed popped out. He ground it under his heel. "That's why your baby's still sleeping alone."

"Good." A breeze knocked down some petals. They drifted down like pink parachutes, pattering around us.

Grover scratched his chest. "You taking a beating won't bring back that dead kid."

My throat went dry.

He said, "The kid's still dead, and in a week or a month or sometime, Chika will find some horny bastard who won't scare her too bad when he asks her to sit in his lap. You get a honking scar out of the deal. A useless gesture won't redeem you Cho Mo."

"In time, the scar will fade," I choked out.

"Yeah, but why the bother? What's the point?"

Another breeze blew through the boughs. No petals fell this time, but they all fluttered, a vast pink comforter whispering overhead. I said, "You've got to do what good you can do, regardless of who you are."

I didn't see Chika on the way out. I never said goodbye, but as I passed Administration, the Asian kid with the twisty scar staggered from his first ET, tears streaming down his face, his eyes unfocused and desperate. He saw me, changed direction, caught me by the shoulders.

"They didn't tell me it'd be like that! I'm not. . .human," he said. "That night in the orchard. I'm so sorry." He rocked his head from side to side, mouth open, until he fell to his knees, then tipped to his side. "They should destroy me," he blubbered. He pulled his knees into his chest, fell to his side, then wrapped his arms around his legs, burying his face. "I'm a mad dog."

The long road from Mola stretched in front of me. At the end I could see the checkout booth and the bus. I knelt beside him, patted him on the back while he shivered. Grover was right: nobody could bring the dead child back, and nobody could forgive me either. All I could do was wait for the scar to become a part of my face and then accept it as my face.

"There are no throw-away people," I said.

The Pair-a-Deuce Comet Casino All-Sol Poker Championships

I am Jared. I don't know about the earlier versions of me that died in their time. They thought of themselves as Jared too, I suppose, but I know who I am. It is frustrating to never remember dying. How did I face it? Everything is clear up to my last save, but not the death itself.

Weeks ago, when I arrived at the Pair-a-Deuce, it was inside Venus's orbit and diving fast. The comet had grown closer through the transport's vids, but nothing compared to the grandeur of stepping into the Casino and seeing the coma effervescing above, lighting the tables and players and the floor show. For the longest time I looked up. The comet's shadow cast a straight, dark tunnel into the twisting gasses. There were faint colors in the veil stretching away, ripples in the shining fabric, writhing around the shadow's contrasting shaft.

With an effort, I looked away. From the transport's high reception area, the casino spread below me. Beyond the dome, and startlingly close, the comet's horizon glowed, as if a sunrise were imminent. I turned in a circle. The same orange hint painted the horizon all the way around. Of the comet's surface itself, I could see little.

"Welcome, Jared," said the concierge. "Your room is ready. After you've settled, you are welcome to inspect the tournament schedule. Also, there are three buffets to choose from, an excellent bar, a spa, a masseuse, and fitness center. Our reset facility is state of the art and open continuously." She handed me a brochure, the same one I'd read on the transport. "Abel, your personal valet during your visit, will direct you to your quarters."

A young-looking man, wearing a gold casino vest and a single brunette braid above his left ear on an otherwise bald head, smiled as he pointed to a commuter rail. "If you'll follow me, sir." He waited until a hand-loop appeared on the rail, then grabbed on. The moving loop pulled him down into the casino, his feet skimming behind him. A bit dizzy, I swallowed. On the transport I chose between the zero gravity of the ship or the artificial gravity of the wheelhouse, and handled both easily, but the comet's micro-gravity was disorienting. It felt as if I were moving up. I glanced overhead. The dome's transparent ceiling remained comfortably distant.

"It takes a bit to get used to," said the concierge. She held my arm and moved me next to the rail. I snagged the next loop, hoping I didn't look too ungraceful. The rail sloped to the casino floor. A row of craps tables packed with patrons passed by on my left. I caught a whiff of alcohol and sweat. Bells clanged somewhere signaling a slot jackpot. Whether it's Vegas or Clarke City at the foot of Olympus Mons or the backside of a comet plunging toward a brush with the sun, a casino is a casino.

Using the loop's thumb controls that moderated speed, I caught up with Abel. "Very good, sir," he said. "You've been to the Pair-a-Deuce before?"

"No. First time."

He raised his eyebrows. "We could ride this rail for a tour of the casino, if you'd like."

I shook my head. My stomach felt coiled, like a snake, and a dose of something to handle motion sickness sounded better than looking around. I'd have days to explore before perihelion anyway.

He said, "We'll have to slow at the next junction to make the transfer."

Ahead, a rail converged on our own. Abel reached across the gap and snagged another loop. I followed.

When we reached my room, he said, "The door is keyed to your palm. If you need anything. . ." he looked at me closely, ". . .a doctor, perhaps. Room service will take care of you."

I nodded gratefully. All I really wanted was some meds and to close my eyes to rest a bit. The brochure hadn't said anything about nausea!

He waited while I moved into the room, a very nice, high-ceilinged Nikka-Hilton suite. My baggage was piled at the foot of the bed. I reached into my pocket for a tip.

"No need, sir," Abel said. "It's included in the bill."

I said, "This trip *is* dangerous, isn't it?"

His face lit up. "Yes, sir! Comets are completely unpredictable. A hunk could break off, and we'd spin right into the sunlight. Wouldn't last ten minutes. This morning's odds were only seven to one we'll make it."

Last I heard they were twelve to one. Maybe they'd learned something new about the comet since I'd last checked. The boy looked so blithe for someone playing Russian roulette. "How old are you, Abel?"

"Twenty-two."

* * *

Abel knew Jared was one of the Patriarchs when he stepped off the transport, just as if he'd been a god. There was something different in their body posture and the way they dealt with the world. Most new guests didn't even look up at first. The casino was noisy, and there was the problem of micro-gravity, but Jared bent his head back to stare at the comet's tail streaming above them. It had a lot to do with immortality. Short timers were busy keeping their houses in order. Abel, for instance, had spent months going through interviews and screenings to get the job on the Pair-a-Deuce. The pay amazed him. It would put him a tenth of the way to his first reset. When he got there, he went to work immediately making contacts. He knew business was about making contacts. He didn't look up, really look up, until he'd been there a week.

But Patriarchs were different. Their value system wasn't geared to the day-to-day. They had so many. So when Jared spent his first minute on the comet gazing at the streaming gasses on fire with the near sun's light, Abel knew.

Not just any Patriarch, either, thought Abel. Jared! *The* Jared. At two hundred and fifty-one years, only eleven resets and a risk rating of 7.8, he was the third highest ranked. This trip could vault him to number one, and Abel would be there to see it. Not only that, but what a contact. If they got along, Jared might be able to help Abel.

After Abel took Jared to his quarters, he accessed his info, what little there was. The immortals were a private lot. Abel studied the holo that had been taken fifteen years earlier. About Abel's height, a shade under two meters, but well-muscled where Abel had a tendency to be scrawny, the effect of a career in low gee. Abel scanned through the record. It'd been forty-one years since Jared's last reset. The summary included his risk-factor activities. There were dozens, including a one-man assault on several of the Valles Marineris's toughest cliffs, which explained the high risk rating. The longest lived of them was a Matriarch with only four resets, and they were all age related. No risk factor at all. She hardly ever left her compound, and, of course, she had no prestige in the immortals' world.

What's the point in living forever if you don't do anything? You either live an adventure forever or die a hero. Why behave any other way? And if you're a Patriarch or Matriarch, you can have them both, over and over, thought Abel.

Abel met Jared the next morning to start his first full day on the casino. Jared had made an appointment at the reset facility.

"Good morning, sir," said Abel. Jared looked much better than he had the day before. His short, dark hair was combed straight back, and he wore a single-piece overall that changed colors depending on how the light hit it.

"Good morning, Abel." Jared's eyes were dark brown, almost black, and he gazed at Abel directly. "Let's take that tour you told me about."

When they reached the surface viewing rooms, Jared let go of his loop, and pushed toward the windows.

"I hadn't imagined so much character to the surface."

Abel joined him. "The comet is composed of loosely packed rocks, dust and volatiles: water ice, frozen carbon dioxide and carbon monoxide." On the horizon directly in front of them, and only a couple of kilometers away, sheets of brilliantly lit crystals flew up to join the display above. Depending on the sun-side jetting, which was irregular, the horizon at any one place could be bright, as it was then, or fairly dark. At their feet, the surface was a bizarre conglomeration of twisted spires reflecting the horizon's orange and yellow glare.

"I thought it would be flat," said Jared. "Flat and black."

"When the sun hits the dark crust, it vaporizes the frozen material beneath, creating pressure that breaks through. The formations are active vents that went from sunlight into the shadow. For a bit, of course, they continued to blow out gasses. As they cooled, the last bit of material, mostly water, froze in the shapes you see. The ice sublimates, but it takes a while."

"They're fantastic!" Jared's eyes were wide, his mouth a little open in wonder, the same as yesterday when he looked up at the million-mile long tail.

Abel faced the window, trying to appreciate the comet the way Jared did. Is this immortality's greatest gift, a more contemplative way to see the universe?

Jared tapped his fingers against the glass. "What are our odds this morning?"

"Still seven to one but they haven't collated all the seismographic data for the day yet."

Abel took me to the reset facility after the casino tour. Every Patriarch and Matriarch handles resets differently. Some are so fearful of losing any of themselves they backup daily. For me, that's obsessive. The Pair-a-Deuce's center looked like mine at home. The same sort of reception area, although the couches here had seat belts so the patrons didn't drift away, the same sort of security procedures to make sure you were who you said you were, not that a counterfeit was likely to slip in here, and the backup room itself was dominated in the same way by the reset imaging machinery, which looked like a giant waffle iron with a space cut out of it for your head and shoulders to fit in as it closed.

"If you'll take your place on the table," said the technician.

He cinched a strap across my chest. A foot above, the top edge of the machinery loomed over me. "This is a good time to backup," said the technician. "You'd hate to lose the trip out here and all the things you've already seen."

The top came down. If the Pair-a-Deuce suffered a catastrophic event, or if my body gave out, or if an angry gambler killed me, the creak of the machinery descending on my upper body, and the oddly electric smell of the room would be my last memory before I woke up in a retraining center. The reset machinery can take a perfect picture of where every neuron in my brain resides, the chemical state of each cell, where individual tendrons connect, where all the nerves lead on to other nerves down to the atomic level, which is an exact portrait of who I am at the moment of the recording, but it takes a while for the new brain to form the copy. For a year I'd be relearning motor control and adapting to the move.

With my eyes closed, I waited for the recording instrument to lock into place. It settled onto my chest. Cool gel flowed around my neck, chin, and the back of my head, over my ears and into them until my head was nearly submerged. Only my nose and mouth were uncovered. Then it solidified. My head was absolutely still. Soft pads settled on my cheeks and pressed against my eyes. Some people hate this part — the claustrophobia — but I like it: the machine's comforting grip.

Depending on what my schedule is, I reset once a month or so. The longest time between reset and death was my first one, four and a half years. What did I know? I was rich as a king and twenty-two. I thought I truly was immortal. Why spend the hour in a reset center when you have your whole life in front of you? I lost a marriage, a son and the four and a half years by not resetting. Six months after that last reset I met someone my age. We fell in love, married and had a child, a boy. He was three when I flew an experimental glider into a flat spin and lost a wing. I've seen the vid: the plane careening. On a closeup I could see my head bent over the controls. I've listened to my communications with the control tower, but I couldn't tell, not really, how I faced death. What was I like in those last few seconds? I don't know.

The tech's voice spoke in my ear, through the solid gel. "We're almost ready, Jared. There may be a moment of discomfort."

I would have nodded if I could. By the time I finished my retraining that first time, almost six years had passed since my last reset. I met my wife outside of the hospital. She was under no legal obligation to come. The man she'd married, the father of her child, died in the plane. I was like his younger brother, and I didn't know her. I remember standing in the lobby, shaking her hand, as if she were a new business associate, while the little boy looked up at me curiously. They had told me about my missing past while I was retraining. I'd seen my wedding vids, but they didn't mean anything. Her hand was warm and limp in mine. Her smile was attractive; I understood what I must have seen in her, but she was *so* old. As far as I was concerned, I was twenty-three and ready to whip the world after a year in a hospital, after dodging death once. How could I have chosen to marry?

Still, there are times when I take out that old wedding album and thumb through the pages.

I started resetting more frequently after that. There's too much to lose if you don't. A memory is more than a limp hand in your own; it's more than a child you don't know looking up at you.

The pain started in the middle of my brain, like a pulsing ember. It swelled suddenly, pushing outward, a supernova behind my eyes, and then, pop, it was gone.

"It will be another moment, Jared," the tech said.

I knew he was checking the recording. If it wasn't perfect, he would have to do it again. There could be no irregularities. Then the recording would be transmitted to the retraining center on Earth where it would be stored. The electric smell was stronger, and the steel-solid gel felt almost hot against my face. Outside of the machine I could feel my palms against the table, sweat-slick and trembling. A "moment of discomfort" indeed!

Abel smiled while watching the hands dealt. There was room for creativity in low grav. The cards were slightly magnetic, and there was metal under the felt, otherwise the slightest breeze might turn up a hole card, but the cards in the air were fun. A good dealer might have dealt the fifth card for five-card draw before the first one had spun down to its spot in front of the player. All the dealt cards rotated in the air at once. Most players didn't deal this way themselves — too easy for a card to twist and be visible — they flicked the cards directly to the table.

Jared, when he dealt, was businesslike.

After lunch, he played aggressively, betting high early to force others to abandon their comfort zones. He bet the maximum often, staying in the game until the end. Abel couldn't find a pattern to when he would fold or bluff. Twice Jared won big pots on great hands, an aces-tens full house, then a straight flush, king high. He also won on pure bluffs. By the end of the session, Abel believed Jared broke even.

Jared's demeanor changed during the day. For a while he was pure poker face, playing like an automaton. Later, though, he smiled often, moved his hands, became talkative. Once, he lost his temper. Flung his cards from the table. They scattered in flat parabolas until wind resistance slowed them, and they began their leisurely descent to the floor.

When the two of them finally headed back to Jared's room on the commuter rail, Jared asked, "Do you know what a 'tell' is?"

Jared turned to the young man, one hand on the loop, the other trailing, dragging lightly on the rail. His expression was serious.

"Sure. It's a mannerism that reveals whether a player is bluffing or not."

"You've been watching me all day; do you know what my tells are?"

Abel laughed. Everything he'd seen today had been a performance. "That was brilliant, sir. It didn't look like it ever mattered to you. I had no ideas what your cards were."

Jared looked at Abel oddly for a moment. "The secret's in caring for it all passionately."

"How's our comet doing?" I asked.

"Ahh! There are three fracture zones the seismo-guys are looking at. One of the techs calls them Usher one, two and three. You know, like that house in the Poe story that looks solid except that it isn't? Pretty funny."

I nodded.

"If the Pair-a-Deuce is above one of them, and the comet splits there, then it would be over, so we try not to camp on top of them. None of them seem very stable, so our odds are down to five to one."

He sounded like he was talking about the trifecta at Camden Downs instead of his own life. "That doesn't worry you?"

"Oh, no, sir. That's just the odds for the casino itself. We have escape pods. Our chances are much better, but I've already put my money on the entire ball of rock making the run safely. They haven't lost a whole casino in twelve years. If you want to make a swing by an observation room, I can show you something worth looking at."

Outside looked much as it had my first time here. Milky-white spires of twisted water ice stuck out of the surface like gnarled fingers, but in between them lay a haziness that at first I thought was in the glass. "Is that fog?"

Abel shook his head. "Carbon dioxide crystals. Look!"

He pointed to my left, and the others at the window crowded against me. A gray plume shot out of the comet, perfectly straight, like a beam of slow light.

"It's a lateral fault. We're only four kilometers from the sunny side where it's 700 degrees. The exposed volatiles are boiling off, but it's darned hot underneath the surface too. Pressure builds up. It vents through weak areas."

I'd never seen anything to match it: the surreal comet landscape; the violent, beautiful geyser flying into the blackness above; the effervescent, shimmering veil fluttering on the horizon, and through the white and yellow display, the laser-steady starlight. I couldn't see the sun, but I could feel it, intolerably huge and flaming on the comet's other side, pulling us in.

"How hot will the surface get at perihelion?"

"Well over a thousand," said Abel.

Someone behind me sucked air between his teeth. I gave my space at the window to another.

Beyond the dome, great sheets of leaping light flowed away. It was like looking through the glass roof of an elevator dropping out of control toward a distant basement, three days from our closest approach and the slingshot gravity boost that would wing the comet back out of the solar system.

The morning the tournament began Abel thought he'd made a connection with Jared, who had been contemplative over breakfast, and when Abel brought up the idea of a good recommendation, he nodded, so Abel decided that meant he had been happy with how he had done his duties.

A bell chimed, and several other players left their meals.

"It's time to start, sir," Abel said.

Jared glanced at him, and the moment vanished. A quick smile. "Let's see whether I remember how to play this game."

The tournament directors had drawn for table assignments. Abel already had Jared's, and he directed him to his seat and pile of chips. The other players were familiar. Jared had beaten them all over the course of the last few days.

A tournament official confirmed that everyone knew the house rules, then play began. Jared dealt the first hand of five card draw, and took that pot on two pair. By lunch, he'd bumped everyone on the table into the loser's bracket and advanced himself into that afternoon's reseed, where table winners played each other. It would take two days to trim the field down to one table full of the big winners for the championship.

Cards flew from dealer to players. Chips clinked against each other. Waiters brought drinks, and players who were concentrating too much to care let the ice melt to nothing, having never touched their glasses. It dizzied Abel. Bets, raises, calls, bluffs, reversals of fortune. Abel liked seven card stud best, where he could see the upturned cards, but mostly he liked watching Jared, whose eyes went from tell to tell. They'd talked about each player. Who had a tendency to raise low when their hand was good. Who laughed longer when they bluffed. Who could be rattled by quick play or frustrated by indecision. Abel knew Jared didn't play his hand; he played the players.

And after a while, they knew it. By the second day the eliminated players started watching Jared. A crowd formed behind the ropes put up to keep the tables clear. Conversation buzzed behind Abel about Jared's play. "I'll bet fifty he's bluffing this time," said someone, and pretty soon, there was a lively set of wagers going on with every one of his hands. The players at the table moaned or grinned at their luck as the crowd reacted to the play.

Abel had never seen a dynamic like it at any other tournament.

Jared won steadily, until, one by one, the other finalists stared at the empty spot on the table where their chips used to rest, then shook his hand. The crowd around the table applauded as the last cards were shown. Jared won on a ten high straight.

"Sometimes it goes that way," he said to Abel as he left the table.

"I've arranged for a reset before the victory party, sir, as you instructed." Jared nodded.

I won the tournament six hours before perihelion. Good players got bad hands at bad times, and everything else went my way. There's magic sitting at a poker table when you know luck is backing you. It's hard to bluff another out of a good hand, and a full house doesn't beat a flush no matter how well you read the other player's face, so it's best to have the flush. You can't control the cards. Poker's mostly damage control and resource management, but I didn't get many damaging hands, and my resources were rich. I think anyone who drew the same cards I did could have been the All-Sol champion this year.

Abel congratulated me as we headed for my room. I wanted to freshen up, and do a reset before the party. When something amazing happens in your life, you don't risk losing it.

"That's incredible," I said as the commuter rail pulled me toward my room. We were only a hundred-thousand miles from the sun, and the comet's tail flared above with squinty-eyed violence.

"They'll be cutting the casino loose soon," said Abel. "We have to move constantly as we go around. The sunrise line will be moving too fast for us to stay anchored."

"What are the odds now?"

Abel laughed. "It's looking a bit dicey, sir. They told me fifty-fifty before breakfast. I've been keeping my eye on the nearest escape pod for you. If you get through this one, your risk rating will be the highest ever. You'll be the top ranked immortal, sir." His eyes practically glowed, and I realized that he worshiped me.

"Only if I survive, Abel. My rating drops if I don't make it."

"No problem, sir. I've got a good feeling about this one. The way the cards were falling for you, if you had a leaky spacesuit and an hour's worth of air, I'd give you ten to one that you could hang onto this rock with one hand, do the hot ride around, and still make your way back to civilization."

He laughed again, and I had to laugh too. His enthusiasm about me was contagious. Maybe I was blessed. Maybe this time I'd make it all the way around, so to speak, and never face my death again. I was still chuckling when the reset machinery clamped down on my head, filling my nose with its strange, electric smell.

At the first observation room, the crowd cheered when Jared entered. Someone pushed a drink into his hand. The tradition in the comet casinos was to spend as much of the trip around the sun drunk. They called it "toasting the toast," and this looked to be a royal party.

At the window Abel saw the comet's surface crawling slowly beneath them as the Pair-a-Deuce glided with the shadow. Wherever the fault lines were, he couldn't see them, and they weren't the only danger. Most venting on the comet's dark side were explosive. If superheated gasses made it this far, they did it under incredible pressure. A large venting beneath them could push the unanchored casino away from the comet's protective bulk and directly into the sunlight. Or even more sudden, a section of rock and solid ice could be blasted into the Pair-a-Deuce's underside and breach the hull.

Abel took his own drink, a glass of water, but only tasted it. He kept his eye on Jared. There was access to escape pods at either end of the room, but the pods only held ten people each, and there were at least fifty partiers crowded against the windows, oohing and aahing at the spectacle outside.

Jared forced his way against the glass. Abel rested a hand on Jared's shoulder so they wouldn't be separated. As they took their place facing the exploding horizon only a couple kilometers away, Abel thought, maybe the comet will tear itself apart as it goes around the sun. Maybe that would be the best thing to happen. If Jared escapes that, then his record will be unassailable.

The two men stood on the far side of the room closest to the escape panel. Abel had just finished thinking, "Maybe the comet will tear itself apart," when the room shuddered, and the klaxons began blaring.

People screamed. In a panic, some tried to run and, instead, they floated helplessly above the floor, their feet and hands flailing about without purchase. ESCAPE PROCEDURE signs lit on the walls, and the escape pod panels were marked with flashing red arrows. "Proceed to your nearest evacuation area," a voice intoned over the intercom.

Someone kicked Abel in the head. He grabbed an ankle and pulled the man down.

"Hold on!" Abel yelled as he put the guest's hand on a bannister.

Where was Jared? Abel turned all the way around.

"Look!" someone yelled. People glanced out the window and most moved, terrified, toward the exits at the back of the room, away from the escape pods.

Where was Jared? He wasn't in the crowd. Where was he? Abel pushed up so he could be above them. Nothing.

Abel turned again. Jared was still at the window, not moving. The floor convulsed. In the distance beyond the observation room back in the casino, Abel heard an impact, or he felt it in his bones, like the thunder of a mountain collapsing. His ears popped, and that, more than anything else, told him the end was near. Air tight doors clanged shut in the distance. Whatever was happening, it was massive.

"You've got to get out, sir!" Abel grabbed Jared's arm, but the man didn't let go of the rail below the window.

"Have you ever seen anything like it?" Jared said, his voice filled with wonder.

Abel pulled again, but Jared still held on. He braced his foot against the wall, ready to force Jared away when he looked out the window, and for a moment, froze.

The horizon had split in a wide crack that led from the incandescent curtain of the comet's tail all the way to the Pair-a-Deuce, like a ravine, and the edges drew slowly apart. At the far end, gasses drove out of the gap, lit from below, intolerably bright, flaming, and as the crack widened, the awful light stretched toward them. Through the veiling gasses, the exploding volatiles boiling away in the thousand degree heat, slowly appeared the surface of the sun.

The room became hot. Abel felt it on his face. Even with his eyes closed, it was too dazzling. He pushed hard to break Jared's hold. Eyes watering, Abel dragged him toward the escape pod. The room had emptied.

If I can get Jared into the pod, Abel thought; if Jared survives this, he'll hold memories that will never be equaled!

Nine of the ten places were occupied. The pod's auto-countdown had engaged. "Twenty seconds to separation. Please exit the takeoff area," the recorded message intoned. Twin airtight doors would shut, sealing the passengers into the pod on one side and protecting the integrity of the casino on the other.

Abel grabbed the last spot's canopy and pulled Jared toward it. He didn't weigh very much, but his mass was the same. Abel grunted with effort.

"Did you see?" he said, his face glowing with joy. "The sun was coming through."

"Get in!" Abel yelled.

Ominous metal shrieking split the air behind them.

Jared's hands caught both sides of the canopy. The acceleration seat waited within.

"Fifteen seconds," chanted the recording.

Abel put a hand in the middle of Jared's back, still keeping a grip with the other. The young man shoved, and somehow Jared shrugged in a complicated way. Instead of pushing against him, Abel's effort thrust him into the pod.

"Don't be ridiculous," Jared said as he swung the canopy shut.

"No!" Abel beat against the descending door.

Jared looked at Abel for the last time. Behind him, the observation room blazed in acetylene brightness.

Against the rising wind within the casino, he shouted, "If you make it, tell myself I died brave. I'm okay with this." He smiled and then the canopy clicked shut.

*　　*　　*

I remember the reset machinery coming down and that peculiar electric smell. Then, I woke up.

At first, I thought my arms were restrained, but it was the combination of Earth gravity and my lack of motor control. I shut my eyes against the familiar sensation of not being able to make my body respond. After all, I'd done this eleven times before.

It took over a month before I was able to manipulate my hands well enough to type out a question for my therapist. Speech would come weeks later.

I laboriously typed, "Did Abel live?"

"Who is Abel?" she said.

Hours passed before an answer came back. I stared at the ceiling, feeling the blood pumping through a body I'd never worn before. Breathing air in lungs that were new to me. Keenly aware that my consciousness had made a transfer that my physical self had not. Was I the same me that just won the All-Sol championship, or was this copy of me flawed in some way? Was the self thinking in my head now a new person or the same one? Was there any way to measure the changes? It was a question I often wrestled with. Of course, it was the same question I asked every morning when I woke up. What happened to the me that fell asleep the night before? What difference was there between sleep and dying?

Anyone who wonders about death and reincarnation need only take a nap.

The therapist finally told me that Abel survived. I'll be released from here before he returns.

Space travel is so slow.

I'll meet him. I hope he saw me in the end. I hope he has news to tell me of myself.

The Stars Underfoot

In the middle of the night, **Dustin edged away** from the frozen shore, careful to keep his weight evenly on both feet. The quarter-mile wide lake had only started freezing a week ago, and no one had made it more than a yard before the ice cracked. Yesterday Kenyon Parker had fallen in up to his knees, and while the gang laughed, he'd run for home, his lips blue with cold. But the temperature had been bitter all day, and once the sun set, the thermometer plunged below zero. I'll be the first across this year, Dustin thought. There's an advantage to being small. He shuffled forward, the ice so thin, he could almost feel it sag under his weight.

A deep breath froze the inside of his nostrils, and it tickled when he wrinkled his nose. So he did it again. I've already established the season's record. I've got to be twenty feet out, he thought. It was hard to tell by starlight what the distance was, so he flicked his flashlight on to check. Yep, twenty feet if it's an inch. Underneath him, trapped bubbles slid away like little jellyfish. The ice was remarkably clear. Dustin crouched, pressed the light against the ice, and played it across the bottom, across silt covered sticks and muddy boulders, much deeper than he was tall. He turned the light off. If anyone in the houses surrounding the park saw him, they would call the police for sure. Last year, *days* after Mike Liddle had made the first crossing, Dustin had been walking alone across the lake, and a lady stuck her head out her back door to yell, "Get off the lake, young man. It's not frozen." Dustin looked down at his feet, at the milky smooth expanse as solid as a marble floor. "Call the Pope, then," he'd called back. "It's a miracle," which he'd thought was a pretty clever thing for a twelve-year old to come up with.

Of course, Mike Liddle had been a hero all winter last year, and Kenyon Parker was one for falling in this year, but no one had ever attempted a night crossing to open the season. No one had ever done it alone. Dustin checked under his coat where the camera was protected from the cold. When he reached the middle, he'd take a picture. Ten bucks at the one-hour developing place, and his name would be carved into neighborhood history.

A splash at the lake's far end. Then, quacking, as if the ducks were right beside him. House lights reflected off the unfrozen part of the lake where they swam, looking like little puppet figures, most with their heads down. Overhead, stars glittered with icy twinkles so sharp that Dustin thought he could surely touch them. He shuffled forward, wary of the slickness, farther from shore, closer to the lake's middle. Another quick check through the ice. His flashlight penetrated deeply, but couldn't reach the bottom now. Green particles drifted through the beam. He wiped the light with his sleeve, standing still, listening to the night sounds. A half hour earlier he'd removed the screen in his bedroom window, lowered himself out, and hiked the mile to the park, crunching through ice-encrusted leaves strewn on pale sidewalks. He'd never walked through the town at night, and now, in the midst of the lake's smooth emptiness, the sounds were amplified: cars shifting gears on streets blocks away, a dog barking, distant laughter from a party. And lights seemed more intense too. Not just the stars, but windows in the homes whose backyards faced the lake. Some glowed in a flickery blue that said a television was on. Rich yellow light poured from others. The air smelled of woodsmoke. Dustin exhaled carefully because he didn't want to disturb the symphony with his own sounds. His glasses fogged from his breathing, so he turned a little into the breeze, and they cleared. The night had never seemed so pure and clean. If he'd known it would be like this, he would have snuck out every night, and he told himself that in the future he would. I'm a superhero, he thought. I'm outside of space and time. I move where no one sees or hears me, while I see and hear all. He chuckled, and it sounded loud in the brittle cold.

A series of snaps, like tiny firecrackers, radiated away from his feet on the next step. He stopped, hands held from his sides as if he were balancing, and his heart raced. I'm in danger! No one knows I'm out here! He shuffled a few feet further, away from the weak area, then stood as motionless as a statue, his hands still out. The ice glittered. It was the stars, perfectly reflected. He stood on a starry table spread beneath him, and he thought about astronauts and space walks. Even the quality of air tasted different, more animated, more primordial. He felt like an explorer, in the center of his own town; he'd discovered a new wilderness. "Trailblazer," he said. "Dustin Boone," the crackling ice already forgotten.

*   *   *

Being small bothered him. He'd never been a hero in anything. Even his friends picked him last when they chose sides, like he was the little brother they had to play with. And the teachers only tolerated him at school, where he earned "C's," because his mom and dad would ground him if he had a "D." He read too much and paid attention too little. He'd stare out the window, cheek resting on his hand, where the mountains rose cool and blue on the horizon, and he imagined undiscovered countries. He watched late-night science fiction and horror movies on Friday and Saturday, when his parents let him. Never the hero. Always the dreamer, the reader, the observer.

A breeze scurried across the surface, kicking the dusting of snow into glowing spirals. Dustin's eyes watered, so he blinked them clear. For a second, he thought a beam of light had flashed up through the ice just in front of him. He blinked again. Nothing other than the little crystal whirlwinds dancing across the lake. He swayed. The stars beneath and above, the wind that switched from front to back, the sense that he wasn't standing on anything substantial dizzied him. For a second, he was afraid he might fall. Surely that would send him through the ice. He remembered rocks they'd thrown into the lake yesterday, orange-sized stones lobbed high that vanished with ragged claps, leaving uneven holes where the water boiled for a second, then was still. The light appeared again, twenty feet away, a distinct glow below the surface.

He moved toward it, careful to keep his feet always against the ice, his body awash with goosebumps. How could there be a light *under* the water? He looked up. Maybe it was a reflection, a plane, a planet, but only the hard-edged stars filled his vision. Maybe it was a ghost, and that nearly stopped him, but maybe it wasn't. He continued on, eyes so wide that he thought they might freeze that way.

The light changed in intensity, dimming, almost disappearing, then growing strong again. It was a beam now, cutting through the water beneath Dustin, so that for a second he saw the floating algae he'd seen early, suspended green specs, then the light pointed away from him. Dustin could see the source, a bright spot three or four feet deep. He held his breath. Could it be a new kind of fish, something that only came out in early winter, never observed before?

*   *   *

Dustin was an imaginative boy. He played by himself in the yard for hours, building kingdoms, then tearing them down. He wrote stories in the back of notebooks, not showing them to anyone. His full life was mostly a secret from his acquaintances. He'd read at family parties, not so much to escape the meaningless chit chat, although that was an advantage, but because he yearned to visit secret worlds. In the books, he saved the day. He solved the problem. He turned the tide. He was not an ordinary boy, because an ordinary boy would not be out on a barely frozen lake in the stars; an ordinary boy would not hope that a picture taken in the middle of the night would make him a hero to his friends.

So he was not ordinary, because an ordinary boy would have run away from the light instead of sliding ever closer, and an ordinary boy would have surely screamed when he saw the light was a flashlight, and holding the flashlight was a hand, and that the hand was attached to an arm wearing a coat somewhat like Dustin's own, and the boy that was wearing the coat stood on the ice just as Dustin did, but upside down, like a bat, walking under the water, pointing his light ahead of him, moving his feet carefully, as if he too might slip and fall

"Hey!" yelled Dustin. His voice echoed from the nearby houses, and the ducks fluttered in response, swimming to their pool's far side. "How can you do that?"

The boy under the ice paused, then swung his light to and fro, as if he'd heard, but didn't know where the question had come from.

Dustin crouched to see better. The soles of the boy's shoes were under Dustin's mittens. Dustin realized the boy didn't look wet. His coat wasn't water sodden, and his hair, from what he could see by the boy's light, was neatly combed. He had a pleasant face, maybe only a year or so older than Dustin, and he wore glasses, but he looked puzzled as he turned slowly, shining his flashlight all around him.

"I'm here," yelled Dustin.

The boy turned his flashlight down. Suddenly Dustin couldn't see. The light blinded him. He threw himself away, slipping on the ice, and there was a sudden cracking. Dustin kept moving, trying to see what was happening. His hands were wet! The ice was broken. He lay flat, spreading his weight, trying to see past the great, black circle that was the flashlight's afterimage.

Something splashed, more ice cracking and a vague scream. No, not vague, muted, like a scream with the volume turned down, a distant sounding "Help! Help!" only ten feet away.

Dustin turned on his flashlight. The boy's legs stuck through the ice and kicked wildly into the air. A movement above him caught Dustin's eye, and he flicked his light toward it. At first, he couldn't tell what it was, then he recognized the boy's flashlight rising from the lake, sinking into the stars. When it turned, its beam glowed dully, then winked out.

Then the ice broke more, and the boy lurched farther into view, his elbows visible now, thrashing at the ice. Dustin glimpsed his face, pulled from the water, and it was frightened, cheeks bulging in a held breath. The boy kicked himself down and tried to pull himself under the surface, but the ice kept breaking. The face appeared. He choked, then lunged down again.

Dustin thought about moving farther away, to keep the cracked ice as far from him as possible. He could retreat to the shore. Whatever was happening here was beyond his ability to understand or explain. Who would believe it? But he didn't move. He watched, his hands bunched into fists so tight he could feel his fingernails digging in, even through the mittens. "Get back!" he yelled. "Get back!" and he didn't mean "get away," but "get back to where you are safe."

The boy floated up, until only his hands remained in the water, flailing. Dustin imagined in a moment, the boy's struggles would weaken. He'd go limp and slowly follow his flashlight into the sky.

Knowing that it was stupid, thinking that the boy drowning in air was probably a hallucination, Dustin left his light on the ice pointed toward the boy and pushed his way forward.

Wet ice. Broken ice. He broke through the ice five feet away. Water. Water like liquid fire, soaking through his pants, weighing down his coat, pulling him deep. Dustin kicked himself forward, so shocked by the water's temperature he couldn't inhale. He kicked himself forward, then grabbed the other boy's wrist that was now a foot above the lake. Dustin pulled hard. The boy moved toward the water, while Dustin's sinking stopped. He pulled again. The boy's face was against his own. They'd both lost their glasses, but by the flashlight's pure light, he saw the boy's eyes, an inch from his own, and they were pleading. Now the boy's head was underwater, while Dustin was clear of the lake to his armpits. He climbed the boy like he would climb a float toy, pulling himself up while pushing the boy down, and the boy helped, thrusting himself deeper. He grabbed Dustin's leg, pinching the skin through his winter pants.

But they weren't stable. Dustin felt the roll begin, and his head was underwater, a thousand cold needles piercing his scalp and peeling back the skin. A scramble to get back on top, desperate to be *above* the water. Knees collided. Hands grabbed coats, tugged, struggled, until there was an equilibrium again, Dustin's head high.

For a moment, he didn't think about saving the boy. Anything to get out of the strangling cold. He'd taken two choking gulps in a row. Coughing ripped his throat, and already his arms felt leaden, his hands like wood. His face burned. He climbed the upside down boy. A promised land of unbroken ice beckoned in front of the flashlight. Dustin reached toward it, careful of their balance, gathered in water and pushed it behind them. They moved a couple of inches. The boy's legs shook under Dustin's hand, but he reached into the lake too, his hand appearing out of the water, mimicking Dustin's movement, and they moved again. Working together, they paddled toward the unbroken ice.

Even Dustin's brain felt cold and sluggish, his thoughts disconnected. Why can't I keep climbing, he thought, until I'm standing on the bottom of his feet and he's standing on the bottoms of mine? We could *walk* out of danger if we always stepped where the other stepped, and the vision seemed so dreamy, for a minute he thought they were already doing it, which frightened him more than anything that had occurred so far because his hand had stopped paddling. He was just holding on, shivering so hard that it was if his muscles had locked up. He forced himself to paddle again. Every inch in the core of him hurt, but he couldn't feel his arms or feet now at all. He had to watch to be sure they were still moving.

The unbroken edge moved closer. The flashlight was only ten feet away. He touched the solid surface, slid his hand across it. Nothing to hold onto, and they almost tipped again. He reached, a little farther this time. For an instant, his wet mitten stuck to the ice, pulling the edge against their hips, but the mitten broke loose. The boy's boot shifted under Dustin's armpit. How could they get back onto the ice without shattering it? Dustin shut his eyes tight, his head so cold that his thoughts flowed like thick jelly. He could push away from the boy and fall flat. If the ice held, he'd be safe, but the boy would be in the middle again. Dustin looked down. The boy held his legs in nearly the same manner. It could work if they leaned at the same time. They'd fall to their sides of the ice, their legs still in the water, but maybe they could scoot to safety. Dustin put his hand flat on the surface. The flashlight beam shone directly on it. If the boy looked, he would see it, a mittened silhouette through the ice. Would he understand?

Breathing hurt. Razor-like crystals seemed to cut into his lungs, his throat. The boy moved — the balance shifted — and through the ice, Dustin saw him reach. Their hands faced palm to palm, only an inch apart. Dustin let go of the boy's leg and twisted as he fell, so that he landed on his stomach. A loud snap. Somewhere, the ice cracked, but it held beneath him. He pulled a knee out of the water, slid forward a few inches. Got the other knee out. Slid. He was clear of the hole, five feet from the flashlight. The boy on the other side pushed forward too.

The light revealed him. Blue eyes to Dustin's brown. Frightened. Hurting, but alive, inhaling. Dustin pushed himself to his hands and knees. If I don't move, I'll freeze to death he thought. He staggered to his feet. Shuffled to the shore, two-hundred yards farther, his coat and pants weighing him down, then lumbered toward home as if Jupiter's gravity was holding him down, water turning to ice in his hair.

What seemed like hours later, he stood in his shower, still in his clothes, his skin tingling in the heat, his un-numbing fingers and toes screaming. Every muscle complaining, he peeled away the coat, dropped the ruined camera to the tile.

I was a hero tonight, he thought as he sat among his lake-soaked clothes, the shower water pounding down, the steam filling the bathroom.

He thought, being a hero isn't about what happened; it's about what didn't. I was a hero tonight, and he was too tired even to cry.

That happened much later that night, and many nights after, when he woke from a dream, where the boy on the other side was dead, his eyes creamy pale and wide, only an inch away beyond the ice, and the boy was him.

The Long Way Home

Marisa kept her back to the door, holding it closed. "Another few minutes and they will have made the jump. You can go home then."

"The war has started," said Jacqueline, the telemetry control engineer. Her face glowed red with panic. "I don't matter. The mission is over. They made the jump *four hours* ago."

Marisa swallowed. If Jacqueline grabbed her, there would be little she could do. The woman outweighed her by thirty pounds, and there were no security forces to help. "Jacqueline, we've come so far."

The bigger woman raised her fist. Marisa tensed but didn't move. Her hands trembled behind her. For a moment, Jacqueline's fist quivered in the air. Beyond her, the last of the mission control crew watched. Most of the stations were empty. The remaining engineers' faces registered no expression. They were too tired to react, but Marisa knew they wanted to leave just as badly.

Then Jacqueline dropped her hand to her side. Her eyes closed. "I don't make a difference," she whispered.

Marisa released a held breath. "We're part of mankind's greatest moment. There's nothing you can do out there." She nodded her head toward the door. "We can't stop what's happening, but we can be witnesses to this. There's hope still."

Several monitors displayed a United States map and a Florida one inset in the corner. Both showed bright yellow blotches. "Areas of lost communication" the key read underneath. Major cities across the country; most of the south-western coast and north-eastern seaboard, glowed bright yellow. In Florida, yellow sunbursts blotted out Miami and Jacksonville. As she watched, another one appeared on Tampa. She glanced at Mission Control's ceiling and the half-dozen skylights. At any moment the ceiling could peel away, awash in nuclear light. She expected it, expected it much earlier, but she'd stayed at her station, recording the four-hour old signals from the *Advent* as it sped toward the solar system's edge, already beyond Neptune's orbit. Would she have any warning? Would there be an instant before the end that she would be aware that it had happened?

Jacqueline sat heavily at her console, and Marisa returned to her station. The data looked good, but it had looked good from the beginning six years earlier when the massive ship ponderously moved out of orbit, all 14,400 passengers hale and hearty. There had been deaths on board, of course. They expected that. Undetected medical conditions. Two homicides. Two suicides, but no major incidents with the ship itself. The hardware performed perfectly, and now, only a few minutes from when the synchronized generators along the ship's perimeter powered up to send the *Advent* into juxtaspace, Mission Control really was redundant. Jacqueline was right.

The room smelled of old coffee and sweat. Many of the controllers had been at their stations for twenty hours or more. As time grew short, they split their attention between their stations and the ubiquitous news displays. A scrolling text readout under the graphics listed unbelievable numbers: estimated dead, radiation readings, cities lost.

Marisa toggled her display. She wanted readouts on the juxtaengines. Mankind *was* going to the stars at last, even if there might be no Earth to return to if they could duplicate the ship to bring them back. "It's easy, having no family," she said under her breath, which wasn't quite true. Her grown son lived in Oceanside, a long commute from southern L.A., but they only talked on the phone at Christmas now. She had to check his photograph to remind himself of what he looked like. A station over, an engineer had his head down on his keyboard, and he sobbed.

Dr. Smalley was the only controller who appeared occupied. He flicked through screen after screen of medical data. The heartbeats of the entire crew drew tiny lines across his display. He looked at Marisa. "We won't know what happens when the shift happens. What will their bodies go through? What a pity they can't signal through the jump."

"If they make the jump at all," moaned Jacqueline.

"We'll know in three minutes," said Marisa. "Regardless of what happens here, we will have saved ourselves."

Dimly, through mission control's thick walls, sirens wailed up and down. The building vibrated, sending a coffee cup off a table's edge and to the floor.

"Maybe if we'd spent the money here, where it could do some good, we'd never come to this," said Jacqueline. "We bankrupted the planet for this mission."

Dr. Smalley studied the heartbeats from the ship. "They're excited. Everyone's pulse is high. Look, I can see everything that's happening in their bodies." He waved a hand at his display. "Their individual transmitters give me more information than if I had them hooked up in a hospital. I wish I was with them."

"Everyone wishes they were with them," said Marisa.

Jacqueline said, "Don't you have a word for it, Doctor, when the patient's condition is fatal, so you decide to try something unproven to save her? That's what we're doing here, aren't we? Humanity is dying, so we try this theoretical treatment."

The countdown clock on the wall showed less than two minutes. The floor shook again, much sharper this time.

"Please, a few more seconds," Marisa said to no one.

So much history happening around her: the first colonial expedition to another star system, and the long-feared global nuclear conflict. The victor had to be the explorers. The names passed through her head: Goddard, Von Braun, Armstrong and the rest of them. It was a way to shut out the death dealers knocking at the door.

"It's an experiment," said Jacqueline, edging on hysteria. "We've never sent a ship even a tenth this big. We've never tied multiple juxtaengines together. What if their fields interact? Instead of sending the ship in one piece, it could tear it apart."

"It's too expensive to try out," Marisa snapped. "It's all or nothing."

"You've been listening to the defeatists," said Dr. Smalley. "The theory is perfect. The math is perfect. In an instant, they will be hundreds of light years from our problems."

Marisa clutched the edge of her monitor. The countdown timer clicked to under a minute. I'm a representative of mankind, she thought. For everyone who has ever wanted to go to the stars, I stand for them. She wished she could see the night sky.

Dr. Smalley hunched toward his computer as if he were trying to climb right through. Jacqueline stared at the television screens with their yellow-specked maps. The images wavered, then turned to gray fuzz. She pressed her knuckles to her mouth.

"Ten seconds," said Marisa. "All systems in the green."

The countdown ticker marched down. Marisa remembered a childhood filled with stories of space, the movies and books set in the universe's grand theater, not the tiny stage lit by a single sun. If only she could have gone too, she could have missed the messy ending mankind had made for itself. The first bombs exploded yesterday morning. Over breakfast, she'd thought it was a hoax. No way people could be so stupid. But the reports continued in, and it wasn't a joke, not in the least.

Eyes toward their readouts, the control engineers monitored *Advent's* last signals. Already at near solar-escape velocity, the *Advent* would leap out of the solar system, riding the unlikely physics of juxtaspace.

"Three. . .two. . .one," someone said. Marisa's screen flipped to the NO SIGNAL message. Analysis indicated the ship had gone. A ragged and weak cheer came from the few engineers in the room.

"She's made the jump," Marisa said. She envisioned the *Advent* obscured in a burst of light as the strange energies from the juxtaengines parted space, allowing the giant ship its trans-light speed journey. For a moment, the space program existed all on its own, separate from the news broadcasts and progress reports, far from the "Areas of lost communication."

"No," said Dr. Smalley. "There should be no telemetry now. They're gone." He touched his fingers to his monitor. Marisa moved to where she could see what he saw. The heart beats on his screen still registered. Brain waves still recorded their spiky paths. He flicked from one screenful of medical transmissions to the next.

"How is that possible?" said Marisa. Jacqueline stood beside her. Other engineers left their stations to crowd behind Smalley's chair.

"They're getting weaker," said Jacqueline.

"No, no, no," said Smalley. His fingers tapped a quick command on his keyboard. A similar display with names and readouts appeared on the screen, but this one showed no activity in the medical area.

"What is that?" asked Marisa. How could there be transmissions? The *Advent* was beyond communication now. They'd never know if she reached her destination. Light speed and relativity created a barrier as imposing as death itself.

"It's their respiration," said Smalley, his voice computer-calm. "They're not breathing." He switched back to the heartbeats. Many of the readouts now showed nothing. A few blinked their pulses slowly, and then those stopped too. Smalley tapped through screen after screen. Every pulse was now zero. Every brain scan showed a flat line.

Marisa's hands rested on the back of Smalley's chair. She could feel him shaking through her fingers. "Check their body temperatures," she said.

He raised his head as if to look back at her. Then he shrugged in understanding. The new display showed core temperatures. As they watched, the numbers clicked down.

"Is it an anomaly?" asked someone. "Are we getting their signals from juxtaspace?"

"The ship blew up," said Jacquline.

Marisa said, "No. We would have received telemetry for that." She held Smalley's chair now so she wouldn't collapse. "It's their real signals from our space." Her face felt cold and her feet numb. A part of her knew she was within an instant of collapsing. "The *Advent* left, but it didn't take them."

Jacqueline said, "Worst case scenario. It was a possibility that the multiple engines wouldn't work the same way as single ones. We dumped everyone into space." Her voice cracked.

"They're dead," said Marisa as the room slowly swooped to her right. I'm falling, she thought. What would a telescope see if it could see that far? After the flash of light? Would it see 14,400 bodies tumbling? What other parts of the ship didn't go?

Her head hit the floor, but it didn't hurt. Nothing hurt, and she was curiously aware of meaningless details: how the tiled floor beneath her felt gritty, how ridiculous the engineers looked staring down at her. Then, oddly, how their faces began to darken. What a curious phenomena, she thought. The fraction of a second before she knew no more, she realized that their faces hadn't darkened. It was the skylights above them. They'd gone brilliantly bright. Surface of the sun bright.

We're not going to the stars, she thought, as the heat of a thousand stars blasted through the ceiling. She would have cried if she had had the time.

Who has died like this? So sudden, the walls shimmered. Then they were gone. The air burst away, much of the ships innards remained, but twisted and ruptured. Torn into parts. The stars swirl around us, and all the eyes see. We all see what we all see, but there isn't a "we" to talk about, just a group consciousness. The 14,400 brains frozen in moments, the neurons firing micro-charges across the supercool gaps. And we continue outward, held together loosely by our tiny gravities, sometimes touching, drifting apart, but never too far. Pluto passed in hardly a thought, and then we were beyond, into the Oort cloud, but who would know it? The sun glimmered brightly behind us, a brighter spot among the other spots, but mostly it was black and oh so cold Time progressed even if we couldn't measure it. Was it days already, or years, or centuries? Out we traveled. Out and out.

* * *

Jonathan shifted the backpack's weight on his shoulders as he tramped down the slope toward Encinitas, then rubbed his hands together against the cold. He'd left his cart filled with trade goods in Leucadia, and it felt good not to be pulling its weight behind him. The sun had set in garish red an hour earlier, and all that guided his footsteps was the well worn path and the waves' steady pounding on the shore to his right. No moon yet, although its diffuse light wouldn't help much anyway. When he'd crested the last hill, though, he'd seen the tiny lights of Encinitas' windows and knew he was close.

He whistled a tune to himself, keeping rhythm with his steps. The harvest was in, and it looked like it would be a good one this year for Encinitas. They'd wired two more greenhouses with grow-lights in the spring, and managed to scare up enough seed for a full planting. For the first time they might even have an excess. If he could broker a deal with the folks in Oceanside, who lost part of their crop with leaf blight, it could be a profitable winter.

A snatch of music came through the ocean sound. Jonathan smiled. Ray Hansen's daughter, Felitia, would be there. Last year she'd danced with him twice, and he imagined her hand lingered as they passed from partner to partner, but she was too young to court then. Not this year, though. It was going to be a good night. Even the icy cold ocean breeze smelled clean. Not so dead. Not like when he was a boy and everyone called it the "stinking sea."

He slowed down. The gate across the path should be coming soon. It stopped the flock of goats from wandering off during the summer. In the winter, of course, they were kept in the barns so they wouldn't freeze. Yes, Encinitas was a rich community to be able to grow enough to feed livestock. Felitia would be a good match for him. She was strong and lively, and her father would certainly welcome him warmly if he was a part of the family. Goat's milk with every meal! He licked his lips, thinking of the cheese that was a part of the harvest celebration.

But what if she didn't want him?

He slowed even more. What wasn't to want about him? He was twenty, and a businessman, but it wasn't like he was around all the time to charm her, and a year was a long time. Maybe she didn't want to travel from village to village, carrying trade goods. And she was a *bookish* girl. People talked about her, Jonathan knew. That was part of her charm. He buried his hands under his armpits. Did it seem unusually cold suddenly, or was it fear that made him shiver?

The gate rattled in the breeze, which saved him bumping into it. Fingers stiff, he unlatched it. Clearly now, the music lilted from over the hill. He hurried, full of hope and dread.

"Jonathan, you are welcome," said Ray Hansen at the door. Hansen looked older than the last time Jonathan had seen him, but he'd always seemed old. He might be forty, which was really getting up in years, Jonathan thought. Beyond, the long tables filled with seedling plants had been pushed to the wall. Everyone in the village seemed to be there. The Yamishitas and Coogans. The Taylors and Van Guys. The Washingtons and Laffertys. Over a hundred people filled the room. Jonathan smiled. "I've come to see your daughter, sir."

The older man smiled wanly. "You'll need to talk to her about that."

Jonathan wondered if Hansen was sick. He seemed much thinner than Jonathan remembered him. Probably the blood disease, he thought. Lots of folks got the blood disease.

The band struck up a reel, and couples formed into squares for the next dance. The caller took his place on the stage. Felitia, in a plain, cotton dress sat on the edge of a table at the far end of the long room, swinging her feet slowly beneath her. Jonathan edged along the dance floor. The music drove the dancers to faster and faster twirls, hands changing hands, heads tossing. He apologized when a woman bumped him, but she was gone so fast he doubted she heard.

Felitia watched him as he made the last few yards, her blues eyes steady, her blonde hair tied primly back. Was she glad to see him? Surely she knew why he was there. He had left her notes every time he passed through Encinitas, and her replies that he retrieved the next trip were chatty enough, but noncommital. She could have been writing her brother for all the passion he found in them.

He sat next to her without saying anything. Now that she was beside him, the speech he'd practiced sounded phony and ridiculous. The villagers rested when the music ended, talking quietly to themselves. On the makeshift stage, the band tuned their instruments. The two guitarists compared notes, while the trumpet player discreetly blew the spit out of his horn.

"This is nice," said Jonathan. He winced. Even that sounded stupid.

"Yes." Her hands were together in her lap. "How were the roads?"

The band started another tune, and soon the crowd wove through the familiar patterns.

"Fine, I guess." Jonathan decided that the best move would be to leave the room. It was one thing to think grand thoughts while pulling his cart down the sea-shore roads, but it was quite another to confront her in the flesh. "I did good business in Oceanside."

"It must be interesting, seeing all those places."

Jonathan swelled. "Oh, yes. I've been even further north than that, you know. I even went to San Clemente once. A few of the buildings still stand.

I wanted to press on to Los Angeles, but you know how cautious the old folks are."

She looked sideways at him.

He cleared his throat. "Just along the beach. Nothing inland, of course. It's ice from the Santa Ana mountains almost to the sea, but they say the snow field is retreating. It's getting warmer, they say."

Felitia sighed. "The dust went up; the dust will go down. I don't know if I believe it. They can call it 'nuclear winter,' but it's more like nuclear eternity to me." She watched the dancers, her face lost and vulnerable. "Encinitas seems so small."

Jonathan gripped the table's edge. What he wanted to ask was on the tip of his tongue. Everything else sounded trivial, but the timing wasn't right. He couldn't just blurt it out. A thought came to him, and with relief he said, "I brought you a present." He slung his backpack off his shoulders and set it between them. Felitia peered inside when he opened it.

"Books!" She clapped her hands.

He dug through the volumes. "There's one I thought you might like especially." At the bottom he found it. "We need to go outside so I can give it to you." He tried to swallow but couldn't. Nothing he'd ever done before felt so bold.

She held his hand as they walked away from the dancers. Her fingers nestled softly in his.

Felitia put on a coat and picked up a storm lamp before they went out the back door. The flame flickered before settling into a steady glow.

"What is it?"

Wind pushed against his face, tasting of salt. It could snow tonight, he thought. First snow of the season. He pulled the book out of his jacket and handed it to her. "Here's as far as you can get from Encinitas."

She opened the book, a paperback edition of Peterson's field guide to the stars and planets. By the storm lamp he could see a color print of the Cone Nebula, a red, clouded background with white blobs poking through.

"Oh, Jonathan. It's beautiful."

Their foreheads touched as they bent over the book.

She turned her face toward his. "My father told me about stars. He said he saw them when he was a boy, before the bad times."

Jonathan glanced up. "My dad said we were going to the stars. His mom helped launch the *Advent*." The uniform black of the night sky greeted him, as indistinguishable as a cave interior. "He said the sky used to be blue, and the sun was as sharp-edged as a gold coin."

He looked down. Felitia's face was only an inch from his own. Without thinking about it, he leaned just enough to kiss her. She didn't move away, and his question was answered before he asked it.

Later, holding her against him, he said, "They say when the dust clears, we'll see the stars again."

And on a calm night, four years later, after Ray Jr. had gone to sleep, Jonathan and Felitia stood outside their house in Oceanside.

"Can you see?" said Felitia. "Do you think that's what I think it is?" She pointed to a spot in the sky.

One hand on her shoulder, Jonathan pulled her tight. "I think it is."

A bright spot glimmered for a second. Another joined it.

They stayed outside until they both grew so cold they could hardly stand it.

We feel space. Neutrinos pass through like sparklers in the group body. Gravity heats our skin. We hear space, not through the frozen cells of our useless ears, but through the sensitive membrane of our group awareness. The stars chime like tiny bells. It has a taste, the vacuum does, dusty and metallic, and it doesn't grow old. We go farther and farther and slower and slower, until we stop, not in equilibrium; the sun won. Gradually, we start back. Apogee past. The Oort cloud. The birthplace of comets. How many years have we gone away?

"Relying on the old knowledge is a mistake." Professor Matsui faced the crowd of academics in the old New Berkeley lecture hall. The new New Berkeley hall wouldn't be done until next year. After a hundred-a-twenty years of use, this one would be torn down. He would miss the old place. "We overemphasize recreating the world we know from the records, but we aren't doing our own work. Where is our originality? Where is our cultural stamp on our scientific progress?" He was glad for the new public address system. His voice wasn't nearly as strong as it had been when he was young.

Matsui watched Dr. Chesnutt, the Reclaimed Technologies chair. He appeared bored, his notebook unopened on his study desk. Languidly he raised his hand. "Point," he said. "Would you have us throw away our ancestor's best work? When we allocate money, should we assign *more* on your 'original research' that may yield nothing, or should we spend wisely, investigating what we *know* will work because it worked before? When we equal the achievements of the past, then it will make sense to invest in your programs. Until then, you divert valuable time and valuable funds."

Pausing for a moment to scan the crowd, Matsui took a deep breath. Were the others with him or against him? The literature department was evenly split between the archivists and the creative writers. Biology, Sociology and Agriscience would lean toward him, as would Astronomy, but the engineers, mathematicians and physicists would cast their vote solidly with Chesnutt, and, as the former head of the School of Medicine, he had probably coerced everyone in the department to vote his way. "Obviously we must continue the good work of learning from the past, but if we throw all our effort, and funds, into that, we risk creating the same mistakes that destroyed their world. You pursue their wisdom without worrying about their folly. Will you follow them down the road that led to nuclear annihilation?"

Chesnutt chuckled. "You can raise the 'nuclear annihilation' demon all you like. As you know, there is no agreement among historians about what caused the great die-off. The nuclear exchange may have been the last symptom of a much deeper problem. We will only avoid their fate if we learn from their triumphs."

Heads nodded in the audience.

Matsui finished his speech, but he could tell Chesnutt had called in all his favors. It didn't matter what value his arguments had, the Research Chair would not gain funding this year. He'd be lucky to hold his committee assignments.

After the meeting, Matsui left the lecture hall in a hurry. He didn't want to deal with the false condolences. The bloodsuckers, he thought. They'll be looking for strategies to make my loss an advantage for their departments in some way or another.

A breeze off the bay cut through his thin coat, sending a translucent veil of clouds across the night sky, and tossing the lights dangling from their poles.

"Wait, Professor," called a voice.

He grimaced, then slowed his pace. Puffing, Leif Henderson, an assistant lecturer in Astronomy, joined him.

"Good speech, sir."

"I'm afraid it was wasted."

"I don't think so. We've got a couple Chesnutt supporters in the department, but I can tell you the grad students aren't interested in making their names in the field by rediscovering all of Jupiter's moons. The younger ones want to do something new."

Matsui pushed his hands deep into his pockets. Maybe he was getting too old for the back-stabbing politics of the University. "Chesnutt has a point. Old Time learning casts a huge shadow. We may never be able to get out from under it, and it doesn't help that whenever original research makes a discovery, the intellectual archeologists dig up some reference to show it's been done before. There's no impetus for innovation."

Henderson matched Matsui's steps. "But the Old Timers didn't know everything. They didn't conquer death. They didn't master themselves." The young man looked into the night sky. "They didn't reach the stars. We should have been receiving the *Advent's* signals for the last fifty years if they made it, or even more likely, they would have come back. They have had four-hundred years to recreate their engines."

"I like to think they arrived, and we just haven't built sensitive enough receivers, or maybe three-hundred and fifty light years is too far for the signal. What they have to wonder is why *we* haven't contacted them, why we didn't *follow* them. The world has gone silent."

The sidewalk split in two in front of them. Astronomy and the physical science buildings were to the right. Administration was to the left. They paused at the junction.

Matsui looked down the familiar path. He'd walked that sidewalk his entire adult life, first as a student, then a graduate assistant, and finally as a professor. From his first day in the classroom he had valued creative thought. That is what the academy is about, he had argued. The Old Timers accomplished noble feats, but they are gone. We should make our own mistakes.

"The world is changing, Henderson. The population will be over one billion in a decade. We survived an extinction event four hundred years ago, so we missed being the last epoch's dinosaurs. We fought our way out of the second dark ages. As a species, we must be fated for greatness, but we're so damned stupid about achieving it." He kicked at the ground bitterly.

Henderson stood quietly for a minute. In the distance, the surf pounded against the rocks. "It's a pendulum, Professor. This year, Chesnutt won. He won't always. If we're going to push knowledge forward, we will escape our past. We'll have to."

Matsui said, "Not in my lifetime, son. It's so frustrating, as a character, humanity has desires. It must. But what they are and how it will go about getting them will remain a mystery to me. There's a big picture that I can't see. Oh, if only there was a longer perspective, it would all make sense."

Henderson didn't reply.

"I'm sorry," said Matsui. "I'm an old man who babbles a bit when it gets late at night. I wax philosophic. It used to take a couple pints of beer, but now cool night air and a bad budget meeting will do it. You'll have to forgive me."

Henderson shuffled his feet. "There's a move in the department to name a comet after you."

Suddenly, Matsui's eyes filled with tears. He was glad the night hid them. "That would be nice, Henderson."

Matsui left Henderson behind, but when Matsui reached the faculty housing, he didn't stop. He kept going until he reached the bluff that overlooked the sea. Condensation dampened the rail protecting the edge of the low bluff, and it felt cold beneath his hands. Moonlight painted the surf's spray a glowing white. He thought about moonlight on water, about starlight on water. Each wave pounding against the cliff shook the rail, and for a moment, he felt connected to it all, to the larger story that was mankind on the planet and the planet in the galaxy. It seemed as if he was feeling the universal pulse.

Much later, he returned to his cottage and his books. He was right. Chesnutt replaced him on the committees, but Matsui wasn't unhappy. He remembered his hands on the rail, the moon like a distant searchlight, and the grander story that he was a part of.

Thoughts come slower, it seems, or events have sped ahead, and we want to sleep. Maybe we have spread out, our individual pieces, a long stream of bodies and ship parts, and odds and ends: books, blankets, tools, chairs, freeze dried foods, scraps of paper, the vast collection of miscellany that humanity thought to bring to a distant star. Or maybe the approaching sun has warmed us. The super-cool state that kept consciousness and connection possible is breaking down. But we know we are accelerating, diving deep into the system that gave us birth. It's been a long trip, out and back, the 14,400. Our individual dreams forgotten, but the group one survived: to travel, to find our way out of the cave, to check over the next hill top. We feel an emotion as the last thoughts fail: something akin to happiness. We're going home.

Captain Fremaria sat on a blanket with her husband on the hill overlooking the launch facility. The lights illuminating the ship had been turned off, but she knew crews were working within the enclosed scaffolding, fueling the engines, running through the last check lists, making sure it would be ready for the dawn liftoff.

"It's just like another test flight, darling," she said to her husband. "I've flown much less reliable crafts." Her heart took a sudden leap as she thought about the mission. She could hear the rockets igniting in her head. Could she do it? The idea of climbing atop the thousands of pounds of propellant had never sounded so foolhardy as it did now. When she was training, the flight remained a theory, an abstraction, but with the ship so close and the schedule coming to its close, she felt like a condemned woman.

"Don't remind me," he said. "I just want to know that you'll be safe. I need a sign."

She sighed. "I wouldn't mind one myself." She did not have to climb aboard the ship. No one could force her to. In fact, she wouldn't really be committed until ignition.

"It's too much history." He moved closer to her so his hand rested on hers. "Mankind returns to space after all these centuries. Everyone wants to know about the impact of this moment. Will we go to the moon next? Will we go to Mars? What will we find there of the old colonies?" He snorted derisively. "I just want to know that you will come back."

Fremaria nodded her head, but he wasn't looking at her. In three hours she would report to launch central, where they would begin preparing her for insertion into the craft that would carry her into orbit. The mission called for ten circuits around the Earth, then a powerless drop back into the atmosphere, where she would fly the stubby-winged ship to a touchdown at Matsui Airbase.

"I won't be that far away. If you could take the train straight up, you'd be there in a couple hours."

Her husband chuckled, but it sounded forced.

For the first time in weeks, the wind was calm. Fremaria had watched the weather reports anxiously, but it looked like the launch would take place in perfect conditions. Not a cloud marred the flawless night sky. The horizon line cut a ragged edge out of the inverted bowl of pristine stars.

"I've never seen it so clear," said her husband.

A green light streaked across the sky.

"Make a wish," said Fremaria.

"You know what it is." He squeezed her hand.

Another meteor flamed above them, brighter than the first.

"That's rare," said Fremaria. "So close together."

Before he could reply, a third and fourth appeared, traveling parallel courses.

"It's beautiful," he said.

She arched her back to see the sky better. "There isn't supposed to be a meteor shower now. The Leonids aren't for another month."

A spectacular meteor crossed half the sky before disappearing.

Fremaria leaned into her husband's shoulder for support. For almost two hours the display continued, often times with multiple meteors visible at once, some so bright that they cast shadows. Then, the intensity dropped until the sky was quiet again.

"Have you ever seen anything like that?" Her husband asked. "Have you even ever *heard* of anything like that?"

"No." She thought about the mysteries of space. "It's a sign."

He laughed. "I guess it might be."

Fremaria glanced at her watch. "It's time for me to go." She brushed her pants after she stood. Her husband held her hand again, but her thoughts now were in the ship. She ran through the takeoff procedure. No mission went without a hitch. They would be depending on her to make corrections, to shake down the craft. A good flight: that was all she wanted, and then a next one and a next one. They began the walk down to the launch facility.

She thought about the centuries. The *Advent* was supposed to go to the stars. Had it made it? No one knew, but they were going again. Her flight would open the door again.

"Are you scared?" her husband asked.

Fremaria paused on the trail. The ship waited for her. She could see that they had cranked part of the scaffolding away from it. Soon it would stand alone, unencumbered. She would sit in the pilot's chair listening to the countdown, prepared to take over from the automated controls if needed. What an experience the rocket's thrust would be! What a joy to feel the weightlessness that awaited her! To break free. To take the first step to the long voyage out.

"I'm ready to go."

A single meteor flickered into existence above them. It glowed brilliantly in its last moment. They watched its path until it vanished.

"They don't last too long, do they?" he said.

Fremaria glanced at the ship, then back at the sky. "No, but they travel a long way first. There's something to be said about making the long trip."

Nothing is Normal

C atdeath snorted two GrieF poppers before deciding on a zebra motif for skinart. A lace band covered her nips without detracting from the herd thundering across her chest and belly, up her neck, across her face and over her shaved head. Still life. After this season, maybe, she could afford animation, and the animals would wander on her, seeking water holes, raising dust, making four-legged love on a dry, Kenya plain. She locked her sleepcot back into place, then checked her look in the mirrored wall. See-through lace shorts. Black tennies. Jungle print bag with a quarter mil of emotiphin poppers individually packaged for quick use. Two large tears tracked down her cheek, over a zebra's back. Good stuff, GrieF. She could really feel it: her stomach ached; her face dragged on the bones with frowning.

She slapped a security jangler on the crib on her way out. Better than a lock, it'd zap an intruder and buzz Scrote two doors down. He'd be out with a tazer before any pop head could bust through and go for the stash. She fronted him an emotiphin a week for the service; used to be he'd go for AmbitioN, but lately he'd been hitting her hard for RegreT. "RegreT lasts longer. It's deeper. Is this the real stuff?" he said. "Best I got," she said. At least he didn't want anything sexual for the service. Not that it would be that bad. He was twenty years older with a skin condition, and a botched retinal replacement that left one eye canted away from the other, but he'd always been kind. There was a lot to be said for pudgy too. "Quit selling," he told her once, even though it would cut off his supply. "Cops don't waste users. Just dealers."

Homeocyte waited for her at the slideway rail. He had to speak up over its perpetual rumble and the talk of commuters sliding past. "J-note's dead. Tunnel cops found him this morning on the east portal station. Said he'd cooled for an hour. He'd been there all that time. Must have been a thousand people stepped over him. Jesus." He staccotoed his fingernails on the rail. Twitchy. Buzzing on something. Maybe AnxiouS or just uppers.

Moonscape skinart spread across his chest. Stubble fuzzed the image. He needed to shave more often. "No load on him. They got him on the way home. Figure he couldn't have been carrying more than two or three doses anyway."

The news didn't effect her more than what she was already experiencing. If she didn't already feel so bad, she would have laughed. The poppers made her feel worse than J-note's death would have if she were straight. "North Tunnel guys?"

"Kids, I figure. Didn't like his skinart, maybe. The burning cross thing again. They slashed it pretty bad."

"You cover his clientele. I'm going down to Georgetown." Catdeath choked back a sob. The GrieF topped out, and everything struck her as stuningly melancholy. Even the graffiti on the walls cried with meaning. Everything touched her.

Homeocyte whistled. "Out of your territory. You'll be staining some slideway yourself." He looked at her shrewdly. "You're emoti-tripping now, aren't you? How many are you popping a day?"

Catdeath wiped her eyes. "Mind your own business. It's a delivery. Take care of subscribers here, and I'll watch after myself."

She stepped forward onto the slideway between a matronly type wearing a house duster's smock, and a scrawny bowlhead. Catdeath couldn't see his face; the bowl covered all but his mouth, but she could hear his music thrumming, and a light flickering in the goggles said he was deep into some v-scape that probably looked a hell of a lot better than this one.

"Hi, beautiful," he said dreamily.

"Sure," she said. In his virtually enhanced world, she could be Aphrodite, for all he knew. He probably thought the middle-aged woman in front of her was a goddess too.

A half mile of residence cribs scrolled at a little better than walking speed on her left. Battered doors, some patched a dozen times over. Burn marks. Steel bars and padlocks. Everyone trying to protect their little bit. She rode the tail end of the GrieF high and mourned not only her fate, but everyone's fate she passed. Over 11,000 workers lived in Shotgun City, the low rent Eisenhower Tunnel projects, converted from auto traffic to housing thirty years earlier. She embraced their lives' sadness. Those that had jobs worked in the I-70 urban corridor from Idaho Springs to Copper Mountain. Food service, household domestics, manual laborers, data manipulators: a river of them moved in and out of the twinned 1.7 mile long tunnels twenty-four hours a day. Flexsteel flooring, thin partitions and an abandonment of anything aesthetically pleasing left over a half-million square feet of cheap residential space. Two twenty-six feet wide, very long cities, connected in numerous ways, side by side, boring through a mountain. A worker's ghetto. Catdeath shifted her bag strap to the other shoulder. The GrieF was wearing off already. Being her own, best customer meant she'd built a tolerance, and the lovely despair slipped away, leaving nothing.

A flashing yellow light on the ceiling, and a bunching up of people on the slideway, told her a cop checkpoint had been set up ahead. They'd be doing ordinary stuff: I.D. confirmation, work permit verification, hidden weapon scan, but she couldn't risk they'd look in her bag. She stepped off the slideway and into a paratobacco kiosk.

"Gotta use your back door," she said, while lifting a panel and crawling under a pipe paraphernalia display. The bored looking clerk whose skinart slowly revolved red and white stripes, like an old-fashioned barber's pole, just nodded.

Catdeath wormed her way into the service passage, the shoulder-width space between the tunnel lining's original tile, and the back of the kiosks and workers' cribs. Wires, cables and pipes competed for space overhead, and she watched her step so as not to bang her head or trip over building substructure as she went around the checkpoint. Condensation ran off the tile, and the air smelled of damp fiberboard and mildew. Shadowy people fled her approach—the lowest of the low, living behind the thin walls.

Through gaps in the paneling, she glimpsed a sushi shop, a home defense weaponry boutique, a skinart emporium, where a young man lay naked on a bench while the tech applied the micro-electric sensitive dyes and the nanochips that controlled the display. "You've got flowers? I like petunias," said the client.

Ten minutes later, she walked behind darkened residences. Most workers were at their jobs, so when she figured she'd gone far enough, she kicked open a weakly latched panel and crawled into a lightless crib. She flashed a penlight around the room the same size as hers, six feet by eight feet. Walls covered with Arabic posters. Two little girls, no more than five or six sat up on the cot, their dark eyes fearful. Probably illigits, or they'd be in day care instead of sitting in the dark. She figured they were lucky. Catdeath put her finger to her lips. "Just passing through."

Outside, beyond the cop stop, she caught the slideway again. The slideway carried her through the long curve to the east portal where she blinked against the open sky's brightness and mid-day sunlight. On the mountain valley's sides, condos, offices, shops and step-malls covered the slopes. Ghostly tendrils of GrieF eddied within her, and she tried to raise the specter of the mountain landscape beneath the cement, but the feeling wouldn't last.

She moved to a tram turnstile, keeping eye for North Tunnel muscle. They ran the business at both portals. It wasn't until she passed her wrist code over the scanner to pay for the tram that she spotted Corvette and Insulin. Corvette was a little guy who had a nasty thing about pain: he bought it, sold it, took it, gave it. Nobody knew what Insulin liked, but he hated South Tunnel action, so Catdeath watched from within the tram as they charged toward her, knocking down a couple of civies at the turnstile, but missing the closing doors by an arm's length. Frustration warped their faces as the car lifted from the platform on its monorail and sped down the valley. She felt around within her bag. The poppers' hard-shelled wrapping didn't tell her their contents. Some SatisfactioN would be good now, or even a whiff of GiddY. With effort, she took her hand from the bag. Temptation pushed her to choose one randomly. Two would be even better. RegreT tinged with TerroR. Maybe a little GuilT and PridE mixed together. Too many people around her. Impossible to tell narcs from civies.

An unbroken line of brick, steel, glass and concrete passed under the tram. City transport. Antiseptic smelling. Cracked seats. Life-dead workers going or coming. Some carried meals in their laps. No children. All in day care. No seniors. An employee's car. Catdeath kept her cheek pressed against the plexiglass, letting the city roll by. The mountain air chilled her. It wasn't tunnel warm or tunnel humid.

Georgetown platform came up too soon. Catdeath thought about finding a rest room where she could pop. Anything to give her an edge, an emotion to swing from, but she needed to be sharp. Big deals don't come along that often, she thought. Have to stay focused.

She glanced around when she stepped off the platform, but the chance a North Tunnel dealer would be this far east was remote. A covered escalator took her into white collar land. Swept streets. No graffiti on walls. Polished glass doorways. Machine conditioned air like rain-washed pine trees. The doorman at Kingston Heights wore tuxedo skinart. Real collar. Real cuffs. Fancy. Expensive work. Impossible to tell he was otherwise naked until she got up close. "Nice suit," she said.

"Nice zebras."

After checking her bonafides, he let her up. The private elevator's walls were mirrors, but the glass floor was utterly clear. The doorman was right; her zebras looked good. The ground dropped away. Catdeath shut her eyes and hummed along with the music, a slow-paced popular commercial instrumental from the week before.

"Do you have it all?" said the buyer. Shimmery gold pants. Black silk codpiece. No shirt. No skinart. Health club musculature beneath a precarcinogenic looking tan. Young body. Old face. He sat on an all white couch. Silver linoleum floor. No scuffs. Catdeath checked the apartment. Glass walls, like the elevator floor. Nothing concealed. Bed. Bathroom. Balcony beyond nearly invisible sliding doors. No sign of a kitchen. She didn't like the set up. A remnant of last night's ParanoiD? She wasn't sure.

"Just like you ordered. An emotiphin smorgasbord." She dumped the bag on the coffee table (real coffee—he offered—she drank).

"Even the tough to get stuff?"

Catdeath held up four caplets "Two LusT, two RagE. Ten months and a neural adjustment just for possession. Make sure you take them in context. Rape on the one and assault on the other. Right situation, right friends, proper supervision, they're fun, but you have to set them up. I wouldn't mix them."

The buyer balanced them on his hand. "Wouldn't you, dear? That's not what I heard. Why don't we both try them and see what happens?"

Catdeath smiled. She knew it disarmed her face. Made her look vulnerable. "I'll pop now and then, but the two I won't mix are business and emotions. Now, what about payment?"

The buyer waved his wrist over a reader built into the table. Account info she couldn't decipher from her angle popped into the air. He manipulated the figures. She gave him her code, and the credits transferred to a roaming, misnumbered account Scrote had set up for her. Number changed constantly. Money stayed with it. Technically invisible to the bank. Only she could access it, and no one could trace it to her, theoretically. "Services rendered," the buyer said. "It'll look like a year of high class domestic work to the Feds. Salary's good when you earn it on your back."

"I wouldn't know." She queried the terminal to confirm the transaction.

"Too bad. We could boost your payday." He grinned, and a network of fine, white scars radiated from the corners of his eyes and mouth. He could be even older than he looked.

She gathered her bag and glanced over her shoulder at the elevator door.

"Why the zebras, dear?" He scooped the caplets into a drawer she hadn't noticed before in the couch's base, and when he closed it, there was no evidence it was there. "They're extinct. Last week, tigers. The week before, wolves. All extinct animals. Why?"

"You've been watching me."

"Smart business to know who you're dealing with. A friend talked with one of your associates. Tried your product. I needed to be sure you weren't working for parties who'd use this little purchase to my disadvantage."

"Politics, it's a bitch. If I get caught selling, ten years and some invasive psychotherapy. Except for those specialty poppers, you get caught using, and it's a fine," she said. She reached into her bag. The bottom supports were snap-away plastic. Fast acting depressants melded into both sharpened ends.

"Appearance, my dear, is sacrosanct to some people."

The elevator door clicked behind her. She didn't wait to see who came in. Left the bag. Cleared the couch on a sprint. Scratched the buyer with the depressant in passing, and knocked a balcony door off its runners going through. As she swung from the railing, she looked back. Tuxedo, hefting a pistol, leaned over the prostrate buyer. Using drugs wasn't that big a deal legally, but hand guns certainly were. She dropped onto the balcony below, slipped into an empty apartment, ran down a hallway, found a maintenance exit locked to the outside and hopped a public escalator down the mountain. White collar holo ads called from the ceiling: clothing, personal services, pharmaceuticals. No one looked up. Most people wore more than she did. No one shaved their heads. Her appearance marked her. Tunnel trash. She knew it. Didn't care.

At the second junction, she transferred to a slideway going east. If the buyer sent a crowd to find her, they'd head west for the tunnel first. Watch the trams. Post spies at the portals. After ten minutes on the slideway, she stepped off. Walked down a broad, stone promenade into an open market, stopped in a skinart shop, bought a popular floral print. The tech reprogrammed her nanochips, changing the dyes' alignment. Zebras faded and a bright cascade of roses bloomed on her arms. Leaves encircled her neck. A spray of petals marked her cheeks.

Next door Catdeath found a floppy hat ("Guaranteed UV compliant!") and jacket, paid for them, then hustled back onto the slideway. Her account was supposed to be untraceable, as long as no one knew it existed. They might find it if they looked hard enough, and the buyer had the her wrist code from a half hour earlier.

Four transfers later, switches of direction each time, she went to ground in an envirobar near Idaho Springs.

"Desert decor today," toned an automatic greeter as she walked in the door. From where she stood, the room opened like the Mojave desert at sunset. Rock-like tables sprinkled across the sand. Long shadows. Vermillion horizon above the sun's edge. The place was nearly empty. She took a table as far away from the door as possible, next to one wall. Up close, the illusion fell apart. The desert display on the near wall blurred out, although across the room the virtual Sierra Nevadas rose up fifty miles away.

Head aching, she ordered an iced camomile tea, rolled the cool glass against her forehead, tried to relax. A whiff of ContentmenT would be nice now, but she didn't know any vendors this far east. Blind buying would put her onto a narc for sure.

Dabney Fortineu, A.K.A. Catdeath. Age twenty-three. Mom: licensed domestic. Father: unknown. Mom transferred Dabney from one corporate daycare to another her first fifteen months before Mom died in an industrial brothel. Cause unknown. Suspected suicide. Social Assistance took ward. Dabney diagnosed with typical reactive attachment disorder at thirty-six months, an endemic fate for poorer children. Corporate provided therapy until seventy-two months. Case worker listed his conclusions upon cessation of treatment, "Muted emotional responses. Near incapacity to form personal relationships. Can't be touched. Expected behavior from a child of her background. Prognosis: normal." In the margin under the dates and signatures, someone had scrawled, "She will never love."

When she was four, she disappeared from her foster crib for two hours. They found her on the slideway, tugging on strangers' sleeves. "Have you seen my daddy?" she asked them.

After two hours, Catdeath moved. Paid for the tea, then hit the slideway running. The buyer might not be tracking her purchases, but she couldn't take the risk. She clenched her hands to keep them from shaking as she transferred from one direction to another. Her mouth's insides stuck to her teeth. She ran her tongue over them, but it didn't help. Signs of emotiphin withdrawal. The headache would get worse, she knew. She'd become weak. Walking would be hard. All she would want to do would be to sleep. If she didn't pop, the symptoms would linger for a week or two. The physical discomfort would taper, but inside she felt nothing — interstellar space nothing. That wouldn't fade. Nothing was normal for Catdeath.

The buyer said he'd "had a talk with one of your associates. Tried your product." No way he could do that. Catdeath sold emotiphins by subscription. Her people ran regular routes, delivered to old customers. Lots of advantage to the system. She never ordered too much material. Only she knew her supplier. Low risk to her runners. She opened up all the new territory and made special deliveries. Tougher for her to be cheated. Tougher for the big hitters to find her operation. So J-note probably hadn't been killed for his skinart. More likely he'd run into Tuxedo, or some other of the buyer's toadies. Wouldn't pony up the goods and ended up dead at the slideway's end.

So why did it go down the way it did? She didn't believe his explanation that he wanted to check her first. There were many ways to do it that didn't involve taking out a low level guy like J-note. In fact, why deal with her at all? Georgetown had its own suppliers. She should have smelled how bad it was, but the credits tempted too much. A month's worth of product moved in one sale. Who could pass that up? Her head hurt. Thinking called up tiny buzz bombs behind her eyes. Sleeping sounded good. She needed to get back home, but to do that required someone to give her an all clear at the east portal. The North Tunnel guys might still be hanging out, waiting for her, or the buyer's crowd could be there, or the cops. She'd have to send one of her people to scout the portal.

Catdeath found a public vidcom booth near a park, a city block of dry looking mountain grass, some natural granite boulders; hands-off wire circled a sickly aspen. She toned Homeocyte's address. Waited for the connection. After forever, a strange face swam into the monitor. Catdeath took it in: two uniforms in the background. Distinctive gray. Homicide. She clicked off, jogged across the park, hopped the back of a delivery cart and rode it for twenty minutes. Found another vidcom, toned her supplier and got an "address not found" message.

She drummed her fingers on the blanked monitor. Her supplier, an augmented paraplegic, ran a chem-shed operation from a false front news stand in South Tunnel. He wasn't going anywhere. He wouldn't go anywhere, so if the address was terminated he probably was too.

The buy was a set up. The buyer was the new man in South Tunnel, and she was the freelancer on the way out. Knowing it didn't help her head.

At fourteen she looked twenty. Long legs, no breasts. Almond eyes, high cheek bones, mahogany skin. Welfare teacher wouldn't leave her alone. Pressured her for "private" lessons. She saw them for what they were. Went to Social Assistance to complain. The case worker set up appointments to work with her. Locked the door behind her one afternoon. Slipped her something in her water. She woke up in South Tunnel. Sore crotch. Quit school. Quit Social Assistance. Met Scrote who gave her a mattress on the crib's floor. "I don't need your help," she told him. He said, "I know," then hacked her into the system. Found her credits to live on by delaying welfare payments to hundreds of recipients for a couple hours each. Money was hers during the interim, and the traveling shortfall didn't show up on the city's audit program long enough to set off an alarm. In a month Dabney Fortineu vanished from the records. Catdeath appeared. For the weeks she lived in Scrote's crib, she waited for him to lower himself off his sleepcot in the middle of the night, to join her on the floor. She expected it. Was resigned to it. Never happened.

Her first skinart: dolphins. Blue dolphins jumping from a green ocean. Grinning faces. Sparkling eyes. Shiny, white foam splashes. Dolphins died in the minor-ozone breach of '48. None left for the major in '54.

Catdeath waited under an arbor at a public access terminal table fifty yards from the vidcom booth. At the next table, a couple prepubescents cruised through porno vids, one after another; a sexless voice interrupted the moaning every minute with the message, "Extended exposure to prurient material may result in antisocial behavior." The boys giggled, and not too subtly checked out Catdeath's legs every chance they could.

A man and woman, skinarted in the same style as Tuxedo, except the man wore a Hawaiian print and the woman wore a French maids outfit, walked briskly to the booth Catdeath had used. The man removed a military issue genescope from his bag and scanned the vidcom's buttons. Meanwhile, the woman, hands behind her back examined the passerbyes' faces. Before she looked in Catdeath's direction, Catdeath ducked beneath her hat's floppy brim and slipped out the arbor's back side.

So the buyer did have her code, and any place she used it, they would be after her. They undoubtably knew what clothes she wore and the skinart.

On the street again, the sun blazed. Everyone wore a hat outside, so she was less conspicuous. The headache escalated into a solid, throbbing pulse. What she wanted to do most was shut her eyes. Dodging would do no good now. They had a map of her purchases, and she realized a half dozen other places required her wrist code where she'd given it without thinking. Within a half mile or so, they knew her location. Artificial Intelligence tracking software probably profiled her moves. The thing to do now was either go to ground and hope they'd miss her in a sweep, or to quit telling them where she was.

A long walk, bypassing slideways that required wristcode for access, brought her to the east portal express tram. She sat to the side, watching as each car filled and departed. No obvious spies here. The platform emptied each time. Perhaps they depended on her code to signal her whereabouts, and they'd be waiting for her at the other end. The billboard beside her changed colors. Became a different ad. If she stood directly in front, she'd hear its message too, but being off center muffled the ad's pitch. She leaned against the slick surface, closed her eyes; envisioned okapi, giraffes, pandas, and they changed into empty jungles, leaves burned black. Then, sullen, gray waters rising in falling in sterile rhythms beneath a searing sun, and the waves rolled into buffalo wandering below her, a brown mass reaching to the horizon. A breeze drifted across the plain, stirring up animal smells and wild wheat. She jerked herself from a doze. How much time had she lost? She couldn't tell. Workers stood on the platform, ready for the tram.

Catdeath rose. Stood beside a tall woman wearing a cellophane raincoat, blazing fireworks skinart underneath, expanding into new colors by the second. An outfit a little extreme for the middle of the afternoon, Catdeath thought. The platform filled; the tram arrived. A line formed. Catdeath stayed close behind the fireworks woman. When she stepped into the turnstile, Catdeath pushed herself against her, forced her knee into the back of the other woman's knee, and almost knocked them both down.

"Sorry," said Catdeath, helping her up.

Fireworks woman's eyes were all pupil. "My fault entirely," she drawled, letting the last sound trail into silence.

They were past the tram's people counter. No alarm. It saw Catdeath and Fireworks as one. No one knew she had boarded. Gentle acceleration pushed her into the bench seat as the tram rose and ascended the mountain. She moved by rote now. Inside, she found no motivation. Couldn't care. Didn't even want to pop. What would it matter? Gummy taste in her mouth. Head a painful heartbeat. Her arms and legs so heavy, she could hardly move them. Catdeath tried to muster a feeling for J-note and Homeocyte, but she found none within her. Even anger at the buyer would be welcome, but she couldn't picture him through the headache. Only sleep would help.

The darkness within frightened more. No glimmer of feeling. Every emotiphin trace washed from her system. Total black hole. Catdeath bent forward to wrap around the emptiness. Her heart sucked it all in, released nothing. An immeasurable void in her chest. She had the headache's pain. She had the texture of her legs beneath her arms. That was all she had.

The tram hurried to the east portal. Catdeath had hardly closed her eyes when the car slowed. People moved to the aisle, ready to depart. She looked up dully. Fireworks rested her arm on the back of Catdeath's seat; a sparkler glittered in the skin of her palm.

* * *

After several years hustling different scams, Catdeath got into emotiphins. Built a customer base. Settled in. She spent most her time in her crib, reading. No social life. She knew dozens of people who believed she was their friend. They weren't. For her, every relationship was a business one. Occasionally Scrote knocked on her door. He'd found a new pastry, and he bought an extra one for her. Sometimes he came in, sat on the sleepcot while she read. Didn't talk much. Programmed her reader to give her free access to the biblioweb. Listened when she told him about muskrats, skunks, raccoon and squirrels, about how they used to be wild everywhere, about how they disappeared.

Emotiphins were good. Like vacations to foreign lands. In between highs, she felt colorless. Tried not to think about meaning. Didn't consider consequences. Just the ever present "now" mattered. Once, when she was ten, she told a teacher, "I used to be a liar, but that was yesterday."

An obese woman, canes for both hands, headed for the exit. Catdeath forced herself up and behind her. She pulled her brim to cover her eyes and crouched a bit. Through the windows, she saw Corvette on a guard rail ten feet above the slideway. No sign of Insulin. Farther on the platform, Tuxedo sat on a bench, a news reader in his lap he wasn't looking at. No cops.

Catdeath used the fat woman for a shield. Stayed low as she stepped off the tram and waddled toward the slideway. At the last second, a few feet from Corvette, Catdeath straightened, took two quick steps and had one hand on Corvette's chest to hold him off balance and the other between his legs.

"Keep your hands clear," she said as he reached for a pocket. She squeezed, and his eyes went wide.

"That hurts so fine. . ." he started to say, and this time she twisted her wrist. His jaw snapped shut as his face paled.

"Too much of a good thing?" Her back was to Tuxedo all the way across the platform. She guessed he probably couldn't see them. Lots of foot traffic into and out of the trams.

"I don't have time to mess with you." She squeezed again for emphasis. He sucked air between his teeth. "There's a guy in a tux sitting near the tunnel entrance."

"Black suit?" said Corvette through white lips.

"Yeah. He's part of a Georgetown crew that's planning on moving poppers in the tunnels. I'm already out. They've scrubbed my people, and my best chance of getting through this alive is to let you know about it."

"Why should I help you?" said Corvette. His hands moved slowly toward his sides. Catdeath pushed him back a bit so he was even more off balance. If she let go, he'd fall off the rail. Just ten feet, but nothing to cushion the blow.

"I don't need your help. He doesn't have your best interests at heart. If they're taking South Tunnel now, they'll be in North Tunnel soon. I know them; *I* can help *you*, but I've got to get in the tunnel first. You distract him, and I'll remember it later. Don't take too long to decide. I've got a headache." She dug her fingernails in a little.

Corvette whispered, "Ouch. All right. You say they killed tunnel people?"

Catdeath nodded, loosened her grip, pulled him upright.

"I think you drew blood," Corvette said.

"Maybe you can get Insulin to kiss it for you later. Get me a few seconds."

Corvette limped into the crowd. Catdeath kept her back to Tuxedo, but turned enough so she could see. Corvette set himself up behind Tuxedo, then nodded her way. She stepped onto the slideway and began moving toward the two. Tuxedo had an unobstructed view of everyone on the slideway. It would be impossible to get by him undetected. As she glided forward, it occurred to her Corvette might do nothing. He could let Tuxedo kill her and still take her warning into North Tunnel. It's what she would do. She watched from under the hat's brim, but she struggled to care one way or the other.

An autocart carrying steaming teas and neuvocoffees rolled by Corvette. He waved his wrist code over the scanner, took a large insulated cups and removed its lid. As Catdeath approached, he raised it to her in a salute, stepped forward and poured the entire cup over Tuxedo's shoulder and onto his naked chest.

Lots of screaming. People rushing about. The last thing she saw as she disappeared into the tunnel was Corvette working his way against the flow of onlookers gathering around Tuxedo.

Ten minutes later, she got off the slideway in front of her crib. Tunnel noises seemed too loud: the slideway's metallic rattle, voices, music, doors closing, bells — too loud, too obtrusive. Catdeath rotated her head on her neck, eyes closed, but even through her eyelids, the lights glared, and overwhelming it all, her head's incessant pounding escalated. It nauseated her. Through a painful squint, she walked to her own crib, reached out to disarm the jangler, then stopped. It wasn't her jangler. Close, but not hers. If she touched it, it would alert whoever put it there. For a moment, she kept her hand poised above the device, and she almost punched in the code anyway. Finally, she sat, knees up, face pressed against her legs.

Everything was gone. She fell over on her side, knees still curled, eyes open, not looking at her door anymore. No emotion, but nothing else either. She tried to think how she ended up this way, but memories wouldn't connect. Her thoughts kept returning to seals, penguins, robins, garter snakes, all gone, all gone. She'd worn them on her skin. Didn't know why, but she liked extinct animal designs. She imagined wearing skinart that rotated images, badgers would rise up, turn away, become tortoises who'd waddle into antelope springing across the prairie. Delicate antelope, impossibly leaping ahead of predators. Beige skin. White rumps. Brilliantly hurtling sagebrush and fences and muddy little creeks. Then, the final transformation. The leaping antelopes would turn into images of Catdeath.

She'd wear herself on her skin.

A herd of Catdeath would wander on her, seeking bars, raising ruckus, making love on a rumbling South Tunnel slideway. She could keep herself alive as she did zebra and tigers, animated on her skin canvas.

But she'd have to get up. Couldn't do it on her own. Had to find help.

She groaned, rolled to her hands and knees, her head like a terrible weight. Staggered to Scrote's door and knocked. Fell into his arms.

Later, she didn't know when, she awoke. For moments she blinked slowly, trying to place herself. Scrote's crib. In his sleepcot. A pale blue monitor glowing, the only light. Her head rested on his leg; his hand cupped her shaved head. He slept sitting up, jammed into the corner of the room, snoring softly, like bubbles rising from the sea bed where dolphins lived.

Catdeath closed her eyes. The top of her head was warm. His fingers traced a path of heat. She didn't feel like brushing it away. For the first time ever, a human touch was good. And deep within, the emotional nothingness twitched. A small twitch, a weak, weak echo of a good emotiphin, but she felt it anyway, stirring in the darkness.

A real feeling, of hope.

DO GOOD

Dedicated to Richard Vernon, Marshall Strickland and Edward Rooney

Vice Principal Welch studied the empty hallway for an hour waiting for ghosts. He stood loosely, leaning against a wall, arms crossed
on his chest, as if watching the Homecoming dance from an out-of-the-
way corner. An empty school is a quiet thing, but it is not silent. He felt as
if he'd put his ear to a seashell, except the seashell had swallowed him, and
the waves rolled, almost forty years of them.

He'd unlocked the front door at 4:30 in the morning, turned off the
alarms and slipped in. The lockers echoed his footsteps, while a security
light at the end of the hall provided illumination, reflecting a thick, moon-
white stripe from the middle of the waxed floor and a bright star on every
locker handle. The hallway smelled of books and old paint. Out of habit, he
looked at his pocket planner. Nothing scheduled until 7:30. He sighed, then
put it away.

Years ago, when Welch took the vice principal job, Principal Robinson,
who retired and died the year after, had taken him to a bar on the far side of
town where Lincoln High parents seldom gathered. He told him after their
third beer, "That school's been there since 1902, Welch, and it started with
greatness. We'd have been the state football champs in our first year, but
the wingback broke his leg in the last game. Think of its tradition. What are
you going to add, Welch? How are you going to make a difference? What
are they going to say about you when you're gone?"

"I don't know," said Welch, his voice sudden and unexpected in the
hallway's quiet.

At 5:30, the heating system kicked on overhead, and a series of sharp
pops ran down the ducts. Lilly, the head custodian, would be coming in
soon, tuning on lights, unlocking doors, opening the school to the Monday
parade. He reached into his wallet for a ten dollar bill, smoothed it against
the wall and wrote, DO GOOD. He thought for a second, then added,
LAUGHING JACK. From his coat pocket he took a roll of tape, put an
inch-long piece on one end of the bill, then walked down the hall. He closed

his eyes, spun around a few times, and then stopped, his hand holding the bill in front of him, finger pointed. Locker 457. His master key opened the door. Books covered the bottom: A.P. ENGLISH, CALCULUS, MODERN U.S. HISTORY, a senior's locker, a senior who evidently didn't have homework over the weekend. Magazine photographs of body builders were stuck to the door's inside along with a valentine neatly inked, TO KIKI FROM HER BUDS. He taped the ten dollar bill next to the valentine before closing the door.

Down the hall, a row of lights flickered on. Lilly had started her rounds.

Welch sighed and headed toward the second floor to his office. No ghosts this morning. Not a one, but that didn't mean the school wasn't haunted. As he walked up the stairs he could feel the crush of students coming down, all those faces across the years streaming around him and through him.

"Good morning, Mr. Welch," said Pamela Howel, the Principal's secretary as she paused outside his door at 6:00, early as always. He glanced up from the bi-monthly incidents summary. She carried a briefcase in one hand and a cellphone in the other. Perfectly coifed black hair. Wire rimmed glasses. Narrow, thirtyish face. Metabolism and personality of a hummingbird. She'd taken the job in September and had already remade the office in her image.

"Hello, Pamela. Good weekend?"

"Nope. Visiting in-laws. Don't forget I need your intention sheet for next year on my desk by Friday."

Welch checked his planner. Written next to Friday's date was the reminder about the retirement intention form.

"Are you going to hang it up?"

Welch shrugged.

"Not that we want you to go," she said before dashing to her office.

Fifteen weapon violations since March 1. Eleven knives, a ninja throwing star, a broken bottle, a BB gun and a sawed off pool stick. Twenty-three fights. Vandalism in the football weight room. Six car burglaries. A fire in the girl's bathroom next to the cafeteria. An attempted suicide. Four incidents of senior hazing, each involving duct tape. And then the folder filled with complaints about Beau Reece, a mouthy second-year freshman who weighed maybe eighty pounds. Welch sighed and pushed it to the side. All in all, a pretty calm two months. He raised his pen to sign the report.

A movement caught his eye. A student in the chair next to the desk crossed his legs.

Welch looked up. No one sat in the chair. He blinked. The skin on his arm prickled as if all the tiny hairs had been tugged. Was it someone he knew? That was the problem: after so many years, it seemed he knew everyone he met. They could be former students or retired teachers or parents he'd met years before. Every face sparked a vague familiarity.

Welch put his head down to look at his papers again, trying to achieve the same state of mind he'd had the moment before, but the chair remained stubbornly empty.

He'd started seeing students who weren't there the week before Christmas break. At first they were a motion in the corner of his eye, but now he saw them straight on. He thought of them as ghosts, but they were more like remnants of the absent. He saw last year's graduates and kids from his first years of teaching, and, occasionally — he shivered to think of it — the dead too.

Twenty minutes later, a pair of noisy baseball players on their way to the gym for before-school throwing practice passed his door. Phones rang. Voices murmured. Doors opened and closed. An unbroken succession of students streamed by. He locked his door behind him, did hall duty until the final bell emptied the passage, hurried a handful of the tardy to class, then slipped into the only empty desk in Miss Knapp's room for a quick evaluation. Thirty-three students filled the rest of the room. A few glanced at him when he sat down. A slender, shiny-cheeked girl who didn't look a day over twelve years old, moved her backpack so Welch had room for his feet.

At the blackboard, red-haired Miss Knapp smiled nervously in his direction. She was fifty or so years old, come late to teaching after decades in the private sector. This was her third year in the building, her tenure year. If her evaluations were good, her job would be much more secure in September. He nodded and opened his notebook.

When Welch was a young teacher, he noticed students stopped talking when he passed. Not all the time, but often enough that when he heard a hushed, "Shh! It's a teacher," he longed to step up to them and ask them to share the secret. He wanted to tell him that five years ago he'd been like them. He was still seventeen in his heart.

It grew worse when he became vice principal. It spread to the teachers. Now he'd been vice principal for so long, he no longer recalled what teachers stopped talking about when an administrator came near. He'd asked his sole friend, Coach Qualls, who taught mythology and the humanities, about it once. "You're the troll, Welch. No one loves the troll."

Miss Knapp trembled slightly as she copied an assignment on the board.

Her fear annoyed him. I'm just a regular guy, he thought. I'm the fellow across the street. He waited until she looked at him, then he frowned and wrote in his notebook, PICK UP GROCERIES TONIGHT. She paled and asked the class for their attention. Welch wrote, BROCCOLI, RYE

BREAD and MUSTARD as if he'd just noticed a critical deficiency in her technique.

He stayed ten minutes until she handed out a worksheet. He had four other teachers to evaluate before first hour ended, so he noted in his planner that he'd observed her class, then rose to leave. Miss Knapp put her book on her desk. "Mr. Welch?"

They talked in the hallway outside the room.

"Can I do anything for you, Mr. Welch? Is this about Beau Reece?" Miss Knapp hid her mouth with her fingertips while holding her wrist. "I didn't see him today, but Friday he provoked the seniors again."

"No. Just a drop-in visit." Welch thought she might be an attractive woman if she didn't suck her cheeks in. He wondered if she was scheduled to supervise the dance this weekend. They might have a chance to talk more casually there.

"My methods, do you think they're sound?"

Suddenly, he felt guilty and mean. He shouldn't have written in his notebook like that. "Yes, of course. You're doing fine." He searched for a more specific observation. "I'm impressed with how you hold the attention of such a full class."

Her eyes darted to his notebook. He could tell she didn't believe him, not for a second. "Oh," she said hopelessly, "my next class is much larger."

"Really? Where would they fit?" He leaned around the corner and looked into her room. Half the desks were empty. The students slouched over their worksheets, their pens a litany of scratching in the silence. The desk where the shiny-cheeked girl had sat was unoccupied, no backpack on the floor. His face felt cold.

"Are you okay, Mr. Welch?"

Welch squinted his eyes shut and rubbed his forehead. "Yes. Have a good day." But as he moved away from her room, he knew she wouldn't. She'd worry all morning about what he'd seen in her room. She'd complain to her friends at lunch, and when she taught in the afternoon, she wouldn't be quite as effective as she would have been if he had never visited. Maybe it would be better if she wasn't coming to the dance. He envisioned two hours of polite conversation filled with bitter subtext.

In Mr. Mendez's Algebra I class, Welch watched the students' backs bent over their work. He'd come in quietly, and only a pimply-faced boy whose purple-penned notes were unreadable noticed when Welch took a seat. Mendez continued sketching a long equation on the board. "The formulas never lie," said Mendez. "Even imaginary numbers tell the truth."

Welch sat for several minutes, his record book unopened. Mendez taught in Lincoln High's original wing. The ceilings rose ten-feet, and rather than the anonymous white tiles and flourescent lighting that marked the new wings, a dozen light fixtures hung down, each bright bulb surrounded by a green reflective collar, like a bed of metal and glass daisies growing from the ceiling. A hundred-year old math room, thought Welch. Over and over, the same lessons: Balance the equation. Seek the lowest common denominator. Chart the axis. Solve for X.

Were any of the students here the least bit. . .nebulous? Welch leaned forward, stretching his trembling fingers toward the pimply student's arm. Mendez kept lecturing. Welch realized the man hadn't faced the students the entire time. The class could sneak out, and Mendez would never know. Welch's hand approached the boy's arm, close enough to touch his sleeve.

Will my fingers slip through?

Welch could see the pores in the boy's hand, the tendons in his wrist.

The boy looked up, his eyes wide, watery and brown. "Yes, sir?"

"Nothing, son. Keep up the good work."

Welch grabbed his notebook, and his pen clattered to the floor.

"Ah, Mr. Welch has joined us," Mendez faced him, chalk in one hand. "Perhaps we could show him the magic of the quadratic."

All heads turned to look at him. Welch backed out of the room. "No, no. I'm just leaving." He fled to the safety of the empty hall, breathing hard. He realized he hadn't touched the student. Now he'd never know.

Coach Qualls, grading papers in the teachers' lounge, looked up when Welch walked in. His bulk swallowed the kid-sized plastic chair. "You all right?" he asked. His jowls were huge and covered with a perpetual five-o'clock dusting of white stubble. At sixty-four years, he was the last staff member who'd been in the building longer than Welch.

Welch sank into a seat of his own. "Yes, of course."

They sat for some time. Qualls moved from paper to paper, check-marking mistakes. Welch looked out the lounge's window, but it faced the side of the school across the open quad below. Sun washed the bricks. No trees or birds or open sky. Just a white wall from top to bottom. Dim sounds from the band room drifted up, throbbing bass notes and the drums. They started and stopped a dozen times, the same thirty seconds of music.

"I turned in my intention form for next year. Time for me to check out," said Qualls. "Are you going to be the old man?"

Welch opened his planner. He hadn't written down anything from Mendez's class, and he wondered if he could count it as an official observation. "Did you accomplish what you wanted by going into this profession?"

Qualls paused, his pen in the air. "Ah, it's one of those days."

"It's just I wonder sometimes if I've done anyone any good. What's my role in the grand scheme? You told me once in the fairy tale that is the school, I'm the troll. I've thought a lot about that." Welch pushed the heels of his hands into his eyes, lighting a thousand sparkles behind his closed lids.

"Was I drunk?" Qualls scratched his chin thoughtfully.

"No. We were between third and fourth hour on a Tuesday."

"Oh, yes. I remember. In the school's mythic landscape, you are in the troll's niche. The teachers are knights, the students are all potential heroes, and you are the dark underpinning. Loved by no one. Intimidating to all. If we just had a bridge to put you under, you'd be perfect."

"That will look damned unimpressive on my tombstone. 'Here lies Vice-Principal Welch, friend to none. Troll to the end.'"

Qualls checked the clock. "Five minutes to the bell. I'm going before the halls crowd up." He stuffed the papers into a briefcase that snapped crisply.

"So, are you a knight? Do knights get to retire?"

Qualls flourished his red pen. "Not me. I'm a wizard, and I'm off to wield my spells one more time. There are kids out there ready to be charmed and bewitched."

For a second, poised at the door to the rest of the school, Welch thought Qualls did look like a wizard under his bushy, white brows.

"I'm seeing ghosts, Coach," said Welch, but Qualls was already gone.

The coffee pot hissed. Above it, on the bulletin board, a sign hung from one thumbtack. DARE TO BELIEVE IN CHILDREN. Stapled beside it, his contribution to the effort, a list of students he'd suspended and a reminder to teachers to provide them with makeup work.

At the end of the day, long after the volleyball team had departed from their spring practice in the gym, and the booster club had left the cafeteria, and the students constructing the set for the musical had put away their power tools and paint brushes, Welch roamed through the school, turning on lights as he went. He checked his pocket planner. Nothing left on the day's schedule. I'm off the planner, he thought. I'm beyond my time. He'd been in the building for the last twenty hours, but he felt restless and antsy instead of tired.

He shook the thought away. Which one would it be tonight? He jangled his keys in his pocket. To his left the lockers gave way to tall windows that looked into the business computer lab. Screen savers swirled in the lab's darkness. He turned right into the freshman hall. Lockers on both sides. Doors into classrooms topped by teacher's names and their subjects. Miss Knapp had added a big smiley face by her name. Welch grimaced when he saw it. Maybe if he dropped a note in her box tomorrow it might make up for his visit to her class.

He stopped by the locker closest to her room. His keys dangled, clinking against the metal. Inside, a cigarette-smelling jacket hung from the hook above a paperback copy of *The Odyssey*. He wrote, DO GOOD on the ten dollar bill he took from his wallet, then signed it, CYCLOPS. When he reached to stick the bill to the inside of the door, he paused. A piece of tape, brittle with age, clung to the spot he always placed the bill. How many years ago had he opened this locker, hoping his gift would make a difference?

It didn't matter. That student had long ago graduated.

Before he could move, though, an arm reached through him, seemed to extend from his own elbow, and stuck a five dollar bill to the spot. The new tape melted into the old and became one.

Blood rushed from his face, and his skin erupted into goose bumps so violently that he thought he might faint. The spectral hand closed the locker, but it was open too, both doors visible to him. Then footsteps echoed in the hallway. Welch turned to see a man walking away. It was himself, darker haired, wearing the horrible gray and red plaid jacket he'd given to the Salvation Army in 1978. Wrestling against his paralysis, Welch forced himself to stir so he could follow, but the man's figure faded into the shadows at the hall's end and the sound of footsteps became the pounding of his heart in his ears.

Welch blinked once, hard, then licked his lips. Of course, it made sense. Still, he was unnerved. He shuddered when he turned back to the locker. The ghost bill had disappeared, and now the locker had just one door, the open one. He put the new tape over the old, then shut the locker as softly as he could, flinching at the mechanism's loud click.

The next morning he started with the Beau Reece folder. Three teacher complaints against him in the previous week. Tardiness, insubordination and inciting a shoving match in the locker room. The two seniors swore Reece started it, but by the time the P.E. teacher arrived, Reece had vanished and the seniors were pushing each other. "I don't doubt the Reece kid had something to do with it," the P.E. teacher said.

As the halls emptied into the first period classes, Welch waited outside the band room, where Reece played the clarinet. The bell rang, and the stragglers hurried to their destinations, casting fearful glances Welch's way. He ignored them. Where was Reece? A few minutes later a student opened the band room door and put the attendance sheet in the folder. The teacher had marked Reece absent.

Ditching or tardy, thought Welch. He checked his watch. Fifteen parent call slips waited on his desk. Last week's athletic eligibility reports needed to be sent to the state for validation. A dozen obligations crowded his planner. He was days behind in teacher evaluations. And, of course, the intention form for next year brooded in his "to do" box. Retire or hang on? What should he do? He filled a cup with coffee in the teacher's lounge, then let himself into the sound booth overlooking the stage. He sat so he could see over the balcony to where the choir practiced. The sopranos stood and held a high note, a long, trembling, wordless vowel. Welch sighed, closed his eyes, letting the cup warm his hands. The altos joined in, then the baritones and bass. Sometimes, when he felt particularly discouraged, after he'd disciplined the umpteenth student for the day, he'd go to the choir room or to the band, or he'd wander through the art classes' galleries, or he'd open the shop's storage room so he could see the shelves and chests and tables students had made. He'd run his hand over the polished joints and glassy smooth wood. The kids can do great things, he'd think. They can be marvelous. But he never worked with those kids. The ones who waited outside his office were the tardy ones, the insubordinate and combative, the criminals.

The bell rang. Welch jumped, spilling the now cool coffee down his leg. He'd fallen asleep. Could he do anything good today? Could he make a difference? He wiped his pants dry as best he could, straightened his tie and headed for the attendance office.

"Can you get me Beau Reece's phone number and his attendance folder?" he said to the secretary, a girl who'd graduated from Lincoln three or four years earlier. She handed him the papers without smiling. When she was a seventeen-year old junior, he'd suspended her for three days for smoking in the girls' locker room.

Naturally, the number was no longer in service. Welch drummed his fingers on his desk, the phone in his other hand. He looked through Reece's attendance records. Although he often skipped classes, he hadn't missed a whole day of school until yesterday. Today didn't look good for him either.

Miss Knapp knocked on his door, looking distraught.

"Have you got a minute?"

Welch nodded. He hadn't put a note in her box yet. Maybe he could just tell her he thought she did a good job.

She sat in the chair next to his desk. "I know you're working very hard to help me be a better teacher, Mr. Welch, but I don't think you get to see the best of me." She kneaded her hands in her lap without looking at him. "I'm a nervous person, Mr. Welch. I'm fine with the kids. When you're in the room, though, I get all tied up."

Welch couldn't speak. He stared at her hands, squeezing so tight the muscles in her arms quivered. He wanted to put his own hands over them and hold them gently. He'd say. "You're going to be an excellent addition to this staff. You already are."

What he said instead was, "Maybe I can arrange for someone else to observe you."

Knapp stood, keeping her hands clasped. "I don't mind you observing me. I just can't teach when you're doing it." Her expression was unreadable, somewhere between misery and confusion. She left the office like a penitent, head down. The whole encounter hadn't lasted thirty seconds. The phone in his hand began beeping, so he hung it up.

Down the hall, he used his key to enter the faculty bathroom. The intercom clicked on for the morning announcements, a litany of club meetings and graduation reminders for seniors. Above the urinal someone had written SQUELCH WELCH. It wouldn't be so bad if this was a student bathroom. He smeared the ink with his thumb.

"Hate graffiti, don't you, son?" said Principal Robinson as he passed behind Welch and let himself into a stall, closing the door behind him. Robinson's belt buckle clinked loudly in the tiled room.

"I'm having a bad day."

"It's the Reece kid, isn't it?" Robinson's voice rose over the partition. "He's the burr under the saddle. You straighten him out, and the other irritations will go away."

Welch closed his eyes and leaned forward, resting his forehead against the cool tile. "Maybe. But if I suspend him, what good will that do?"

"You've got to find him first."

The toilet flushed.

Welch looked at the partition. There were no feet visible below it.

He gasped, then leapt to the door, breaking the latch when he banged it open. No one sat there. In the bowl, the water swirled.

Welch stepped back and bumped into the wall. His legs shook and he almost fell. Then, suddenly, he laughed. The water slowed its circular path and grew still while Welch's laughs subsided to chuckles. He wiped tears off his cheeks. Now he knew a secret, not that he'd ever heard anyone ask it, but he knew. Ghosts used bathrooms.

He started to laugh again. It welled within him, but he clenched his jaw tight against it. He could see himself in three of the mirrors above the sinks, his wild eyes; his disheveled hair. "I'm hallucinating," he said. "I'm going to wake up in my bed, and I'll be twenty-two again, wondering if I should go on the motorcycle trip into Mexico with Harold." Welch remembered his brother's postcards that came every week his first year of teaching and how he put them aside while planning lessons.

"Now I'm talking to myself in the bathroom." Welch stepped to a sink, washed his face. He straightened his tie, then dabbed a paper towel at his chin where a single drop of water glistened. Maybe when I open the door, he thought, there won't be a school there at all. It could be a desert or an ocean or a blank wall. He remembered the white wall across the school's courtyard through the teacher lounge window. How many years had he spent staring at that featureless expanse?

He pushed the door open tentatively. Pamela Howel strode toward him, a clipboard under one arm. She had her "I have to deliver a hand grenade" expression.

"We have a situation, Mr. Welch."

Welch nodded, but he started making his strategy. If I visit every one of Reece's classes, I'm bound to run into him. I have a quest, a mission to turn this boy around. I don't have to be the troll. I can be Odysseus. Ten years of war. Ten years of exile, and then a just reward. He smiled as he headed toward his office, picturing Reece's schedule sitting on his desk.

Howell grabbed his arm earnestly. "Did you hear what I said?"

Surprised to see her still there, he shook his head.

"The boy who tried to commit suicide last week named you in his note. The school board put you on their schedule for tonight. You need to be there at 7:00 sharp." She pivoted on one heel and went back the way she had come.

Welch reeled; he couldn't even remember the kid. He rubbed his fingers hard into his forehead while scrinching his eyes closed. Nope. No memory at all of his connection with the boy. One thing at a time, he thought, as he wrote in his planner, SCHOOL BOARD MEETING, 7:00, SUICIDE.

First, find Beau Reece. Outside Reece's second class, Welch stood by the doorway, hands in his pockets, watching students enter. Most ignored him. Some looked at him curiously. A few kept their eyes averted. The stream slowed. The bell rang. No Reece.

Welch walked off school grounds to "skid row," where the smokers, skateboarders, goths and dropouts went when they were ditching class. He flushed a couple out of the high jump pit by the football field, encouraged three boys sitting on their skateboards in the alley beside the track to move on, then strode behind the convenience store across the street from the high school, surprising a pack of kids smoking, mostly tobacco, but he caught a whiff of pot too. Eyes went wide as cigarettes disappeared behind backs. Most of them had been in his office at one time or another.

"Have any of you seen Beau Reece?" he asked without real hope.

No answer for a long minute.

A boy wearing black leather pants and a spiked dog collar said, "He played with the jazz band yesterday before school."

Reece didn't go to any of his classes yesterday. Welch assumed he must have been sick. "Really?"

The boy nodded. The rest of the group stood silently, little whiffs of smoke curling behind them. "He missed this morning," the boy added.

"Thanks," said Welch, then he turned toward the school.

"Umm. . ." a girl with a violet top knot but shaved close above her ears said. "Aren't you going to yell at us to get back to class?"

Welch looked up at the perfect cotton-ball clouded sky. He shrugged. "Do what you want."

Ten paces away though, he stopped and went back. The kids hadn't moved. "All of you are underage to be smoking. Throw those things away, and I'll forget I saw you." He tried to bluster, but it came flat and without conviction.

"Are you all right, Mr. Welch?" asked the violet top knot.

Welch sighed as if he'd been punctured. "Just get away from the store. They're business folks and you kids leave a mess back here."

When Welch reached the school, he looked at the convenience store. None of the kids had left.

For the rest of the morning, he patrolled the building in a daze. He pulled the records of the student who'd tried to commit suicide, but Welch's encounter with him had been in December when the boy had been suspended with three others for throwing snowballs at the busses. Even when Welch looked at the boy's picture, he couldn't remember him. Why would he name me in a suicide note? wondered Welch, and what did the school board want? He walked a long circuit from the agriculture building, past the swimming pool, then out to the driver's ed. course. In all his years in education, he'd never been teacher of the year, or even teacher of the month. He'd never been recognized by the board for an "Excellence in Education" award. He'd never been asked to speak at graduation. No one ever gave him a yearbook to sign. Maybe the board would ask for his resignation, or worse, the ignominy of a forced retirement.

What did Odysseus feel like after twenty years? Cursed by the gods. All his men dead. Not even sure his wife remembered him. Hope must have dwindled within him, thought Welch. What did the troll under the bridge feel? How did he feel about his place in the world?

He added up all the sick days he'd never taken. If he handed in his retirement intention sheet now, he could call in sick for the rest of the year and not even go to the school board meeting. Who needed the grief?

The bell rang, sending the students to lunch. Welch walked on the left side of the hall against the flow of traffic, glad for the contact when students bumped into him, even if they did shoot him annoyed glances. At least they were real, and he was real too. A short boy passed on Welch's right. Welch grabbed the boy's shoulder.

"Beau?" he said, but it wasn't him.

School ended. The busses left. Teams practiced. Clubs met, and, gradually, the building emptied. Once again, Welch wandered the hallways. The sun, low in the sky, sent long beams of light through the windows next to the doors and down the main hall. Only one day in the spring the windows lined up with the sun on the horizon so the light reached all the way to the other end.

He felt like he walked in a tunnel of light as he fingered the ten dollar bill in his pocket. In fifteen minutes he would have to leave. His planner was very exact about it: SCHOOL BOARD MEETING, 7:00, SUICIDE.

Years and years earlier he'd started taping money to the inside of lockers, one or two bills a week. Sometimes more if there were a lot of kids through his office. DO GOOD, he wrote, but in all that time he'd never heard anyone talk about the mystery presents. He never heard what the kids did with the cash. It reminded him of standing on the edge of the Grand Canyon, flicking pebbles over the edge. They vanished into the depths without a sound. How come our *good* deeds never come back to haunt us? He checked the slip in his hand. Beau Reece used locker 1209.

The doors behind him crashed open, flooding the hall with sun. The silhouetted form of a half-dozen boys filled the space, and hard-soled shoes clicked against the floor.

"What are we gonna do?" cried one. As they came closer, Welch could see they were football players carrying a boy on a stretcher. For a moment Welch was disoriented. Football in the spring? Football ended months ago.

"I think his leg is broke," said another. They rushed by Welch. Dirt and grass stains marred their thick sweaters with an "L" sewn to the front.

The boy on the stretcher moaned, his face streaked with tears. "I'm sorry, guys," he said.

"We can't be best in the state without our wingback," said a third.

"Welch could save the day," sobbed the boy on the stretcher. "He could carry the ball for us."

"What?" stammered Welch. "What did you say?"

But the team hurried down the hall, the sun glaring on their backs, and they dissolved into dust motes before reaching the end.

The hallway dimmed as the doors closed. Welch looked back at the windows. The sun touched the horizon, a perfect, crimson globe beyond the glass. In minutes the hall would be dark and it would be next fall before the sun lined up once more. He glanced at his watch. Time to go.

Taking a deep breath, he found Beau Reece's locker. He flattened the bill against the metal and wrote DO GOOD. He thought for a second about signing it ODYSSEUS. He shook his head. Odysseus didn't fit. If he was anyone from that story, it would be Paris, whose bad judgements destroyed heroes, so he signed it, THE TROLL.

The key slid into the lock, but the door resisted. Welch leaned into it to take the pressure off the internal mechanisms so he could pop the latch. The door swung open. Then, slowly, a body fell out. A ghost in the locker! Welch thought, his heart fisted tight. He took it in at once. The band of duct tape around the body's torso, pinning his arms to his side. The tape around the ankles. The broad band of dull silver across the ghost's mouth. And still, it fell, until at the last second, Welch stepped forward and caught it before it hit the floor.

A solid weight in his hands, Welch sat back in surprise. No ghost. It was a real boy, a small one, unconscious or dead. Welch pressed his fingers to the boy's throat where a pulse beat firmly. He worked his fingers under one edge of the tape, and carefully pulled it away from the child's mouth.

It wasn't until the kid opened his eyes blearily and croaked, "Mr. Welch?" that he realized he held Beau Reece.

Near midnight, while sitting in the hospital's waiting room, it occurred to him he'd missed the school board meeting. It didn't matter. He couldn't help smiling. The doctor told him Beau was dehydrated but would be fine. "Don't you have rules against hazing?" asked the doctor.

The glass pneumatic doors from the parking lot wheezed open. Coach Qualls and two other teachers came in.

"What are you doing here?" said Welch. Qualls looked so misplaced, and Welch realized in three decades he'd only seen him at school.

"The night nurse is the superintendent's wife, and she called him. His cell phone went off right in the middle of his closing comments. We came straight over. Good work, man." Qualls slapped him on the shoulder.

Welch shrugged. "Just luck, really."

Qualls sat next to him. "That's not what I heard. The secretaries told me you'd been looking for Reece since yesterday. Good instincts, I'd say."

Welch sighed and let himself sink deeper into the chair. The day had been a long one. Another teacher walked in, and before the doors closed, Miss Knapp entered, rubbing her coat sleeves against the cold of the spring evening.

"You were all at the meeting?" asked Welch. Through the doors he could see other teachers in the parking lot heading toward them.

"Sure," said Qualls. "Weren't you supposed to be there too? That kid who tried to commit suicide named twenty-four of us in his note. Typical school board over-reaction. They wanted to talk to us about sensitivity. Did you hear how he tried to do himself?"

Welch shook his head. The room filled with teachers.

"Four bottles of antacid pills." Qualls laughed. "He thought an overdose of anything would kill him."

The superintendent of schools joined the crowd, spotted Welch. "It's caring educators like yourself who make us proud to be teachers." He squeezed Welch's hand. "Forty years in education, and you're still making a difference. You saved that boy's life."

A news truck pulled up to the doors.

Welch stood next to Qualls. Teachers filled the room. Qualls raised his hand and waved, then slowly dropped it, turning toward Welch.

"What?" said Welch.

"It's the darndest thing."

"What?"

"I thought I saw Principal Robinson. For a second I thought it was Robinson over there."

Welch sighed. "It happens to me all the time."

"Where's this Welch fellow?" said a man with a television camera tucked under his arm.

"Must be a slow news night," said Welch, suddenly so embarrassed that he looked for a door to duck into, but the teachers surrounded him.

Afterwards, when the television crew departed, and most of the teachers had trickled away, Miss Knapp approached him, still in her coat.

"This was marvelous." She looked around the room. "So many of us came."

Welch didn't know what to say. Outside of the school, he had no words for her. But he wanted them, words that wouldn't make her nervous. Surely he could talk to her about subjects other than attendance and discipline and teaching strategies.

Something in her expression seemed strained, then a realization dawned on him. "Qualls did this, didn't he?"

Miss Knapp blushed. "No. . .oh, no. We really were glad to come, really. Well. . .he said you'd been a little down. You're not angry, are you?"

Welch shook his head. They stood without speaking for a few seconds, then she put out her hand. "I have to get going. Congratulations, though. You did a good thing. Will you be at the dance Friday?" Her delicate and cool fingers rested against his palm.

   Dances featured ear-crushing music by groups he didn't recognize, gate-crashers from other schools who had to be tossed out, kids who came to the school drunk or who snuck into their cars for a beer or a joint before trying to get past him, and afterwards there would be torn confetti and crushed paper cups and decorations to be taken down. That's the way it always was. But he also knew the dance floor would be full of students and ghosts. He could live with the ghosts. And for the real kids? Warm hands on bare backs during the slow songs. Shy smiles. Genuine laughter. He would stand to the side, arms crossed on his chest, watching, like a knight on a castle wall.

   "Save a dance for me," he said.

   It was his place.

The Safety Of the Herd

Cringing from the press of bodies, Shotgun City detective Toyas Midtmann missed the beginning of the confrontation. He pushed his elbows against the commuters penning him in to give himself a little room, shutting his eyes against the mass of heads swaying to the tram's movement. A cop who loathes people shouldn't be a public servant, he thought. If he were a lion strolling alone across an African steppe where hills rose in the distance, shimmering in the heat, he would be happy. An uneasy murmur brought him back.

He eyed the tram securitycams, three black-lensed bubbles hanging from the roof. A red light blinked in two of them, but the one directly overhead looked dead, which either meant the vid *was* dead or the light didn't work. Regardless, the two toughs facing each other a few feet away weren't paying attention. Toyas squeezed between a couple of business types, trying to get close before things got worse. Everyone leaned away, though, and there wasn't room to move. Toyas shifted to get his stun prod out of its holster; but a heavyset guy in a gray overcoat trapped his arm against him.

A young tough said to an older man, "Are you pulling blade on me?" A skinart forest fire blazed on the young man's face and shaved head. Flame images circled his cool, blue eyes. He tapped his dueling knife's hilt that hung on his chest just below his shoulder, handle down for a quick draw.

The older one, dark-bearded, wearing pale leather, held his knife delicately between thumb and finger, sliding it slowly in and out of its chest sheath. "I'm pulling it."

"But are you pulling on me?"

Faces surrounded them, mostly Shotgun City domestics heading down canyon for day jobs. They pushed back, creating a four-foot arena. Behind them, the curious stood on their toes, peering over heads for a better look. The tram rocked, and through the windows, building after building whipped by.

The tableau froze, pale-leather holding his blade so an inch gleamed; fire-face resting a finger on the hilt. Toyas yelled, "Break it up! Police!"

Fire-face turned toward him, and the tram lurched. Pale-leather lunged forward, blade beside his ear.

Someone screamed. People pushed together so hard Toyas lost his breath. The tram slid onto the platform and stopped. Doors on one side opened, releasing the commuters. Behind him, other doors opened and new commuters pushed in. Toyas rode the crush out, panning the crowd for the two toughs. Nothing. People riding slideways and escalators. Others milled around soy and drink kiosks, steam rising from heating pans.

He almost tripped over the body ten feet later. Lying on his back, fire-face stared into the sky. Toyas felt for a pulse but knew the boy was dead. A stab wound just left of center bled little. The blade had gone straight to the heart, a rare thrust for a dueling knife, which by law could be no longer than three inches.

The neck was warm and placid. Sweat slick. Toyas guessed the boy died before he left the tram, but the crowd carried him upright to this point before he dropped. Fire images still crawled up his cheeks, licked his ears, flickered across his forehead, the skinart dyes following their programmed display, living on the dead skin. False fire. No heat. A woman brushed against him, her eyes locked forward; he was sure she didn't see him. "Step wide!" he called. "Crime scene. Step wide!" Still, they came. Crouched over the body, he saw knees and feet. A flattened cup leaked coffee until someone kicked it, and only the stain remained.

Toyas tongued a transmit switch on the back of a tooth and called for clean up. He ordered a tracer on the tram and a download of the securitycam files, but he held little hope they'd show much: backs of heads, fuzzy faces, motion — not enough for court-worthy IDs. Another corpse — fifteen to twenty a day on this tram line alone.

Tiny voices filled his ear: a rolling riot had spread to Idaho Springs, fifteen miles down canyon; there was a hostage situation in Dillon and another in Shotgun City. A dozen All Points Bulletins. Another cop called for a clean up while he waited. The violent recital: situations droned on. He half listened, tuning in to his calls and not the others, but he had nothing to do, leaning over the dead boy.

People stepped over the body. Toyas fended them off the best he could until clean up arrived. The human tide inexorably flowed, a herd on the move.

By the time he got to Bellamy Labs where he was to arrest Reanna Loveday for unauthorized genetic manipulation, it had turned into a suicide standoff.

Not much to the building itself. Undistinguished signs marked the slideway platform as private, and the afternoon's light reflected off the door's muted silver sheen. People in a steady procession on the slideway moved up and down canyon behind him. Toyas arched back; the sky, a luminous blue ribbon cut by walks and bridges, stretched between the buildings' tops. Trams scooted overhead on magnetic rails. The population's weight pressed around him, above him, below him; going its varied ways. It smelled of fish and deodorizers, of dusty, clammy skin that never saw the sun and slept too close together. This is no place for a Masai warrior, he thought. I should be trotting across a grassy plain, spear in hand, my fate's master. Not that there are any Masai left, or grassy plains for that matter.

He imagined how easy it would be to pull his dueling blade in a crowded tram too and stab and stab and stab, for the room, for the dull hatred. He rubbed his hands together. He still felt the dead boy's sweat on his fingertips.

The door scanner okayed his warrant, opening to a wide hallway crowded with frightened lab staff. A young man in a medical smock turned to him when he came in the door. Something in his eyes struck Toyas. They darted wildly, and the man trembled. A skinart rose rotated slowly on his cheek, and Toyas thought about the dead tough, fire crawling on his head. "It'll be fine," said Toyas. "We do this all the time."

Sub-detective Clancey waved from the far end, looking small in his new uniform, his police academy chevrons still shiny. "She's blocked herself into a back office on the other side of her lab with a vial of something poisonous. Nobody knows what it is." He'd unholstered his stun-prod and slapped it nervously into his hand. "I figured I'd wait until you got here."

"Her lab's through there?" A skinny window beside the door revealed another hallway punctuated with doors.

Clancey nodded, then wiped his sleeve across his forehead. "She's got DNA stuff back there, they say. Maybe some wacky diseases. I don't know. Something exotic and incurable. Make your skin fall off."

Toyas shook his head. "Not a contract gene shop like this. Worst she could do is change your rhododendrons."

A shaky voice behind him said, "Her specialties are genetically-based animal behavior modification and natural vectoring. She finds traits we like from one kind of animal to replace traits we don't like in another animal."

Toyas turned.

Another man in a medical smock. Close set eyes. Fiftyish. Name tag read "Hirhito Blevins." He extended a hand. "Loveday is working on the pigeon problem for the city. Wonderful mind. Wonderful, but touchy. She has a lab to herself. Over a hundred square feet of space, and she bullied the others out. Hates crowds, she says. Terribly inefficient. Three employees generally work a lab that size. We leave her alone, though. Genius can be eccentric."

Toyas tried to back away from the man, but the room was too crowded. "Can't you let these people go home? They'll just be in the way."

Blevins shook his head. "They're hourlies. Automatically docked if they leave the building."

Toyas rubbed his eyes and held back an urge to yell. Clancey downloaded the situation file and Loveday's psychiatric and work profiles into Toyas' palmtop. Intelligence rating off the scale, but mediocre school records. She'd worked continuously for the last four years, moving from one contract to the next — a rarity for most employees — flawless performance numbers. She must be good, Toyas thought. She'd tried killing herself when she was a teenager. Clancey peeked over his shoulder at the display. "See, she's serious about this."

Loveday's portrait came up. An unsmiling, thin-faced blonde in her mid-twenties.

"Any clue what set her off?"

Blevins said, "I was talking, very calmly, and she started raving. Threw a clipboard at me. Totally unprovoked. She's unbalanced. Always has been, but we need her."

Toyas guessed the conversation wasn't that innocent but didn't say so. The case profile noted that Blevins had turned in the original complaint for unauthorized computer use. Loveday's user history showed hours of research on human gene patterns, mostly centering on socialization behavior. "This is all outside her specialty, isn't it?"

Blevins said, "Oh, yes. Completely misplaced effort. Her real gift is natural vectoring for animals. Most genetic manipulation happens under controlled conditions: a livestock breeding facility, for example, or a doctor's office. But sometimes we want to spread a genetic change where the subjects are difficult to reach, so we have to find a way to introduce and disseminate the mutagen naturally. A parasite or a disease. Something infectious, easily transferred, but not fatal. She was piggybacking a mutagen to a weakened form of avian influenza for the pigeon problem. This investigation into human genetic patterns is not a part of her contract. There are federal laws, and, besides, she stole computer time and lab space. It reflects on my evaluation."

Toyas gave his stun prod to Clancey, then opened the door into the empty hallway. His palmtop went back into its fanny pack. "Why'd she try to kill herself the first time?"

Clancey scanned his display. "Doesn't say, but her parents died two months before in a rolling riot." He read further. "Looks like they got caught at a restaurant. Six others died there too. The report doesn't implicate them. Might be a connection."

"Give me an hour."

The door closed. Toyas walked past open offices toward Loveday's lab. He turned off his earplug, and the crime litany stopped. His steps clicked loudly in the silence, and he realized for the first time in days, he couldn't hear a human voice. The police station rang with sounds; human commerce filled the shops and streets; his tiny Shotgun City apartment never completely shut out the slideway's rumble and the rise and fall of human murmur twenty-four hours a day. Everywhere he went, thousands of people within a mile of him. The entire Denver to Salt Lake City inter-mountain urban corridor crowded with them. They'd even filled the twin Eisenhower tunnels that used to be a part of the highway system with apartments and shops to create Shotgun City.

He slowed to enjoy the moment. Took a deep breath. Here the air smelled antiseptic, scrubbed clean, slightly chemical, not close and clammy. Not like the tram. He walked in the middle of the hall and thought about extending his arms as wings; they wouldn't touch either side. In his apartment, he kept a recording of a Greater Flamingo taking off from the shore of lake Samburu — a tremendous bird fighting its way into the air. He could spin around here, his arms out, and not touch anything.

Toyas glanced back; in the window behind him, Clancey and several others peered through. He kept his arms down, but for the first time today he felt relaxed. If the tram hadn't been so crowded, if it had been like this hallway, the fight might never have happened. The flame-faced boy would still be alive, the fires washing over his lips and sweeping around his eyes. Before the fight started, the people close by had pushed away, but the people farther back had leaned in, not wanting to miss the action. Their heads bobbed between shoulders, craning for a view. A violence hunger. They wanted to see, and the ones close didn't want to be hurt, but none of them had reached forward to stop the fight. Toyas thought everyone on the tram should have been arrested. Co-conspirators. Accessories to a homicide.

Most of them wore blades. Old folks, children, clergy — it didn't matter. A knife was a fashion statement. Illegal to use outside the dueling halls, but people had them just the same. Toyas thought about his luck that the tram had pulled into the platform when it did. That close, blood's smell in the air, a chain reaction could have started. Everyone stabbing everyone else out of. . .what? Fear? Hatred? Hysteria? It didn't matter. Mass stabbings had happened before. Like a rolling riot. No explanation. Violence breaking out in one spot, spreading to another, leaving destruction and injury before moving on. Sometimes lasting for weeks and traveling for miles, like fire.

Loveday's lab door wasn't closed tight. Toyas pushed it open with his foot, letting the room unfold before him as the door swept wide. She wasn't there. A long table in the middle was clean, a clipboard on the floor the only sign of disarray. On the wall, between open cabinets filled with equipment, several posters hung. All historical scenes. In one, a herd of cows grazed at sunset, their backs golden in the slanted light. Another showed a hundred buffalo, their heads up and alert, as if a wolf had appeared just off the poster's edge. He touched it, and it crackled under his fingers. Real paper. Very expensive.

"Reanna Loveday?" Toyas called. He thought the partly closed door at the back of the lab must be her office. The light was off. "My name's Toyas. Shotgun City police, Reanna. I need to talk to you. We don't want you to hurt yourself. Your friends are concerned about you."

"Blevins isn't a friend," said a voice from the dark. A bitter laugh. "He's an accounting geek. Right now he's adding up lost productivity." A shuffling noise. A click of metal on metal. "Toyas? Good, African name. Are you a rat or a snake, Officer Toyas?"

Toyas sat on the table's edge. He liked the empty room. He liked the posters. There was no reason to rush. Unless someone buzzed his palmtop, he was unreachable for the moment.

"I don't know. What's the difference?" he said. She didn't reply. "Must be nice to have a big place like this to work in." Blevins was right about the room: it was about ten by ten feet, which made it two feet longer and four feet wider than Toyas' Shotgun City apartment. "They said you were going to kill yourself."

Loveday didn't speak for a while. There was only one way out of the lab, and it was past him, so she wasn't going anywhere. Toyas stretched his legs.

"I might," she said. Her voice didn't sound stressed. Tired, but not stressed. Not like she was poised on the precipice. "Rats kill themselves. Snakes don't."

"Any particular reason?"

"Genetics. It's all in the genes."

"I didn't know animals could commit suicide," said Toyas. She actually sounded pleasant. A little stuffed up perhaps. She sniffed in the darkened office and blew her nose. "Do you want to come out here to tell me about it?"

"I don't like people. Did they tell you that?"

"Who does?" Toyas got up. Walked around the room. It was amazing. Step after step without running into someone. His knuckles brushed against the wall as he went by.

"Snakes do."

"Like people?"

"No, each other. You could fill a box with snakes and they wouldn't know the difference. Some of them spend the winter crammed into a little hole, hundreds of them. There was a story once of a Texas rancher who broke into a snake den while digging a cellar. Ten-foot thick ball of rattlers snoozing away."

Toyas wrinkled his brow. The conversation had taken an odd turn. Still, standard procedure in a suicide situation was to keep the victim talking. "Snakes aren't people, though."

"My point exactly! At least most of them," she said, as if she'd won an argument. "But we can't avoid them! I had a reservation to go camping next month. I've held it for four years. Three days and two nights in a real forest. It's with a group, of course, but you can hike by yourself. There's a stream and a lake, they say. I've seen the brochure. There's a picture of one person, just one, sitting on a rock at a meadow's edge."

Toyas nodded sympathetically. For the last three years he had submitted requests to visit Mt. Kenya Park. He wanted to see *Kere Nyaga*, the Kikuyu name for Mount Kenya, the Mountain of Brightness.

She sneezed. "Sorry, allergies." She wiped at her nose. "They canceled my reservation."

"Why?" Toyas paused in front of a complicated computer display: twisted strands braiding among each other, numbered and lettered notation labeling the strand's bumps. He scrolled to the display's top. Human Gene Segment, L14d.

"People won't come out. Not enough snakes. Too many rats. They closed the park. They've closed all of them. There's no place to go to get away. There are too many people who are rats. We've got to get rid of the rats."

Toyas glanced sharply at the office door. Her voice sounded odd on the last statement, ominous or desperate. He remembered Clancey's fear that she'd made a disease. It was unlikely — anticipation of just such an event had prompted hundreds of checks in the system — but maybe she'd figured a way around the security. He reached behind him for his palmtop, and pressed the emergency call to bring a squad to isolate the building. This might not be just one detective talking a person out of suicide anymore. Soon, experts by the score would dissect her notes and computer, revealing everything she'd worked on in all the time she'd been here.

"That's why you wanted to kill yourself? Because you lost a camping reservation?" Keeping his tone calm, he clicked backwards through screen after screen of genetic code, but his fingers quivered on the keys. All beyond him, the cryptic notations giving no clue of her intent. Was this a suicide situation or a threat to public safety? "And what does this have to do with rats?"

"No. Not the camping." The ominous tone dropped away, and now she sounded exhausted, like she was giving up. "An experiment went wrong. I thought I'd solved a problem, but it didn't work. I couldn't change a rat. Physician Rat, heal thyself."

"Blevins said you worked with pigeons."

She laughed. "Those stupid pigeons. Do you know what the city wanted me to do? Stop pigeon droppings. Millions of dollars over the years cleaning buildings. They contracted me to change pigeon pooping behavior. I think I solved it. Pigeons poop everywhere. Cats are clean about it. A cut here, a splice there, and I'll have all the pigeons in the world scratching their droppings into the dirt. No, the experiment was with me. My self experiment failed. I'm genetically resistant."

Toyas transferred everything in her computer onto his palmtop. It only took a few seconds. The experts could look at it later if there was a need. He didn't see her own palmtop. Probably had it on her. Incriminating evidence might be there.

"Genetically resistant?" he said, mostly to keep her talking while he waited for reinforcements.

She sneezed again. "Yes. Not everyone's genes are malleable. Some resist mutagens better than others."

A chair scraped. Her pale hand appeared on the door jamb, and the door swung open. "Are you by yourself?" She stood in the shadows.

He nodded.

After several minutes without moving — he could feel her eyes on him, sizing him up — she said, "I'm agoraphobic. Really bad. You know, panic attacks." She slid around the door's edge, keeping her back to the wall. The palmtop picture didn't flatter her. Even in the lab's harsh light, her features were softer, younger, color high in her cheeks. "It's hard to breathe with you here." There was nothing in her hands—no poison or way to kill herself—nothing frightening about her. She might have a syringe in the lab coat, though, thought Toyas, something that would take just a pressure on the pocket to inject.

The file transfer finished. Toyas moved to the other end of the room. "Have you always been that way?"

She touched a button near the computer, and the doubled-helix on the screen cleared. "Since I was a kid. The doctors call it trauma induced social anxiety disorder. It got worse after my parents died. Rats in the box."

"Rats?" He checked his palmtop. The files were all there. Crisis intervention reported they were in the lobby.

She looked directly at him for the first time since she'd come out, her eyes bright, fevered. "Rats attack each other in a box. They're social, but you can't overcrowd them. They'll even bite themselves. Snakes don't. Herd animals don't. Pressed together in pens, they're content. Nothing bothers them. It's genetic. Mom and Dad died in a restaurant, killed with butter knives and forks. The box was too crowded. The rats got them. So, are you a rat or a snake?"

A bustle in the hallway behind him, and the door shattered inward. Loveday shrieked, leaping for her office door, but a tangle-burst got her. She went down in a tightening confusion of fine mesh that pulled her arms into her sides and bound her legs. Masked intervention operatives poured into the room, fifteen or twenty of them. There was little room to move. Toyas backed against the wall.

"Did she say anything?" someone shouted to him. "Did she make a threat?" Someone else pushed a re-breather into his hands, but he didn't put it on. Operatives opened drawers, poking gene-scanner proboscises into the depths, the hand-held units sucking air to their tiny, automated analysis chambers. "Nothing here," said one operative, the re-breathing unit muffling his voice. "Pigeon DNA," said another. "More pigeon. And cat. I have cat."

Blevins voice came from the door; Toyas couldn't see him past the officers. "Those are authorized. We have papers for them!" Blevins followed the officers, showing them clearances for everything they found: dog, cow, octopus, mosquito, several others, but no snake. Toyas shook his head. Why no snake? That's what she said she'd been doing. There wasn't rat either.

Loveday kept shrieking wordlessly.

"What are you looking for?" said Toyas, flinching against her voice. "Can I help?" He sidled along the wall toward Loveday. Two officers held her down while a third ran a see-all over her tangle-webbed lab coat.

"Nothing in the pockets. She's clean." The officer searching her looked up at Toyas. "If she's made a pathogen, she needs a way to distribute it. Powder, pills, liquid spray — it could be anywhere. We've got a squad doing her apartment too."

Another officer ground his knee into Loveday's back, squeezing her screams thin. Toyas grabbed his collar and pulled him off. "She's not going anywhere," said Toyas. "No need to hurt her." Only the man's eyes were visible above his re-breather, dark and enigmatic. Toyas suspected the man liked what he had been doing. Loveday stopped screaming.

They ripped posters off the walls, scanned behind them; emptied cabinets, broke jars, poured out chemicals, cut open notebook covers, all efficiently. In fifteen minutes they'd taken the lab apart and found no deadly viruses or evidence that she'd worked on one.

An officer came out of her office, a melted palmtop in his hand. "She torched it," he said. "We may never know what was on this." He dropped it into a plastic bag for later analysis.

Toyas stayed close to Loveday, keeping his hand on her arm. "She just wanted to go to a park," he said under his breath. Knees and feet passed around him. He fended them off so no one stepped on her. It reminded him of the dead boy from the tram. No reason for all these people to be here, thought Toyas. They're scaring her, and it made his skin creep. Too much jostling.

Finally the officers stood around Loveday, discussing whether they should take her to the patrol house for questioning or to a hospital for observation. She breathed through her mouth. "Officer Toyas," she whispered. "I need to blow my nose." Stuffed up, her arms tight to her side, she sounded pathetic. Toyas found a tissue in his fannypack and held it for her. She blew noisily against his hand. When they picked her up, still horizontal, facing the floor, she rose until her red-rimmed eyes were level with his. "Thanks," she said, and sneezed in his face.

When the squad left, Toyas looked around the room. The litter had been swept up, but broken glass in a fine dust sparkled at the lab table's end. They'd taken the computer and her notes. A poster dangled from one corner on the wall. He pressed it back up. Sheep on a hillside, covering it so tightly he could see no grass, just backs and heads. In the middle, a single tree rose above them, its greenery a sharp contrast to the sheep's white and black.

Toyas couldn't sleep that night. The slideway's constant rumble bothered him. He could feel crowds passing past his doorway. He tried staring at his prints on the wall: a brightly lit view of Mt. Kilimanjaro, a sunrise on the Indian Ocean at the Kenyan coast, a lone giraffe. But it didn't help. After he turned down the light, he imagined his neighbor's breathing to his left and right. The weight from neighbors above seemed to bow the roof. Sometimes he heard them in bed, their apartment no larger than his own, moving rhythmically.

When he finally dozed, he dreamt of crawling in a tunnel, deep underground, moist dirt falling on his neck, slipping under his hands. After a dozen turns, the tunnel grew tighter until he squirmed on his belly. Then, the

ceiling rose away. His fingers hooked over an earthen edge. A dim light
glowed in the huge room below him, and it was filled. Thousands of naked
people, intertwined, moving slowly in sleep — a giant people ball. The
closest parted, as if they knew he was there, to give him a space in the
mass. He slithered from the hole, put his hands on legs and arms, pulled
himself in. No one woke, but they moved aside, let him burrow deeply in
their phosphorescence. He pushed his knee against a shoulder, levered
himself between two backs, their ribs and backbones sliding over him, swimming in people, and then he reached the middle. He rested. Everything tight
and cozy, warm and friendly, until he heard a vibration, a quiet rattle rising
in the mass. The leg above his head grew cool. Pressing against his side, a
thigh thinned, became slick and scaled. Air buzzed, and pressure rose. He
struggled to breathe. A fanged face pressed against his head, black marble
eye unblinking. It slid by. All snakes, everywhere. No people. He gasped.
Lungs ached. Arms trapped. No breath.

He flailed in the darkness, throwing his blanket aside. One hand slapped
against the wall, and his neighbor rapped back a muffled curse. Toyas lay
gasping, his throat coated and his nose stuffed up. By bed light he found
tissue, but blowing didn't clear his nasal passages. A couple pillows propped
beneath his head stopped the worst of the draining, and when the antihista-
mine and decongestant began to work, he fell asleep again, this time without dreams.

The next morning after he stepped outside his apartment door, he keyed
for an update on Loveday. The palmtop showed they'd checked her in for
observation. A couple screens later he found the hospital had put her in a
private room. She'll like that, he thought. Other than disrupting the peace,
no indictments had been issued. A blinking icon at the screen's bottom
indicated "Under Investigation." Another one said, "Possible Biohazard."
He clicked the unit closed, waited for an opening, then stepped on the
slideway. Before he reached the Shotgun City limit sign and the end of the
city's long tunnel, he'd sneezed half a dozen times. "Sorry," he said each
time to annoyed commuters. "Allergies." The decongestants kept his breathing clear, but his nose itched and he had a sore throat. Not bad, but it hurt to
swallow.

He checked in so that headquarters would transmit his cases, a short
list this morning, only three homicides. On the tram ride, he mulled over the
dream, and as an afterthought checked on the stabbing from yesterday. As
he'd feared, the securitycams didn't show enough to advance an investigation. No blood on flame-face's knife. No witnesses who could help. No
specific similarities to other stabbings to indicate a pattern. Probably random, Toyas thought, one act of violence by a man who had never done

such a thing before and probably never would again, not that finding the killer would help the dead boy anyway.

The tram missed the first Dillon platform. The rolling riot was too close. Police shut off the platforms, rerouted slideway traffic and shut down bridges and elevators through the district in an attempt to choke the fighting off. As the tram slid past the platform, Toyas saw yelling people standing on the edge, trying to get out. Rats and snakes, Loveday had called them. With no room to move, rats turned on each other. The box was too small. She'd asked him which one was he. That must mean I could be either, he thought. Not everyone hates the crowding. He sneezed again. Couldn't even get his hand up over his mouth in the tram's tight quarters. A lady in front of him flinched and wiped at the back of her neck.

The second Dillon platform passed, and the third. An angry mumble rose in the tram. People missing their stops would either have to walk up canyon to get to work, or they wouldn't be able to get there at all. Most employees were hourlies. They were paid only for time on the job, regardless of the excuse. Somebody pushed someone else, and for a few seconds shouting filled the tram. Toyas held his palmtop tight. With the right combination of commands, he could have the car flooded with sleepy-gas. He wondered how long ago it had been since he'd been gas-proofed, and if it would still keep him conscious. The yelling subsided, though, and he relaxed, swallowing in relief. It hurt.

His all-call squeaked in his ear, and headquarters queried him on his position. "Emergency override," the earphone said. "Debark at Silverthorne #4." He shrugged and worked his hand up to his face so he could wipe his nose. The tram followed a long curve in its track, making everyone lean. A man next to Toyas stumbled a little and caught Toyas' sleeve to keep his balance. "Pardon," he said.

"It's OK." Except for his sneezing, Toyas didn't feel bad this morning. Not like yesterday when he might have thrown an elbow to keep the stranger off him. It's not their fault, thought Toyas. They're missing work.

He couldn't see a window. Somehow he'd ended up in the middle, but he knew the upper canyon complexes were passing by. In a minute, they'd be at Silverthorne and he could find out what the emergency was. In the meantime, he let the tram's gentle motion lull him. People pressed against him, moving with the sway. Very soothing.

Then, Toyas saw him, the pale-leather tough from yesterday. His hand rested on his dueling blade, a line of gleaming metal showing it was part way out of its sheath, and Pale-leather scowled around him, his dark beard disarrayed, his expression filled with hate. Toyas tongued a transmission and subvocalized a report. It took a few seconds to clear his stun-prod from its holster. He didn't want to be caught unprepared this time.

The tram slid toward Silverthorne station. Pale-leather glared at the crowd, his hand tight on the dueling blade, obviously within an instant of pulling it out. Toyas brought the stun-prod up, next to his chest. If the man drew the blade, Toyas figured he could just reach him over the intervening heads. They held the pose until the tram slowed down for the platform. Pale-leather closed his eyes for a moment, as if in relief, and Toyas felt suddenly inside the man's head. It was the closing of the eyes that did it. It wasn't people the man hated, but the pressure against him, the constant touching. He didn't want to hurt anyone, but he would. A rat in the box, ready to bite, his rodent-like instincts playing themselves through, nearly beyond his control, and Toyas knew that was him too, yesterday, an inch from stabbing out himself.

Doors opened, and a line of policeman waited on the platform, standing steady against the stream flowing from the car. Toyas maneuvered himself behind Pale-leather, letting the traffic carry him out. He reached to snag the man's shoulder when something grabbed him on both sides.

They spun him around, a policeman on each arm. Toyas barely saw the helmet coming before it was over his head.

"He's escaping!" yelled Toyas, and struggled to get an arm free. They held too tightly though, and through the helmet's glass, Toyas glimpsed Pale-leather stepping onto a slideway. The other officers formed a barricade around them that diverted foot traffic. Blevins' face floated into view as he sealed the helmet at Toyas' neck. A circulation fan kicked on, sending a sweet tasting wash of bottled air across his forehead. The policemen didn't say anything as they half-carried Toyas to a cruiser and pushed him into the holding tank. Blevins and an officer followed.

Blevins said, "Did Loveday cough on you? Did you touch her hands or face? How close did you get?" The officer ran a gene-scanner over Toyas' clothes. On the officer's shoulders were biotech chevrons and captain's bars. Toyas had never met a captain before. He searched for something to say.

"Oh, man," the captain said. "He's loaded."

Blevins paled. "It's not our fault. We admit no liability. Her actions were not sanctioned by the lab. Pure pirate stuff."

"What's going on?" said Toyas. His head wobbled, and he wondered blearily if the air in the helmet was doped.

Blevins ignored him. "If your people could have salvaged her palmtop sooner, none of this would have happened. Remember, we reported her. We deserve a medal."

The captain leaned back. A lurch indicated the cruiser had taken off. Where? Toyas wondered, sure now he was drugged.

"Shut up, Blevins," said the captain tiredly. "The courts will decide what to do with your company. In the meantime, how can we stop this?"

Blevins licked his lips. Toyas watched the man's lips part in slow motion, his tongue moving at quarter speed. Funny, Toyas thought, that their speech sounds fine, but they've slowed down so much.

"She tied the mutagen to a cold virus. That's her specialty, natural vectoring. Maybe we can quarantine the area, contain it all."

The captain kept his eyes closed, defeated. "We've ordered it already."

Toyas formed his words carefully. "Was it snake genes? She said something about snakes. Am I going to die?" The question felt academic, and he almost giggled.

Blevins looked at him. "No, not snakes. Why would you say that? It was a part of cow genetics. We don't know what part yet. We don't know what she wanted to do, but it's a human mutagen. She was immune."

Toyas' head dipped and circled. He was sure they could see it, although they didn't seem to notice. The world felt buttery and soft. He didn't even mind being transported to an unknown destination. In the background, the cruiser's hum sounded like bees, African bees, and he thought about Kenya, the great, wind-swept plains, and the long extinct animals. But not a lion. He pictured zebras instead, a congregation of them, heads down at the water hole. Toyas wished he were there, shoulder to shoulder in the population, at peace, taking water. He could almost feel them around him. The dust they kicked up a comforting layer on his back. The safety of the herd.

A tendril of fear eddied in him for a second. His lips parted heavily; he could barely shape the words. "They won't lock me up, will they?" He saw himself thrown in an empty hospital room. A viral contagion ward. No one to lean against. No one to reach out and touch.

Toyas held onto consciousness long enough to say, "Don't let them put me in. . .isolation."

The Sound of
One Foot Dancing

I shook the chains holding the sound stage's side doors locked, then started the long walk through the darkened studio to check the front. The day had been a full one. Mr. Sandrich, the director, had the crew knock down the Lincoln Day set and assemble the 4th of July one. He didn't like three of the flats, and they had to be redone. The dancers and extras got antsy, and all the while reporters were trying to get in to interview Fred Astaire about how he felt about yesterday's declaration of war. In the meantime, one of our cameramen had a son on the Arizona, and he didn't come to work because the navy hadn't told him whether his boy was alive or not, so I doubled as studio security and camera grip. I'd been thinking about quitting, you know, joining the war effort and all.

It was 3:00 in the morning, and I should have been going home myself, but a percussive tapping from the Holiday Inn set kept me here. Tired as I was, I had to smile. Astaire was practicing by himself again. It didn't matter when Sandrich called the day, Astaire stayed to work. I'd heard he weighed 140 pounds when the picture started. The Paramount doctor said he was down to 126 and prescribed thick steaks, which were delivered from the commissary every night at 7:00. He hardly touched them.

The front doors were locked too, so I found a chair in the dark beside the set and watched Fred Astaire dance. Only one overhead spot was turned on that isolated him in its lighted circle. His hands were in his pockets, and he danced with only one foot. The taps flew briskly, different rhythms, slow at first, a quick rattle, then a steady syncopation. He switched, so now his other foot beat out a rhythm. His head was down. I'd seen him do this before, a dancer's warmup. Soon, though, he started moving on the stage, more ice-skating than dancing, in and out of the light.

I relaxed into the seat. The steady tapping of his flashing feet lulled me and excited me too. No one could be so tired that watching Fred Astaire wouldn't wake him. Without music, he made tunes. Without a partner, he made a duet. His hands were out, practicing one side of a routine I recognized. It was the part from *Flying Down to Rio* where he and Ginger Rogers danced across seven white grand pianos. He hummed the tune, turning, turning, dipping and sliding, in the light and out. I could almost see Ginger, dress flying, anticipating his moves. He'd told me once, "Of course Ginger was able to accomplish sex through dance. We told more through our movements instead of the big clinch. We did it all through dance."

Astaire accelerated. His feet hardly touched the stage, while his tapping seemed not to come from him, but to be an accompaniment. I'd seen him dance many nights, but not like this, one hand curled around an invisible waist, the other in the air, holding an invisible hand. Round and round. Through the light, brilliantly lit, and than back to the dark, a gray shape swirling, tapping, humming his musical part.

Then, he stopped. "Where'd you go?" he said, his voice echoing in the empty studio. "Where'd you go?"

I cleared my throat. He jumped. He didn't know I'd been watching. "Where'd who go, Mr. Astaire?"

"Is that you, Pop?" He shaded his eyes from the spot and peered toward me.

"Yes, sir. Nice dancing, sir."

"Where'd the girl go?" He looked at his empty hand, puzzled.

"Girl, sir? We're alone. Studio's locked up."

"There was a girl. . .about yay tall. Dark hair. Round face." His voice trailed off. "We were dancing."

I stood, my skin as cold as marble. "You must be tired, sir. It's time to go home."

He looked at me, his forehead and cheeks white in the spot, his eyes deeply shadowed. Then he glanced behind him as if he'd heard a noise. "I was holding a girl, I could have swore. . ."

I rattled my keys. "It's been a long day, Mr. Astaire. I'll open the door for you."

When he was gone, I crossed the cavernous space, past the Valentine Day's set, through the little tree-lined road for the carriage ride, where Bing Crosby sang "Easter Parade" to Marjorie Reynolds, through the Holiday Inn set itself — the Christmas tree was next to the piano; they'd do the "White Christmas" bit this week — and then to the north doors.

They were secure, I knew they were, but I checked them anyway. When I came to *the* door, my hand trembled. The big deadlock turned stiffly — the door wasn't used much — and I pushed it open with my shoulder. Outside in the California night I saw a narrow alley, a low wall, and on the other side, shining in the star light, the glistening mausoleums and tombstones of the Hollywood Memorial Cemetery. Rudi Valentino is buried there, and so is Douglas Fairbanks. I also saw Lillian's grave, not so new now, tucked away inconspicuously next to the gaudier displays.

Lillian, who answered a call for dancers last year, another anonymous girl hoping for a movie part, who lined up with the rest, who made the first cut because she wasn't too tall, or too short, or too fat, who waited for her chance to dance, and when they called her name she stood, took her spot on the stage, put her hands on her hips, poised for the music to begin, like a thousand other girls over the years. I watched her because I always watch the dancers' auditions. Except this time, for this girl, before the music started, she swayed and fell.

I sighed. Lots of girls faint. They stand around all day, their hopes in their throats, and then their turn comes. So I walked forward, fingering the smelling salts in my pocket. She'd come to, another embarrassed performer. But she didn't. The studio doctor got there within minutes. The other dancers, all hopefuls, surrounded us. "She's gone," the doctor said.

A dancer shrieked. "It was just sleeping pills! It couldn't have killed her."

I learned that day how strong, how *obsessive*, the Hollywood dream is. Lillian had looked like a shoe-in for the part. If she flubbed her audition, then the other dancer thought she'd have a better chance, so she'd slipped her the drugs.

The doctor told me later, "Lillian must have had a weak heart, Pop, for her to collapse that way."

I don't know what killed her, but I don't believe it was a weak heart. Not *her* heart.

Lillian's tombstone glowed grayly among the others. There's something in the real dancers, like Fred Astaire, that won't quit, some steel-barred determination that keeps them on their feet long after the rest have gone to bed. I looked up and down the alley, the door's handle cool under my hand. "Go to sleep," I said into the empty night. "Go to sleep, Lillian. Quit coming back."

Most of the sound stages at Paramount have a haunt or two. It's an old studio. The first film was shot here in 1917, DeMille's *The Squaw Man*. Valentino shot *The Sheik* here in 1921, and *Wings*, which won the first ever Academy Award for best picture, was filmed here in 1927. Casts by the hundreds have come through Paramount's gates. All those dreamers filming dreams. But doors swing open on empty stages. Equipment moves.

An actress can walk from one spot to another ten feet away and suddenly shiver. "It's so cold here," she'll say, her hands wrapped round her arms.

I saw Lillian the first time a week after she died, her back to me, standing in an open door. "You can't be here, Miss. We're closed," I said. Then she turned, and I recognized her as she faded away. She returned two or three times a week, looking sad. I followed her once, walking slowly from set to set. At the end she met my eyes. I blinked, and she was gone.

I asked around. None of the other security guards knew about her. Only me. I thought, why me? Why do I always see her? Was it because I held her head as she died on the stage, so young, so unfulfilled, still waiting for her musical cue? Was that it?

When I returned to the sound stage at noon, filming had already been going for four hours. Jimmy, the morning guard, told me that Astaire was waiting at the gates at 6:00 and danced for two hours before the rest of the cast arrived. Firecrackers popped within the studio.

"He's doing the 4th of July routine again?" I asked.

Jimmy shook his head, then nodded. "The man's unstoppable."

There was applause as I approached the set. The camera crew and extras clapped. Astaire stood in the middle of the stage surrounded by wisps of firecracker smoke. "Not right yet. Let's shoot it again," he said. Then he took his starting position behind the curtains.

Mr. Sandrich looked like he wanted to say something, but he swallowed the thought, shrugged and said, "Cue the music. Take twenty-one. Cameras, action."

Astaire came through the curtains, all movement and rhythm and timing. This was supposed to be a spontaneous routine. In the story, Marjorie Reynolds, his partner, doesn't show up and two important Hollywood executives are in the audience. He grabs a handful of pocket torpedoes, and as he dances, he throws them against the ground, an explosive counterpoint to his own pyrotechnics. It's the most amazing dance routine I'd ever seen.

He turns. Bam! He skips twice, does a half pirouette. Bam! Bam! He lights an entire string of firecrackers, then dances among the explosions. All to the music. All looking like he was making it up on the spot. It was stunning.

When he finished, he didn't even appear to be breathing hard. Everyone applauded again. My hands sting with enthusiasm.

"No. It's still not right. Let's do it again." He disappeared behind the curtains.

A familiar voice said over my shoulder, "Pop, he's getting so thin, I could spit through him."

"Yes, sir, Mr. Crosby."

He shook his head in wonder as he walked away toward the sound proof practice rooms. Martha Mears, Miss Reynolds' voice double, was with him. They'd been working on the harmonies for "White Christmas" since last week.

All in all, Astaire did the firecracker routine for the cameras thirty-eight times and it was late at night before he said it was good enough. Only the essential crew members were left in the studio.

"Go home, boys," he said. "I want to get in another step or two."

The lights shut down, except for the spot he'd danced to the night before. I checked the doors. In the year since she'd died, I'd never seen Lillian dance. She walked or stood. She found me, then locked her eyes on mine, straining to communicate a mute message from beyond her grave I never understood.

Tapping came from the stage again. One foot.

"Hey, Pop," he said as I took a seat in the dark. "Let's see if we can get a curtain call from our mystery dancer."

He beat out his complicated, one-footed rhythm, hands deep in his pockets again. "You know, my character in the film is searching for a dance partner." He changed to the other foot without breaking the beat. It scraped, skipped, heel-toed, variation on variation. "I know what it's like to look for a partner. One dance. One supreme dance to glory." He sounded whimsical. "Sometimes when the music starts, it's like. . .well. . .it's like. . ." He trailed into silence, his eyes tracking off stage. "Ahh," he sighed.

I couldn't see her! Why couldn't I see her? Astaire glided to center stage. Offered his hand. Curled the other around the small of her invisible back.

I've seen Astaire dance with Ginger Rogers, with Eleanor Powell, Rita Hayworth and Grace Kelly. He's redefined what a human can do with his body to music. But I'd never seen a dance like this. Not before. Not since.

And they danced. The room grew cold. Not just a spot, but the whole studio, thousands of square feet. My exhalations were frosty plumes. I found that I was crying, the tears freezing on my cheeks, and I suddenly felt like an intruder, a peeping tom. I left. Walked through the Holiday Inn interior. The Christmas tree glittered in the little light. Bing Crosby's pipe lay on the piano top. I could almost hear him singing, "I'm dreaming of a white Christmas. . .where children listen for sleigh bells in the snow."

Then I exited. Now I stood in the Holiday Inn exterior. Impossibly, the snow machine above turned on. Oatmeal flakes tumbled down around me. I was freezing in a fake snowstorm while Fred Astaire danced with the ghost of dead girl who never made it into the pictures.

I unlocked a north door. Crossed the alley. Leapt the low wall, then walked home through the Hollywood Memorial Cemetery. I never went back to the studio. I mailed my resignation.

They released *Holiday Inn* in August of 1942. A Japanese U-boat shelled a Santa Barbara oil refinery in January. Corrigedor fell in May. We beat the Japs at Coral Sea and again at Midway, but the losses were terrible. I tried to enlist. The army wasn't interested in a prematurely gray, heavy, flat-footed thirty-two-year-old ex-security guard.

In September, finally, I went to see the movie. Someone told me that they'd seen me in the film, and I remembered that on a lark they'd used me in one scene. Didn't even change my name. I'm standing at a security door when the filming of the final Holiday Inn sequence starts, and I tell Fred Astaire and his agent they can't come in. I have one line. Behind the door, Bing Crosby and Marjorie Reynolds finally get together. If you watch the movie, you'll see me.

But that's not what's important.

I settled into the theater seat. The movie was pretty popular. That song, "White Christmas," just seemed perfect for our boys overseas, but this was a weekday matinee, and I almost had the house to myself.

It's a sweet story. I'd almost forgotten. Bing Crosby loses his girl to Fred Astaire, and then he has a bad go of it as a farmer, then he tries show business again at Holiday Inn, a nightclub only open on holidays. Crosby meets Reynolds, and they fall in love, only to have Astaire come along and try to steal her too. I waited for the 4th of July number. How would it play on the screen? Would anyone see that Astaire used thirty-eight takes to look like he'd made it up on the spot?

The scene approached. There's a ensemble song and dance number before Astaire's firecracker routine. I was watching, my eyes half closed. A line of girls comes onto the stage from one side, a line of guys from the other. They're singing a patriotic tune about the 4th. The guys group at the back of the stage singing the bass line. Half the girls split off into the audience, the other half, six girls, have formed three pairs, backs to the camera. The first pair faces the audience to sing, "Let's salute our native land." The next pair turns, "Roman candles in each hand." Then the last pair sings, "While the Yankee doodle band."

I don't hear any more. I'm standing in the theater, pointing at the screen.

The girl on the right is Lillian. She sings and dances through the rest of the scene. It's Lillian.

Astaire danced her right into the movie. He got her a part. Rent the video if you don't believe me.

I never saw Fred Astaire again.

After Astaire died at eighty-eight, Mikhaile Baryshinikov said, "It's no secret we hate him. He gives us complexes because he's too perfect. His perfection is an absurdity."

They buried him at Oakwood Memorial Park not far from Ginger Rogers' grave.

I wish they'd put him at Hollywood Memorial, where his real partner rests, the one who danced her way into *Holiday Inn*. The only one light enough on her feet to match him, step for step.

A Flock of Birds

The starlings wheeled like a giant blanket flung into the sky, like sentient smoke, banking and turning in unison. They passed overhead so close that Carson heard their wings ripping the air, and when the flock flew in front of the sun, the world grew gray. Carson shivered even though it was only early September and warm enough for a short-sleeved shirt. This close he could smell them, all dark-feathered and frantic and dry and biting.

He estimated maybe 50,000 birds. Not the largest flock he'd seen this year, but one of the bigger ones, and certainly bigger than anything he'd seen last year. Of course, the summer before that he didn't watch the birds. No one did. No chance to add to his life list that year. No winter count either. The Colorado Field Ornithology office closed.

He leaned back in his lawn chair. The bird vortex moved east, over the wheat-grass plain until the sun brightened again, pressing pleasant heat against the back of his hands and arms. He was glad for the hat that protected his head and its middle-aged bald spot. This wasn't the time to mess with skin cancer, he thought, not a good time at all. He was glad his teeth were generally healthy and his eyesight was keen.

The binoculars were excellent, Bausch & Lomb Elite. Wide field of vision. Top notch optics. Treated lenses. He'd picked them up from a sporting goods store in Littleton's South Glenn Mall. Through them the birds became singular. He followed discrete groups. They swirled, coming straight toward him for a moment, then sliding away. Slowly he scanned the flight until he reached the leading edge. Birds on one half and sky on the other. They switched direction and the leaders became the followers. He took the binoculars away and blinked at their loss of individuality. In the middle, where the birds were thickest, the shape was black, a sinuous, twisting dark chord. One dot separated itself from the others, flying against the current. Carson only saw it for a second, but it was distinctly larger than the starlings, and its wing beat was different. He focused the binoculars again, his breath coming fast, and scanned the flock. It would be unusual for a single bird of a different species to fly with the starlings.

Nothing for several minutes other than the hordes streaming by, then the strange bird emerged. Long, slender wings, a reddish breast, and it was *fast*. Much faster than the starlings and twice their size. The cloud shifted, swallowing it, as the entire flock drifted slowly east, farther into the plains.

The bird looked familiar. Not one from his journals, but one he'd seen a picture of before. Something tropical perhaps that had drifted north? Every once in a while a single representative of a species would be spotted, hundreds, sometimes thousands of miles from where it was normally found. The birder who saw it could only hope that someone else confirmed the sighting or that he got a picture, otherwise it would be discounted and couldn't be legitimately added to a life list. If he could add a new bird to his list, maybe that would make things better. A new bird! He could concentrate on that. Something good to cling to.

The flock grew small in the distance.

Carson sighed, put the binoculars back in their case, then packed the rest of his gear into the truck. He checked the straps that held his motorcycle in place. They were tight. The tie-down holding the extra batteries for the truck and motorcycle were secure too. From his spot on the hill he could see the dirt road he'd taken from the highway and the long stretch of I-25 that reached north toward Denver and south to Colorado Springs. No traffic. The air above the Denver skyline was crystalline. He strained his ears, tilting his head from one side then the other. He hadn't heard a car on the highway behind him all afternoon. Grass rustle. Moldy-leaf smells, nothing else, and when he finally opened the truck's door, the metallic click was foreign and loud.

Back at his house in Littleton, he checked the photoelectric panels' gauges inside the front door. It had been sunny for the last week, so the system was full. The water tower showed only four-hundred gallons though. He'd have to go water scavenging again in the next few days.

"I'm home," he called. His voice echoed off the tiled foyer. "Tillie?"

The living room was empty, and so were the kitchen and bedrooms. Carson stepped into the bathroom, his hand on his chest where his heart beat fast, but the sleeping pills in the cabinet looked undisturbed. "Tillie?"

He found her sitting in the back yard beneath the globe willow, still in her robe. The nightgown beneath it was yellowed and tattered. In her dresser he'd put a dozen new ones, but she'd only wear the one she had in her suitcase when he'd picked her up, wandering through the Denver Botanical Gardens two years ago.

He sat on the grass next to her. She was fifty or so. Lots of gray in her blond hair. Slender wrists. Narrow face. Strikingly blue eyes that hardly ever focused on anything.

"How's that cough?" he asked.

"We never play bridge anymore, Bob Robert."

Carson stretched out. A day with binoculars pressed to his face and his elbows braced on his knees hurt his back. "Tough to get partners," he said. Then he added out of habit, "And I'm not Bob Robert."

She picked at a loose thread in the robe, pulling at it until it broke free. "Have you seen the garden? Not a flower in it. A single geranium or a daisy would give me hope. If just one dead thing would come back."

"I've brought you seeds," he said. "You just need to plant them."

She wrapped the thread around her fingertip tightly. "I waited for the pool man, but he never came. I hate skimming." She raised her fist to her mouth and coughed primly behind it twice, grimacing each time.

Carson raised his head. Other than the grass under the tree, most of the yard was dirt. The lot was longer than it was wide. At the end farthest from the house a chicken wire enclosure surrounded the poultry. A couple hens sat in the shade by the coop. No pool. When he'd gone house hunting, he'd toyed with the idea of a pool, but the thought of trying to keep it filled and the inevitable problems with water chemistry made him decide against it. The house on the other side of the privacy fence had a pool as did most of the houses in the neighborhood, now empty except for the scummy pond in the deep end. In the spring he'd found a deer, its neck bent unnaturally back, at the bottom of one a block over. Evidently it had jumped the fence and gone straight in.

"Are you hungry?" Carson asked.

Tillie tilted her head to the side. "When will the garden grow again?"

He pushed himself off the ground. "I'll fix eggs."

Later that evening, he tucked Tillie in bed. The room smelled of peppermint. From the bulge in her cheek, he guessed she was sucking on one. In a little-girl voice, she said, "Can you put in my video?" Her expression was alert, but her eyes were red-rimmed and watery. He smiled. This was as good as she got. Sometimes he could play gin rummy with her and she'd stay focused for an hour or so before she drifted away. If he asked her about her past, she'd be unresponsive for days. All he knew about her came from the suitcase she carried when he'd found her. There was a sheet of letterhead with a name at the top: "Tillie Waterhouse, Marketing Executive," and an athletic club identification card with her picture and name. But there was no Tillie Waterhouse in the Denver phone book. Could she have wandered away from the airport when air travel was canceled?

The first words she had said to him, when she finally spoke, were, "How do you bear it?"

"Did you have a good day?" He turned on the television and pressed rewind on the VCR.

Her hands peeked out from under the covers and pulled them tight under her chin. "Something magical is going to happen. The leaves whispered to me."

The video clicked to a stop. "I'm glad to hear that," he said. The television flickered as the tape started, a documentary on the 2001 New York City Marathon a decade earlier. It opened with a helicopter flyover of the racers crossing the Verrazano-Narrows Bridge into Brooklyn. The human crowd surged forward, packed elbow to elbow, long as the eye could see. Then the camera cut to ankle level. Feet ran past for five minutes. Then it went to face level at a turn in the course. The starting crush had spread out, but the runners still jogged within an arm's length of each other, thousands of them. Carson had watched the video with her the first few times. The video was a celebration of numbers. Thirty-thousand athletes straining over the twenty-six mile course through New York City's five boroughs.

"Here's the remote if you want to watch it again."

"So many American flags," she said.

"It was only a month after that first terrorist thing." Carson sat on the end of her bed. Some runners wore stars and stripes singlets or racing shorts. Others carried small flags and waved them at the camera as they passed.

"I won't be able to sleep," she said.

He nodded. "Me either."

Before he left, he pressed his hand to her forehead. She looked up briefly, the blanket still snug against her chin. A little fever and her breath sounded wheezy.

Later that night he made careful entries in his day book. A breeze through the open window freshened the room. He'd spotted a mountain plover, a long-billed curlew, a burrowing owl and a horned lark, plus the usual assortment of lark sparrows, yellow warblers, western meadowlarks, red-winged blackbirds, crows, black terns and mourning doves. Nothing unusual beside the strange bird in the starling flock. Idly he thumbed through his bird identification handbook. No help there. Could it actually be a new bird? Something to add to his life list?

Tomorrow he'd take the camera. Several major flocks roosted in the elms along the Platte River. He hadn't done a riparian count in a couple months anyway. After visiting the distribution center, he'd go to the river. With an early enough start, he would still have ten hours of sun to work with.

He shut the book and turned off his desk light. Gradually his eyes adjusted as he looked out the window. A full moon illuminated the scene. From his chair he could see three houses bathed in the leaden glow, their windows black as basalt. His neighbor's minivan rested on its rims, all four tires long gone flat. Carson tried to come up with the guy's name, but it remained elusive. Generally he tried not to think about his neighbors or their empty houses.

He couldn't hear anything other than the wind moving over the silent city. Not sleepy at all, he watched the shadows slide slowly across the lawn. Just after 2:00 a.m., a pair of coyotes trotted up the middle of the street. Their toenails clicked loudly against the asphalt. Carson finally rose, took two sleeping pills and went to bed.

"The woman who stays with me is sick," said Carson. He rested his arm against his truck, supplies requisition list in hand.

The distribution center manager nodded dourly. "Oh, the sweet sorrow of parting." He hooked his grimy thumbs in his overalls. Through the warehouse doors behind him Carson saw white plastic wrapped bales, four feet to a side, stacked five bales high and reaching to the warehouse's far end. They contained bags of flour, corn, cloth, paper, a little bit of everything. Emergency stores.

Carson blanched. "It's not that. She just has a cough and a bit of fever. If it's bacterial, an antibiotic might knock it right out."

"T.B. or not T.B. That is congestion, Carson," he said, laughing through yellow teeth. Carson guessed he might be fifty-five or sixty.

Carson smiled. "You're pretty sharp today."

"Finest collection of video theater this side of hell. Watched Lawrence Olivier last night until 3:00 or 4:00." The manager consulted his clipboard. "No new pharmaceuticals in a couple months, and I haven't seen antibiotics in over a year. I could have my assistant keep an eye open for you, but he hasn't come in for a week. Lookin' sickly his last day, you know?" The manager rubbed his fingers on his chest. "Could be that I've lost him. Have you tried a tablespoon of honey in a shot glass of bourbon? Works for me every time."

A car pulled into the huge, empty parking lot behind Carson's truck, but whoever was inside didn't get out. Carson nodded in the car's direction. Evidently they wanted to wait for Carson to finish his business.

He handed the manager the list. "Can you also give me cornmeal and sugar? A mix of canned vegetables would be nice too."

"That I've got." The manager hopped on a forklift. "Tomorrow may creep in a petty pace, but I shouldn't be a minute."

When he returned with the goods he said, "The quality of mercy is not strained here. I'm not doing anything this afternoon. I'll dig some for you. Few months back I heard a pharmacy in an Albertson's burned down. Looters overlooked it. Might be something there. I've got your address." He waved the requisition list. "I could bring it by your house."

Carson loaded boxes of canned soup and vegetables into the truck. "What about the warehouse?"

The manager shrugged. "Guess we're on an honor system now. Only a dozen or so customers a day. Maybe a couple hundred total. I'll bet there aren't 50,000 people alive in the whole country. I'll leave the doors open." For a moment the manager stared into the distance, as if he'd lost his thought. Behind them, the waiting car rumbled. "You know how they say that if you put a jellybean in a jar every time you make love the first year that you're married, and you take one out every time you make love after that, that the jar will never be empty? This warehouse is a little like that."

When Carson started the truck, the manager leaned into the window, resting his arms on the car door. This close, Carson could see how greasy the man's hair was, and it smelled like old lard.

The manager's smile was gone. "How long have you known me?" he said, looking Carson straight in the eye. His voice was suddenly so serious.

Carson tried not to shrink away. He thought back. "I don't know. Six-teen months?"

The manager grimaced. "That makes you my oldest friend. There isn't anyone alive that I've known longer."

For a second, Carson was afraid the man would begin crying. Instead, he straightened, his hands still on the door.

Tentatively, Carson said, "I'm sorry. I don't think I've ever asked what your name was."

"Nope, nope, no need," the manager barked, smiling again. "A rose by any other moniker, as they say. I'll see what I can find you in the coughing line. Don't know about antibiotics. Come back tomorrow."

It wasn't until Carson had driven blocks away toward the river, as he watched the boarded up stores slide by, as he moved down the empty streets, past the mute houses that he realized, other than Tillie, the manager was his oldest friend too.

* * *

Sitting on his camp chair, Carson had a panoramic river view. On the horizon to the west, the mountains rose steeply, only a remnant of last winter's snow clinging to the tops of the tallest peaks. Fifty yards away at the bottom of a short bluff, the river itself, at its lowest level of the season, rolled sluggishly. Long gravel tongues protruded into the water where little long legged birds searched for insects between the rocks. A bald eagle swept low over the water going south. Carson marked it in his notebook.

Across the river stood clumps of elm and willows. He didn't need his binoculars to see the branches were heavy with roosting starlings. Counting individuals was impossible. He'd have to estimate. He wondered what the distribution manager would make of the birds. After all, they had something in common. If it weren't for Shakespeare, the starlings wouldn't be here at all. In the early 1890s, a club of New York Anglophiles thought it would be comforting if all the birds mentioned in Shakespeare's plays lived in America. They tried nightingales and chaffinches and various thrushes, but none succeeded like the 100 European starlings they released in Central Park. By the last count there were over two-hundred million of them. He'd read an article in one of his bird books that called them "avian cockroaches."

He set up his camera on a tripod and scanned the trees with the telephoto. Not only were there starlings, but also red winged blackbirds, an aggressive, native species. They could hold their own against invaders.

Carson clicked a few shots. He could edit the photos out of the camera's memory later if he needed the space. A group of starlings lifted from some of the trees. Maybe something disturbed them? He looked for a deer or racoon on the ground below, but couldn't see anything. The birds swirled upwards before sweeping down river. He thought about invaders, like infection, spreading across the country. Carp were invaders. So were zebra mussels that hitchhiked in ships' ballast water and became a scourge, attaching themselves to the inside of pipes used to draw water into power plants.

It wasn't just animals either. Crabgrass, dandelions, kudzu, knotweed, tamarisk, leafy spurge and norway maple, pushing native species to extinction.

Infection. Extinction. And extinct meant you'd never come back. No hope.

Empty houses. Empty shopping malls. Empty theaters. Contrail-free skies. Static on the radio. Traffic-free highways. The creak of wind-pushed swing sets in dusty playgrounds. He pictured Tillie's video, the endless runners pouring across the bridge.

Carson shook his head. He'd never get the count done if he day-dreamed. Last year he spotted 131 species in the fall count. Maybe this year he'd find more. Maybe he'd see something rare, like a yellow-billed loon or a fulvous whistling duck.

Methodically, he moved his focus from tree to tree. Mostly starlings, their beaks resting on their breasts. Five-hundred in one tree. A thousand in the next. He held the binoculars in his left hand while writing the numbers with his right. Later he'd fill out a complete report for the Colorado Field Ornithologists. A stack of reports sat on his desk at home, undeliverable.

He couldn't hear the birds from here, but their chirping calls would be overwhelming if he could walk beneath them.

A feathered blur whipped through his field of vision. Carson looked over the top of his binoculars. Two birds skimmed the tree tops, heading upriver. He stood, breath coming quick. Narrow wings. Right size. He found them in the binoculars. Were they the same kind of bird he'd seen yesterday? What luck! But they flew too fast and they were going away. He'd never be able to identify them from this distance. If only they'd circle back. Then, unbelievably, they turned, crossing the river, coming toward him. The binoculars thumped against his chest when he dropped them, as he picked up the camera, tripod and all. He found the birds, focused, and snapped a picture. They kept coming. He snapped again, both birds in view. Closer even still until just one bird filled the frame. Snap. Then they whipped past, only twenty feet overhead. And fast! Faster than any bird he'd seen except a peregrine falcon on a dive.

His hands trembled. Definitely a bird new to him. A new species to add to his life list. And the bird he'd seen yesterday couldn't be a single, mis-placed wanderer, not if there were two of them here. Maybe a flock had been blown into the area. He knew Colorado birds, and these weren't native.

He stayed another hour, counting starlings and recording the other river birds that crossed his path, but his heart wasn't in it. In his camera waited the image of the new bird, but he'd have to transfer it to the computer where he could study it.

Tillie was in bed. Beside her, on the night stand, were packets of seeds. She hadn't moved them since he'd brought them to her in the spring. The television was on. There were, of course, no broadcasts, so gray snow filled the screen, and the set softly hissed. Carson turned it off, darkening the room. Sun light leaked around the closed curtains, but after the brightness outside, he could barely see. In the silence, Tillie's breathing rasped. He tiptoed around her bed to put his hand to her forehead. Distinctly warm. She didn't move when he touched her.

"Tillie?" he said.

She mumbled but didn't open her eyes.

Carson turned on her reading light, painting her face in highlights and sharp shadows. He knelt beside her. Her lips were parted slightly, and she licked them before taking her next rattling breath. He wanted to jostle her awake. She slept so poorly most nights that he resisted. The fever startled him. As long as it was just a cough, he hadn't worried much. A cough, that could be a cold or an allergy. But a fever, that was a red flag. He remembered all the home defense brochures with their sobering titles: FAMILY TRIAGE and KNOW YOUR SYMPTOMS. "Tillie, I need to check your chest."

His fingers shook as he pulled the blanket away from her chin. Her neck was clammy, and underneath the covers she was sweating. She *smelled* warm and damp. Clumsily he unbuttoned her nightgown's top buttons, then he moved the light so he could see better. No rash. She wasn't wearing a bra, so he could see that the tops of her breasts looked smooth. "Tillie?" he whispered, really not wanting to wake her. Her eyes moved under her eyelids. Maybe she dreamed of other places, the places she would never talk to him about. Gently he rubbed his fingertips over the skin below her collarbones. No boils. No "bumpy swellings" the brochures described.

Tillie mumbled again. "Bob Robert," she said.

"I'll get some aspirin and water." He pulled the blanket back up. She didn't move.

"You're nice," she said, but her head was turned away, and he wasn't sure if she was talking to him or continuing a conversation in her dream.

As he poured water from a bottle in the refrigerator, he realized that it would be difficult to tell if Tillie became delirious. If she started talking sense, *then* he'd have to worry about her.

The distribution manager had said to come back the next day, so there was nothing to do other than to give her aspirin and keep her comfortable. She woke up enough to take the medicine, but closed her eyes immediately. Carson patted her on the top of her hands, made sure the water pitcher was full, then went to his office where he printed the pictures from his camera. The last one was quite good. Full view of the bird's beak, head, neck, breast, wing shape and tail feathers. Identification should have been easy, but nothing matched in his books. He needed better resources.

Driving to Littleton library meant passing the landfill. Most days Carson tried to ignore it — it reminded him of Arlington Cemetery without the tombstones — but today he stopped at the side of the road. He needed a place to think, and the broad, featureless land lent itself to meditations. Last year swarms of gulls circled, waiting for places to set down. The ones on the ground picked at the remnants of flags that covered the low hills. The year before, wreaths and flags and sticks festooned with ribbons dotted the mounds while earth movers ripped long ditches and chugged diesel exhaust. Today, though, no birds. He supposed there was nothing left for them to eat. No smells to attract them. The earth movers were parked off to the side in a neat row. Dust swirled across the dirt in tiny eddies that danced for a moment, then dissipated into nothing. The ground looked as plain as his back yard. Not a tree anywhere or grass. He thought about Tillie searching for a geranium.

He looked up. The sky was completely empty. No hawks. Could it be that not even a mouse lived in the landfill?

What would he do if she left? He leaned against the car, his hands deep in his pockets, chin on his chest. What if she were gone? So many had departed: the girl at the magazine stand, the counter people at the bagel shop, his coworkers. What was it he used to do? He could barely remember, just like he couldn't picture his wife's face clearly anymore. All of them, slipping away.

He slid his fingers inside his shirt. No bumps there either. Why not, and were they inevitable?

A wind kicked across the plain, scurrying scraps of paper and more dust toward him in a wave. He could taste rain in the air. Weather's changing, he thought, and climbed back into the car before the wind reached him.

Skylights illuminated the library's main room. Except for the stale smell and the thin coating of neglect on the countertops and the leather chairs arranged in cozy reading circles, it could be open for business. Carson saw no evidence that anyone had been here since his last visit a month ago. He checked his flashlight. Sunlight didn't penetrate to the back stacks where the bird books were, and he wanted to make sure he didn't miss any.

On the bulletin board inside the front doors hung civil defense and the Center for Disease Control posters filled with the familiar advice: avoid crowds, get good sleep, report symptoms immediately. The civil defense poster reminded him that PATRIOTS PROTECT THEIR IMMUNE SYS-TEMS and the depressing, REMEMBER, IT GOT THEM FIRST.

The cart he found had a wheel that shook and didn't track with the others. It pulled to the left and squeaked loudly as he pushed it between the rows. In the big building, the noise felt out of place. Absurdly, Carson almost said, "Shhh!" A library was *supposed* to be quiet, even if he was the only one in it.

Back at the bird books, he ran his flashlight across the titles, all his favorite tomes: the Audubon books and the National Geographic ones. The two huge volumes of Bailey and Niedriach's *Birds of Colorado* with their beautiful photographs and drawings. He placed them in the cart lovingly. By the time he finished, he'd arranged thirty-five books on the cart, every bird reference they had. He shivered as he straightened the collection. The back of the library had never felt cold before.

At the checkout desk, he agonized over what to do. When he was a child, the librarian filled out a card that was tucked in the book's front cover. Everything was computerized now. How was he going to check the books out? Not that it was likely anyone would want them, but it didn't feel right, just taking them. Finally he wrote a note with all the titles listed. He stuck it to the librarian's computer, thought about it for a second, then wrote a second one to put into the gap he'd left in the shelves. He added his address and a p.s., "If you really need these books, please contact me."

Before going, he wandered into the medical section. Infectious diseases were in the 600 area. There wasn't a title left. He took a deep breath that tickled his throat. It felt odd, so he did it again, provoking a string of deep coughs. It's just the dust in here, he thought, but his lungs felt heavy, and he realized he'd been holding off the cough all day.

Carson stopped at the distribution center on the way home. The parking lot was empty. He wandered through the warehouse, between the high stacks, down the long rows. No manager. No assistant. Last year Carson had hauled a diesel generator into a theater near his house. He'd rigged it to power a projector so he could watch a movie on the big screen, but the empty room with all the empty seats gave him the creeps. He'd fled the theater without even turning off the generator. The warehouse felt like that. As he walked toward the exit, his strides became faster and faster until he was running.

As the sun set into the heavy clouds on the horizon, he accepted the obvious. Whatever Tillie had, he had too. She breathed shallowly between coughing fits, and, although the fever responded to aspirin, it rebounded quickly. The aspirin helped with his own fever, but he felt headachy and tired.

Sitting beside her bed, he put his hand on her arm. "I'm going to go back to the Distribution Center tomorrow, Tillie. He said he might find some medicine."

Tillie turned toward him, her eyes gummy and bloodshot. "Don't go," she said. Her voice quivered, but she looked directly at him. No drifting. Speaking deliberately, she said, "Everybody I know has gone away."

Carson looked out the window. It would be dark soon.

Tillie's arm burned beneath his fingertips. He could almost feel the heated blood rushing through her. "I've got to do something. You might have pneumonia."

She inhaled several times. Carson imagined the pain; an echo of it pulsed in his own chest.

"Could you stay in the neighborhood?" she asked.

He nodded.

Tillie closed her eyes. "When it started, I watched TV all the time. That's all I did, was watch TV. My friends watched TV. They played it at work. 'A Nation Under Quarantine' the newscasters called it. And then I couldn't watch any more."

Carson blinked his eyes shut against the burning. That's where he didn't want to go, into *those* memories. It's what he didn't think about when he sat in his camp chair counting birds. It's what he didn't picture when he bolted solar cells onto the roof, when he gathered wood for the new wood stove he'd installed in the living room, when he pumped gasoline out of underground tanks at silent gas stations. Sometimes he had a hard time imagining anything was wrong at all. When he drove, the car still responded to his touch. The wind whistled tunelessly past his window. How could the world still be so familiar and normal and yet so badly skewed?

"Well, we keep doing what has to be done, despite it all," he said.

"I was innocent." Her gaze slid away from his, and she smiled. Carson saw her connection to him sever. The shift was nearly audible. "I don't want to see the news tonight. Maybe there will be a nice rerun later. *Friends* or *Cheers* would be good. I'll go to the mall in the morning. The fall fashions should be in." She settled into her pillow as if to go to sleep.

Carson set up a vaporizer, hoping that would make her breathing easier, then quietly shut her door before leaving.

Crowbar in hand, he crossed the dirt expanse that was his front yard, stepped over the dry-leafed hedge between his yard and the neighbors. The deadbolt splintered out of the frame when he leaned on the crowbar, and one kick opened the door. The curtains were closed, darkening the living room. Carson wrinkled his nose at the house's mustiness. Under that smell lingered something rotten, like mildew and bad vegetables gone slimy and black.

He flicked on his flashlight. The living room was neat, magazines fanned across a coffee table for easy selection, glass coasters piled on a small stand by a lounge chair and family photos arranged on the wall. Three bedroom doors opened into the main hallway. In one, a crib stood empty beneath a Mickey Mouse mobile. In the second, his light played across an office desk, a fax machine and a laptop computer, its top popped open and keyboard waiting.

The third door led to the master bedroom. In the bathroom medicine cabinet he found antacids, vitamins and birth control pills, but no antibiotics. When he left the house, he closed the front door as best he could.

An hour later he'd circled the block, breaking into every house along the way. Two of the houses had already been looted. The door on the first hung from only one hinge. In the second, the furniture was overturned, and a complicated series of cracks emanated from a single bullet hole in the living room window. In some of the houses the bed sheets covered long lumps. He stayed out of the bedrooms. No antibiotics.

His chest heavy, barely able to lift his feet, he trudged across the last lawn to his house where one window was lit. Whatever the illness was, it felt serious. Not a cold or flu, but down deep malignant, sincere, like nothing he'd ever had before. This was how he felt, and he'd started in good shape, but Tillie hardly ever ate well. She never exercised. Her system would be especially vulnerable. He pictured his house empty. No Tillie gazing over her cards before drawing. No Tillie wandering in the yard, looking for a single geranium to give her hope. "How do you bear it?" she'd asked.

Tillie was sleeping, her fever down again, but her breathing was just as hoarse. In his own lungs, each inhalation fluttered and buzzed. He imagined a thousand tiny pinwheels whirling away inside him.

Carson started the New York City Marathon video, then returned to the chair next to Tillie's bed. He wet a washcloth then pressed it against her forehead. She didn't move. "What a celebration of life," said the announcer. "In the shadow of disaster, athletes have gathered to say we can't be beat in the long run." A map of the course winding through the five boroughs appeared on the screen. Then a camera angle from a helicopter skimming over the streets showing the human river. At one point a dozen birds flew between the camera and the ground. "Doves," thought Carson, feeling flush. Even his eyes felt warm, and when he finally rested his head on Tillie's arm, he couldn't feel a difference in their temperatures.

*   *   *

He dreamed about bird books spread across a desk in front of him, but he wasn't in his office. Other desks filled the room, and at each one a person sat, studying books. In the desk beside his, a man with tremendous sideburns that drooped to the sides of his neck picked up a dead bird, spread its wing feathers apart, scrutinizing each connection. He placed the bird back on his desk, then added a few lines to a drawing of it on an easel.

"Purple finch," said the man, and Carson knew with dreamlike certainty that it was John Audubon. "A painting is forever, even if the bird is not." Audubon poked at the feathered pile. "It's a pity I have to kill them to preserve them."

"I'm searching for a bird's name," said Carson. Some of the people at the other desks looked up in interest. He described the bird. "I've only seen three of them flying with European starlings."

"Only three?" Audubon looked puzzled. "They flew in flocks that filled the sky for days. Outside of Louisville, the people were all in arms. The banks of the Ohio were crowded with men and boys, incessantly shooting at the birds. Multitudes were destroyed, and for a week or more the population fed on no other flesh, and you saw only three?"

Carson nodded.

"With European starlings?"

Carson was at a loss. How could he explain to Audubon about birds introduced to America after his death? He said instead, "But what is the bird's name?"

"Purple finch, I told you."

"No, I mean the bird I described."

Audubon picked up his pencil and added another line to the drawing. He mumbled an answer.

"Excuse me?" said Carson.

More mumbling. Audubon continued drawing. The bird didn't look like a finch, purple or otherwise. His lines grew wilder as the bird became more and more fantastic. He sketched flames below it with quick, sure strokes, all the while mumbling, louder and louder.

Carson strained to understand him. What was the bird? What was it? And he became aware that the mumbling was hot and moist in his ear. With a jerk, he sat up. Tillie's lips were moving, but her eyes were shut. What time was it? Where was he? For a moment he felt completely dissociated from the world.

Two aspirins in hand, he tried waking her up, but she refused to open her eyes. Her cheeks were red, and in between incoherent bursts of speech, her breathing was labored, as if she were a deep-sea diver, bubbling from the depths. Her forehead felt hot again. A sudden shivering attack took him, and for a minute it was all he could do to grit his teeth against the shaking. When it passed, he swallowed the aspirins he'd brought for her. Maybe there might be antibiotics in one of the houses a block over.

He put on a coat against his chills, grabbed the crowbar and flashlight, then crossed the street. In the night air, his head seemed light and large, but walking was a strain. The crowbar weighed a thousand pounds.

In the second house he found a plastic bottle marked PENICILLIN in a medicine cabinet. He laughed in relief, then coughed until he sat on the bathroom floor, the flashlight beside him casting long, weird shadows. Only two tablets, 250 mg. each. They hardly weighed anything in his hand. What was an adult dosage? Was penicillin the right treatment for pneumonia? What if she didn't have pneumonia, or she did but it was viral instead of bacterial?

Carson staggered back home. After fifteen minutes, he was able to rouse Tillie enough to take the pills and the aspirin. Exhausted, he collapsed on the chair by her bed. He put his head back and stared at the ceiling. Swirls and broad lines marked the plaster. For a moment he thought they were clouds, and in the clouds he saw a bird, the narrow winged one that he'd seen by the river, the one Audubon said he knew, and suddenly, Carson knew too. He'd always known, and he laughed. No wonder it looked familiar. Of course he couldn't find it in his bird books.

Smiling, holding Tillie's hand, he fell asleep.

A pounding roused him.

Thump, thump, thump. Like a heartbeat. His eyelids came apart reluctantly and gradually he focused on the length of bedspread that started at his cheek and reached to the bed's end. Without moving, without even really knowing where he was, he knew he was sick. Sickness can't be forgotten. Even in his sleep, he must have been aware of the micro war within. It surged through him, alienating his organs, his skin. The machine is breaking down, he thought.

"Someone's at the door," said Tillie. She stirred beside him. "It might be the pool man."

Carson pushed himself from the bed, his back cracking in protest. His legs felt wooden. How long had he been next to her?

She was sitting up, blankets over her legs, an open book face down under her hands. "You've been sleeping, Bob Robert," she said brightly.

He put a hand against her forehead, then against his own. "I'm not Bob Robert." She was cooler, and the wheezing in her chest didn't sound quite as bad. The empty penicillin bottle sat on the night stand beneath her reading light. Could antibiotics work that fast? Even if they did, one dose wouldn't cure whatever they had. She'd relapse. He'd get sicker. He needed to find more.

A pounding from the front of the house again.

He stood shakily, his chest aching on each breath.

"I'll be back," he said.

"Oh, I'm all right. A bit of reading will do me good." She opened the book. It was one from his office. Sometime during the night she must have gotten out of bed.

Carson braced himself against the hallway wall as he walked to the front door, hunched over from the illness. His head throbbed and the sunlight through the front window was too bright.

"Carson, are you in there?" a voice yelled. "Birnam wood has come to Elsinore," it shouted.

Through the pain and fever, Carson squinted. He opened the door. "Isn't it Dunsinane that Birnam comes to?"

The warehouse manager balanced a box on his hip. "I saw the damndest thing on the way here." He started. " Jeeze, man! You look terrible."

Carson nodded, trying to put the scene together. The manager's truck was parked next to his own in the driveway. The sun lingered high in the sky.

How long had he been sleeping? Carson forced the words out in little gasps. "What are you doing?"

Grabbing Carson's arm, the manager helped him into the living room onto the couch. "I found the antibiotics I told you about," he said. "It wasn't in the pharmacy. The place burned to the ground." The manager ripped open the box lid. Inside were rows of small, white boxes. Inside the first box were hundreds of pills. He plucked two out. "But in the delivery area behind the store, there was a UPS truck chock full of medicine."

Carson blinked, and the manager offered him a glass of water for the pills. When did he get up to fetch the water?

"Your chest is heavy, right, and you're feverish and tired?"

"Yes," croaked Carson.

"I can hear your lungs from here. Pneumonia, for sure, I'll bet. If we're lucky, this'll knock it right out."

Carson swallowed the pills. Sitting, he felt better. It took the pressure off his breathing. Tillie had looked healthier. Maybe the penicillin helped her, and if it helped her, it could help him.

The manager walked around the room, stopping at the photoelectric panel's gauges. "You have a sweet set up here. Did you do the wiring yourself?"

Carson nodded. He croaked, "Why aren't you at the warehouse?" The light in the room flickered. Ponderously, Carson turned his head. Through the picture window, it seemed for a moment as if shadows raced over the houses, but when he checked again, the sun shone steadily.

Without looking at him, the manager said, "Time to move on. That warehouse paralyzed me. I've been waiting, I think. Olivier's Hamlet said last night, 'If it be now, tis not to come; if it be not to come it will be now.'"

"What was he talking about?" asked Carson.

"Fear of death. Grief," said the manager. "The readiness is all, he said. Ah, who is this?"

Tillie stood at the entrance to the hallway. She'd changed into jeans and a work shirt. Her face was still feverish and she swayed a little. "Oh, good, the pool man," she said. Without pausing for a reply, she waved a handful of packets at them. "I'm tired of waiting for flowers, Carson. I'm going to plant something."

Confused, he said, "It's nearly winter," but she'd already disappeared. He rubbed his brow, and his hand came away wet with sweat. "Did she call me Carson?"

Shadows hurried across the street again, and this time the manager looked too.

"What is that?" asked Carson.

"I was going to ask you." The manager stepped out the door and glanced up. "I saw them on the way over. They're funny birds."

Carson heaved himself out of the couch. His head swam so violently that he nearly fell, but he caught himself and made it to the door. He held the manager's arm to stay steady.

Overhead, the flock streamed across the sky, barely above the rooftops. Making no sound. Hundreds of them. Narrow wings. Red breasts.

"What are they?" asked the manager.

Carson straightened. Even sickness couldn't knock him down for this. The birds zoomed like feathered jets. Where had they been all these years? Had there just been a few hidden in the remotest forests, avoiding human eyes? Had they teetered on the edge of extinction for a century without actually disappearing despite all evidence to the contrary? Was it conceivable to return to their glory?

Carson said, "They're passenger pigeons."

The manager said, "What's a passenger pigeon?"

It's an addition to my life list, thought Carson. Audubon said they'd darkened the skies for days. Carson remembered the New York City Marathon. The people kept running and running and running. They filled the Verrazano-Narrows Bridge.

"I guess sometimes things can come back," said Carson.

The impossible birds wheeled to the east.

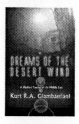

About the Author

James Van Pelt ws born in 1954 in Akron, Ohio, but grew up in Littleton, Colorado, not too far from Martin Marrietta's rocket engine testing plant in the Waterton Canyon. When the weather conditions were right, test firings rattled the windows in his house.

He graduated Metro State College in Denver in 1978 with a bachelor's degree in English and history and a high school teaching certificate. He earned an M.A. in creative writing from the University of California at Davis in 1990. His poetry, non-fiction and stories have appeared in numerous magazines and anthologies, including *Asimov's, Analog, Alfred Hitchcock's Mystery Magazine, Realms of Fantasy, Talebones* and many others. His stories have been reprinted in Gardner Dozois's *Year's Best Science Fiction*, David Hartwell's *Year's Best Fantasy*, and Stephen Jones's *The Mammoth Book of New Horror*. "The Last of the O-Forms" was a Nebula finalist in 2004. Other stories have

been recommended for Nebula and Stoker awards, and included in both Dozois's and Ellen Datlow's year's best honorable mention lists. In 1999, Van Pelt was a finalist for the John W. Campbell Award for Best New Writer.

Strangers and Beggars, his first collection, was named by the American Library Association as a Best Book for Young Adults. It also was a finalist for the Colorado Blue Spruce Young Adult Book Award.

When he's not writing, he teaches high school and college English in Grand Junction, Colorado. His wife and three sons have grown accustomed to his long, motionless moments hunched over his laptop, punctuated by wild bursts of typing.

More information about current projects and upcoming publications can be found at his home page at http://www.sff.net/people/james.van.pelt. He welcomes e-mail about writing, teaching and science fiction at Vvanp@aol.com.

Printed in the United States
50051LVS00006B/160-174